The Wedding Band

By Cara Connelly

The Wedding Band
The Wedding Vow
The Wedding Favor
The Wedding Date

The Wedding Band

A SAVE THE DATE NOVEL

CARA CONNELLY

AVON IMPULSE
An Imprint of HarperCollins Publishers

Excerpt from *Various States of Undress: Georgia* copyright © 2014 by Laura Simcox.
Excerpt from *Make It Last* copyright © 2014 by Megan Erickson.
Excerpt from *Hero By Night* copyright © 2014 by Sara Jane Stone.
Excerpt from *Mayhem* copyright © 2014 by Jamie Shaw.
Excerpt from *Sinful Rewards 1* copyright © 2014 by Cynthia Sax.
Excerpt from *Forbidden* copyright © 2014 by Charlotte Stein.
Excerpt from *Her Highland Fling* copyright © 2014 by Jennifer McQuiston.

EPub Edition FEBRUARY 2015 ISBN: 9780062282385
Print Edition ISBN: 9780062282378

10 9 8 7 6 5 4 3 2

Chapter One

DAKOTA RAIN TOOK a good hard look in the bathroom mirror and inventoried the assets.

Piercing blue eyes? Check.

Sexy stubble? Check.

Sun-streaked blond hair? Check.

Movie-star smile?

Uh-oh.

In the doorway, his assistant rolled her eyes and hit speed dial. "Emily Fazzone here," she said. "Mr. Rain needs to see Dr. Spade this morning. Another cap." She listened a moment, then snorted a laugh. "You're telling me. Might as well cap them all and be done with it."

In the mirror Dakota gave her his hit man squint. "No extra caps."

"Weenie," she said, pocketing her phone. "You don't have time today, anyway. Spade's squeezing you in, as usual. Then you're due at the studio at eleven for the voice-over. It'll be tight, so step on it."

Deliberately, Dakota turned to his reflection again. Tilted his head. Pulled at his cheeks like he was contemplating a shave.

Emily did another eye roll. Muttering something that might have been either "Get to work" or "What a jerk," she disappeared into his closet, emerging a minute later with jeans, T-shirt, and boxer briefs. She stacked them on the granite vanity, then pulled out her phone again and scrolled through the calendar.

"You've got a twelve o'clock with Peter at his office about the Levi's endorsement, then a one-thirty fitting for your tux. Mercer's coming here at two-thirty to talk about security for the wedding . . ."

Dakota tuned her out. His schedule didn't worry him. Emily would get him where he needed to be. If he ran a little late and a few people had to cool their heels, well, they were used to dealing with movie stars. Hell, they'd be disappointed if he behaved like regular folk.

Taking his sweet time, he shucked yesterday's briefs and meandered naked to the shower without thinking twice. He knew Emily wouldn't bat an eye. After ten years nursing him through injuries and illness, puking and pain, she'd seen all there was to see. Broad shoulders? Tight buns? She was immune.

And besides, she was gay.

Jacking the water temp to scalding, he stuck his head under the spray, wincing when it found the goose egg on the back of his skull. He measured it with his fingers, two inches around.

The same right hook that chipped his tooth had bounced his head off a concrete wall.

Emily rapped on the glass. He rubbed a clear spot in the steam and gave her the hard eye for pestering him in the shower.

She was immune to that too. "I asked you if we're looking at a lawsuit."

"Damn straight." He was all indignation. "We're suing The Combat Zone. Tubby busted my tooth and gave me a concussion to boot."

She sighed. "I meant, are *we* getting sued? Tubby's a good bouncer. If he popped you, you gave him a reason."

Dakota put a world of aggrievement into his Western drawl. "Why do you always take everybody else's side? You weren't there. You don't know what happened."

"Sure I do. It's October, isn't it? The month you start howling at the moon and throwing punches at bystanders. It's an annual event. The lawyers are on standby. I just want to know if I should call them."

He did the snarl that sent villains and virgins running for their mamas. Emily folded her arms.

He stuck his head out the door. "Feel that." He pointed at the lump.

She jabbed it.

"Ow! Damn it, Em, you're mean as a snake." He shut off the water, dripped his way across the bathroom, and twisted around in front of the mirror, trying to see the back of his head.

"Was Montana with you?"

"No." Little brother's clubbing days were over. Montana spent his evenings with his fiancée now.

"Witnesses?"

"Plenty."

"Paparazzi?"

"Are you kidding?" He was always tripping over those leeches. October usually ended with one of them on the ground, Dakota punching the snot out of him while the rest of the bloodsuckers streamed it live.

Em dragged her phone out again. "Hi, Peter. Yeah, Dakota got into it with Tubby last night. Just a broken tooth and a knot on his thick skull. But the press was there, so expect pictures. Okay, later."

Dakota gave up on the lump. His hair was too thick.

And too damn long, an inch past his chin for the Western he'd start filming next month. Seemed like a lot of trouble for what amounted to another shoot-'em-up just like the last one, and the one before that. This time there'd be horses instead of hot rods, and six-guns instead of Uzis. But no real surprises, just lots of dead bodies.

Em handed him a towel. "Car?"

He glanced out the window. No surprises there either. Another sunny day in L.A. "Porsche. The black one."

She walked out of the bathroom, tapping her phone. "Tony, bring the black Porsche around, will you? And drop the top."

GOOSING THE GAS, Dakota squirted between a glossy Lexus and a pimped-out Civic, then shot through a yellow light and squealed a hard right into the In-N-Out Burger, braking at the drive-thru.

"Gimme a three-by-three, fries, and a chocolate shake, will ya, darlin'?" He glanced at Em. "The usual?"

She nodded, phone to her ear.

"Throw in a grilled cheese for the meat-hater. And an extra straw." He pulled forward behind a yellow Hummer.

Still talking, Em opened her iPad, fiddled around, then held it up for him to see. Pictures of his go-round with Tubby.

He shrugged like it didn't bother him, but it did. Oh, he didn't care if people knew he'd had his ass handed to him. That was inevitable; nobody beat Tubby.

What pissed him off were the damn paparazzi.

Everyone—Peter, Em, even Montana—told him the media was a fact of celebrity life. A necessary evil. And maybe that was true.

But he'd never forgive them for Charlie. For driving a good man to suicide, then tearing at his remains like the flesh-eating vultures they were.

And it wasn't only the paparazzi who'd made money and careers off Charlie's life and death. "Legitimate" journalists waded in too, exploiting his best friend's disintegration, never letting humanity get in the way of a good story.

The day they spread Charlie's corpse across the front page, Dakota swore off "news" forever. No papers, no magazines, no CNN. Never again in this life.

Pulling up to the window, he set aside his resentment and laid a practiced smile on the redhead inside. "Hey, Sandy-girl. What's shakin'?"

"Hey, Kota." Her Jersey accent spread his nickname like butter. "I like the hair."

"You can have it when I cut it off." He tipped her fifty bucks and she blew him a kiss.

Peeling out of the lot, he handed off the bag to Em. She was still uh-huhing into her phone, so he plucked it from her hand.

"Hey! That was Peter."

"We just saw him twenty minutes ago." He rattled the bag.

"Honest to God." She unwrapped his burger and spread a napkin on his lap. Then she stuck both straws in the shake, took a long pull, and passed it over, half turning in her seat to eyeball him. "So what happened last night?"

He sucked down two inches of shake, then tucked it between his thighs. "Some asshole was hassling this girl. Feeling her up." Manhandling the poor kid. Pinning her to the wall and rubbing all over her.

"Tell me you didn't hit him."

"I was about to." And wouldn't it have felt great to lay that pretty boy out? "I pulled him off her. Then Tubby waded in and spoiled my fun."

"And the October madness begins." Em tipped back her head and stared up at blue sky. "Why, oh why, couldn't Montana get married in September? Or November?"

"Why does he have to get married at all?" It made no

sense. Montana—or Tana, as he was known to family, friends, and his legions of Twitter followers—had the world by the balls. Women loved him. Hollywood loved him. The critics loved him. He was the indie darling, offered one challenging, nuanced role after another, while Kota got stuck blowing up cities and machine-gunning armies single-handedly.

Sure, Kota made bigger box office. But Tana had the talent in the family.

"Sasha's a great girl," Em pointed out.

"Yeah, she's a peach. But peaches grow on trees in California. Why settle for one when you can have the orchard?"

Em punched his shoulder. "That's for peaches everywhere, especially California."

Kota grinned and passed her the shake. "Call Mercer, will you, and tell him we're running behind. I don't want him getting pissed at us."

"Pfft. You never worry about anybody else's feelings."

"Because they can't kill us just by looking at us."

"See? You're scared of him too." She crossed her arms. "I wish you hadn't hired him."

"So you've said about a million times. But Tana put me in charge of security, and Mercer's the best." His guys were ex-Rangers and Navy SEALs. "He says he'll keep the press out, and I believe him."

"Well good luck with that. They always manage to sneak somebody inside."

"Not this time," Kota vowed. A beach wedding might be a security nightmare—not to mention just plain pointless, since everyone was zipped into tents and couldn't see the water anyway—but Mercer had it covered. Airtight perimeter, no-fly zone. Saturday's guests and employees would be bussed in from a remote parking lot and wanded before admittance. Anyone caught with a recording device would be summarily executed—er, ejected.

Kota gave a grim smile. "Believe me, Em, Mercer's got it locked down. Not a single, slimy, sleazy reporter is getting into that wedding."

"You're getting into that wedding." Reed aimed a finger at Chris. "Don't bother arguing. It's that, or clean out your desk."

"This is bullshit, Reed! Archie admitted it was his screwup."

"And his desk is already empty. But your ass is still in a sling, Christine. Your name was on that story."

"I told him not to go to print until I verified it! If he'd waited till I gave him the go-ahead—"

"You're missing the point. Senator Buckley saw *your name*—Christine Case—on the front page. *You* accused her of mishandling campaign contributions. It's *your* blood she wants." Reed's chair scraped back. "You wanted to do hard news, now you've got to take the heat."

Chris rubbed her temple. "I earned my byline, Reed." With two years of writing fluff for the Living section. It finally seemed to pay off when one of Buckley's PR flacks—a guy Chris knew from covering the senator's thousand-dollar-a-plate fund-raisers—handed her the story of a lifetime. Her big break. Guaranteed to run front page above the fold.

Reed had no sympathy. "You should've held onto the story until you locked it up. You handed Archie a stick of dynamite."

Oh yes she had. And it blew up in her face.

Reed was right. She bore a big chunk of the blame. She was lucky he hadn't fired her outright.

"Listen, Chris." Reed came around the desk, propped himself on the edge. "Your mother's a hero to a whole generation of reporters. Emma Case's coverage of Vietnam changed history. That's why you're still sitting here, getting another chance. That, and the fact that your father's the entertainment at Montana Rain's wedding."

"So now we're competing with the *Enquirer*? Sneaking into celebrity weddings? For God's sake, we're the *Los Angeles Sentinel*. Is this what journalism has come to?"

Wrong question. Reed stiffened. "Don't preach to me, young lady. I grew up in this business, and I can tell you the world's changed. Newspapers all over the country are hanging by a thread."

"The scoop on this wedding won't make or break the *Sentinel*."

"Maybe not. But it'll make or break your future here. I went to the mat for you, and now you'll return the favor. I promised Owen an exclusive. *Where the Stars Are* rolls out in two weeks, and Montana Rain's wedding *will* be the centerfold spread."

"Come on, Reed. It's no better than a tabloid—"

He cut her off ruthlessly. "Your opinion's irrelevant.

Owen's the publisher, and it's his baby. He's expecting it to boost Sunday circulation, and if it goes down in flames, it won't be because this office didn't do its damnedest."

Chris tried to stare him down, but Reed was master of the stare down. She crossed her arms. He crossed his.

Sand trickled through the hourglass.

Chris dropped her eyes. Thought about her mother, how proud she'd been when Chris graduated from Columbia with her master's in journalism. How disappointed when she didn't use her degree, choosing a troubadour's life with her father instead.

Well, it was too late to redeem herself in her mother's eyes. Alzheimer's had dulled Emma Case's razor-sharp mind. The woman Chris admired and resented and loved with all her heart was, in so many of the ways that matter, already lost to her.

Emma would never know that Chris was finally following in her footsteps. Or that her old friend Reed, managing editor of the *Sentinel*, had given Chris that chance.

But Chris knew. With no references except her family name, Reed had taken it on faith that she'd bring the same commitment to the *Sentinel* that Emma had brought to her Pulitzer Prize–winning career.

But sneaking into celebrity weddings, dishing on who wore what and who canoodled with who . . . well, nobody won awards for that.

Still, she owed Reed. And with the balance sheet so far out of whack, what could she do but suck it up, sing with her father's band at Montana Rain's overblown extravaganza of a wedding, and bring back some useless gossip to hype Owen's pet project.

Then, with that humiliation behind her, she'd ride out her time in the penalty box until she got another crack at hard news.

Next time, she'd use better judgment, double-check her sources.

Next time, she'd do her mother proud.

Refusing to meet Reed's eyes, Chris punched in her famous father's private number. He answered on the first ring.

"Hi, honey pie."

"Hi, Dad." She cut to the chase. "Listen, is the offer still open? Can I do the wedding this weekend?"

"Abso-fucking-lutely." Zach Gray didn't miss a beat. "I'll work up a new set list and shoot it to you. We hit at two. And honey, security's tighter than a gnat's asshole. No phones, no nothing. Expect to strip down to your skivvies."

And the hits just kept on coming.

Chapter Two

THE WEDDING GUESTS drifted into the reception; A-listers, arm candy, and a few normal people who stood out like sore thumbs.

Through a gap in the backstage curtain, Chris watched them stake out tables with purses and wraps, then amble off in search of drinks. Like guests at any other wedding, but not.

Across the half-acre tent, a string quartet played Mozart while wannabe actors passed hors d'oeuvres, playing the role of obsequious staff.

Well, she was role-playing herself, wasn't she? The difference was, her role hadn't always been an act.

Long before turning herself into earnest journalist Christine Case, she'd been sultry chanteuse Christy Gray, touring with Zach and his big band, playing Europe and Vegas and zillion-dollar weddings like this one.

Zach sauntered over. "You okay, honey pie? It's been a while."

She forced a show-must-go-on smile. "Like riding a bike."

He rubbed her arm. "You're a pro, babe." He left the rest unsaid, but she'd heard it before: *That's why you belong in the spotlight, singing for thousands instead of churning out boring stories a hundred people might skim.*

Easy for him to say. He didn't know what it was like to be Emma Case's daughter. To Zach, Emma was just another one-night stand, noteworthy because she'd been a great lay, twice his age at the time, and a famous journalist, in that order of importance.

He likely would have forgotten all about her if she hadn't given him Chris: his first child, his only daughter, and, as he frequently told her, the best torch singer he'd ever had the pleasure to work with.

He wanted her to follow in his footsteps every bit as much as Emma wanted Chris to follow in hers. The upshot was that Chris's life had never been her own, just a choice to be made between their two extremes.

Today, though, Chris and Christy shared the stage, the singer and reporter rubbing against each other like wool and silk, making static. Making her sweat.

With one hand, she squeezed the knots in her neck. If she was going to get through this without disgracing herself, she had to stay calm. Avoid surprises, complications, and messy entanglements—

Zach peeked through the curtain and broke out in a

grin. "Well, well. This should be interesting." He stepped back.

The curtain parted and a big man strode through.

A big man.

In her heels, Chris stood six feet tall, but this man had four inches on her, a chest like a billboard, and shoulders that could hold up the tent if it started to fold.

Dakota Rain. *Wow*.

"Zach, right?" He stuck out a hand built to wield Thor's hammer. "I'm a big fan." His deep drawl rumbled like distant thunder.

Then his eyes—bluer than a Highland sky—shifted from Zach to her. And popped.

For a moment those startled eyes stared. Then down they inched, peeling her gown to her ankles, leaving it in a puddle while they cruised back up, erasing her panties, her bra. Igniting her skin, lingering on her lips, until finally they settled on her eyes and held there while his Adam's apple bobbed.

"My daughter, Christy," she heard Zach say through the ringing in her ears.

"Nice. Dress." The words came out on a rasp that seemed to stick in Dakota's throat.

She was tongue-tied herself, awash in a flood of testosterone. The man pumped it out with every breath.

They shook hands and held on, caught in a mutual spell, until a petite woman with short black hair and a pointy elbow jabbed him in the ribs. "Reel your tongue in before you step on it."

Dakota dropped his gaze to give her the hard eye.

"This is Em. She used to be my assistant. Now she's looking for a job."

"It's nice to meet you both." Em shook their hands. "If you need anything, just let me know and I'll make sure you get it."

"Appreciate it," said Zach, "but we've got everything we need."

"Okay, then we'll leave you alone." She clamped a hand on Dakota's wrist and headed back out through the curtain. He let her tug his arm out straight, but his body didn't budge. She could have been hauling on a Cadillac.

"Zach"—his rumbling drawl again—"my ma's been a fan from day one. Mind if I bring her backstage?"

"Not at all. We'd love to meet her."

Dakota nodded, then scorched Chris with a last searing look before letting Em drag him away.

"Honey pie, you watch out for him. He's a player."

Chris managed a shaky laugh. "Takes one to know one."

"Damn right. But even *I'm* not in his league. The dude sweats sex. If I can feel it, women must fall like timber."

Yes, and if the media had it right, he'd felled forests.

"Not this woman." Chris had enough celebrities in her life. With few exceptions, they were self-centered, thin-skinned, narcissistic attention whores.

And Dakota Rain, Hollywood's biggest box office star, was the ultimate celebrity. So what if his gaze burned straight through her dress? There was a reason the man got paid millions just to squint.

Zach looped an arm around her shoulders. "The smart

money says if he turns on the charm, he'll have you flat on your back before you can whistle Dixie."

She laid a hand on her heart. "Gee Dad, I love our father-daughter talks."

He chucked her chin. "I know you don't need me to tell you about the birds and the bees. But, sweetie, the king of the jungle just got your scent. Trust me, he'll be back."

"WHAT THE FUCK, Em?"

"The fuck is, you were drooling on your shoes."

"Did you *see* her?" Supermodel tall, with bombshell curves, yards of chestnut waves, and a face to make Da Vinci weep.

"Yeah, I saw her. I saw you eye-fuck her right under her father's nose."

Kota started to deny it. Then, "She eye-fucked me back."

"Hers was more of an eye-fondle. Obviously, she's not the slut you are."

Points in her favor. "How come I've never seen her before?"

"Because she doesn't tour much anymore." Em kept them moving, maneuvering between tables, dodging potential waylayers. "Sasha saw her sing with Zach in Vegas a couple years ago. She brought the house down. Then she dropped off the radar."

"To do what?"

"Maybe she had a baby. Or a nervous breakdown.

Anyway, Sasha was over the moon when Zach said she was coming today."

Kota was stuck on the baby. "She's married?" He'd been too discombobulated to check for a ring.

"I don't know her whole story. Sasha only mentioned her to Mercer this morning. He went ballistic, of course. No time for a background check, blah blah. So watch yourself, she might be a terrorist."

"I should frisk her."

"I'm sure you will. Do me a favor, though, and get through the reception first. Spare your parents the spectacle that would surely ensue."

Good point. His track record with weddings wasn't the best. They tended to get messy when, say, a bridesmaid's father caught him with his pants down and broke a chair over his head.

"I'll save it for the after-party," he decided. "You're coming, right?"

"Half an hour, tops. Then"—toothy grin—"I'm on vacation."

What was he thinking, giving her the week off?

"Forget vacation," he said. "I need your help with the getaway." An elaborate scheme involving look-alikes conspicuously exiting the party to jet to Italy in his Cessna, while the newlyweds tiptoed to a friend's Gulfstream for a paparazzi-free honeymoon on Kota's private island.

"You don't need me," Em said. "Mercer's all over it. I'd just get in the way." She steered him toward the head table. "Now let's get this show on the road. I need you on that airplane."

"You could come with us." He dangled the bait. "A week on the beach. No phone, no internet . . ."

"Just what Tana needs, *more* people horning in on his honeymoon."

"I'm not horning in. I'm staying in the guesthouse clear across the island. Besides, you told me I should hole up in October."

"I meant a month on the space station, or dogsledding to the South Pole. Not tagging along with your brother and his bride."

"They'll never even know I'm there."

"Pfft. You'll get lonely and start pestering them after twenty minutes."

She might be right. A solitary week reading scripts and watching the Pacific sunset sounded idyllic a month ago, when he was humping rocket launchers through steaming jungle and deadlifting bodies into helicopters.

But once his latest film wrapped and he got back to L.A., all that alone time started to hang heavy.

Em muscled him into his chair. The head table was empty at the moment, the bride and groom still with the photographer. Propping her butt on the edge, she looked him in the eye.

When she spoke, her tone was softer and gentler than usual. "You'll be fine. Tana's still your little brother. You're not going to lose him."

Sometimes Em saw too damn much.

"You and Tana," she said, "are closer than any two people I know. Nobody can come between you. And it's got to be obvious even to a bonehead like you that Sasha doesn't want to. She likes you."

"I like her too." And he couldn't deny that she encouraged Tana to hang out with him. It wasn't her fault his brother preferred her company most of the time. The guy was gone for her.

"I know you're used to having Tana to yourself," Em said. "Jetting off to Vegas or Miami or New York on a whim. Taking armfuls of women to the island instead of a wife and a boring pile of scripts. But Kota, come on, you're thirty-five next month."

Ouch. "Thirty-five's not old."

"No, but it's mature, or it should be." She cocked her head. "I think a week alone is just what you need. You can clear your head. Think about what comes next."

Which was exactly the problem. He didn't want to think about what came next.

Desperation made him reckless. "I'll give you a month off when we get back."

Her smile was sad. "That's bullshit. You wouldn't last a day in L.A. without me. And besides, I've got plans with Jackie this week."

"Bring her along." Talk about reckless; Jackie drove him nuts.

"I can't. We're Houston bound. She's finally going to tell her parents."

He snorted. "They'll probably shoot you. Best case, they'll stick you in separate bedrooms. No sex all week."

"Maybe. But *I* can go without sex for a week. *You'll* be chasing the sheep around the island."

He smiled, as she'd meant him to. "You've got a sick mind, Em. That's why I love you."

"I love you too," she said. And with a bracing shoulder punch to offset the mushiness, she left him to fend for himself.

No easy feat once the happy couple arrived.

"Congratulations," Kota made himself say, earning an Oscar nomination. Not that he wasn't happy for them. He was. It was himself he was miserable for.

"Thanks, man." Tana's eyes, the same changeable blue as Kota's, crinkled at the corners when he grinned.

Tana pulled out Sasha's chair, settling her like a princess on a throne before taking his place beside her.

Kota leaned forward to see around his brother's big frame. "Sasha, sweetheart, you're the prettiest bride to ever walk down the aisle."

"Oh, Kota." A fat teardrop leaked from one emerald eye. "Thank you. I'm so happy." She reached out a slender hand. He squeezed it lightly.

She really was a nice girl. If Tana *had* to have a wife, he couldn't have chosen better. Sasha was kind, thoughtful, and sweet as . . . well, a peach.

Somebody clinked a glass with a spoon. Another hundred people took it up, and the newlyweds got back to what they were best at—making out like the last two people on earth.

Kota broke it up by getting to his feet. Time to get the toast over with. The room quieted as a thousand eyes turned toward him. Even the newlyweds unlocked their lips.

He hadn't prepared anything. No need, since he planned to keep it short and sweet. A quick poke at Tana, a few words welcoming Sasha to the family, and then he could hit the bar.

With that in mind, he ran through the standard intro, thanking folks for coming, giving a shout-out to this one and that. Inviting everybody to the after-party at his Beverly Hills mansion.

Then he dropped a hand on his brother's shoulder, leaving it there while he scanned the faces of friends and colleagues, most of them people they'd worked with in their fifteen years in the business.

Movie people appreciated a dramatic pause, so he drew it out, built the suspense. After all, this was the fun part, where he'd pull out one of a hundred hilarious stories about Tana. These folks expected it. They were all ears.

Then he caught his ma's eye, brimming with unshed tears. And for the first time it struck him that while his own feelings about Tana's marriage were mixed, for Ma it was a dream come true.

She'd nearly given up on her boys settling down and giving her grandchildren. Now Tana was halfway there, and she'd expect Kota to mark the occasion with something more poignant than a bachelor-party roast.

He didn't have it in him to disappoint her.

He took a deep breath and began. "You all know the story of the Rain boys. A couple of delinquents kicking around the system, booted out of one foster home after another. And for damn good reason. We were trouble with a capital T."

He spread his palms, did his scallywag smile. "Some things haven't changed."

Laughter rolled through the tent.

He gave it a minute, then let his smile slide sideways, toward rueful. "We were hard to handle, for sure. Big and bad and mad at the world. Our motto was hit first, hit hard, and deal with the fallout later.

"The social workers didn't know what to do with us. They tried splitting us up. Even shipped us to different states." He left out the panic, the fury, the near insanity that gripped him when they tore Tana away.

Instead, he said, mildly, "That really pissed us off," and got another laugh at the understatement.

"But being smarter than we looked, we cooked up a plan. It was simple, and it went like this. No matter where they sent us, we ran away, then hitched a ride back to Wyoming. Back to Roy and Verna Rain's ranch."

He cut a glance at his folks, seated in the place of honor nearby. With her unretouched wrinkles and department store dress, Verna should have looked out of place in such glitzy company. But to Kota, she outshone the rest.

And Roy, he was six feet of gristle in a stiff black suit. The strongest, truest man Kota knew.

"The Rains were good folks with no kids of their own. They'd taken a chance on us early on, showed us love and kindness. But surly brats that we were, we'd blown it to hell and they sent us packing.

"We never forgot 'em, though. And they never forgot us either. How could they, when we kept turning up on their doorstep like bad pennies? Two strapping boys with man-sized chips on our shoulders, we were too proud to ask out loud for another chance, and too desperate not to want one."

Hollywood fell away as he remembered how it was.

"The first few times we showed up, Verna fed us a big meal. Turkey and gravy, or steak and potatoes. We were always hungry. Then, when supper was over, Roy loaded us in the pickup and drove us back to the county home, thinking that'd be the last they saw of us.

"But Tana and me, we're stubborn as stumps. We knew there was work enough for ten men on that ranch, so we figured if we put our backs into toting bales and shoveling sh—" He cut a sheepish glance at Verna, which raised a chuckle.

He shrugged and half-smiled. "Anyway, maybe it was all that toting and shoveling, or maybe they just got tired of driving ninety miles to the home, but one day Pops left the truck in the barn. A couple months later they adopted us. And that's when everything changed for Tana and me."

He paused. "You've all heard it said that saving one dog won't change the world, but it'll change the world for that one dog. Well, the same goes for kids."

The tent had gone quiet; only silence and sniffles.

Kota squeezed his brother's shoulder. "We survived," he weighted every word, "because of each other. And we thrived because of Roy and Verna Rain. That's why, for Tana and me, family always comes first."

Stepping around his brother, Kota took Sasha's hand and pulled her gently to her feet. Solemn as a preacher, he said, "Welcome to the family, darlin'."

And he wrapped her in a hug to a thunder of applause.

Chapter Three

ONE EAR PRESSED to the curtain, Chris scribbled notes on the back of an envelope with an eyebrow pencil.

It was messy, but what could she do? She'd left her pad and pen at home. After a hundred society soirees, remembering who wore which designer dress was second nature. No need to write it down.

But when Dakota Rain started talking in that spellbinding drawl, speaking from the heart about his legendary messed-up childhood, she knew she had to get every word. Moving, personal, and exclusive, it was exactly what Reed wanted.

If this didn't save her job, nothing would.

"Watcha doing, honey pie?"

She whirled, scrunching the envelope. "Just making a crib sheet for the first set. Um, we're doing 'Fever' in A, right?"

"Just like always." Zach cocked his head. "Nervous?"

"Do I seem nervous?" She flipped her hair, affecting nonchalance.

"More like jumpy." He grinned. "Dakota got to you, didn't he?"

"Pfft. No."

"Well, sweetie, you got to him."

She eye-rolled. "Yeah, he was all atwitter."

"He's not the first guy to get tongue-tied around a beautiful woman."

She jerked a thumb toward the crowd. "Did you get a look out there? There's at least two hundred beautiful women."

"Of course there are, this is Cali-fucking-fornia."

"So let's see how tongue-tied he is." She pulled back the curtain.

Half the guests were up and circulating while their seventy-five-dollar-a-head appetizers went cold on their tables. But then, this *was* Cali-fucking-fornia. Most of these women topped out at five hundred calories a day. They wouldn't fritter them away on appetizers, no matter how famous the chef.

Instead, they orbited Dakota, who was yakking away with no sign of a knot in his tongue.

She smirked triumphantly, but Zach only shrugged. "Just proves you knocked his socks off."

"No, Dad, it proves some women will listen to any dreck that falls from celebrity lips."

She gazed out at Dakota, the sun at the center of his own solar system. "He assumes he's fascinating, and why wouldn't he, when our celebrity-infatuated culture hangs on his words? As if being born good-looking makes him inherently interesting." She lifted one shoulder, let it fall. "I almost can't blame him for thinking he's God's gift."

Zach poked her. "You're a smarty-pants, just like your mother."

She dropped the curtain. It was too easy to stare, to be blinded by the sun.

She focused on Zach. "Speaking of Mom. I haven't told you because . . . well, I haven't told anyone." She swallowed hard. "Mom's got Alzheimer's."

"Oh, sweetie, I'm sorry." He pulled her into a hug.

She rested her cheek on his shoulder. "Don't tell anyone, okay?"

"It's a disease, Christy. Nothing to be ashamed of."

"I'm not ashamed. It's just that Mom would hate the headlines. 'Groundbreaking War Correspondent No Longer Knows Her Own Name.'"

Zach winced. "She's that bad?"

"Not yet. But reporters are always looking for a hook." The irony didn't escape her. "I wouldn't put it past them to"—air quotes—"*interview* her, especially the ones she's pissed off over the years. And there are legions."

"Yeah, I get you." Privacy invasion was something Zach understood too well.

His dry tone made Chris ask, "How are *you* doing?"

"One day at a time. Sometimes, one minute at a time."

She tightened her arms around him. What could she say that hadn't already been said?

Zach's whole adult life had been a hedonist's wet dream. He'd finally checked himself into Betty Ford.

Now he was seven weeks clean and sober, and each morning when he woke up, he started from scratch.

He stepped back and gave her a bracing smile. "Don't worry about me, sweetie. I've got this."

She wasn't so sure, but she nodded.

Balling his hands in his pockets, he put a twist in his smile to lighten the mood. "As I was saying, you're a smarty-pants. But sometimes you outsmart yourself."

She played along, played it up. "As *I* was saying, Dakota Rain's a raging egomaniac and a dimwit to boot. Have you seen his movies? He's all bulging muscles and squinty eyes. He snarls and spits out two words at a time. 'Nice. Dress.'" She grunted it out like an ape.

And the curtain drew back. Mr. Bulging Muscles himself.

Mortified, she stared helplessly as a hot flush shot from her neck to her crown.

But if he'd heard her dissing him, he hid it behind a smile. And there was nothing disparaging to be said about that Smile. He flashed it around in every film, and it sold as many tickets to red-blooded women as his body count did to their bloodthirsty boyfriends.

"Zach." His deep drawl rumbled. "I got someone here who's dying to meet you."

Stepping aside, he touched a big hand to his mother's slender shoulder, and Chris got her first good look at the woman who'd housebroken the Rain boys.

If size had been what counted, those boys would have

run roughshod over her. Fine-boned and slender, Verna Rain could have walked under Dakota's outstretched arm without mussing her snowy wash-and-set.

But there was more to her than flesh and bone. Kindness, humor, and determination were etched on her face. She would have needed all three to raise the self-professed bad boys into Hollywood's biggest stars.

Yet she could still be starstruck herself. Staring up at Zach, her cornflower eyes went round, and her cheeks glowed apple red.

Zach took it in stride, placing a gallant kiss on her knuckles. "It's a pleasure to meet you, Mrs. Rain."

"Oh. Oh dear." She went a deeper red. "Mr. Gray, I've been a fan for a long time. Ever since *Precious Love*."

Zach grinned. "Well, that *is* a long time, isn't it? And none of this 'Mr. Gray' business. I'm Zach to my friends."

"Oh. Oh my." She fluttered like a bird.

Chris slanted a glance at Dakota. He looked amused, and a little perplexed. He caught her eye, and the grin he gave her was boyish, spontaneous. And twice as appealing as the Smile.

Her heart sped up in response, and she smiled back without thinking.

Instantly, his eyes glazed. He focused on her lips.

She clamped them shut.

Zach touched her arm. "May I present my daughter, Christy?"

Chris pried her lips open. "I'm delighted to meet you, Mrs. Rain."

"Please, call me Verna." Her handshake was firm, but her fingers felt like twigs.

"What a lovely name. I've never heard it before."

"Oh, I don't imagine you have many Vernas in Los Angeles anymore. But there's a few of us in Wyoming yet." She touched Dakota's sleeve. "Remember Verna Presky? You had such a crush on her in sixth grade. She wouldn't look at you twice."

Zach let out a laugh. "Bet that hasn't happened lately," he said to Dakota.

"You'd be surprised" was the wry reply.

Chris felt his gaze on her face. She darted a glance at him.

And Verna caught them red-handed. A slow smile curved her lips. "Christy, dear, are you married?"

"Um, no." In Chris's world, marital role models were thin on the ground. So were marital prospects.

Verna patted her wrist. "Don't worry, dear. The right man will come along. Maybe sooner than you think." Deliberately, she looked up at her son. "I met your father at a wedding, you know."

"Yeah, Ma, I know. A hundred people and your eyes met across the room."

"That's just how it was." She turned to Chris. "My second cousin Noreen's wedding reception. I was sixteen, in a sprigged muslin dress I made for the occasion, the most formfitting thing I'd ever worn."

One hand floated over her hip. "I was just filling out, and that dress caught the boys' eyes. They gathered round as boys do, but I knew them all from school and wasn't interested in a one of them.

"Then Roy walked in." Her eyes sparkled. "He was older, from a few towns over. We'd never met, but he took one look at me, I took one look at him, and we beat a path to the preacher."

She lowered her voice. "In those days, you know, marriage came before sex, so there was no time to waste. Roy was that handsome."

Dakota drew back, shock on his face. "Whoa, wait. You mean you and Pops have had sex?"

"Oh, a time or two. But even though we gave him ample opportunity, the Lord chose not to give us children until you and your brother came along." She patted Dakota's cheek. "And the moral of that story is, be careful what you pray for."

Dakota caught her thin hand and pressed a kiss to her palm. "God works in mysterious ways."

"That he does, my boy." She smiled boundless love at him. Then she tucked her hand in his arm. "We've pestered these nice folks long enough. Take me back to your father."

"Yes, ma'am."

Chris watched them go, the broad-shouldered man in the bespoke tuxedo towering over the tiny woman in the off-the-rack dress.

Zach shoulder-bumped her. "A guy who loves his mom can't be all bad."

"I didn't say he's bad. I said he's light in the brainpan."

But she had to admit it was hard not to like a guy who treated his mom like a queen.

And it would be harder still to exploit their relationship for the *Sentinel*.

KOTA SMILED AT the wannabe starlet manning the bar. "Gimme a Johnnie Walker, will you, sweetheart?"

"Would that be red, black, blue or platinum, Mr. Rain?" She tilted strawberry lips, did a slow blink of bluebonnet eyes.

"Make it red, honey, I'm a simple man." Since it was expected, he dropped his gaze to the breasts bubbling out of her two-sizes-too-small vest, let it linger long enough to show he appreciated the goods, then wrapped up the show with a rueful half smile that said, *If only I didn't have other plans for the night.*

It was the work of a moment that hit all the right notes, and when she handed him his drink, they parted with good feelings all around.

Sipping his whiskey, he wandered the room, making small talk, passing out compliments like lollipops. Flirting perfunctorily. But he was restless. Unsatisfied.

After a few sips, he left his whiskey on a tray. It wasn't what he wanted.

What he wanted was backstage.

But panting after a woman wasn't his style. So he forced himself to walk in the opposite direction, circling back to his folks' table.

He found his old man in a snit. "I suppose you fawned

all over *Zach*," Roy was saying to Verna, his still-sturdy arms crossed over his chest.

"She fawned, all right," Kota drawled, stirring up trouble. Sixty years married and Pops still got jealous. Every man should be so lucky.

Spinning a chair around, Kota straddled it. Ma swatted his arm, a feather fanning a tree limb. "Look who's talking. You're smitten with Christy."

"'Smitten'? That's a word?"

"Don't play doofus with me, Mr. Valedictorian. It's about time a girl turned your head. You should ask her out."

He made a rude noise that earned another swat. He could barely feel it, but he said, "Ow," just to humor her.

"Quit trying to marry him off," Pops grumbled. "Let him sow his oats."

Now Ma made the rude noise. "He's sown oats aplenty—"

"He's the Johnny Appleseed of oats," said Tana, arriving just in time to butt in.

Straddling another chair, he clapped Kota on the back. That, Kota felt. He curled a lip at his brother, who laughed.

"I was just saying," Ma forged on, "that your brother should ask Zach's daughter for a date."

Tana smirked. "I hate to tell you, Ma, but it usually works the other way around. The ladies stalk Kota."

"This one won't," Ma predicted. "She's a class act, all the way."

"In that case"—Tana threw down the dare—"she won't go out with him anyway."

That was the excuse Kota needed. Heaving a put-upon sigh, he pushed back his chair.

"Where you going?" Tana asked him.

"To hit on Christy Gray, where else? Ma won't quit till I do."

"*I do*," Ma repeated. "Music to my ears."

This time Pops made the rude noise.

Kota found Christy backstage, scribbling on a crinkled envelope.

"Hi," he said.

She leaped out of her shoes.

He held up his hands. "Sorry. Didn't mean to spook you."

She crushed the envelope in her fist. "If you're looking for Dad, he's in his dressing room." She pointed, then set off toward her own.

He pursued, weaving through band members and roadies loitering outside the makeshift dressing rooms. "Actually, I was looking for you. You made quite an impression on Ma."

"She's an extraordinary woman," she said over her shoulder.

"She wants me to ask you out."

Christy stopped outside her dressing room. The canvas flap that served as a door was closed. She made no move to lift it.

Instead, she quirked an amused brow. "Your mother does your matchmaking?"

"Not usually, but the wedding's addled her." He twirled a finger by his temple. "She's fragile right now. I think we should humor her."

Christy laughed, low and sultry and rich enough to roll around in naked.

"I'm serious," he said. "She could snap any time."

Again with the sultry laugh. He hooked a finger in his collar, which seemed to be shrinking as fast as his underwear.

"I'm sure she'll survive," she said. Then she did the unthinkable. She lifted the flap, blowing him off.

It was unprecedented. Completely off script.

So he improvised. Touching a palm to the small of her back, he slid smoothly into the dressing room alongside her.

By movie-star standards, it was cramped. He took it in with one glance. Faded Levi's and a pink tee draped over a chair. Flip-flops kicked underneath it. Department-store cosmetics spilling onto the dressing table from a worn canvas bag.

Offstage, it seemed, Christy Gray was no diva.

"So, I guess you're seeing somebody," he said, continuing the conversation as if he hadn't barged into her space.

"No, I'm not seeing anyone." Slightly annoyed.

"In love with a married man? Saving yourself for Jesus?"

She half smiled, half smirked. "I know the usual line is 'It's not you, it's me.' But this time, it's not me. It's you."

"Ouch." He rubbed his chest like she'd punched him.

"Sorry, but I'm allergic to celebrities."

"Why? We're just people."

"And the bird flu's just a virus."

"What if I wasn't a celebrity?"

"What else would you be?"

"A veterinarian." He threw it out there.

"That takes brains," she said, like they were lacking.

He dunce-scratched his head. "Now you're just confusin' me."

She laughed again. It was killing him by inches.

He went all in. "Listen, Ma won't quit hounding me till we go on a date. It can be a pity-date. I'm okay with that, as long as she thinks you're into it." He did an aw-shucks smile. "Make an old lady's day and date her shiftless son."

"I don't—"

"At least come to the after-party. Let her get a look at you before she and Pops totter off to bed. It'll be kinda like a date, but not really."

He smiled again, and for a minute she looked tempted, like maybe she was so incredibly turned on by him that her perfectly sensible aversion to celebrities suddenly seemed asinine.

A man could hope.

But then, like a slow-motion action sequence, the kind where the bloodletting's drawn out for maximum cinematic effect, she started . . . to . . . shake . . . her . . . head . . .

And as if on cue, Zach called, "Knock knock," and stuck his shoulders through the flap. Spotting Kota, he said, "Hey, man. Sounds like a kick-ass after-party."

"You'll be there, right?"

"Abso-fucking-lutely."

Kota bit back a grin. Sometimes just when things were

going to shit, up through the manure popped a big red rose.

Christy jumped in. "Dad, really?"

"Really." He chucked her chin. "You worry too much, honey pie. We're on in ten."

On that note he ducked out. She swung around, glaring daggers at Kota. "You *know* he just got out of rehab."

Of course he knew. Just like he knew she'd feel obliged to chaperone. His inner scoundrel mentally rubbed his hands. But the decent guy Ma raised made himself say, "I'll uninvite him if you want me to."

She glared some more. Then she huffed out a sigh. "He has to get back into circulation sometime."

A solemn nod. "You'll probably want to keep an eye on him, though."

"Convenient, isn't it?"

"I'm just sayin'." He shrugged.

"And I'm *just sayin'* . . ." She stuffed the crumpled envelope into her bag. " . . . it's *not* a date. So you can wipe the smug look off your mug."

And with a toss of her head she strode from the tent, every inch a diva.

Chapter Four

CHRIS SQUEALED AROUND the hairpin turn like she was racing her Eos through the streets of Monaco instead of sleepy Laurel Canyon. Screeching to a stop in her driveway, she grabbed her bag and hotfooted through the back door.

Her roomie, Raylene, leaped out of her path. "Chris! What the hell?" She licked up the Riesling that slopped over her knuckles.

"Sorry, I'm in a hurry." Chris barreled across the kitchen and sprinted up the spiral staircase.

"No kidding. Where's the fire?"

"At Dakota Rain's," Chris called down two flights. Her bedroom occupied the entire third floor, which wasn't as impressive as it sounded, since the whole house was a shoebox standing on end, balanced on a million-dollar postage stamp.

Raylene followed her up the corkscrew stairs. "You're going to Dakota Rain's? Can I come?"

"No." Chris pawed through her walk-in closet. Off came the pink T-shirt, replaced by a shimmery gold tank. "I have to keep an eye on my father. I can't supervise you too."

"I'll be good."

"You'll be trouble."

Raylene pouted. "I'm off probation in two weeks."

"Unless you're arrested tonight. Then you'll go to jail for six months."

Raylene's third DUI had finally landed her in hot water. College chum or not, if she stayed on that road, Chris was kicking her out. She didn't have room in her life for two alcoholics.

While Raylene moped, Chris shucked her jeans and shimmied into a black skirt with a ruffle at midthigh.

"I want your legs," Raylene said grumpily. "And your ass."

"I want your tits and your triceps," said Chris. "So we're even."

She ducked into the bathroom to strip off her stage makeup. Raylene called through the door. "What if I promise not to drink?"

"I've heard it before, Ray. I can't deal with you tonight."

"Fine. Be that way." Ray clumped down the stairs.

Chris let her go. No time to smooth feathers; she had to get to Dakota's drunken orgy before Zach tumbled down all twelve steps and landed in a bottle of Beefeater.

Tail on fire, she hit her cheeks with blush, her lips with gloss, and scooped up five-inch gold Louboutins that would cut into Dakota's vertical advantage. She was on a beeline for the stairs when Reed rang her cell.

"Pack your things," he said without preamble, "and get out."

She froze in midstride. "You can't fire me, I got the story!"

"I mean get out of L.A. The senator's suing the paper. The sheriff's deputy just served me, and you're next on the list."

"Well, shit." Chris slewed a looked around her room. No place to hide.

"If you're home, get out of the house," Reed said. "Get out of L.A. Out of the country if you can. I'll tell everyone you're on assignment. That'll slow things down while Owen works on Buckley to drop the suit."

Chris clutched her forehead. "What if she won't?"

Unemployment and disgrace, that's what.

"Listen, Chris, Buckley's pissed right now. She wants to turn the knife. So she'll make tomorrow's Sunday morning rounds, blast the liberal press, discredit the paper, and when she can't get any more mileage, she'll *graciously* accept our apology." He snorted. "Trust me, no politician wants a judge scrutinizing their spending. She'll pull the plug before it gets to court."

That sounded good, but something smelled fishy. "If you're so sure she'll drop it, why do I need to disappear?"

"Because Owen's easiest play here is to offer up a sacrificial lamb."

"Baaaaa."

"Exactly. So we'll remove temptation. Make him do it the hard way."

Chris slumped against the railing. "This is all my fault. Maybe I should fall on my sword."

"Like hell." Reed put steel in his tone. "I'll let you know when your career's over, Christine. In the meantime, I'm not telling Emma Case I stood back while her daughter took the fall for some overeager editor trying to make a name for himself."

That only made her sadder. "Thanks, Reed, but don't worry about Mom. She wouldn't know what you were talking about."

"*I'd* know. Now grab your passport and get on a plane. Call me in a week. This whole thing might blow over by then, but if not, make damn sure your wedding exclusive is juicy enough to convince Owen you're indispensable."

"No problem there. I got Dakota's toast word for word. Met his mother. Lots of good stuff." Enough to impress Owen, especially with the potential after-party scoop.

"Good," Reed said. "Now turn off your phone until you call me next week. When I tell Owen you're incommunicado, I don't want my eye to twitch."

"But Seacrest"—Emma's facility—"won't be able to reach me."

"I'm second on their call list. If something comes up, I'll handle it. Now pack your bags and get the hell out of Dodge."

Five minutes later Chris was rocketing down the mountain, suitcase in the trunk, passport in her purse, guilty conscience riding shotgun.

MEN IN BLACK ringed Dakota Rain's Beverly Hills mansion, a formidable perimeter even the brashest paparazzi didn't have the balls to breach.

Standing in the circular driveway—barely inside that perimeter—Chris chewed a Tums while the goon who'd all but cavity-searched her gave the same top-to-bottom treatment to her VW.

"You'd think POTUS was on site," she muttered under her breath.

Hell, maybe he was. The Rains were Hollywood royalty. Why wouldn't the president slobber all over them like everybody else did?

She handed off her keys to a steely-eyed SEAL type standing in as valet, then passed under a temporary portico meant to guard against eyes-in-the-sky. Making for the wide double doors, she froze when a whip-thin woman braced her, armed with an iPad and, possibly, a Glock.

"Name," the woman stated.

"Christy Gray."

Flat pewter eyes studied Chris down to her pores, then lowered to the iPad. She scrolled, while ice water trickled down Chris's spine. This woman could eat the tough guys outside for breakfast. If she discovered Chris's double identity, her body would never be found.

A long moment stretched as the hangman knotted the noose, then those unnerving eyes rose again. Another ice-cold inspection and a terse "You're good to go."

Chris managed a nothing-to-hide stroll across the arena-sized foyer, then ducked through the first open doorway, finding herself in a game room tricked out with every diversion from vintage pinball to top-of-the-line gaming chairs. The current focal point was a pool table overhung by a Tiffany lamp and surrounded by a rowdy crowd.

Ignoring the hooting and hollering, Chris snagged a champagne flute from a passing tray, downed the bubbly like water, then blotted her neck with the tiny bar napkin.

Her nerves were jangling, and for good reason. She was running from the law. Worrying about her father, her mother, and her job.

And now she was undercover behind enemy lines.

"Hi, Christy."

"Agh!" She fumbled her glass, catching it before it hit the floor.

"Sorry." Em touched her arm. "I didn't mean to startle you."

Funny how she'd been hearing that all day.

"Not your fault," Chris said. "I'm a little jumpy. Nurse Ratched freaked me out."

Em made a face; half smile, half apology. "Believe it or not, she's the goodwill ambassador in that bunch. Kota went overboard with security."

"Threats?" A fact of celebrity life.

"Just the usual whackos. No, this whole security blitz is about keeping the press out."

Nausea rolled through Chris's gut. "That seems extreme."

"Kota's an extreme kind of guy." Em took her arm. "Come on, let's move before anyone notices you're here."

Chris turned to stone. "What do you mean?" Were they on to her already? Was Nurse Ratched locking down the estate, preparing to stuff Chris in a trunk for a trip to the tar pits?

"What I mean," Em said with a grin, "is that you're the hottest ticket at this party. You stole the show today. Everyone wants to meet you."

"Oh, if that's all." Whew.

Em poked her chin at the pool table. "When that breaks up, they'll spot you. I'm sure you've been mobbed by fans before, but nobody does it like the Hollywood set."

That wasn't good either. There was always a chance, slim but real, that someone in the crowd knew her backstory. She needed to check on Zach and get out before her cover was blown.

"Have you seen my father?"

"He's out by the pool. I'll take you."

Em led her across the hallway into a dim room lined with bookshelves—*Dakota Rain has a library?*—then out through French doors into a rose garden, blooming lavishly.

"Wow." The heady scent hung on the moist evening air. But the benches were empty. "I'm surprised no one's out here."

"Kota made this for Verna. He keeps it private." Em nudged her along a path that followed the line of the house. "You might've noticed I used a palm plate to get into the library. That's off limits too. Kota's all about privacy."

Chris glanced back at the house, at the wings stretching ahead and behind. She was no stranger to wealth. Zach had millions, and she was well off herself. But Dakota was in another league. "How many rooms?"

"I'm not really sure. It's got all the usual stuff—solarium, gallery, theater, blah blah. But Kota only uses a handful of rooms." She shrugged. "I told him not to build this monster, but boys will be boys."

Ahead, the enormous terrace surrounding the lake-sized swimming pool was packed with partiers. Torchlight sparked off sequins and jewels. Waiters circulated with champagne. The bar was three deep. Chris scanned the faces for Zach's, praying she wouldn't spot a martini in his hand.

"Don't worry," said Em. "We've got a man on him."

Chris's head swung around. "I beg your pardon?"

"Kota knows you're worried about him, so he's got a guy positioned to run interference if anyone throws temptation in his path."

"Oh. That's . . . nice?"

Em shrugged. "Kota's sensitive to addiction issues. He's lost people. And he probably feels guilty, because if I know him—and I do—he used Zach to lure you here."

A lightbulb went on in Chris's brain. The nerve.

Em must have seen her eyes widen, because she

shrugged again. "Yeah, he's kind of a dick that way. But surprisingly thoughtful at the same time." She checked her phone. "Zach's about ten feet north of the grill."

She pointed past a stainless-steel monster as long as a limo, manned by four men in chef's hats. And there stood Zach, Pepsi in hand, bantering with the usual bevy of beauties.

As so often before, Chris envied his ease. Zach knew exactly who he was, where he fit, while she was a square peg in a world of round holes.

"He looks okay," she admitted. Which meant it was safe to ditch Christy Gray and get Christine Case on the first plane out of LAX.

Then Em pointed again, toward the house. And Chris followed her finger.

Big mistake.

Onto the terrace strode Dakota, invading it with his presence, towering over the mere mortals in his sphere. Torchlight cast his Viking cheekbones in bas-relief and glinted like fire off the streaks in his mane.

Chris went wet everywhere. Her armpits, her panties. Saliva pooled on her tongue.

Talk about mouthwatering.

He'd traded his tux for a simple white button-down, tailored to his gladiator's frame. The sleeves were rolled to the elbows, exposing forearms snaked with muscle, and the tails were tucked into Levi's that cupped an ass so fine his billboards sold millions of boxer briefs, mostly to women hoping to mold their man's butt into something similar.

Never gonna happen. God only made one.

And the guy who owned it had gone to some trouble to lure her to his house. Meaning she could, if she wanted, get her hands on that butt.

She wanted. Oh boy, she wanted. In fact, if she weren't two weeks away from splashing his brother's wedding across the *Sentinel*'s centerfold, she might just blink her no-celebrity rule for one night of anything-goes sex with the hottest guy on the planet.

But damn it, given the circumstances, that would be wrong. More wrong than simply spying on him and exploiting his family.

Even *her* shaky ethics balked at screwing him, and then *screwing* him.

Still, it couldn't hurt to say a polite hello. To catch one last whiff of panty-melting pheromones before morphing back into boring Christine Case.

She let Em propel her toward the light.

KOTA SCANNED THE terrace from his superior height. He'd gotten word from Mercer that Christy was on site. But where?

Craning his neck, he almost tripped over tiny Danni Devine. "Hey, Kota." She shook back silky blond hair and winked one amber cat's eye.

"Hey, Danni." Decency required he give her a minute. Just last month he'd carried her half-naked body over his shoulder as they'd run from Colombian drug lords. They'd followed up the rescue with sweaty jungle sex— on camera and off.

She'd been angling for an encore ever since, and under normal circumstances, he'd be up for it. But these weren't normal circumstances. Even when she laid the flat of her hand on his chest and cocked her head expectantly, he couldn't bring her into focus.

It was all Christy's fault. From the first moment, she'd possessed him with her gorgeousness, her curves, and her irresistibly indifferent attitude.

And then, sweet Jesus, she'd stepped onto the stage, and he'd lost his mind completely.

The spotlight loved her, sparkling off sequins and glossy chestnut waves, catching her pale throat when her head fell back. She was pure sensuality, holding the mic like a lover, her body swaying like a palm tree on a sultry summer night.

He'd seen nothing like her, ever.

And her looks were just part of it. Her voice, Lord, her voice—that's what really undid him. Low and lush, it wrapped around him like velvet, conjuring dark, steamy bedrooms and hot, slippery bodies tangling in sweaty sheets.

Standing at the back of the tent, gazing at her like a love-struck groupie, he'd believed to his core that she sang just for him.

He'd damn near come in his pants.

Then she left the stage, and reality tipped an icy pail over his head as a quick look around showed him every man felt the same.

Since then, nothing mattered except getting close to her and publicly staking his claim. And if he had to mow down every male in Hollywood to do it, somebody better call 911, because there'd be heavy casualties.

Danni fingered a button. "The bride and groom look happy. But their best man looks out of sorts." She slid her palm up and down, a suggestive stroke. "Bet I can put a smile on his face."

He should know how to respond; it was wired into his brain. But Christy had fried his circuits.

Undaunted, Danni inched up under his nose. The scent of her shampoo wafted up—peaches.

She took advantage of a bump from behind to smush her chest against his, drawing attention to the melons threatening to roll up out of her top. She licked cherry lips. "Whatcha thinking about?"

"Fruit."

She blinked. "Fruit? Is that a euphemism?"

"Usually," he said, puzzled. "But at the moment, it's just fruit."

A commotion broke out off to his right. "There she is." "That's her." "Is she alone?"

His pulse leaped, and like everyone else, he stared as Christy stepped from the shadows, smile on her lips, glossy waves curling over pale, naked shoulders.

The crowd blocked his view of her body, so he zeroed in on her eyes. Warm and welcoming, they locked with his, and he forgot where he was. Every drop of blood in his veins sizzled.

She came toward him, and magically, the crowd parted, clearing a path between them. She shimmered like a vision. Glimmered like flame.

Then her gaze dropped from his eyes to his chest, and her smile flattened into a cynical line.

Uh-oh.

He looked down. Danni clung like a vine.

And for some reason, probably instinct, he was cupping her ass.

He dropped it, raising his hands like a crook. Christy came to a standstill just out of arm's reach.

She ran an eye over Danni. "Nice dress," she said, dropping his own words like turds.

Danni looked dubious. "Um, thanks?"

"I mean it." Christy gave her a smile. "I wish I could wear that style."

Danni beamed, and unclung to do a dainty pirouette. "It's adorable, right?"

Christy's reply was swallowed up as the sharks surrounded her—every unattached man and a few who'd shaken off their dates.

Kota got busy shaking off Danni. "Scorsese's over by the band—"

Enough said. She disappeared like smoke.

He turned back to Christy. At the center of the feeding frenzy, her low, husky laugh was chum in the water. The little sharks gobbled it up, embarrassing themselves. Pretty-boy Gosling flirted like a teenager. And Clooney, the old fart, had his hand on her elbow.

Kota waded in, the great white, the biggest and baddest shark in the sea.

Shoulder-bumping Clooney, strafing Gosling and the rest with a get-back glare, he hooked a hand around

Christy's waist. "Zach's looking for you," he lied. And stiff-arming a path through the diehards, he hustled her into the house.

Another mob met them there, and he shoved through it bodyguard-style, pushing his way down the hall, through the gallery, the media room, using his size the way God intended, to carry his woman back to his cave.

Palming into the library at last, he slapped the door shut behind them.

Then he stepped away from her. Big men could be scary, or so Ma had drilled into his head. He didn't want to scare Christy. He wanted her to come to him.

She didn't.

Instead, she put a hand to her brow and peered around like she was searching for land. "It's kind of dark," she said, "but I think I'd see my father if he was here."

He hit a light switch. A single reading lamp came on, throwing a warm glow at one end of the sofa. "He's outside. I can get him."

"Or you can send your spy for him."

"Or that." He moved toward the sofa, hoping she'd follow. "I thought you'd be glad someone's keeping an eye on him."

She drifted deeper into the room, but toward the desk, not the sofa. "That would mean I don't trust him."

"Hard to trust an addict."

She ran a hand over mahogany, then propped her fine ass on the edge and brought her gaze around to him at last.

It tingled like electricity over his skin.

"That sounds like the voice of experience," she said.

He shrugged a shoulder, gave an answer no one could dispute. "This is Hollywood."

He sat on the sofa, stretching his arm along the back, body language for *Come on over and join me*.

She crossed her arms.

Okay, he could do conversation if he had to. "So, you live in L.A.?"

"Yes." No details.

"Surprised I haven't seen you around."

"I'm not much for the party scene."

"Clubs?"

"Not the ones you frequent."

That made him smile. "You know which clubs I frequent?"

"Doesn't everyone? I thought that was the point of brawling on the sidewalk. If they're not paying you for that kind of publicity, you should bill them."

He spread his palms. "Then I'd have to give my agent fifteen percent. The IRS would stick their hands out too. The damned extras would want scale." He shook his head. "Hardly worth it."

She laughed. It shivered through him. He gripped the arm of the sofa so he wouldn't get up and go to her.

"So, how long you been singing with Zach?"

"Years, on and off. Mostly outside the States." She uncrossed her arms and braced her hands on the desk. Her shimmery blouse went taut across her breasts.

Somehow, he kept his eyes on her face. "Ma's got all his CDs. She says you're not on any of them."

"I don't like the studio."

"So you've never recorded?"

"It doesn't feel like performing. There's no give-and-take with the audience." She shifted again, picking up a glass paperweight shaped like a dachshund.

Holding it up to the light, she frowned. "This dog has three legs."

"Tripod," he said. "He's my dog. Want to meet him?"

"Um, what about my father?"

"Sure, he can meet him too." Popping up before she could gather her thoughts, he put a hand on the small of her back and steered her out through the glass doors, where the rose garden's scent rolled over them like a wave.

She paused, inhaling. "Em brought me through here earlier," she said. "It's lovely."

"Yeah, Ma's into roses." While the scent had her dazzled, he linked his fingers through hers and got her moving toward his part of the house. "Speaking of Ma, remember, she's supposed to think we're on a date."

"Whoa." The effect of the roses wore off. "This isn't a date."

"We'll pretend. Just to make her happy."

Keeping hold of her hand, he palmed them through another door, into his living room. Ma and Pops were stretched out in recliners, sound asleep in front of the tube.

He shut the door with a thud, and Christy hissed. "Quiet, you'll wake them."

He opened the door again. Slammed it.

Nothing.

"They slept through a tornado once," he said in a normal tone.

But Tripod woke up and popped off Ma's lap to sprint-hop to him. He scooped the runt up in the crook of his arm.

"What happened to him?" Christy asked, eyeing the scar where the missing front leg should have been.

"It was already gone when I found him wandering on Sunset." Kota tickled Tripod's belly so he wriggled like an eel.

She reached out and did a one-finger scratch. "Who named him Tripod?"

"Me. I call him Tri, for short." He grinned. "Cute, right?"

"And original." She looked up at him.

And she smiled.

His swallow stuck in his throat like a piece of steak. For a moment he gagged. Then he blasted a cough, a titanic explosion that made Tri lunge for safety.

Safety, meaning Christy. The dog hit her chest like a bowling ball. Her arms clutched him instinctively, but Tri wasn't satisfied. Down her shirt he went, nose in her bra, tail sticking out the neckline.

Christy squealed, staggering backward, hitting a lamp that hit the floor like a gong. Her heels skidded on wood. She scrabbled for traction.

Before she could fall, Kota caught her arm and reeled her in against his chest. Tri's ass wriggled between them. They each stuck an arm down her shirt.

Kota felt around more than he had to.

And together they pulled Tripod up and out.

Chapter Five

TRI SNUGGLED IN the crook of Kota's arm. The dog's silly grin and wagging tail seemed to say, *Big fun for the guys*. Kota didn't disagree.

Tugging at her sagging neckline, Christy narrowed her eyes at him. "You groped me."

He was all innocence. "Must've been Tri."

"Please. He's got one foot. You've got five fingers."

"We could replay it in slo-mo, see who did what." He shifted Tri closer, peering down her still-gaping blouse.

Her hand slapped her chest. "I know the difference between a hand and a paw."

She was blushing, he noticed, right down to her bra. The heat rose in waves from her skin, stirring his blood like a mating call. He tightened the arm that still cinched her waist, pinning her with his biceps.

She moved her hand from her chest to his, but she didn't push him away. Her eyes went dark, almost black. Her lips parted, drawing his gaze. Drawing him in.

He dipped his chin . . . and Pops farted in his sleep.

Instantly, she pulled back and gave Kota's chest a hard shove. And the gentleman Ma raised loosened his grip, even as the animal within roared his fury.

Ma sat up, wakened by Pops's fart, when she could sleep through Armageddon. "Kota?"

"Right here, Ma. Christy's with me."

"Oh dear. You caught us napping." She reached over and shook Pops. "Wake up, Roy, we've got company."

Pops scrubbed a palm over his face. "I wasn't asleep."

The same conversation they'd been having for years.

Kota nudged Christy forward. "Pops, this is Christy."

"Hello, young lady." He stood up from his chair and gave her hand a courtly kiss. "I hear you've got my boy in a tizzy."

"I do?"

"You must. He hasn't brought a girl home to meet me since sixth grade. And that Verna Presky wasn't nearly as pretty as you are."

Christy smiled, then she laughed, a happy, husky sound that had Pop's eyes going wide. The look he shot Kota said he got it, all right.

Ma took things in hand. "Christy, dear, you sit right here." She directed her to the love seat that right-angled the recliners. "Roy, turn that TV off. Kota, get the poor girl some dinner."

Good thinking. She looked kind of peaked. Kota hit a

button on his phone. "Tony, get some food to the family room, stat."

"I'm fine, really," Christy said to Ma. "I know I look like a mess—"

"Don't blame me," Kota cut in. "Tri nosedived down her shirt."

Ma snorted a laugh. "The little pervert does that to me all the time."

Kota dropped the little pervert on her lap. Tri turned a tight circle, then settled down with both eyes on Christy.

There was a tap on the door, and a waiter wheeled in a cart loaded with covered dishes.

"That was fast," Christy said.

"When Kota says jump, they jump." Ma wagged her head like she couldn't understand it.

Kota started lifting covers. "We got steaks, ribs, shrimp skewers, lobster tails." He looked up, gauging Christy's interest. "Don't like meat? There's pasta six different ways. Green stuff."

"He means salad," Ma put in.

"That's what I said." He raised another lid. *Eww.* "This looks like risotto, with some kind of lumps in it."

"Mushrooms," said Ma. "I had some. It's delicious."

Pops made a face. "Stick with the steak. You can't go wrong with beef."

Kota nodded. "You got that right, Pops. Beef built this house."

Ma gave him the hard eye. "You know I don't like it when you say that." She turned to Christy. "Kota likes to say that beef built his muscles, his muscles made his money, and his money built this house. It's his way of discounting his talent."

She shifted back to Kota. "Make your girl a plate with a little of everything."

Christy popped up like a cork. "No, thanks. I can do it." She joined him at the cart, clearly anxious to prove she wasn't his girl.

Yet.

He crowded her. He'd gotten a noseful of her scent when he'd held her tight. Now he took another whiff. She smelled like roses.

Not like peaches at all.

"Tell me what you want," he murmured, "and I'll give it to you."

Her half smirk said she caught his double meaning. "Thanks, but I'll take care of myself."

Now there was a picture to stick in his mind.

She bent over to get a plate from the bottom of the tray. He stepped back to take in the view of her ass. Two round cheeks ample enough to fill even his big hands.

Her legs, all five miles of them, were tanned and toned and built to cinch his waist. And the toes peeping out of her shoes were pink tipped and suckable.

He'd never been a toe man, but this woman could change that.

Then she stood up and he forgot about her toes, because her breasts were under his nose again. He'd copped a feel, and they were prime. A solid C, all natural, and silkier even than the bra that housed them.

He was dying for another handful.

He shoved his fists in his pockets.

She poked around the pastas, spooned a few onto her plate. No beef, but at least she wasn't scared of carbs. Thank God for that.

Beef might've built his muscles, but pasta built her ass.

Ma caught him staring. He couldn't pretend to feel guilty about it.

"Christy might like some wine," Ma said mildly.

"Right." How was he supposed to remember his manners when all the blood had gone from his head to his pants? "Red? White?"

"Whatever you're having," said Christy. "You're eating too, aren't you?"

"Yeah, sure." He threw a steak on a plate, poured two Cabernets, and carried everything to the coffee table.

"So, Christy." Ma leaned forward to begin the interrogation. "Do you live nearby?"

Kota was all ears.

"In the canyon," she said. "A few miles from here."

Excellent news.

"By yourself?"

"With a roommate."

Uh-oh.

"A girlfriend?"

Nice one, Ma.

"Yes, a college friend."

Whew.

Christy twirled her linguini. Cream sauce dripped from her fork, and she caught it with her tongue.

Kota forgot to chew his steak.

Then her lips closed around the fork, sucking it clean, and his knife slipped from his fingers. It clattered on his plate, and Ma threw him a mind-your-manners look. *Right*. He should mind his manners while Christy had sex with her pasta.

Ma smoothed her skirt, smiling at Christy, deceptively casual. "Tell me, dear," she drilled down, "what do you do with yourself when you're not singing?"

Kota leaned in.

And Pops ruined everything. "Je-*sus*. Let the poor girl eat. You're as bad as the dentist, asking questions while he's got his hand in your mouth."

Ma gave a light laugh. "Roy's right. I'm just curious, is all. Here you are, such a talented singer. Why, you took my breath away. Stole it right out of my lungs. And nobody seems to know anything about you."

"Maybe she likes it that way," Pops butted in. "Everybody doesn't have to go on *Oprah*. Some folks still know the meaning of privacy."

Ma folded her hands. "We're just conversing. Nobody's prying."

"Oh you're prying, all right. Sizing her up for a wedding band."

Christy coughed out Cabernet.

Ma reached over and patted her back. "Don't mind Roy. He's up past his bedtime."

"Yeah, Pops," Kota said, "you can turn in anytime."

"Don't you start too," Pops said. "You're not the boss of me."

Kota rolled his eyes.

"And don't sass me either. I'm not one of your ass kissers."

At that, something crashed into the door, rattling the frame.

"Now you've done it, Roy," said Ma.

She rose and opened the door, and a slavering blur of fur exploded into the room.

WITH NO THOUGHT involved, just fight or flight, Chris leaped up on the love seat as the monster dove at Kota, bared teeth aimed at his throat.

It landed in his lap. Paws on his shoulders, it slobbered all over him, hugging him, if a dog could be said to hug.

"Je-*sus*," said Roy, rising to give Chris a hand down.

Verna was laughing. "Cy can't stand it when Roy chides Kota. He has to comfort him."

Kota wrestled the creature to the floor. He was laughing too.

Chris didn't see the humor. She'd have sworn the animal meant to rip all four of them to bloody shreds. She still wasn't sure it wouldn't, so she balanced her butt on the edge of her seat, poised to run for her life.

"Sit," said Kota, and the creature sat. "Say hi to Christy."

The boxy head swung her way, and she recoiled instinctively.

Staring at her from his one and only eye was the ugliest dog in the world.

"He's a lover," said Kota, rubbing the dog's barrel chest.

"Uh." Words failed her.

The dog's square, brindle face was a ghastly patchwork of scars, the most vicious a white slash bisecting his sewn-shut socket. His mangled lips gave him a perpetual snarl. Even his lolling tongue looked like he'd licked razor wire.

"I call him Cyclops," said Kota. "Cy for short. He had a run-in with some barbwire, and the barbwire won."

"Ah." Compassion pushed past revulsion.

"He's part pit bull, part wussy, aren't you, boy?"

Cy rolled his adoring eye toward Kota, who kissed him on the nose.

Chris's heart turned over with a thud.

Verna must have heard it, because she smiled. "Kota's got a hand with animals. Always has. The hurt ones find their way to him."

Roy made a face. "Lame coyotes, orphan jackrabbits. He should've been shootin' 'em like every other self-respecting rancher. But no, he's out in the barn nursin' 'em instead."

"My boys have big hearts," said Verna.

Kota turned red. "Enough, Ma." He aimed a pointed look at the clock.

She took the hint. "Will you look at that. Midnight's come and gone. Come on, Roy, let's go to bed."

"Now you're talking." Roy shot his recliner upright. "Take care of yourself, young lady." He gave Chris's knuckles another gallant kiss. "Until we meet again."

"Good night," she said, wishing it wasn't good-bye forever. Unexpected emotion put a catch in her voice. She had a mom-crush on Verna. And who wouldn't love Roy?

Verna took Chris's hands in her own. "Why don't you come back tomorrow, dear? There's a pretty little rose garden out behind the house. We'll have lunch before Roy and I head home."

It was out of the question, but still, temptation made Chris hesitate. The Rains were nice, down-to-earth people, the kind of folks who lived in the same house for fifty years. The opposite of her rootless parents. She loved Zach and Emma, but they'd never been much in the stability department.

Still, that didn't give her the right to lean on these fine people, not when she carried betrayal in her heart. If Verna knew how Chris meant to exploit her precious sons, she'd never befriend her. She'd cut her off at the knees.

And Chris would deserve it.

So she rose, smoothing her skirt. "I wish I could, but I only stopped in for a minute. I'm heading out of town for a while."

Verna's disappointment seemed genuine. "Business or pleasure?"

"A bit of both." If she had to go into exile, it would damn sure be someplace warm and sunny.

"Another time, then." Verna patted her arm, then turned to her son. "Kota, you take care of your brother."

"Yes, ma'am." He kissed her cheek, shook hands with his father, and off they went.

Some of the warmth left the room with them.

"I should get going," Chris said. "You've got Dad covered. He doesn't need me."

She would've moved toward the door, but Kota stood in the way, too big to get around without touching, and too hot to touch without getting burned.

"No problem," he said. "I'll walk you out."

That was too easy.

Then, he added, "Okay if I finish my steak first? I hardly ate a bite all day."

She eyed him. He blinked innocently.

"I don't like being manipulated," she said.

"I don't like eating alone," he replied.

Then he smiled at her. She tried not to be dazzled, but she found herself back on the love seat anyway.

He dug into his steak, then aimed his fork at the pasta she'd scarcely touched. "If you don't like it, take something else."

"It's delicious. I'm just not hungry." She sat back with her wine to wait out her sentence. Surely God was punishing her duplicity by waving Kota under her nose.

Tri hopped off Verna's chair and up onto the love seat. His skinny tail wagged. He eyed her neckline.

She covered it with her free hand.

"Down, Tri," Kota said, and the little shrimp stretched out along her leg, nose pointed at her pasta. Kota slid the dish to the middle of the table.

Cy licked his chops. Kota gave him a look, and Cy lay down too, head on his paws, lone eye fixed on the love of his life.

"They're devoted to you," Chris said. She didn't know what to make of it. She had no experience sharing space with animals. Neither of her parents had stayed in one place long enough for pets. And she'd bought her own house just six months before, barely time enough to consider it home, much less add a pet to it.

Kota shrugged one shoulder. "Dogs are easy. Give 'em love and some food and they'll give you their soul. Take Cy here." Kota fed him a nibble of steak. "Some asshole kept him tied out on a four-foot lead. He got away, snarled himself up in barbwire, and the asshole never even took him to the vet. Just tied him back on the lead."

He rubbed the dog with his toe. Cy panted his devotion.

"Mailman called it in, but not in time to save the eye. Then nobody wanted him because the scars make him look like he was trained to fight."

And because he was gruesome to look at. "How'd he end up here?"

"A girl I know down at the shelter asked me to take him."

That seemed odd. "Why'd she ask *you*?"

He smiled at her, gorgeously. "Because I'm the end of the line. The last stop for the halt and the lame, as Tana likes to say."

She touched Tri with her fingertips. He rolled over like a hot dog on a griddle.

Kota leaned across Chris, his blue eyes filled with humor and heat. He scratched Tri an inch above his stubby penis. "He likes it right there. So do I."

Deliberately, she dropped her gaze to Tri's nubbin. "You two probably have a lot in common."

"Hell, yeah. For a dachshund, my man Tri is hung."

She laughed because it was a good one, but the heat flushing her body was no laughing matter. She raised her wineglass and glug-glugged, trying to put out the flame.

But throwing alcohol on fire only made it burn hotter.

She glared at his steak. "Aren't you done yet?"

"What's your hurry? Got a plane to catch?"

"As a matter of fact."

He forked a dainty sliver of meat into his mouth. "So, where you headed on business-slash-pleasure?"

"Good question. I'll figure it out when I get to the airport."

He perked up. "No destination in mind? Just going where the wind takes you?"

"Something like that." She set her glass on the table. Wine loosened her lips. It had a similar effect on her legs. Two things best kept pressed together around Kota.

"I'm taking a trip myself." He checked the clock. "A few hours from now. Want to come along?"

"No." As if she'd jet off with him for a week like one of his bimbos.

"Why not?" He abandoned his steak and leaned in, eyes gleaming. "It'll be fun. We're going to my island. Me and Tana and Sasha."

"You're horning in on their honeymoon?"

He threw up his hands. "Why does everyone keep saying that?"

"Because you are?"

"I'm not. I'm giving them the big house, and I'm staying in the guesthouse *across the island*."

"Alone? No starlets and supermodels to keep you company?"

"Not a one."

"Stop the presses."

"Speaking of the press." He grinned. "We're pulling a fast one. Sending look-alikes to Italy in my jet while we sneak out the back door to my buddy Adam's plane. He's dropping us at my island on his way to some big board meeting somewhere."

She covered her ears. "You shouldn't tell me that."

"You're right. Now I'll have to kill you. Unless you come along." He put her glass in her hand. "Imagine," he said, seduction in every word, "a whole island to ourselves. Nothing but sun, sand, and surf."

She poured more wine on the fire.

"Palm trees, white sand. Crystal-clear water." He painted a tempting picture. "We'll sunbathe. We'll snorkel. We'll swim."

Her mind went to him in a swimsuit.

Or out of it.

She stood up abruptly. "Thanks, but I forgot to pack my grass skirt. Besides, I have some writing to do."

Kota rose too. So tall. So broad. His shoulders must be three feet across.

"You're a writer?" He looked interested. Too interested.

"I'm working on a book." That much was true. She

was writing her mother's biography, a story that deserved to be told.

"That's cool," he said. "You can have your own wing. All the privacy your heart desires." He smiled, devastatingly. "And when you desire something else, you can come on over to my wing."

Just like a celebrity to assume every woman would throw herself at him.

"No thanks," she said, sidestepping toward the door.

He matched her step for step. "No phone." He dangled the bait. "No internet. No TV. No Twitter."

It sounded like paradise.

"Why would that appeal to me?" she said to be contrary.

"Because you're tired of all that." He was close enough to touch her, but he didn't. His voice stroked her instead. "You want peace and quiet. Waves lapping the shore."

He was hypnotizing her. Putting her into a sensual trance—

A sharp knock on the door broke the spell. Kota yanked it open. "Not a good time, Tony."

"Sorry, but there's a deputy sheriff at the door. He's looking for a woman, a Christine Case."

Chris went ice cold.

"She on the list?" Kota asked.

"No. I told him if she's not on the list, she wouldn't get in. But he claims her roommate said she was headed here, so he wants permission to come in and look around."

Cold sweat trickled down her spine.

"Not happening," said Kota. "Tell him he can wait

outside the perimeter with the media assholes and grab her if she comes out. Which she won't, since she's not on the list."

Tony left, and Kota curled his lip in disgust. "Now the idiot reporters'll say I'm harboring fugitives."

Chris offered a sympathetic nod like she knew all about the prying press—which she did, since she was one of them—and kicked herself in the ass for lollygagging around the mansion sucking on eye candy instead of getting the hell out of Dodge.

Now it was too late. She was trapped. When the deputy snagged her leaving the premises, not only would he serve her with summons in the lawsuit, thereby pissing off Owen beyond all redemption, but the phalanx of cameras stationed outside the perimeter would capture the whole nasty business on film.

With so little real news to report about the wedding of the year, the juicy story of the undercover reporter would flash around the globe, further embarrassing the *Sentinel*, destroying Chris's last shred of journalistic credibility, and, worst of all, exposing her treachery to the entire Rain clan.

She'd hoped to spare all of them—and her parents— that final insult by posting the wedding story under an anonymous byline. She'd never get away with that now.

Unless . . .

Casually, she strolled to the food cart and plucked a chocolate-covered strawberry from a silver bowl set in ice. "So, tell me more about your island."

Chapter Six

THE GETAWAY PLANE was gassed up and waiting on the runway at Burbank. Shaking hands with its owner, billionaire playboy Adam LeCroix, Chris realized that he was everything the press made him out to be—tall, dark, and impossibly handsome, with a presence that made men do his bidding and women do anything.

But in Kota, he'd met his equal. Watching them clasp hands, Chris decided they were two sides of the same coin, cast in bronze by a beneficent god. A female god. Who liked tall men with extremely awesome arms.

Adam's fiancée, Maddie, a bite-sized blonde with a killer sense of humor, knew exactly how to play both of them. Elbow-bumping Chris, she murmured, "Watch this."

As Kota turned to greet her with his thousand-watt smile, Maddie's eyes glazed. Her body went limp as a noodle. "Hi, Dakota." A breathy whisper.

"Maddie darlin'." He kissed one cheek. Then the other. Held her tiny hands in both of his.

And Adam busted in. "That's enough of that, unless you've got someone else willing to fly a thousand miles out of his way to drop you on your island."

Kota released Maddie's hands with a show of reluctance. She let out a tremulous sigh.

"Christ Jesus," Adam muttered, his European accent making blasphemy sound sexy.

Maddie dropped a wink at Chris, who bit back a grin.

The pilot's voice piped through the speaker, advising them to buckle up for takeoff. Adam guided Maddie to a pair of cushy leather seats, while Kota steered Chris into the facing pair. Sasha and Tana buckled in on the sofa, where they could canoodle in relative privacy.

Kota murmured in Chris's ear. "Maddie's not a great flier. She'd probably feel better if you held my hand."

"How do you figure?"

"See how she's clinging to Adam? She gets embarrassed about that. So if you were holding my hand, snuggling into my shoulder like you were scared too, she wouldn't feel like such an oddball."

Tempting. Even more tempting when he traced a pattern on her wrist with one fingertip.

"If I didn't know better," she said, "I'd think you were trying to seduce me."

"If I was, would it be working?"

She let out a soft snort. "Forget it. You promised me solitude. I'll see you next Sunday when we're back on the plane."

The fingertip moved up her arm, a slow, slippery slide to the inside of her elbow.

How did he know that was her second-most erogenous zone?

He lingered there, his touch feather light, raising goose bumps that shivered up her arm and down her spine, all the way to her first-most erogenous zone.

She steeled herself. "There are those among us who can resist you," she said. "Women who can say no to Dakota Rain."

He leaned in so his hair brushed her shoulder. His voice was a whisper. "Name one."

"Me," she whispered back.

"We'll see." His breath was warm on her neck. "Try again."

"Maddie."

He pulled back enough to give her a get-real stare.

She put on a pitying look. "You realize she's not really into you, right? She goes googly-eyed just to annoy Adam."

"Pfft. I could have her like that." He snapped his fingers.

"I wouldn't mention that to Adam. Twenty thousand feet is a long way to fall."

"Hell, I can take him."

She gave Adam a slow study. "Hmm, I don't think so."

"You're kidding. Feel this." He picked up her hand and wrapped it around his arm.

Biceps built to make women weep.

His lips brushed her ear. "Still think he can beat me?"

"I think—" Well, that was a lie. She couldn't think. Her brain had melted.

She brought her other hand up, a vain attempt to circle his arm.

"Ooooh," she breathed.

He flexed, and her mouth went bone dry.

"Big," she got out, reduced to one syllable. "Hard."

KOTA MET CHRISTY'S eloquence with silence, not trusting himself to speak.

Big and hard was right. And he didn't mean his arm.

Then she lifted her hot gaze to his face, and the hunger in her eyes pushed his control to the limit. He had two choices: get it on with her, or get away from her.

Now.

Plane sex was out, so he hit his seat belt release, managed a muttered "Excuse me," and made tracks for the bathroom, holing up in there for as long as he decently could.

As it was, when he came out Tana quirked a brow at him. "Feeling okay? You ran for the can like you ate some bad clams."

"I'm fine," Kota said. Soaking his head in cold water had driven some desperately needed blood back up north to his brain. "I just needed a minute. Long day."

"Tell me about it." Tana was sitting on the couch, one hand stroking Sasha's shoulder as she slept with her head on his lap.

Kota climbed over Cy and Adam's dog, John Doe,

both of them flaked out on the floor and snoring like chain saws.

Taking the captain's chair across from his brother, Kota swung it side to side with one foot. "So. How's it feel?"

"Scary. Like, I'm scared something'll happen to Sasha. She'll get hurt, or . . . you know."

Yeah, he knew. Their mother disappeared thirty years ago this month, when they weren't much more than toddlers. Then their dad went looking for her, and they lost him too.

Scary shit for a kid.

Scary shit for a husband.

Kota leaned over and patted Tana's knee. "Nothing's gonna happen to your wife. That's a promise." Sasha was family now.

Tana looked grim. "Nobody can control everything, man. Not even you."

"Doesn't stop me from trying." As Em loved to point out.

They brooded in silence for a while, but gloom wasn't their natural state. Tana shook it off first, poking his chin in Christy's direction. "How'd you pull that off?"

Kota scratched his head. "I don't really know. One minute she didn't want any part of the island, and the next she was raring to go."

"Playing hard to get?"

"She doesn't have to play. She *is* hard to get." Christy might be hot for him, but she wouldn't be jumping in the sack without a lot of persuasion. The movie star thing that made other women's clothes fall off actually seemed to be a negative to her. Besides, "I'm not sure, but I don't think she likes me."

Tana laughed, and laughed.

Kota gave him the finger.

Heading back to his seat, he found Christy chatting with Adam and Maddie like they were old cronies, blabbing about the Riviera and St. Tropez and some restaurant at the top of the Eiffel Tower.

"We're getting married on my yacht next month," Adam mentioned. "Then we'll cruise the Greek islands. Maddie's never been."

Maddie rolled her eyes. "Yachts and cruises and weddings. I don't remember signing on for any of it."

"You will, darling." Adam brought her hand to his lips and trailed kisses over her knuckles.

Maddie went starry-eyed.

Kota stroked Christy's arm, stealing her attention for himself. "We're still a couple hours out," he said. "That seat reclines if you want a nap."

"No thanks." She rolled her shoulders.

"I can rub those for you. Get out the kinks." He flexed his hands. Women liked his big hands. And who didn't like a shoulder massage?

"No thanks."

The woman was work. "A drink? Some food? There must be something I can do for you." He laid on the double meaning.

She raised an eyebrow. "No. Thanks."

Okay then, back to conversation. "What're you writing about?"

That got her attention. She went bright pink. "What do you mean? I'm not writing anything. I don't know what you're talking about."

"Didn't you say you're writing a book?"

"Oh." She breathed out. "Right. The book. It's a biography."

"Of?"

"A journalist."

His back went up. "A *reporter*?"

"A war correspondent. She covered Vietnam. Bosnia. Somalia. The first Gulf War. She's a hero."

"Okay." He tried to compartmentalize heroic war correspondents on one side of his brain, the rest of the media on the other. But it wouldn't compute, so he changed the subject instead. "So you're a writer? That's your job?"

"Mmm-hmm."

"Why'd you stop touring with Zach?"

"Life on the road." She shrugged. "You know how it is."

Finally, something in common.

"Zach seems to like it," he said.

"It's all he knows. He's got a house in the canyon not far from mine, but he's hardly ever there."

He liked watching her talk, the way her lips moved, the line of her jaw. And her voice mesmerized him. Throaty, like she'd shot whiskey. Sexy, like she'd just come.

A foot tapped his leg—Tri looking for a lift. Kota one-handed him onto his lap. The pervert propped his front foot on the armrest, eyeballing Christy.

She put a hand on her chest.

Tri gave up and rolled over on Kota's thigh, all three feet in the air. Kota scratched him an inch from his junk, and Tri wriggled in glee.

Christy snorted. "Men."

"We're easy, just rub us in the right spot." He grinned. "I'll show you mine if you show me yours."

She laughed her husky laugh. He hadn't heard it since they boarded the plane, and now he wanted nothing but to hear it again, against his throat, ruffling his hair.

Everything about Christy—everything—called out to him on an atomic level. She was gorgeous and smart and funny, and totally bullshit-proof.

And she wanted him. Or she wanted his body, anyway. He didn't care that it was purely physical at this point. Once he got her clothes off, they'd burn up the island.

After that, who knew where things would go? All he knew for sure was that they had a whole week to find out.

CHRIS RUBBED HER temple. Why, oh why, hadn't she stowed away in a catering truck? She'd be halfway to Cabo by now instead of an hour into the flight of the damned.

This whole situation could only be cosmic justice, meted out by the patron saint of journalists to punish her fall from grace.

And it couldn't have been more torturously crafted.

A week on a tropical island with the hottest guy on the planet. A guy who was coming on to her with every breath, who her whole body was begging to bang.

A guy she was deceiving just by sitting beside him.

Already she was in agony. How would she endure seven days? It might as well be an eternity.

She shifted in her seat, wishing for a continent between them instead of an armrest. "I think I'll take a nap after all."

"Good idea." Kota folded the armrest up. "Want to put your head on my shoulder?"

Oh boy, did she want to.

"No, I'm good," she said.

"Then how 'bout I put my head on yours?"

She gave him a get-over-yourself look. "Maybe I'll forget about the nap." She put the armrest down.

He put it up again. "Seriously, you should sleep. I won't pester you."

"I don't believe you."

He made an X on his heart, and she smiled in spite of herself.

When she woke up hours later, he was holding her hand. Or more like cupping it in his upturned palm, as if he'd worked his hand under hers where it rested on the seat.

She couldn't fairly call it pestering, but it was its own brand of torment. Because Kota was proving to be disarmingly sweet. Hot and sweet was a deadly combination.

At the moment, though, he was harmless, sleeping

like a baby. For the first time she could study him un-observed, seeking out the inevitable imperfections that would prove he was mortal.

And there were many, as her scrutiny revealed. She worked her way down from the top.

For starters, his widow's peak was off center, his hair was too thick for a normal comb, and his lashes were too long and too lush for anyone but a mascara model.

His nose was a half centimeter too wide, his lips too full for a man who got paid millions to snarl, and his arms . . .

Okay, so he had one perfect feature.

But his chest was so broad that he'd need custom-made shirts, his waist was narrower than hers, and his package—

Whoa, his package. Hello, morning wood. Morning redwood. Like, two-thousand-year-old Sequoia—

"Hey, gorgeous. Like what you see?"

Of course he'd caught her ogling.

She covered by stretching and blinking as if she'd just opened her eyes. Like she'd coincidentally woken up staring at his bulge but hadn't really noticed it.

His smirk said he was on to her.

Damn it, why did she feel so outclassed? Hadn't she just finished logging his imperfections? The man was a troll.

Then he caught her in his bluer-than-blue gaze and scooped back his sleep-tousled hair, and she had to call bullshit on herself.

The truth was that the gods, in their wisdom, had

plucked one of their own from his throne and sent him to Hollywood. And she was as bedazzled as the rest of womankind.

Thor, or Zeus, or whoever he was, reached over and hooked his pinky under a lock of her hair. Gently, he unstuck it from her cheek, then pulled it slowly through his fingers to the end.

"How can you look so good after sleeping in a chair?" he said.

She could ask him the same question, but that way lay madness.

"Are we there yet?" she asked instead.

He slid his hand out from under hers to look at his watch. "Twenty minutes, give or take."

She couldn't decide if that was good or bad. The plane was purgatory, but the island would be hell.

Heading for the bathroom, she noticed that everyone else was still asleep. Maddie and Adam snuggled together like puppies. Sasha's new husband spooned her on the sofa. Everyone looked snug and content and utterly peaceful. And why wouldn't they? They'd each found the other half of their own happy couple.

Locking herself in, Chris leaned against the door, and for the first time in weeks, she thought about Jason.

After a year together, they'd broken up last April, when the Dodgers traded him to Boston. Now she wondered what would have happened if she'd gone with him, or if he'd stayed in L.A.

Would they be married? Happy?

She'd never know, because when push came to shove,

neither of them was willing to sacrifice their career for the other.

Still, they'd had fun together. She missed him sometimes. And she definitely missed having a man in her life.

A six-month dry spell wasn't helping her resist Kota's charms.

Back in the cabin, she found everyone waking up, rubbing their eyes, raising the shades to look out. She took her seat, and a few minutes later the plane banked to the left. Dawn broke across her lap, glinting off the choppy sea.

Kota leaned across her to point at the archipelago curled in a comma to the east. Most of the islands were overspread with dense foliage from sea to sea.

But the largest had a house on either side, a landing strip at one end, and a wide swath of meadow dotted with . . .

"Sheep?"

"Mmm-hmm. And horses." He pointed out a small herd. "Goats. Chickens. You name it."

The window was small, their heads close together. His bristles grazed her ear. His hair tickled her shoulder.

She drew a deep, secret breath through her nose, taking in his scent. Not cologne but the man himself, spicy and exotic. She licked her lips. Would he taste as delicious?

Tri hopped from Kota's lap to hers and propped his foot on the windowsill. The three of them couldn't get closer unless they all went down her shirt again.

Then the pilot said to buckle up. Kota sat back in his

seat. Tri tucked himself between their hips. It was all so cozy.

Too cozy. Too tempting.

A great big mistake waiting to happen.

Unless . . .

Chris smiled over at Maddie and Adam. "So, where are you two heading from here?"

Chapter Seven

CHINA. THE ONE place Chris wouldn't dare test her passport.

Twenty years ago, the Chinese had cordially but categorically invited Emma Case to leave their country, and to take her entourage of cameraman, editorial assistant, and ten-year-old daughter with her.

While it was unlikely they'd continue to bar Chris at this point, she'd certainly be pulled out of line for questioning. When Adam inevitably tried to intervene, he'd discover under the worst possible circumstances that she was a journalist.

He'd then inform his good friend Dakota that he'd been harboring a spy.

Chris couldn't let that happen, not while a chance remained to preserve her anonymity. Her own self-respect had been an early casualty in this ruse, but she couldn't stomach Verna and Roy—and Kota—knowing she'd deceived them.

As Adam's plane disappeared in the distance, Kota revved the golf cart. "You ready?"

She'd better be, because she was stuck.

Tri hopped from the backseat into her lap, and Cy hung over her shoulder, fanning her cheek with hot breath while Kota gave her the tour.

"The island's five miles long and two miles wide. The big house looks out on the bay." He gestured off to the right, where Tana and Sasha had disappeared along a rutted lane in their own golf cart. "They get the sunset."

Kota took a hard left onto a similar lane, carved through a sea of ferns and canopied by coconut palms. "The guesthouse is on a pretty little inlet. We get the sunrise."

He looked over and gave her a smile, and she noticed he looked lighter, more relaxed. Not that he ever really seemed stressed. Just the opposite; he radiated laid-back confidence. But now that she knew him a little, the contrast was marked.

He seemed looser, happier. His drawl was deeper.

And his eyes couldn't be bluer without extending the spectrum to include a shade previously unknown to man.

"The guesthouse is half the size," he said. "Cozier. And the truth is, I like it better than the big house. But keep that under your hat."

"It's a secret?"

"Hell yeah. My brand depends on Dakota Rain demanding the biggest and the best. The most expensive everything."

He spoke as if Kota and Dakota were two different people.

"So you spend a fortune on big houses you don't want to live in? That makes no sense."

"Nothing about celebrity makes sense," he said, the most sensible thing she'd ever heard him say.

"But you love it, don't you? The women, the fawning, the obscene amounts of money?"

"Any man who says he doesn't want women falling in his lap is lying through his teeth. And the money's great." They emerged from the foliage to pause on a rise overlooking the sea. "How many people own a tropical island?"

"Not many," she admitted. She drank in the view: water sparkling like diamonds; waves lapping at white sand on a crescent beach; and in the curve of the cove, a villa-style house with flowering gardens, wide covered porches, and an Olympic-sized pool. All of it, the entire lovely estate, was surrounded by palm trees on three sides and the endless ocean on the other.

"It's paradise," she said.

"Damn right."

"Who takes care of it?"

"Selena and Jaime. But they went home for the week to visit their folks. We've got the place to ourselves."

Oh no. She'd counted on a housekeeper, a cook. Even a gardener would've been some kind of chaperone.

She should've known better. Kota was famed for hedonism. In full swing, this place probably made the Playboy Mansion seem like Disney.

Pointing the cart downhill, Kota picked his way over rough ground as Chris fought down panic.

"There's really no phone?" she said. "What if there's an emergency?"

"There's a satellite phone we can call out on in a crisis, but my folks are the only ones who can call in. Even Em doesn't have the number."

"And no internet? What's that like?"

"Relaxing." He said it emphatically. "No checking e-mail or Twitter or CNN. No looking up every word you don't know, or checking who starred in what TV show from back when you were a kid." He braked in the courtyard. "It reminds you everything doesn't have to happen this minute."

While the dogs hopped out and commenced sniffing, he sat still, gazing at the hibiscus that bloomed outside the back door. "It reminds you," he said, "to pay attention to what's around you."

Chris didn't need any help with that. Her challenge was to *ignore* what was around her.

As if to drive home just how impossible that would be, he tipped his head back and finger-combed his mane off his forehead, a careless move that bunched his shoulders and flexed his forearms and could have sold rumpled white shirts by the thousands.

He seemed unaware of his own hotness, but it scorched

Chris like a blowtorch. Seven days! They closed in on her like the fires of hell.

There was no time to waste. She had to get to her room, lock the door, and stay there, living off the three granola bars in her purse until the plane came back and carried her away from temptation.

Throwing both legs out of the cart at once, she forgot about the five-inch heels she'd never bothered to change. They sank into the dirt and she fell back against the cart, cracking her elbow so pain sang up her arm.

"Ow!" She clutched her funny bone.

Kota sprinted around the cart. The dogs came running. Her face flamed, and embarrassment pushed her already jumbled emotions into full-fledged chaos.

"I'm fine," she snapped, shaking off his hand, shooing the dogs.

"Did you twist anything?" Kota dropped to his knees and wrapped his warm hands around her ankles.

"No!" She yanked a foot from his grip, whacking her heel on the running board. "Ow!"

He looked up at her like he was assessing her sanity, and his squint only emphasized the azure of his eyes. The sun kissed his streaks and caught the blond in his stubble. And his frown was as heart-stopping as his smile.

No wonder her sanity was on the line. The magnitude of her bad decision had grown blindingly clear.

Then in one fluid movement he rose, and suddenly she was looking up at him. He cupped her sore elbow. "You don't have to be nervous."

"I'm not nervous." She jerked her elbow, but he had a firm hold on it.

"Well, whatever you are, you better get a grip. I've got a first-aid kit here, but the way you're going, we'll have to call in the navy."

He was right; she had to calm down. This was only Day One.

Slowly, deeply, she sucked in a breath, then blew it out through her nose. Carefully, deliberately, she took possession of her arm and sidestepped out of his aura.

"I'm overtired," she said curtly. "And I didn't expect to be stranded on Gilligan's Island. I assumed there'd be other people."

How could he have left out such a crucial detail?

It must have been premeditated. And premeditated seduction, like premeditated murder, made the perp more culpable.

Which gave her every right to push back. She was on her own with no backup. She'd have to shoot first and make it count.

"I assumed," she added in her most condescending tone, "there'd at least be someone *interesting* to talk to."

KOTA TOOK THE bullet straight through the heart.

Christy's message was clear: *You might be hot. But you're dumb as a stump.*

Well, why should she think any differently than the rest of the world?

He hoisted her suitcase out of the cart and headed

for the house. "Sorry to disappoint," he said over his shoulder. "I'll stay out of your way so I don't bore you to death."

He felt her eyes on his back. His big, strong back. He was a meat suit to her, nothing more.

Storming through the back door, he charged through the kitchen without appreciating it, even though it was his favorite room. He'd designed it to be the heart of the house, state of the art but cozy, opening to the courtyard in back and the covered porch in front.

"Your wing's this way." He left her to trail behind as he took a hard right. Courtesy was beyond him at the moment. He had nothing to prove to Christy Gray.

As long as she screwed him, he couldn't care less what she thought of his mind.

He strode down the hall. "You can work in there." He chin-pointed at a den and kept going, dropping her bag on the floor of an ocean-view sitting room. "There's three bedrooms further down. Take your pick. Meanwhile, you can sit in here and talk to yourself so you won't be bored."

Appalled at his own bad manners but too stung to fake it, he turned his back and strode out.

He kept walking, going out the way he came in, through the kitchen, the courtyard. He passed by the golf cart, long legs eating up ground. The dogs swung in alongside him, Tri struggling to keep up with his furious stride.

Scooping the innocent dog up to his chest, he forged into the ferns, covering the narrow path to the meadow in under a minute.

When it opened before him, he made himself stop and take it in.

And then he simply stood there and let them come to him.

The chestnut found him first, seventeen hands, as sleek as a seal. She poked his shirt pocket with her blaze-white nose. He scratched her chin. "Sorry, Sugar, I left 'em in my suitcase." A Ziploc full of Jolly Ranchers, her favorite.

A second horse gave him a shove from behind. Blackie, of course. The big gelding liked to swap shoulder bumps with him. Kota gave him one back and Blackie nodded as if to say, *Glad to see you've been working out.*

From all across the meadow they drifted toward him. Nosing his pockets, snuffling his hair, lip-nibbling Tri, sidestepping Cy, who crisscrossed underfoot.

Tana would laugh if he saw it. He'd call him "Kota the horse whisperer." Kota didn't mind. He let them love him. He drank it in.

When they'd all had their chance and he'd had a word with each one, he tucked Tri down his shirt, grabbed a fistful of Sugar's mane, and swung onto her back.

And he let her run, racing the wind through the meadow, the herd thundering around them, Cy running wide on the flank.

Stretched out over Sugar's neck, Kota forgot everything but the wind strafing his cheeks, tearing at his hair, stripping the dregs of frustration and disappointment from his mind.

His body was one with Sugar's, muscles taut and

straining. His legs gripped her sides. They urged each other on, and on. Tears streaked his cheeks. He blamed them on the wind.

When Sugar pulled up, breathing hard, they'd left the full length of the island behind them. Kota wiped his face with his sleeve and tipped his head to soak up the sun.

He was back where he belonged. Back in control. And feeling better than he'd felt in weeks.

CHRIS KNEW A pissed-off man when she saw one.

Towing her carry-on into a bedroom fit for a princess, she tried not to add guilt to the list of things to despise herself for. She'd only meant to brush Kota back, not cut him to the bone.

Who knew he was so sensitive? After all, he made a fortune playing brawn-over-brains on screen. He wouldn't choose those roles unless they came naturally.

Still, he probably didn't like being reminded that he was no Einstein, especially since his brother had hit the genetic jackpot in both looks and IQ.

In any case, she'd rather have him pissed off at her than chasing her around the kitchen. Because, let's face it, now that she was out of testosterone range, she could admit that three granola bars weren't going to cut it. She was already starving, and the bowl of fruit she'd spotted on the counter was too tempting to resist.

But first she'd take a few minutes to unjangle her nerves.

She started with a warm shower and a leisurely dry-off with a fluffy bath sheet as big as a bed. Then she took her time getting dressed in one of the two sundresses she'd packed.

Things looked brighter already. More manageable. Less stressful.

She hung the other sundress in the walk-in closet and tossed a pair of capris, a T-shirt, and a handful of panties in the twenty-drawer bureau. So much for buying what she needed when she got where she was going. She'd have to make do. Things could be worse. As long as she stayed calm—

"Aagh!" A brush of fur on her calf scared her out of her shoes. She leaped up on the bed, heart pounding, eyes frantically scanning the room.

A black cat sat, sphinxlike, beside the bureau.

"You." She gave it a slit-lidded stare. One of those freaky earless cats she'd seen on Facebook.

It blinked bored emerald eyes.

Refusing to concede to a cat, she dropped her butt down on the bed and jounced a few times, like she'd been planning to test the mattress all along.

Yep, it was firm. With just enough give to make it perfect for sex. And wide enough for half the football team to join in.

Or one supersized underwear model.

Gee thanks, devil kitty, for starting that train of thought.

At that, the cat rose abruptly and strutted out, as if to say that its work here was done.

Flopping back on fluffy pillows, Chris stared at the

ceiling, where a slow-thwapping fan stirred the warm, humid air.

Gone was the illusion of equanimity she'd constructed in the shower. She was back where she started, her nerves sizzling and snapping like electric lines brought down in a hurricane.

Seven days.

They yawned ominously.

Seven days to resist the irresistible Kota.

Seven days to write the story that would salvage her career.

Seven days to pretend she was someone she wasn't.

Good times.

KOTA'S SHIRT CLUNG to his back. He peeled it off.

His jeans were lead weight. He dropped them on the sand.

His sweaty underwear strangled his nuts. He hooked his thumbs in the waistband . . . and paused.

God*damn* it. The island was for skinny-dipping, free of long-range lenses angling for a shot of his junk. His usual companions were good with that, and just as happy to get naked themselves.

But Christy would freak.

The devil on his shoulder hissed, *So what? She doesn't like you anyway.*

But Ma's son had promised Christy she had nothing to fear. And a naked man, especially a naked man who outweighed her two to one, was bound to make her nervous.

So he waded into the waves in his boxer briefs, warm saltwater lapping his thighs. When it tickled his balls, he dove under, surfacing in a crawl.

Paralleling the shoreline, he stroked until his shoulders begged for mercy, then rolled onto his back and floated, bobbing on the swells, his gaze following a lone fair-weather cloud drifting lazily above him.

And he wondered what Tana was doing. Well, not *exactly* what he was doing. He had a pretty good idea about that. But what he was doing in general, with his new, married life.

Making plans with his wife, most likely. Plans to build a new house, probably outside of L.A. Plans to get pregnant and start a family.

He should be happy for Tana. And he was. He really was.

So why did he feel so sad?

Damn it, this was why he'd begged Em to come with him. She'd have teased him out of his melancholy by now.

Instead he had Christy, who thought he was boring.

Well, he wasn't boring in bed, and he had the testimonials to prove it. If he got her in the sack, she wouldn't be thinking about conversation, that's for damn sure. What she'd be thinking about was his body, and all the things he could do to her with it.

Hell, she was already thinking about that, and she hadn't even seen the good stuff yet. She'd melted down over his arms. Wait'll she got a load of his chest, not to mention the rest of the goods.

A gull circled overhead, checking him out. He waved

at it to prove he wasn't carrion, and it lost interest and flew off.

Yep, he was just a meat suit to birds and humans alike.

Well, if his body was Christy's weakness, it was his strength. He'd been working it for years, on screen and off. It was his ticket to stardom, and into any bed he wanted.

Right now, that was Christy's bed.

Striking out for shore, he spotted her sitting on the porch swing in a bright fuchsia dress. Bare arms and bare feet, hair piled in a loose knot.

She pretended to look out to sea, but he felt her gaze on his skin.

Oh yeah, he knew just how to play this scene.

Hang onto your panties, baby. It's showtime.

Chapter Eight

Kota walked out of the waves like Poseidon surfacing from the sea; bronzed, built, and seriously godlike.

Chris tried not to look.

Yeah, right.

Pausing on the beach, he slicked back his hair with both hands. The move spread his elbows into a perfect V that tapered down to his granite chest, past his ripped abs and narrow hips, to end in a conspicuous point, shrink-wrapped by his clinging wet briefs.

Oh God.

She dragged her gaze away from that point, but not until she'd gotten an eyeful.

It would fuel her fantasies for months to come.

She made herself focus on the dogs going nuts at his feet, as if he'd been lost at sea for a month and they'd surrendered all hope of seeing him again. They circled him like planets as he strode toward the porch, water sluicing down his gleaming chest.

Why, oh why, hadn't she taken her mango and run back to her room? Because she felt bad about hurting his feelings, that's why. Her conscience couldn't handle being a bitch on top of everything else.

Besides, it was simply too beautiful here to stay inside. The scenery was spectacular.

And getting better all the time.

But that was beside the point. She wasn't here to pant and drool. She was here to be civil, even friendly. And if his body made it hard to think about anything but sex, she'd just have to brazen it out, as if she encountered Poseidon daily and wasn't impressed.

At the foot of the steps he bent over to pick up a rubber ball. His quadriceps flexed, long and powerful. Then he turned and hurled it into the waves, making deltoids bunch and ripple.

Cy bounded after it, or at least Chris assumed he did. Her attention was riveted much closer to home, on the muscled back blocking out the sun. Kota planted his hands on his hips, and her eyes followed them, then dropped lower, to white cotton stretched over marble-carved buns.

She licked her lips. Swallowed. Tugged on her neckline with one finger and blew down her dress.

Cy came bounding back and dropped the ball at Kota's feet, but instead of throwing it again, Kota stepped up on the porch, tossing it from hand to hand.

"Nice dress," he drawled.

"You'll be sick of it before I leave. I'm short on clothes."

"That's okay, they're optional here."

"So I see."

Grinning, he leaned his butt on the railing—a mere arm's length in front of her—and crossed his ankles.

She kept the swing swinging with one foot, and her eyes nailed to his face.

Don't look down. Don't look down.

He tossed the ball to her, so she had to look down.

Wow.

It hit her in the chin. The ball, that is.

"Oops," he said. Twisting from the waist, he reached out one arm and snagged it as it bounced. "You okay?"

"Yes." She made herself stare at the ball. Red rubber, hollow. She memorized its detail. Anything not to look at the bait he was dangling.

"If I toss it again, can you catch it?"

That irked her. "Of course. You took me by surprise."

"Daydreaming?"

"Thinking."

"About what?"

She drew a blank.

He laughed, pulling her gaze from the ball to his face. Poseidon never looked so good.

"Admit it," he said. "You were thinking about me."

"Oh please. What an ego."

"Well, I *am* standing right in front of you."

"Blocking my view." She leaned left to look around him.

He took it as an invitation to sit on the swing, which was built for two normal-sized people who liked each other a lot.

His thigh hairs prickled the bare part of her leg. His arm rubbed against hers as he tossed the ball from hand to hand.

Cy pestered him until he hurled it, an explosion of muscle power that juddered the swing.

"Geez, you'll bring the whole thing down."

"I doubt it." He tugged one of the chains supporting the swing. It could have moored a cruise ship without feeling the strain.

She used it as an excuse to abandon the swing anyway. Taking his place at the railing, she slapped at the damp spot he'd made on her dress. "Look at this. You got me wet."

His smile grew slowly this time, giving her space to think about what she'd said. She felt the flush start at her nethers and rise like the tide to her cheeks, firing her skin all the way.

Still, she pretended not to catch on. "I've only got two dresses with me. I don't need you dripping on them."

His smile widened. He rose.

With both of them barefoot, he had eight inches on her. She sidestepped—not a retreat, just a change of position—and Tri let out a blood-curdling squeal.

"Oh God, oh no." Chris dropped to her knees, patting the small body, terrified she'd paralyzed him.

He rolled over to give her his belly.

Laughing, Kota squatted and scratched Tri's fun spot. "He's a drama queen. Any excuse."

She sat back on her heels. "The men around here."

"Lovable, right?"

"Not the word I was thinking of." Cy chose that moment to bump her with his socket. "More like needy," she said, rubbing his gnarled head.

"We're easy. Scratch us in the right place and we'll follow you anywhere."

She rolled her eyes. "Speaking of following me, an earless black cat snuck into my room and tried to hex me."

"That'd be Van Gogh. He lost his ears somewhere."

"He wasn't born that way?"

"Nope." Kota dropped down cross-legged, putting everything on display. She buried her face in Cy's neck. Any port in a storm.

"Van Gogh had a tough life," Kota said. "He was next up for the needle when I got the call."

"Your friend at the shelter again?"

"Mmm-hmm. Black cats don't get adopted too often. Earless black cats, never."

"And now he's in paradise."

"Shows you never know from one day to the next."

So true. Twenty-four hours ago, Chris had no idea she'd wind up here on Kota's island.

"Are there more?" she asked. More like her and Van Gogh. More refugees.

"Eight cats, last I counted. Probably under the porch." He knocked on the floor. "They'll come around when they get used to you."

"And the horses?"

"Starving to death on a farm outside Sacramento."

"How'd you get them here?"

"On a ship."

"I see." But she didn't, not really. It seemed a soft heart beat beneath those iron pecs. Not what she'd expected.

His body wasn't what she'd expected either. He was big, oh yes, but not bulky like a juiced-up bodybuilder. Defined, God yes, but not cut to shreds like a cartoon character.

His body, in all its glory, looked one hundred percent authentic, like it was built by beef and hard work, and he wore it like he owned it, not like a costume he put on for the camera.

It was who he was. It suited him down to the ground.

And she wanted to touch it. Just a squeeze here and there.

And yes, there too.

As if he read her mind, he leaned back on his hands, a devastating move that contracted his abs, flexed those pecs, and displayed his arms at a new and interesting angle. She could study them all day and never get bored.

Tempting fate, she flicked a glance at his face. Indigo eyes caught hers and held fast.

He wasn't laughing now.

"Go ahead," he said. "Touch me."

She licked her lips. "Pfft. Get over yourself."

"Then I'll touch you." His gaze was steady, intense. He reached out and traced a fingertip up the back of her arm.

She should stop him. Immediately.

She moved her arm.

Closer to him.

Over her shoulder he skimmed, then down the front of her arm, adding fingers along the way.

In the crook of her elbow, he drew a circle with the pad of his thumb, a barely-there touch, lighter than a breeze, warmer than the sun. Sensual as sin.

She held herself still, afraid to move. Afraid he'd keep touching her.

More afraid that he'd stop.

THERE, RIGHT THERE. The crook of her elbow was silky and tender, and he'd swear it was wired straight to her pussy.

Once more Kota stroked it, the sweep of a feather, then drew his finger up and away, and saw her strain not to chase it.

Over her shoulder he traced a path, then down the back of her arm, raising goose bumps in his wake. She shivered, and he cupped her elbow. Slid his thumb once more into the crook and felt her pulse going wild.

He was half wild himself, hard as a nail and ready to yank her by that elbow into his lap, shred the dress she wouldn't need anymore, and pull her down on his cock as he drove up hard.

But he willed himself to cradle her elbow lightly, to slide his thumb back and forth. To stoke the flame that would, soon enough, scorch her panties right off.

He only had to wait, the hardest thing he'd ever done. Wait for her to make the next move, to need him inside her like she needed her next breath.

Then she'd tear off her own dress. Climb into his lap, onto his cock. She'd rake his shoulders with her nails, arch her back, cry his name—

"Quit it." She shook off his hand. "I'm not one of your pets. I'm not going to roll over and beg you to scratch my belly."

Leaning back on his elbows, he pulled his knees up before she got a look at the tent in his briefs. He hid surprise and frustration behind amusement. "We'll see," was all he said.

"No, we won't *see*. So you can wipe that smirk off your face."

He exaggerated a poker face, which seemed to irk her even more.

"I've been around celebrities all my life," she went on. "I know you're used to women peeling off their clothes every chance they get. You expect it. Well, not me, buster."

She shook her head positively, her umbrage patently fueled by bottled-up lust. "So don't bother strutting around half naked, waving your muscles and your . . . everything else under my nose."

"My everything else?" He wrinkled his brow. "You'll have to be more specific."

She glared.

He shrugged. "Then don't blame me if I keep waving whatever it is under your nose."

"Very funny."

"Just trying to be a good host."

"You can be a good host by delivering what you promised. Peace and quiet."

If those were really what she wanted, she would've stayed in her wing. But for some reason she was denying herself—and him—the hot sex she craved.

She couldn't hold out for long.

He rose, careful to keep his back to her, since his "everything else" hadn't gotten the message that sex was on hold.

"You want privacy, you got it," he said obligingly. "But if you're hungry"—he rolled it over his shoulder as he strolled through the door—"I'm making pasta."

Mmm, pasta. Her stomach growled. The mango had been a drop in a very empty bucket.

Through the open window, she heard Kota banging around in the kitchen. Running water. Opening drawers.

Like one of Pavlov's dogs, her mouth watered.

What harm could there be in sharing lunch? She'd straightened him out on the sex thing. As in, there wouldn't be any. So what could it hurt?

Not that she rushed to the kitchen on his heels. She waited a decent interval, then drifted in casually.

Ignoring his bare chest behind the center island, she opened the fridge as if considering a cold drink.

"Got some sav blanc right here," he said.

She pulled her head out of the fridge. The ice bucket sweated on the granite island; the wine gleamed pale gold in his glass.

He tipped his head at a cabinet. She got a glass, and he filled it.

What could it hurt?

Settling on a stool, she leaned an elbow on the counter. On the other side of the island, he was busy kneading dough with the heels of his hands.

"You're making it fresh. Color me impressed."

"Fettuccini okay?" He lifted his glass with a floury hand. She watched his throat move as he swallowed.

"Sure." She dropped her gaze to the dough. He worked it expertly. His hands were big but not clumsy. They knew how to exert precisely the right amount of pressure.

As her elbow knew from experience.

Other parts of her body were pretty sure of it too.

Leaving the dough to rest, he lifted a pasta maker from a low shelf, displaying an ass she was—okay—sorry to see he'd dressed in board shorts.

Still, it was riveting.

She kept her eyes on it as he moved around the kitchen, setting a pot of water to boil on the stove, chopping broccoli, then stir-frying it on a second burner, melting butter in a saucepan on a third.

That was three times more burners than she'd ever used at once.

Tripod tapped her leg with his foot.

"He likes to watch," Kota said. So she picked him up and put him on the other stool. He jumped over on her lap. Kota laughed. "Given a choice, guys take lap every time."

She sipped her wine. "That's why it's best not to give them a choice."

He smiled, wickedly.

"I'm serious," she said. "I'm not here for sex." Unfortunately.

"I hear you."

"But you don't believe me."

Patiently, he rolled out the dough. "I believe you believe it."

"What's that supposed to mean?"

He fed the dough into the pasta maker, catching strands of fettuccini as they came out the other end. "It means I believe you think you didn't come here for sex."

"Oh, you think I deluded myself? That I subconsciously knew I wouldn't be able to resist you?"

He spread the pasta on parchment. "Something like that."

She huffed. "The arrogance."

"I almost had you on the porch."

"Pfft. I had an itch on my arm and you happened to scratch it."

He snickered.

She took a measured sip of wine. It wouldn't do to get drunk. Besides, even if it was noon in L.A., it was breakfast time here.

Which meant she was drinking with breakfast. Way to kick off the week.

She set her glass on the counter. "It can't be nine o'clock yet. Wouldn't bacon and eggs be more like it?"

"Look around," he said. "You see any clocks?"

She looked. No clocks.

"I don't know about you," he said, "but my life's scheduled down to the minute. Studio, set, meetings, read-throughs, more meetings, photo shoots, interviews."

He spread another handful of pasta on parchment. "When I come here, I don't give a shit what time it is. I do what I want, when I want." He shrugged. "Pasta for breakfast? Why not? With wine? Why not?"

She couldn't think of a good reason. Besides, she'd been up all night, with just a nap on the plane. She'd eaten next to nothing for twenty-four hours. And, well, pasta.

She picked up her glass. "Okay, I'm good with that."

THEY ATE ALFREDO in the deep shade of the porch, at a café table barely big enough for their plates.

At a table that small, intimacy was on the menu, which was exactly why Kota chose it. He was close enough to see the gold flecks in Christy's caramel eyes.

Lunch had lightened her mood. "This is amazing." Her eyes rolled in ecstasy. "The pasta, oh God. And the sauce. So creamy, but so light."

He topped off her wine, even though it would probably put her to sleep. The truth was, he could use some shuteye himself. Just a catnap before sex. Then another one after.

Meanwhile, he enjoyed her enjoyment, happy to contribute to her wonderful ass.

Around them, peace reigned. The dogs snored under the table. Sunlight glinted off the water. A breeze fanned the stray hairs trailing from Christy's messy bun.

His gaze lingered on creamy shoulders. "You'll want to stay in the shade at midday, or you'll burn to a crisp."

"No problem. I'm going straight from this table to bed."

He smiled.

"For a nap," she clarified.

"Sure." He nodded agreeably. "A nap sounds good."

"Alone."

"Up to you. I'll fight you for the hammock." He aimed a thumb over his shoulder where it swayed in the breeze. "Or we can share. It's big enough for two."

"That'll be the day."

"Your loss. It's the best napping spot on the island. And it's not like we could have sex in it, if that's what you're worried about."

She rolled her eyes.

"Believe me, I've tried," he went on, "and I'm too damn big."

"And so modest."

He wagged his head. "You've got a dirty mind. I noticed it before, the way you always find a double meaning—a *sexual* meaning—in every innocent remark."

She snorted. "No, that would be you."

He gave her a pitying look. "You can try turning it around on me, but we both know you just proved my point with the hammock thing. What I *meant* is I'm too heavy. I start moving around and the hammock always flips over. And nothing kills the mood like a face-plant on the floor."

He spread his hands. "As for what you *thought* I meant, well, I've never gotten that far before flipping. But now that you mention it, you're probably right. I'm probably too big."

"Wait a minute. *I* didn't say you were too big."

"And why would you? It's nothing to complain about, right? I mean, I get a lot of oohing and aahing, but no complaints."

She laughed, finally, just when he was starting to wonder if she'd left her sense of humor on the plane.

With a lazy turn of her wrist, she wound her fork in the pasta, then she sucked it off—just a quick slurp and a flash of tongue—and his head spun a dizzy loop.

Maybe it was the wine. Maybe it was the woman. Either way, he liked it.

Under the tiny table, their knees brushed lightly. And she didn't pull away.

WINE FOR BREAKFAST didn't seem like such a bad idea anymore.

Honestly, through wine goggles, Chris's situation looked a lot less dire. Sure, she was stranded on a desert island with a guy her body wanted to jump but her mind said was off limits. That part was no fun.

But there was plenty of good stuff too.

For one, he could cook. For another, he'd showed her the wine cellar—stocked! For another, he was funny. For another, he was hot.

Oh wait, hot wasn't good. Hot made her life suck.

She pushed her wineglass away, better late than before she did something stupid.

Like put her hand on his thigh.

His thigh, which was muscled and tanned and so close to hers that their knees were touching. Not her fault! The table was teeny-weeny. Four legs couldn't fit under it without making contact.

Anyway, back to handling his thigh. She couldn't. But she wanted to. His legs were *soooo* long and lean.

She sat back in her chair to steal a look. Sneakily and unobtrusively. And he just happened to lift his foot to scratch Cy, making his quadriceps flex in all their magnificence.

Go figure. All her life she'd been an arm girl. Now she was a leg girl too. All because of that thigh. And his calf was glorious too.

Even his foot was nice. Even his toes.

Who had nice toes? Only Kota. He could be a toe model.

She reached for her wine again. Might as well, right? Enjoy the buzz before she crashed. Cuz when she woke up, she'd be back to reality. Back to fretting about her precarious career and her nerve-wracking plot to salvage it—

Nope, don't go there now. Just enjoy the buzz.

"We can arm wrestle for the hammock," Kota offered.

She laughed. "Gee, I wonder who'll win."

"I'll give you a handicap." He set their empty plates on the floor and propped his elbow on the table.

When she simply looked at him, he took her wineglass and set that on the floor too, then positioned her elbow on the table and clasped her hand in an arm wrestler's grip.

She laughed again at the comical contrast; his arm made four of hers, and her hand disappeared in his grip.

She went for a quick slam, hoping to catch him off guard.

He gave her a pitying smile.

She shrugged. "Worth a shot."

"Whatever. Now listen up, because I'm gonna teach you how to win any match with any man. It'll come in handy if you're ever down on your luck and need to make a quick buck."

"Let me guess. I should flash some tit." She whipped her shoulder strap down. His eyes darted to her breast, and—wham—she took him down.

Then up went her strap.

"What the hell!"

She snorted a laugh. "I traveled with a *band*. I know the power of the tit."

He looked stunned, then offended. "So you flashed 'em around to get what you wanted? A little nipple for a better seat on the tour bus?"

"Don't talk to me about flashing the goods." She drilled a finger into his biceps.

He didn't deign to answer.

Instead, he positioned their arms for another round. "Let's try that again."

Down went her strap; slam went his hand.

"I can do this all day," she said.

"Me too." He grinned.

"Perv." She shook off his hand and stood up. "Out of my way, loser. I've got a date with the hammock."

HALF-DOLLAR-SIZED AND ROSE-PETAL pink, Christy's nipple was burned into Kota's brain.

He watched her sashay to the hammock, then roll in like a sack of potatoes. Tri danced around underneath until she scooped him up, showing a mile of leg and almost landing on the floor in the process.

Then the lucky dog snuggled into her armpit and the pair of them corked off in five seconds flat.

Rubbing his knuckles where they'd whacked the table—twice—he considered the awesome power of the tit. Muscles were no match for it. Money? A joke. Brains? Get real.

The tit reigned supreme.

Now for another glimpse.

He left Cy cleaning the plates and tiptoed across the porch. Carefully, he sat on the side of the hammock. Then, in one suave move, he straightened and rolled, pushed her up on her side, and spooned her, all with barely a ripple.

Tri wriggled out from under her side, shot him a dirty look, then curled up against her breasts and corked off again.

Christy snored through the whole thing.

Which was a major disappointment. He'd hoped for some groggy, half-drunk, half-asleep horniness, where her defenses dropped and she melted into him and they ended up on the floor, but not until he'd proven he wasn't too big for hammock sex after all.

Instead, she slept on, while his conscience fought a dirty little war with desire.

Desire had him sliding the strap down her shoulder, not far enough to see more than the swell but enough to slip his hand inside if he wanted to. He wanted to. And what was the harm? He'd felt up sleeping women before.

Sleeping women, his conscience pointed out, who'd already let him feel them up when they were awake.

Conscience had Ma on its side.

With a sigh of defeat, he lifted her head and slipped his arm under to pillow it. Then he burrowed his nose in her rose-scented hair and dropped off to sleep curled around her.

Chapter Nine

CHRIS WOKE UP sweating, sandwiched between a tiny fur ball and a giant man.

Sweating was her least favorite temperature. When she exercised, she always chose an air-conditioned gym over a sticky set of tennis.

Normally she'd elbow her way out of a sweat sandwich as fast as she could.

Normally.

Instead she lay still, more focused on the hunk at her back than the hair stuck to her neck. Kota's long legs spooned hers, a perfect fit. One arm pillowed her head—and what a pillow it made. The other lay along her side, his big hand cupping her thigh.

And that wasn't the half of it. His chest—that monument to chests the world over—curved around her back. And his groin—enough said—cradled her butt like a sling.

No, she wasn't going anywhere. Not yet. Not for a while.

She dozed instead, in and out, half-thinking, half-dreaming. Enjoying.

Until Kota came to.

It was a process. A deeper breath, a twitch of her pillow. A squeeze of her thigh, probably a reflex.

Then he was awake, conscious. And instantly aroused.

She pretended she was still asleep as his erection grew from average to Kota-sized.

He gave her thigh another squeeze, then a stroke. Then his thumb slid up under her hem. She could actually feel him fight the urge to go all the way up to her ass. When he didn't, she gave him points for decency, then took some back when he crept up to the edge of her panties.

He settled there, apparently satisfied with sweeping his thumb back and forth.

The problem was, *she* wasn't satisfied.

It was wrong, she knew that. She was worse than a betrayer, she was a horny betrayer, this close to doing something so skeevy, so unforgivable that she might just as well throw herself into the sea and be done with it.

And yet, his thumb. His chest.

Then he moved his leg, a sensuous slide that elevated the back of her knees to first place on her list of erogenous zones.

He blew on her neck, a silky movement of air that only made her hotter.

He must have noticed the change in her breathing,

because his teeth came out, scraping over her shoulder. His hand on her thigh moved higher, his thumb hooking under the lace edge of her panties.

Time to stop this, stop him. Some lines simply couldn't be crossed.

Then he nosed her ear. "Your scent drives me crazy." His gruff, sexy whisper made her mouth water.

"I-I don't wear perfume."

"I know." His leg kept up that slow slide. His hand crept higher. And higher.

"Listen, Kota—"

His teeth closed on her earlobe, possessively. His thumb pushed higher, lifting the elastic, clearing the way for the rest of his fingers.

Into her panties they slid, sliding over her belly, and lower. She forgot what she was saying as the doors of hell swung open. The flames leaped and snapped.

Then from under the table, Cy shot from a doze to DEFCON 5 in one beat of a heart. Tri sprang off the hammock to rush to his side. Chris tried to sit up, Kota tried to hold her down, and in a blink and a blur, they landed on the floor.

"God*damn* it, Cy!" Kota's roar deafened Chris. "There better be goddamn insurgents on the beach."

Flat on his back underneath her, Kota had taken the brunt of the fall. She tried to roll off him, but his arms caged her. "You okay, sweetheart?" he asked in a much gentler tone.

"I cracked my funny bone again. Otherwise I'm good." Too good. Good enough to pick up where they left off.

Which wouldn't be good at all.

Kota must have had the same idea, because he didn't waste any time. Her thighs were spread now, instead of glued together. He went straight for the wet and the heat . . .

And Cy trotted around the corner with the newlyweds in tow.

"Howdy, neighbors," Tana sang out. Then he spotted them on the floor. "Shit, Kota, I told you to put a mattress under that thing."

Kota clunked his head on the floor. Clunk clunk clunk, like if he clunked it enough he'd wake up from a bad dream.

Helping Chris to her feet, he addressed his brother through his teeth. "Nothing better to do on your first day of marriage than pester us?"

"We're ready for a break. Figured you would be too." Tana grinned, and Chris felt a flush wash over her; embarrassment and residual arousal. Dropping her eyes, she brushed uselessly at her wrinkled sweat rag of a dress.

Kota tugged her against his chest, probably to hide the erection digging into her spine. But his hands on her shoulders felt supportive. And possessive.

"We were napping," he said with an edge.

Tana's "mmm-hmm" sounded as skeptical as the situation deserved. He hooked an arm around his wife's waist. "I told Sasha about your horse whispering. She wants to see for herself."

Chris could hear Kota's teeth grind. But he did a fair job of giving in gracefully to his new sister-in-law.

"Sure," he said, "we'll meet you in the meadow." And turning Chris by the shoulders, he hustled her through the door.

INSIDE, KOTA PUSHED her against the wall.

"I can rip this dress off you now," he said, "and get this done quick. Or we can wait and take our time once we get rid of my idiot brother. Your call."

He voted for *now,* quick and dirty, to take the edge off the lust that was tearing him apart. She was rumpled and tousled, her skin sheened with sweat, and he wanted to fuck her more than he wanted to breathe.

But he didn't want to scare her, so he gave her a choice while he shamelessly cheated, catching her face in his hands, thumbing her cheeks, taking her lips in a kiss that left nothing to chance.

And it worked, of course it did. She caught his wrists and held on as she kissed him back, knees buckling, hips grinding.

Then . . . footsteps on the porch.

What the fuck?

The screen door opened and he stepped back from Christy, her shape tattooed in fire on his skin.

"Oh, hey." Sasha had the decency to look contrite, unlike Tana, who grinned shamelessly over her shoulder. "Sorry to bother you again," she said, "but can I use your bathroom?"

Kota pointed down the hall, too frustrated for words.

Christy took off in the other direction, red as a tomato.

Tana took a step back, out of arm's reach, taunting him with that grin. "Don't blame Sasha. I put the notion in her head that she had to pee. Told her she shouldn't drop her panties in the woods, what with all the spiders and snakes."

Kota advanced on him.

Tana broke up laughing. "You shoulda seen your face, man. Both times."

Kota shoved him out the door. Tana kept laughing.

Off the porch. Still laughing.

"You got a death wish, you little shit?"

More side-clutching hilarity.

Then Kota started laughing too, at his idiot brother, at the look he imagined on his own face.

That was the great thing about Tana. He put things in perspective just by being alive.

THE SUN WAS low in the sky when they reached the meadow. Leaving the others to wait in the shadows that reached out from the woods, Kota stepped into the light, moving slowly, fanning the tall grass with his fingertips.

The horses sensed him immediately. Sugar lifted her head, nostrils flaring. She started forward, then stopped, scenting the other humans standing in the shadows. She'd learned caution the hard way.

But Kota's pull was strong. He clicked his tongue and she nickered back at him, carving a line through the grass until he was scratching her chin. She nuzzled the jeans he'd put on, going for the Jolly Ranchers stuffed in the pocket.

"Pushy girl, aren't you? Like all the ladies around here." He unwrapped one and she took it from his palm with soft, whiskery lips.

Cy thought he wanted one too, until he tried it. He spit it out on the ground, where Blackie scooped it up.

From across the meadow, they came to Kota as they had before, circling and prodding. He handed out Ranchers all around, with a second for Sugar because she loved them the best.

Then, patting her neck, he whispered in her ear. "Time to show off for those pushy ladies. You play the traumatized horse, I'll play the hero who tamed you."

Curling a hand in her mane, he boosted onto her back and used his knees to urge her toward the trees.

CHRIS WATCHED THEM come with her heart in her throat. It was breathtaking, like a scene from a movie, the bare-chested warrior returning from battle astride his proud destrier, both of them washed in golden sunlight.

"Wow," Sasha breathed beside her. "That's"—she swallowed audibly—"amazing."

Fanned out behind him, the other horses followed, trusting Kota's lead. He held the whole herd in the palm of his hand.

Drawing up, he swung the chestnut so she stood broadside to Chris. And he beckoned her.

Without hesitation she raised her arms, and he lifted her up in front of him. "Swing a leg over her head," he said, and she did, glad she'd put on capris. Then he locked an arm across her middle, crushing her against him, and with a squeeze of his knees, they were running.

"Eee!" The wind whipped her shriek into thin air and tore her hair from its bun. Lacing her fingers through the chestnut's mane, she hung on for dear life as the mighty muscles pistoned beneath her, while behind her, all around her, Kota shielded her like a fortress, his body effortlessly in synch with the horse, as if they shared one mind.

Across the meadow they tore, Tana and Sasha streaking alongside them astride a great black horse. Sasha's eyes were wide and wild. She held her arms up like she was riding a roller coaster, trusting Tana to keep her safe.

"I want to do that," Chris shouted into the wind.

"Go ahead, I've got you." Kota's arm cinched her tighter.

One hand at a time, she released the horse's mane, only to cling to the strong arm at her waist.

Then she let go, reaching for the sky, taking the wind square on the chest. She felt herself come unmoored, held fast only by Kota, but that was enough.

Inside her, a reckless laugh spiraled up and up, until out it spilled, happier than song, wilder than sex. It was joy unleashed.

It was awesome.

And it changed everything.

Chapter Ten

"OH MY GOD, oh my God!" Sasha couldn't stop talking about it. "That was *amazing*."

She clutched Tana with one hand, Kota with the other. "How do you do it? How do you get them to accept you like that, to *worship* you?"

Chris wanted to know the answer herself, but she couldn't marshal the words to ask. She was well and truly awestruck.

Tana, for once, didn't poke fun at his brother. "It's all Kota. He's got a way with animals. Always has."

To Chris's mind, it was more than "a way." It was mystical.

After riding breakneck for miles, they'd walked back through the meadow with the horses milling around them, as if the humans were part of the herd. The black one—Blackie, another Kota original—kept bumping Kota like they were schoolyard chums. The chestnut—

Sugar—practically had her nose in his pocket. And the others, all of them, had jostled for position, trying to get next to him.

"Kota vouches for me," Tana went on, "or they wouldn't let me near them. And considering the hellhole he saved them from, I wouldn't blame them for never trusting a human again."

"You must be so proud," Sasha said, beaming at Kota. "Of changing their lives. Making them whole."

Kota shrugged. "They keep the grass cut so I don't have to mow it."

Tana scoffed. "Don't let him kid you. He's got ranches in six states. Horses, dogs, cats, hamsters—"

"Just the one hamster," Kota cut in. "A friend of a friend's."

"Not to mention that he's overrun Ma and Pops's ranch with rescues. He's the softest touch in the west." Tana snorted a laugh. "If people only knew Mr. Gun 'Em Down can't watch a cute kitten video without bawling."

"I think that's sweet." Sasha rubbed Kota's arm. "And I happen to know your brother's just as sappy."

She slid an arm around Tana's waist. "Don't worry, boys, your secret's safe with Christy and me. Right, Christy?" She gave Chris a wink like they were best girlfriends.

Chris managed a watered-down smile, while inside she was going to pieces.

She'd had Kota all wrong. Sure, he was arrogant and horny, and he expected her to fall into bed with him like every other woman on earth.

But he was also loyal and generous and not dumb at all.

She'd been in denial, probably so she could justify betraying him, but the evidence was irrefutable. Her first clue was the wedding toast, an ode to family and fortitude that didn't leave a dry eye in the house. Then there was Em, the kind of woman who wouldn't have given Kota ten minutes, much less ten years, if he wasn't worthy of it.

Then his parents, so down-to-earth and normal, and obviously the most important people in Kota's world. Then Cy and Tri and Van Gogh, all of them damaged throwaways to most people, and that much more precious to Kota because of it.

And now . . . now this thing with the horses.

He was some kind of shaman.

Tana, the other man she was poised to betray, was kind and funny, and loved his brother and his wife and his parents wholeheartedly. And Sasha was sweet and sincere and ready to befriend Chris, never knowing she was a spy bent on exploiting every intimacy to save her own sorry ass.

They reached the guesthouse, pausing at the porch steps. "Are you okay?" Sasha asked, touching Chris's arm in a way that was friendly and comforting, and so, so undeserved by the traitor in their midst.

"I'm a little queasy." True. "Probably too much sun." A lie.

"I've been there," said Sasha. "Drink lots of water. Kota, you make sure she drinks lots of water."

"I'm on it." He stroked Chris's shoulder, his hand so gentle she could scarcely bear it.

Tana took his wife's hand. "Don't worry, honey, Kota knows what to do." He shot Chris a friendly smile as they arced off toward the main house. "You'll feel better in the morning," he said.

But she doubted it. She doubted it very much.

THEY WOULDN'T BE picking up where they left off, Kota realized, not with Christy so pale.

He scooped her up in his arms and headed for her bedroom.

"Hey." Even her protest was feeble.

"Don't worry, I won't take advantage of your weakened condition." He kissed her wan cheek. "You need a cool shower, a tall glass of water, and a good night's sleep."

He nudged her door with his foot, set her down in the bathroom, and turned on the shower. "You take the shower, I'll get the water, and we'll both tuck you in."

Afraid to leave her alone for too long, he sprinted to the kitchen, poured an ice water and piled some berries in a bowl, and got back to her room before she was out of the shower.

He stuck his head in the bathroom. "Need anything?" It didn't hurt to ask. Maybe the cool water revived her and she wanted help soaping up.

"No thanks." She still sounded peaked.

The shower turned off, and a minute later she emerged in a cotton nightie that hit her midthigh. His adrenaline spiked, but he kept lust off his face. She must really be hurting if she waltzed out in front of him without seeming to care.

She headed straight for the bed. He pulled back the cotton sheet, watching her nightie ride up as she slid under it.

Then he sat on the edge of the bed. "Drink this." She drank it, then sank back against the pillows. Her face was as white as the linen. "Are you hungry?"

She shook her head, staring up at the fan. He stroked her forehead with one hand and held her wrist with the other. Her pulse tripped crazily under his thumb.

If she'd been beautiful to him before, she was breathtaking now, her eyes dark pools, haunted and mysterious.

The need to care for her overwhelmed him. "I can stay with you, sweetheart. This bed's so big you won't even know I'm here."

That should've prompted a snide remark, even though he meant every word. But all she said was "No thanks, I'll be okay."

So he kissed her cheek, her palm, ran a knuckle over her jaw. And reluctantly, he left her.

In the kitchen, he tended the animals. The dogs got the dregs of Alfredo mixed into their supper. The cats got the food he'd had specially formulated and manufactured to his exact specifications. Everyone got fresh water, and he got a Corona. He took it out on the porch swing.

Twilight was his favorite time on the island. Over the ocean, stars sparkled like diamonds flung across midnight blue velvet. Creatures rustled in the foliage, coming out to hunt in the cool evening air.

As it always did, the island's serenity soothed his mind and made him more contemplative than usual.

Sipping his beer, he wondered idly what would have happened if he'd stuck with his original plans. If he'd finished college and continued on to veterinary school instead of going off to L.A. with Tana.

He wouldn't be sitting here, that was for damn sure. And God knows what would've happened to Tana, alone in the wilds of Hollywood. He shuddered to think of it. There was damn little in his life to be proud of, but he'd always taken care of his brother.

Rocking the swing with one foot, he reflected on the wedding, feeling rightfully smug. Security-wise, it was an unmitigated success. No problems with nut jobs or overenthused fans, and not a single reporter wriggled through the net.

Take that, Em. She loved to mock his control-freakishness. So did Tana. But nobody complained when things went off without a hitch.

In fact, the wedding's only unforeseen complication was Christy. Their instant attraction had punched him in the gut, and he couldn't seem to catch his breath.

From the moment he'd met her, she'd run roughshod over his plans. He'd done everything he could think of to herd her into line, but she was completely unpredictable. Her emotions were all over the map. One minute she was hot as a pistol, the next she cut him off at the knees. He still wasn't sure where he stood with her.

In fact, the only thing about Christy that he could be sure of was that he couldn't be sure of anything.

Cy wandered over to sit in front of him, giving him the one-eyed stare. Kota dropped one eyelid and gave it back to him.

Cy blinked first, then slunk off to lie in the doorway, hinting at bedtime. Tri was nowhere to be seen, probably snuggled in bed with his new girlfriend Christy.

The sky had gone full dark while he ruminated. The only light on the porch was what spilled from the kitchen.

Up at the main house Tana and Sasha would be banging away. Good for them. Sasha was a nice girl. He liked her. Ma and Pops liked her. So did Em.

Charlie would've liked her too.

That thought snuck out of the shadows and stabbed Kota's chest, stealing his breath. Sweat broke out on his brow.

His instinct was to flinch away from the pain, to shift his thoughts elsewhere, like he usually did.

But tonight he was tired and lonely, a deadly combination. Gloom settled on his shoulders like a shroud. What right did he have to push Charlie out of his mind? The first and best friend he'd made in L.A. was dead, and he was partly to blame.

The least he could do was respect his memory.

He drained his Corona and held the bottle up to the light. What had he been drinking the day he'd met Charlie? Something cheap, for sure, since he and Tana had just rolled into town.

They'd been half drunk when a casting agent spotted them at the bar. Recognizing fresh meat on the hoof, he made them an offer on the spot—starring roles in the movie he was casting. All they had to do was sign on the dotted line.

Being smarter than they looked, they tried to read the contract. The agent got pissy and summoned his friend, a guy so big he made two of Kota.

Things were shaping up to get ugly when Charlie entered the scene. Pushing his Ray-Bans to the top of his head, he said with a smirk, "Eugene, does your parole officer know you're back at it? Coercing innocent young men into making porn?"

Eugene tried to save face, but all he could come up with was "Fuck you, Charlie Brown."

He slithered out the door with his muscle, and Charlie watched them go. Then he said, "If you boys are looking to make porn, you can do better than Eugene. If you'd rather keep your clothes on, come with me and I'll buy you a burger. Ever been to In-N-Out?"

And that's how Charlie came into their lives.

He was an agent, but he didn't sign them that day. He didn't sign them at all. He befriended them, and in Hollywood a friend can be harder to find than an agent.

With Charlie's help, they scored jobs as PAs on the set of a blockbuster, where they rubbed elbows with megastars and a famous director. That led to more jobs, a few minor roles, a lot of wild parties, and a mind-blowing profusion of pussy.

And through it all, Charlie kept them from blundering. He genuinely had their best interests at heart. So much so that when another agent—a big one—offered to sign both brothers, Charlie urged Kota to bow out and let Tana travel the Hollywood road alone.

"Once you start making real money," he said in words that would prove to be prophesy, "you won't be able to walk away. You can kiss vet school good-bye."

At the time, Kota had scoffed. But look at him now. Fifteen years in the business, zillions in the bank, his next three movies lined up, and he'd yet to finish college.

He wouldn't complain, not when so many had so little. And besides, he wouldn't do anything differently. Who knew what disaster might have befallen his brother if Kota hadn't hovered in the wings?

But things had changed. Tana was settled now. Established, mature, content.

Married.

He didn't need Kota anymore, not like he had before. And Charlie, well, he was long gone. Ten years dead and buried.

So, what now? For the first time, Kota's life had no purpose.

For the first time, the man with the plan didn't have one.

Chapter Eleven

WHEN CHRIS WALKED into the sunny kitchen, she found Kota on a stool, working his way through a crossword and a big mug of coffee.

"Mornin', gorgeous," he said, and the smile that broke over his face made her heart skip three beats. He got up and poured her a mug. "Feeling better?"

"Much." Ten hours without brooding, fretting, or lusting—thanks to a seldom-used sleeping pill—and she felt almost normal.

But it wouldn't last, not unless she stayed well away from that smile. "I'll be working today"—sequestered in her room—"so you don't mind if I take my breakfast in there, do you? Maybe some cereal?"

His smile fell, and she felt a pang in her chest. In a perfect world, the whole week would be a sun-soaked sex romp with Poseidon, cavorting in the sea, riding horses, riding him. She'd almost gone there yesterday, a mistake she blamed on too much wine and not enough sleep.

She could only be grateful that Tana and Sasha had appeared before she'd damned herself for all eternity. Bad enough she was a two-faced liar. She drew the line at being a two-faced liar who slept with the person she was lying to.

And after yesterday, there was more than just her ethics at stake. Now that she realized Kota wasn't just a pretty celebrity face but a truly extraordinary man, it was personal. She respected him. She couldn't stomach the thought that if he someday learned she'd authored the forthcoming wedding exposé, he'd believe she'd whored herself out for a story.

"Suit yourself," he said, "but I'm making French toast." He set a bottle on the counter. Pure Vermont maple syrup.

That was dirty pool. She bit her lip.

"With strawberries," he said.

Mmm, strawberries. Harmless little berries, so plump and so sweet. Piled on harmless French toast. Drizzled with harmless syrup.

He pulled out a stool invitingly.

Her good intentions crouched on the windowsill, one foot in, one foot out. Then Tri tapped her ankle and—poof—out the window they went.

Telling herself that it was, after all, only polite to share breakfast with her host, she scooped up the little dog and parked her butt on the stool.

She'd sequester herself *after* breakfast. For the rest of the day. And night.

Meanwhile, the view. Shirtless again, Kota moved around the kitchen, pulling out flour and eggs, a loaf of French bread. When he glanced her way, she had to ask, "You used blue tile on purpose, didn't you, to bring out your eyes?"

He grinned. "Did it work?"

Like a charm.

She dropped her gaze to the mixing bowl. It looked like a toy in his hands, but he handled it like a pro. "Who taught you to cook?"

"Ma. She wanted her boys to be self-sufficient when we went out in the world. I can press a shirt, scrub a tub till it shines, and cook damn near anything that walks, swims, or grows in the dirt."

He smiled, a crooked curve of his lips more beguiling to her than his movie-star smile. "I'm rusty on the pressing and scrubbing, but I keep my kitchen skills sharp." He pointed his wooden spoon at her. "The ladies worship a man who can cook. Don't try to deny it."

She realized she was smiling too, a little dreamy, a lot bedazzled. "I can't deny it." What was the point, when she kept falling at his feet every time he picked up that spoon? "Does Verna know you use your cooking skills for seduction?"

He looked offended. "I've never cooked for sex. Well, not until yesterday, and look where that got me. It put you right to sleep." He drizzled milk into the bowl. "What

I cook for is *better* sex. A well-fed woman is a happy woman, and a happy woman is more fun in bed."

Amused, she lifted a brow. "Is that a scientific conclusion based on thousands of case studies?"

"Hundreds, not thousands. I can't cook for *all* of them. Who has the time?"

She laughed. His humor seldom came out in his movies, and never in the interviews he visibly suffered through when promoting a new film. But his timing was spot on.

"You should make a comedy," she said.

"It would flop. People don't want to see me crack jokes. They want to see me crack heads."

"I don't know about that." She cupped her mug in both hands. "You're pretty hot when you laugh. Trust me, the ladies would pay money to see it."

"But their boyfriends would stay home in droves. I'd lose my tough-guy cred. Damage my badass brand. Or so my agent tells me."

"Your agent should get a load of you now," she said as he poured coffee with one hand and stirred batter with the other. "He'd be on the phone to the Food Network. *Cooking with Kota.*"

"Think it would catch on?" He hardened his jaw, narrowed his eyes to a squint. He *did* look like a badass. A superhot, mostly naked badass. With flour on his cheek.

She swallowed. "Yeah, I kinda do."

Oh, she had it bad.

Tucking Tri under her arm, she went to cool off by

sticking her head in the fridge, where she found a pitcher of fresh-squeezed orange juice.

"Pour me some, will you, sweetheart?"

She did, wondering why *sweetheart* didn't piss her off like it should.

She poured herself one too, then loitered at the stove, pretending to watch his process instead of his biceps as he soaked the bread.

No harm in looking, she told herself. What could it hurt?

Nothing . . . until the first slice hit the griddle with a sizzle and pop, setting off a chain reaction. Hot butter spattered his abs. He skipped back with an "Ow."

And then, oh God, then he curled his chin down to look at his stomach, a move that carved his three rows into six perfect bricks.

Dazzled, she watched him dab the butter with a finger, then lick it off with his tongue.

God help her, she wanted to *be* the butter.

Whirling away, she started opening random cabinets, searching for plates. Anything to stop staring. No one could really be built like him. He must be Photoshopped.

"Plates are warming in the oven," he said, a sea of calm to her tempest. "But you can pop the champagne and pour it into the OJ. You like mimosas, don't you?"

KOTA SMILED TO himself as he walked the plates to the porch. He couldn't have planned that better if he'd tried.

Day two of "muscling" Christy into bed—har har—was underway. She could fight it, but it was a losing battle for sure, when a few drops of butter could take her down at the knees.

And that hadn't even been intentional. Wait till he put his back into it, so to speak.

Setting the plates on the table, he gave her a minute to get settled before he bent over for Cy's ball, twisting—just a little—so her eyes locked onto his abs. Then he straightened up—a little slow motion there—and hurled the ball all the way to the water, twisting the other way to give her a shot of his back.

He heard her breath catch. Satisfied, he took his own seat and quit posing long enough to let the French toast do its thing.

She drowned it with syrup and took a bite. Her head went back. Her eyes closed like she was coming. "Good. So good." She drew it out in a moan.

He smiled. The next time she moaned like that, she'd be in his bed. Or his shower. Or under the hammock.

He refilled her mimosa. In a replay of yesterday, he slipped his knee between hers. Everything was working according to plan.

Until she moved her knees away.

What the—

He played it cool. "I'll throw a couple more on the griddle."

In the kitchen, he studied her through the window. Today's sundress was grape, sprinkled with tiny white flowers and their tiny green stems. Her bare arms looped loosely around Tri on her lap, and her hair, thick and glossy as mink, was caught up in another of those messy buns.

An artist could make her face a life's work, but it was the newly etched crease between her brows that caught his attention. Because it meant she was worried. About him.

As she should be. He was scaling her fortress. He'd be over the walls before dark.

Back at the table, he slid another slice onto her plate. "Thanks," she said. "For feeding me. And for this." She swept an arm toward the sea.

"I'm glad you're here." He leaned back and sipped his mimosa. He enjoyed watching her eat. He liked hearing her voice, her husky laugh.

"So you live in the canyon?" he said. "Whereabouts?"

"Oh, it's hard to describe. The roads are . . ." She did a windy path with her hand.

"I know my way around. My agent's on Willow Glen. And my best friend lived in the canyon for years."

"He moved?"

"He died."

"I'm sorry." She lowered her fork, sympathy in her eyes. "Was he ill?"

"Overdose." How did they get on this topic? He didn't want to talk about Charlie.

Before he could change the subject, she said, "I lost a friend that way too. Kind of a boyfriend, or I thought he was. He was in the band—the sax player—back when I was barely legal." Her finger stroked absently at the condensation on her glass. "I didn't know the signs back then. I'm smarter about it now."

"My buddy was clean when I met him, back when I first came to L.A. But he had secrets. They got out. And instead of coming to me, he found a dealer." Kota tipped the last drops from his glass down his dry throat. That was more than he'd meant to say about Charlie.

He refilled their glasses. "So you don't want to tell me where you live, is that it?"

She shrugged. "It's a habit."

"I promise I won't follow you home and howl under your window."

"I've heard that before."

"Bad experience?"

"More than one."

"Online dating?"

"Crazy fans. I'm sure you know what I mean, times ten."

Did he ever. Which meant that the more he pestered her, the less likely she'd tell him. Not that he couldn't find out by other means. But now he understood that if she told him herself, it would mean something.

He wanted it to mean something.

Soft fur brushed their legs, and they both peered under the table. "Oh no." Christy's voice broke with pity. "What happened to him?"

"That's Scar. Some fucked-up individual dunked his tail in lighter fluid and set it on fire." The cat's back end looked like it had been peeled and boiled.

"My God." Christy swallowed down revulsion with a

visible gulp, then reached down to stroke his orange head. "I can't fathom the mind of someone who'd do that."

Kota couldn't either. But he knew how hard it was for most people—even extremely compassionate people—to accept the animals that looked so hideous.

That Christy could—that she went further and embraced them—made her more beautiful to him than any of the gifts lavished upon her at birth.

Emotion, raw and deep, tightened his chest. "I gotta tell you, sweetheart. I think I'm in love."

CHRIS'S HAND FROZE on the orange cat's head. "You're kidding, right?"

That was a dumb question. Of course he was kidding. Nobody fell in love in forty-eight hours.

He only smiled a crooked smile. "Another slice?"

She laid a hand on her stomach. "If I grow out of this dress, I'll have nothing to wear."

His smile widened. "Coming right up."

She smirked and stacked their plates. He shrugged like she didn't know what she was missing. Which was completely wrong, because she actually had a pretty good idea what she was missing.

Scooping up their glasses, he followed her inside, then waved her out of the way while he got busy cleaning up.

From her perch on the stool, she ogled his butt as he loaded the dishwasher, a drawn-out process that involved a lot of bending and stretching and twisting, and more bending. She didn't mind a bit. "*Cooking with Kota* is my new must-see TV."

His quick grin told her lust must be written on her face.

She wiped it off and groped for casual conversation. "Speaking of Kota," she said, "is Dakota your real name?"

"Yep." He dried his hands on a towel, folded it neatly. "Our parents—our birth parents—got around. Mostly skipping out on the rent. I was born somewhere in South Dakota. Tana was born in Butte."

She sensed some embarrassment there, best defused with humor. Holding Tri up in front of her face, she said to the dog, very seriously, "This explains his knack for original names. It's genetic."

Kota looked startled. "Well, hell."

She smiled. "Some things are coded in. Like this." She raced up the major scale from C to C and back down.

His eyes glazed. "Do that again."

She did it again.

He let the towel fall to the counter. "Will you sing for me?"

Men had asked her before; it wasn't unusual. The difference was that Kota's request didn't make her self-conscious. It felt like part of the conversation.

He spread his hands. "Anything. The theme from *Cheers*."

She sang a verse.

He grinned like a kid. "How about Adele? Or wait, do you have originals? Do you write songs—"

She held up a hand. "No, I don't write songs. Dad's

written some for me, but let's wait on that." Singing was intimate. A funny thing to say about something she did before thousands. But one-on-one it was intimate.

The last thing this situation needed was more intimacy.

She set Tri down on all threes. "Thanks for breakfast, but I've got . . . stuff."

His hands fell to his sides. "Okay. All right. I've got stuff too. Scripts and shit."

She turned to go, dragging her feet, secretly wishing—

"The thing is," he said, and she turned back, all ears. "I could use some help with Blackie's leg. You might've seen the bandage."

"I didn't notice. What happened?"

"Just a scratch, but in this climate . . ." He shrugged one shoulder. One awesome shoulder. "Anyway, if you're busy—"

"No, I'll get my sandals."

In her room, sanity grabbed her by her shoulders and gave her a hard shake. "It's bullshit, and you know it," she told herself in the mirror. "Blackie would walk on his hind legs for Kota. He'll certainly stand still for a bandage."

She paced. "I should stay away. He's too hot. I mean, come on, those abs." She shivered. "And I like him. Why do I like him?"

Van Gogh strolled into the room. Chris pointed at him. "You. The earless cat. That's why I like him." He did a silent meow. She clutched her head. "What's happening to me? How can I do this?"

She even wasn't sure what "this" was. Visit the horses

with Kota? Make it through the next week? Write a story exploiting his brother? Throw in some juicy stuff about their deadbeat parents?

"Take your pick," she told Van Gogh. "They're just points on the continuum of fraud and deception."

"Hey, babe?" Kota called down the hallway. "Wear something you can ride in and we'll take Sugar for a run."

Her conscience scraped pointy claws across her brain. *Pull out,* it said. *Tell him you changed your mind. You've got to buckle down to work. No time for racing through the meadow bareback with his arms wrapped around you.*

She opened her mouth with the best of intentions. And out came "Sounds good. I'll be right there."

Conscience reared up again, but Denial kicked it in the balls.

Get over yourself. It's just a ride through the meadow. What can it hurt?

Chapter Twelve

WITH HIS LEAD tied loosely to the wall of the shed, Blackie stood perfectly still while Kota unwrapped his foreleg and gave the scratch a long study. "Looks good," he said, satisfied. He rose and patted the horse's shoulder.

Blackie gave him a solid bump.

"Easy, boy. Let me wrap you up before you start your shenanigans." Kota squatted to slather on salve. Christy stood behind him, peering over his shoulder.

When he was done, he passed her the jar. She turned it over. "There's no label," she said. "What is it?"

"A little something I mixed up."

"You *invented* it?" She sounded flabbergasted.

"*Invented* might be a strong word." He wound the bandage around Blackie's leg, snipped it off, and stood up. "I combined some common natural remedies in proportions I thought would be most effective."

She looked stumped.

He hooked a finger under her chin. "If it makes you feel better, sweetheart, I think with my dick most of the time and only fall back on my brain in a crisis."

That got a smile out of her. And what a smile it was, a curve of luscious lips that cut off his brain and went straight to his dick. He had to taste her.

Cupping her cheek, he dipped his chin, angled his head for a kiss . . . and Blackie body-slammed him, catching him flatfooted. "Shit!" He staggered sideways and cartwheeled over a hay bale.

"God*damn* it."

He sat up, nursing his elbow and glaring at Blackie, who laughed his secret horse laugh.

Christy was no better. She had her hands on her knees, busting a gut at his expense.

"What if I broke something?" he threw out at the pair of them. "Then how would you feel?"

It fell on deaf ears.

He faked a limp but that got him nowhere, so he untied Blackie's lead and pointed out of the shed. "Go tell your friends how you messed up our first kiss. I bet they'll have something to say about it."

Christy leaned against the wall, wiping her eyes. "If only I had that on film. I'd run it backwards and forwards."

He pointed his elbow at her accusingly, showing a big, dirty scrape.

She held up a finger. "I've got just the thing." She balanced the jar on her palm. "A miracle salve made from common natural remedies blended together in their most effective proportions."

He plucked the jar from her hand and tossed it over his shoulder. "Very funny." He backed her against the wall.

"You have no idea." She drilled a finger in his ribs.

He flinched, then gave her his famous you-fucked-with-the-wrong-guy squint. "I don't like being tickled."

She squinted back. "I don't like being crowded."

"Liar," he murmured, moving in until there was no space between them. He pushed his hands into her hair. It slid through his fingers, softer than satin. He lowered his chin and went in for the kiss he'd been robbed of.

And she cut her eyes to the left. "Blackie!"

He whirled, duped like an amateur, while she slipped through his fingers and out of the shed.

He found her in the trees, doubled over. "You need to work out more," he informed her tartly, "so you don't have a heart attack." But when she looked up, he realized she wasn't winded. She was laughing her ass off. He did his ruthless-killer squint.

"Oooooh, Mr. Badass, don't hurt me." She clutched her side.

That did it. He put her over his shoulder.

Laughter morphed to outrage. "Hey!" She drummed his back with her fists as he walked five steps to Sugar, who'd trailed him like a kid sister.

Flopping her over Sugar's back, he said, "You'll enjoy

this more sitting up, but I'm good either way." He slapped her luscious flank smartly. "Your call."

"I'll sit up." Her words were muffled, but her tone was clear, and deadly. "You'll want to watch your back from now on."

"Yeah, yeah." He lifted her easily and set her on the horse right-side up. Then he scooped up Tri. "Hang onto him, he gets wiggly."

And grabbing a handful of mane, he leaped up behind her.

TALK ABOUT INTIMATE. What could be more intimate than a Kota-cocoon? His arms caged hers; his groin cradled her butt. His heat soaked through her thin cotton tee.

It was all so wrong, but it felt so right.

He held Sugar to an amble, meandering through meadow and ferns, sunlight and shade. The herd moseyed alongside. Birds chirped and twittered.

Chris knew she should be mad about his manhandling, but really, she'd asked for it. And how could she complain when she was right where she wanted to be?

They poked along in silence, and it occurred to Chris that Kota was utterly relaxed, perfectly content here among the horses.

It made her ask, "Why Hollywood?" She'd never wondered before, because it seemed obvious: He'd gone to Hollywood to become famous, feed his bottomless ego, and make money hand over fist.

It didn't seem obvious anymore. "Why didn't you work with animals? That's where your heart is."

"Vet school was the plan," he said. "I got sidetracked."

That sounded more like it, except, "Isn't it really hard to get into vet school? Academically, I mean."

"I know this'll shock you, but I had a 4.0 when I dropped out of college."

"Get out."

"Already accepted to vet school at Cornell."

"*Seriously?* I mean, wow. Huh."

"Gee, thanks." Dry as dust.

"Listen, I'm sorry. But it's not like you advertise your IQ. Your films—"

"Gross hundreds of millions, of which I get a fat percentage."

"Okay, but—"

He cut in, clearly pissed. "I'm filthy fucking rich. I couldn't spend it in three lifetimes."

"But—"

He exploded. "What part don't you get? Money, fame, women. Cars, a jet, a fucking island all my own. It's the American dream, baby. Whatever I want, I can have." He caught her chin and took her lips in a fierce kiss that had nothing to do with desire and everything to do with control.

She didn't try to resist; she simply reached behind her back and grabbed a handful of nuts.

He froze.

She pulled her head away. "Say you're sorry," she gritted past clenched teeth.

Tension vibrated through his huge frame. Sugar stopped walking. The herd gathered round.

Then, like steam through a pressure valve, he blew out a breath. His body deflated. "I'm sorry. I'm a dick."

"You *are*. You are *such* a dick." She resisted the urge to give a hard squeeze before she unhanded him. "What the hell got into you?"

He shook his head like he couldn't explain it.

"You upset everyone," she said.

"I know. My bad." He stroked Tri till he stopped quivering. The horses went back to their business; Cy resumed his patrol.

But Chris wasn't letting him off that easy. He hadn't hurt her, but he'd startled the hell out of her. "You're too big to pull that shit. It's scary."

His whole body telegraphed remorse. "It won't happen again. I promise."

"I'd feel better if I knew why you did it the first time."

Sugar topped out on a bluff, and for a moment they simply sat and took in the view, the sea stretching to the horizon, glittering and empty and vast.

Then he nudged Sugar down the path toward the beach below. When her hooves sank into the sand, he stopped her with a word and slid from her back.

He lifted Chris down, holding onto her waist even after her feet touched the ground.

"I can't explain," he said, "without sounding like an ungrateful asshole. I *am* rich and famous. I *do* have everything money can buy. There's not a handful of men in the world who wouldn't trade places with me."

Looking up at him, she saw past the movie star to the troubled man inside. "Except you," she said. "You wouldn't trade places with you."

"Ungrateful asshole that I am."

She touched his cheek, and he smiled. The shadows melted from his eyes. Kota couldn't seem to hold onto a bad mood—another thing she liked about him. The list kept growing.

"Don't get me wrong," he said, "there's a lot to love about my life, and I make the most of it." He turned her around to face the water. "This right here is one of the highlights. And it's all ours, so strip down and let's get wet."

It was too good to resist, but she fought it anyway. "I don't think—"

"Good idea, don't think. Just swim." He pulled off his boots, unbuttoned his Levi's. Her eyes followed his zipper.

He paused, jeans still hooked on his hips. "Sweetheart, that water's warm and wet, and once we're in it we'll both feel a whole lot better. So strip down to your skivvies and I promise I won't do anything you don't want me to."

But that was the problem, wasn't it? She couldn't think of anything she didn't want him to do.

WADING IN, KOTA tried to focus on the waves breaking against his thighs instead of Christy's hot pink panties and bra.

Hot. Pink.

The color was burned into his retinas. He dove

through a chest-high wave and swam out past the breakers. Treading water, he tried not to stare, but damn it, she took her time wading in, foam spraying her skin as the waves licked at her legs.

Then she knifed through a wave, surfacing to breast-stroke toward him, sleek as a seal.

She stopped at arm's length to tread water, squinting in the sunlight. "Are there sharks out here?"

"I don't know. Let me check." Ducking under, he got a shark's-eye view of flashing silver legs and pink-wrapped cheeks.

Circling her thighs, he skimmed fingertips over slippery skin, snapped elastic with one finger, caught her big toe and released it.

Then he peeled away and popped up where he started. "Only one, but he's big."

She smirked, then dove. Silver and pink flickered around his thighs as she circled, more mermaid than shark. He waited, heart racing, for the stroke of her hand on bare skin—

And she pinched him.

"Ow!"

She broke the surface, laughing.

He closed in until they were just inches apart, close enough to see the gold ring around her irises. Their legs brushed as they treaded water, neither giving ground.

"First you tickle me," he said, "then you strangle my nuts, and now you pinch me. You're such a girl." He made it a taunt.

"First you crush me to the wall, then you throw me over your shoulder, then you abduct me on your horse. You're such a caveman." She made it a sneer.

He went nose to nose. "Me Tarzan, you Jane."

"Speak for yourself."

"Cavemen don't talk much. We drag women around by their hair." He took a handful of hers.

"You wouldn't dare."

"There's not much I wouldn't dare." He released her hair and gripped her hips with both hands. She was built for him, her curves a perfect fit in his palms.

He tugged her to him, and her breasts swelled against his chest, ballooning up from her pretty pink bra.

Until he unhooked it with two fingers.

He pulled back just enough to let it float out of the way. Then he slid a hand up to cup her. Her nipple hardened as he felt her up.

"Yep, you're definitely a girl."

"And you're definitely a caveman." Husky, like she liked cavemen a lot. "But—"

"Okay." He grabbed a handful of butt too.

"Not that kind of but."

But . . . she didn't dislodge his hand. Their legs undulated in tandem. Her lips glistened with seawater. He licked it off with a slow stroke of his tongue.

She let out a little moan. Slid her palms up his arms and got a grip on his shoulders. Her breasts slipped and slid over his pecs. "We have to stop," she murmured.

"No we don't." His splayed hand crushed her against

his hard-on. She resisted by wriggling, making both of them hotter.

He licked her lips again. "Baby, let me in."

She shook her head, but weakly. She was folding like paper.

Then he pushed his fingers inside those hot pink panties, and damned if her eyes didn't glaze with pure lust. It unchained his own, and he reached for the heat, finding it with his fingertips, wetter than water.

Christy quit resisting. She let him in, all right, between her legs, between her lips, kissing like she sang, with her whole body and soul. She tasted like salt and surrender, and he wanted to eat her alive.

They fought the swells, thrashing their legs, dragging each other under. On land he'd be inside her by now. But strong and motivated as he was, in choppy ten-foot water, they were drowning.

He broke away at last. "The beach," he got out. And they swam like Jaws was chasing them.

CHRIS STAGGERED THROUGH the shallows to dry land, hands on her knees, sucking wind.

Kota charged up behind her, catching her waist, turning her, lifting her so her legs naturally hooked over his hips.

One huge hand cupped the back of her head, bracing it as he took her mouth, her tongue. His other hand supported her ass, fingers inside her panties, inside her.

Her conscience squawked. She ignored it, scraping nails over bunched shoulders, along straining triceps. Kissing him, soaking up his heat, his awesome strength.

He released her lips to drag kisses down her throat. "Baby." His breath was a rasp. "It's a long shot, but you got any condoms on you?"

She huffed out a laugh; frustration and dismay. "Yeah, right here in my pocket."

He dropped his forehead on her shoulder and shuddered out a breath. When he lifted his head, his jaw was tight, but his eyes were hot. "I'm not coming till I'm inside you, but there's no reason you have to wait."

He pressed deeper, and her head lolled back. Oh God, if he could do that with only two fingers . . .

"How long to get home?" she asked. If it was more than ten minutes . . .

"Ten minutes at a gallop."

She unlocked her ankles and let her legs slide down his thighs, sopping pink silk dragging over bulging white cotton.

The man was big everywhere. Every. Where.

Then he split her eardrums with a whistle. Sugar came at a run.

"You'll want your pants," he said, releasing her to snatch up his own.

She worked wet legs into capris that seemed two sizes too small, then looked around for her T-shirt. She spotted it hanging from the back of the jeans he hadn't bothered to button.

"Hey." She reached for it.

He swiveled away. "You don't need a shirt to ride." His smile had plans in it.

"What about sunburn?"

"I'll cover you."

She made another grab. He danced away, then circled back, catching her waist and boosting her up on Sugar.

In a finger snap he'd plopped Tri on her lap and leaped up behind her. "Sugar baby," he called out in his powerful drawl. "Run like the wind!"

He was as good as his word, keeping the sun off her back with his big body, and off her front with his free hand. His palm fit her breast like a glove, and watching him handle her while they streaked through the meadow was the hottest thing she'd ever seen.

They pulled up on a dime at the shed, and Kota had all three of them on the ground in a heartbeat, hurrying Chris down the path toward the house.

"I could carry you," he offered, as if she was dawdling.

"I'm not a sack of potatoes." Flopping over his shoulder was no fun.

"How about this?" He scooped her up with one arm under her knees, the other under her back.

Not bad.

Then, "Nope, I can't do it. I can't look at your tits without touching 'em."

He dropped her legs and backed her up to a tree, one big hand behind her so the bark wouldn't scrape her, the other taking the weight of one breast.

"Beautiful." He dipped his head and licked her nipple

with the flat of his tongue, then pulled back to blow on it. She hardened to a point.

"My breasts"—her breath caught as he went in for another taste—"don't usually do much for me." They simply weren't that sensitive.

"Baby, they're doing plenty for me." He moved her hand from his waist to his erection, stroking himself with the flat of her palm.

The last shreds of her reason fell in tatters to the ground.

Shaking off his hand, she shoved hers down his pants, palming him, velvet over steel.

He sucked air through his teeth, bracing a hand on the tree. "Just for a second," he whispered as she stroked. "Just a second."

Leaning in, he let out a low moan, swelling in her hand. Throbbing against her palm.

Then he straightened and yanked her hand out. She tried to get back in, to grab hold of what she wanted, but he cuffed her wrist. Squeezed his eyes shut, held his breath.

Seconds ticked. Then he hissed it out slowly and opened glazed eyes. "That was close."

She smiled. Oh, she'd liked having all that power in her hands. All that *everything* in her hands.

"Let's go." Taking her elbow, he barreled down the path, hustling her along in front of him.

They'd reached the edge of the woods, the home stretch, with the house in sight, when they heard *knock knock knock*.

"Kota?" Sasha's voice. "Are you home?"

They slammed on the brakes, then backtracked into the trees while the dogs charged ahead, giving them away.

"God*damn* it." Kota kicked a stump. "For a desert island, it's pretty fucking crowded."

"Give me my shirt."

He whipped it out of his jeans and held it over his head.

"Seriously?" She put a hand on her hip.

He eyed her pose. "Keep that up and you'll never get it back."

She dropped her arm. "Is this how you want your new sister-in-law to find you? Acting like a caveman?"

He grinned like an idiot. She made a grab for her shirt. He let her catch hold, then used it to pull her close and wrap an arm around her waist.

"You can have it," he said, nuzzling her ear, "if you promise to take it off again as soon as she goes."

That was easy. "I promise."

"Cross your heart?"

She drew an X on her breast. He dropped a kiss on top of it, turned it into a bite. The scrape of his teeth shouldn't be so arousing—

"Kota?" Sasha sounded concerned now, striding toward the path, the dogs racing ahead.

Chris shrugged on her shirt, then casually, as if she hadn't just had a hand down Kota's pants, she stepped out of the trees with him at her heels.

"Hey, there you are." Sasha looked relieved. "I got worried when the dogs showed up without you."

"Just lollygagging, enjoying the day." Kota's smile was genuine.

Sasha's gaze zeroed on Chris's pink T-shirt just long enough to remind Chris that it was wrinkled and wet, and probably transparent.

Chris's face heated, and embarrassment gave conscience a foothold. It reared up, reminding her she had no business getting naked with Dakota Rain. She was a spy, hiding out on his island to pen an article about his brother and this very nice woman who'd never done her any harm.

Suddenly, Kota's hand on her waist felt all wrong. She stepped away, scooping up Tri, keeping her distance from Kota.

"I guess you were riding," Sasha said. "And swimming. And stuff."

"Yep," Kota said. "Surprised to see you up at this hour, being on your honeymoon and all."

Sasha smiled, a sparkle in her eye. "We went to bed early. Besides, I'm usually up before dawn. Which makes this a late start for me, especially since we're a couple of time zones over."

Kota caught Chris's eye. He rubbed his chest with the flat of his hand, a riveting move. She gulped, then forced herself to look at Sasha, who was still chattering away cluelessly.

"— so I thought I'd stop by and invite you to dinner. Tana's dying to try out your new grill." Sasha flashed a friendly smile at Chris. "Wait'll you see it. It's so Kota. As big as a bus. You herd the cow in one end and steaks come out medium rare on the other."

Chris's half-assed smile was less than Sasha deserved but all Chris could manage.

"Sure, dinner sounds good." Kota shuffled his feet, practically herding Sasha along.

She got the hint at last. "Okay then, come on over when you get hungry."

She'd scarcely disappeared around the corner when Kota caught Chris's hand.

"Come on, babe. I need you under me *now*."

Chapter Thirteen

KOTA PRACTICALLY DRAGGED Christy to the house. She balked when they got to the steps.

"Listen—" she said.

"Later," he cut in. No sentence that started with "Listen" ever went anywhere good. "You can talk my ear off later and I'll memorize every word. But right now, my balls are turning fifty shades of blue."

He started up the steps, tugging at her hand. She held her ground.

"I can't do this," she said.

"Sweetheart, we've been doing it for an hour. We're just getting to the good part."

She looked down at her toes.

Jesus, he was losing her. Swallowing exasperation, he fell back on proven methods.

"Okay. It's your call." He made it sound like gracious surrender. When she lifted her head, he raised his arms and slicked back his hair with both hands, then locked them behind his head in his billboard pose.

He pretended to study the sea while she looked her fill. Then he dropped his hands to his hips. Rolled his shoulders like he was shaking it off. Rubbed a palm across his abs, slowly, like he was thinking about something else . . .

And she bolted past him, up the stairs, and down the hall toward her room. A door slammed in the distance.

"Well, fuck," he muttered.

Tri hopped up the steps and went after her, the traitor.

Kota glared at Cy. "Go ahead, why don't you? You know you want to." Cy tucked his tail, guilty as sin.

"Whatever." Kota stomped down the other hall and slammed his own bedroom door.

A cold shower helped for about five minutes, until he flopped facedown on the bed. The bed where Christy should've been spread underneath him.

What the fuck?

Everything had been going according to plan. Even better, in fact, what with the hot-buttered abs opening the show with a bang.

Then there was the foreplay in the shed, in the water, on the sand. If he'd just remembered a goddamn rubber, they'd have gotten it done right there.

He rolled over on his back and stared at the fan going round and round. His cock pulsed with each heartbeat. Why hadn't he let her get him off in the woods? He'd had to channel a fucking Jedi to keep from coming. And for what? Sasha showed up and that was that.

What the fuck?

He punched a pillow into shape and stuffed it under his head. God*damn* it. He had a few things to say to Christy Gray, that was for damn sure. But he'd be a gibbering nutcase unless he finished himself off like a goddamned teenager first.

Taking himself in hand, he crossed an arm over his eyes and summoned her tits.

CHRIS CUPPED HER breasts and stroked her thumbs over the nipples.

Nothing. As usual. Her breasts were dead zones. Nobody had ever gotten into her panties by way of her breasts.

Except Kota. His palms conducted some kind of current that zapped life into her breasts and made her nipples stand at attention.

Was it because his hands were rougher than a pampered movie star's should be, as if he actually *did* something with them?

No. Jason's palms were calloused from years of baseball, but her breasts slept through their whole relationship.

Whatever. It was irrelevant. What mattered was that she was out of control.

Eyes on the prize, Christine. Keep your job, save your career, and do Emma proud. Even though she has no idea.

Especially because she has no idea.

That made it even more meaningful, didn't it? More

honorable. This wasn't some lame attempt to win Emma's approval. That ship had sailed.

No, Chris would become a top-notch journalist because Emma deserved a daughter who was a credit to her. One who'd carry her torch into the future, who her colleagues would say was a chip off the old block.

Or maybe Chris would become a top-notch journalist to silence the doubting voice in her head, the voice that said she didn't have the drive to be the journalist her mother was.

Or, for that matter, the serious singer her father was, although that was a whole different can of worms.

One disappointed parent at a time, please. Take a number.

Back to Emma. Reed. The *Sentinel*.

Chris tried to focus her thoughts, but Kota kept ambling across her brainpan, distracting her with his arms, his chest. His package.

"Leave me alone," she muttered. Stepping into the shower, she braced one hand on the tile wall and turned on the cold water. Goose bumps shivered over her skin. She gritted her teeth.

So it was uncomfortable, so what? It was no more than she deserved. She was a wanton woman. An old-fashioned phrase, but it summed up her morning. Thank God Kota hadn't had a condom, or she would have surrendered her last sliver of self-respect right there on the sand.

But at least sexual frustration wouldn't be gnawing her alive.

Disgusted with herself, she gave up on the shower,

wrapped herself in a fluffy towel, and flopped on the bed. Tri tapped her ankle until she hoisted him up. He snuggled against her side.

She watched the ceiling fan's lazy sweep. Why, oh why, couldn't Kota be the obnoxious idiot he was supposed to be?

Thump thump thump. A fist shook the door.

"God*damn* it, Christy, open up."

"And speaking of obnoxious idiots . . ." She strode to the door and yanked it open. "What's your problem?"

Barging in, he shot out one accusing finger at Tri. Then he swung around to point it at her. "You promised."

She let her eyebrows ask what the hell he was talking about.

"You promised to take your shirt off as soon as Sasha left."

She looked down at her chest, then up at him. His eyes blazed blue flame. She fanned it for fun. "Do you see a shirt?"

"No. And I don't see your tits either. Which was the whole point."

"That may have been *your* point. *My* point was to get my shirt back before *Sasha* saw my tits." The same traitorous tits that perked up the minute he charged through the door.

He advanced on her until she had to look up to hold his gaze. "It was implied by the context." He tucked a finger into the towel between her breasts. They seemed to swell of their own volition, forming cleavage just to snuggle up to his finger.

"The context," he went on, "was heavy foreplay, as in you were playing with my dick and I was playing with your tits. And the implication was that we'd get back to playing just as soon as we got rid of Sasha."

He tugged. The towel slithered to the floor.

She stood perfectly still while his eyes devoured her breasts, then inched lower, and lower, as hot as a blowtorch.

When he spoke, his drawl was ragged and deep. "God must've built you just for me."

He touched her breasts, the barest drift of fingertips over the outer swells. He trailed them down her sides, tickling her waist, skimming her hips. Then moved them up again, lighter than a breeze, raising goose bumps in their wake.

It was so erotic she could've climbed out of her skin.

He dug a handful of condoms from his pocket and tossed them on the bed. "Baby, we're gonna do everything two people can do. And we're gonna start right now."

She couldn't breathe, couldn't swallow.

He stepped in.

She stepped back, guided by her last working brain cell. "I-I can't."

"You can." He closed the distance.

"No." Firmer now. "I just met you. I don't have casual sex." That was the truth, even if not the whole truth.

"Sweetheart, there's nothing casual about this." Conviction burned in his eyes.

"I'm serious, Kota. Two days together might make us

old cronies to you. But not to me. I don't make friends easily, and no matter how tempted I am, I don't have sex with a man until I'm comfortable with him."

That stopped him short. His brow creased in confusion. "You're not comfortable with me?"

"All evidence to the contrary"—she gestured to her own nakedness—"no, I'm not. But if it's any consolation to your ego, no man's ever seen my breasts after forty-eight hours—or had my hand down his pants, for that matter—so you're in a class by yourself."

"And you want me, right?"

She made a "duh" face.

He seemed slightly mollified, but his gaze was sharp. "So when you get to know me, we can do it?"

A loaded question, but she'd walked into it. And she couldn't fault his logic, based on the facts as she'd stated them. The problem was, she'd left out a few things she was in no position to reveal.

So she hedged. "When I get to know you, I might not like you."

"Damn, you're making this complicated."

You have no idea.

He got a crafty look in his eye. "Temptation might get the best of you."

He tempted her just by breathing. "We'll see about that." She squatted to scoop up her towel. When she rose, he was grinning. "What's so funny?"

He pointed behind her. She turned.

A full-length mirror.

CHRISTY'S FACE WENT up in flames. Wrapping up like a burrito, she said, "That's cheating—"

He lifted a hand to cut her off. "All's fair, darlin', and just so you know, I aim to cheat every way I can think of. And I can think of *lots* of ways."

He rubbed his jaw contemplatively, and the scrape of knuckles over stubble put stars in her eyes. He bit back a grin. The poor thing thought she could hold out until she "got to know him," whatever that meant. Not that he didn't respect her for it. It was a nice change of pace.

But her admirable morals were mighty inconvenient. Even after taking the edge off back in his room, he was hornier than a seventeen-year-old, and not fucking her *right this minute* was harder than anything—*anything*—he'd ever done in his life.

Well, if she was into torture, two could play at that game. Tempting her to bend her rules was really just another brand of foreplay. The higher he stoked the fire, the hotter the main event would be.

With one last, slow scratch of bristles that left her wanting more, he hooked his thumbs in his pockets, drawing her eyes to his crotch. He tapped his fingers as he rocked back on his heels.

She played with the ends of her towel, trying not to stare.

"Hungry?" he asked.

She shrugged. "I could eat."

"Meet me in the kitchen"—a last tap of fingers on denim—"and I'll feed you."

She showed up ten minutes later with the grape sundress covering too damned much skin.

Enjoy the pursuit, he reminded himself. *The endgame is inevitable, and it'll be all the sweeter.*

"Pasta okay?" A rhetorical question if ever there was one. He dusted the countertop with flour. "Want to help?"

She looked dubious. "I've never made pasta."

"And you're not starting today. Amateurs get chopping duty." He set two fat red tomatoes in front of her.

She eyed them like they might bite. "Um, there's a reason I eat out a lot."

"You're kidding me." Anyone could chop tomatoes.

"I spent my childhood on the road with one parent or other. Nary a Verna in sight."

With a long-suffering sigh, he took up the knife. After all, she had other attributes that couldn't be taught.

"Like this." He diced a tomato in slow motion.

"Huh. They do it so much faster on the Food Network."

He chopped the other at full speed.

She slid a cheek onto a stool, gave a Cheshire cat smile. "How will I learn if you do everything for me?"

"Smart-ass." He went back to his dough. "Don't put your feet up yet, you're not done. There's an herb garden around the south side of the porch." He pointed, for the directionally challenged. "Think you can handle snipping some basil?"

"It's green, right?"

"Right. Just like all the other herbs." Picking up the scissors, he stared at her until she slid off the stool, reluctantly.

"You're supposed to be tempting me," she groused as he shuffled her toward the door. "Making me work isn't the key to my heart."

He paused in the doorway. "You could sing for your supper."

She smirked a little smile and plucked the scissors from his hand. "Never mind. I'll figure out which one's basil."

She brought back an armful that made his eyes pop. "Pesto it is," he said, and got busy washing and chopping.

Christy picked up the pepper mill to use as a mic. "Welcome, all you horny ladies at home. It's Man Candy Monday on *Cooking with Kota*. Today he'll demonstrate the proper use of pectorals when slicing basil."

KOTA GLANCED UP, and the blue of his eyes stole Chris's breath. Then he flexed, and she lost her voice too.

"You asked for it," he said.

She set the pepper mill on the counter. What was she thinking? She was playing with fire. She should go to her room. She even turned to flee.

And—"Whoa"—a white cat prowled into the room, skinny as a toothpick.

"There you are, Bumble." Kota squatted and made kissy noises. "You must be hungry."

"Hungry? He should be dead." Chris squatted down next to Kota. "What's wrong with him?'

The scrawny thing rubbed between Kota's knees. Kota tipped its pointy face toward Chris and pulled back its lips.

No teeth.

"I'm not even gonna ask," she said.

"I wouldn't tell you if you did." Kota opened a can and set a bowl of soft food on the floor, aiming a get-back finger at Van Gogh.

Bumble crept up on the bowl and commenced gumming.

"Why Bumble?" Chris asked.

"Because Bumbles bounce."

It took her a minute, then she laughed, muffling it when Bumble cast a nervous glance over his shoulder.

"He's shy," Kota said, sitting cross-legged next to Chris. He skimmed a hand down the cat's knobby spine. "He never shows himself to anybody but me."

"I guess I have a way with the halt and the lame," she said, surprised to realize it was true.

"Yeah, you do." Kota stroked his other hand down her hair. "I like that about you."

She opened her mouth to respond, but a rush of emotion left her speechless.

Kota and his animals were wrapping around her heart.

His hand slid under her hair and cupped her nape. "I can help with these knots," he murmured, squeezing gently.

A moan slipped through her lips, acquiescence, a plea, and he shifted around behind her, legs splayed so she fit snugly in the V.

Using both hands, he worked the steel cables that tied her head to her shoulders. "Baby, it's a good thing you came to the island. You need a vacation."

She laughed weakly. If only. If only it was really a vacation. If only her whole presence wasn't a lie.

But she'd think about that later. For now, she swallowed her drool. "God, that's good."

He nuzzled her ear, his breath warm on her skin. "I can do better."

"Better might kill me."

"I haven't lost anyone yet." His teeth scraped her lobe as his thumbs broke up knots, turning her shoulders to jelly. "I can take every bit of this tension away." A seductive whisper. "Let me get you off. You'll relax. I promise."

Talk about tempting. It would be so easy to lean back against him. To give in to his magic hands.

"You're cheating again," she got out, holding herself upright by will.

"It's working, isn't it?"

"Not yet, but keep trying. You never know."

He laughed, a deep rumble that tightened her belly and her nipples, drawing everything up with anticipation. Sapping her resistance.

Then his hands stilled. "Well hell," he said, reverently.

"What? Wait. Don't stop." She opened her eyes. She was cross-legged, her dress hiked up way too high, and Bumble stepped cautiously into the open space between her thighs.

"Bumble's never sat on anyone's lap but mine."

"So we should keep the karma flowing." She shrugged to give him a hint.

His hands went back to work. She stroked a finger along Bumble's throat, drawing out a thready purr. Nice kitty. Useful kitty. He took sex off the table. Kota wouldn't disturb Bumble, even to get laid.

Or so she thought until he unzipped her dress.

"Better access," he said before she could object.

"To what?"

"Your shoulders, what else?"

He brushed fabric aside, and she couldn't deny that skin-on-skin gave him better purchase. Knots fell like timber before the awesome power of his thumbs.

She arched, eyes rolling back as he moved lower, his long fingers circling her waist as his thumbs worked her low back.

"Yoga," he said. "I'll show you some poses."

Ugh. Yoga wasn't her thing. But at least he wasn't talking about sex anymore.

"Orgasm first," he said on cue, "to loosen you up. Then yoga to keep you flexible." He leaned in, bare chest to bare shoulders, and scraped his scruff along her cheek. "I got you covered on both ends. So to speak."

She laughed, because he was funny and she liked him, and because she had to break the spell he was weaving before his thumbs inched any lower.

It was time to stop the madness. And she would.

But first she took one long, last moment to soak up the sexiest man alive. His chest, his stubble, his almighty hands. The warm, hot happiness spreading through her limbs.

Then, like ripping off a Band-Aid, she pulled away. She set Bumble on his feet and climbed to her own. And made the mistake of looking down at Kota, a sexy mess with his jeans unbuttoned and his hard-on bulging along his thigh.

He forked his fingers through tumbled blond silk and squinted disgruntled blue eyes.

"You know we're gonna do it," he grumbled. "Why make it so hard?"

Chapter Fourteen

CHRISTY SMILED, A slow curve of luscious lips punctuated by a pointed look at his boner. "You're blaming *me* for making it hard?"

"As a matter of fact, I am." He got to his feet and menaced her with a look that had zero effect. Then he twirled his finger.

She menaced him with a look of her own, but she let him zip her up. He managed to cop a feel while he was at it. She danced away, but not as fast as she could have.

Hornier than ever but satisfied he'd made progress, he went back to the pasta while Christy took her usual seat with Tri on her lap. Cy snored like a chain saw. Bumble stink-eyed Van Gogh as the earless cat slunk over to sniff the empty bowl.

It made a uniquely domestic tableau, and warmth bloomed unexpectedly in his chest. An overwhelming desire to protect and defend. A surge of affection not just for the animals but for Christy as well.

What the hell?

Lust, he understood. It was a daily event, prompted in different degrees by all kinds of women. True, Christy had blazed new ground. But the bottom line was that she was a woman he wanted to have sex with. That made it familiar, if uncharted, territory.

On the other hand, this warm, fuzzy fullness curling around his heart was reserved for family, a few close friends, and all four-footed creatures.

So what was she doing in the middle of it? Why did he have to fight down the urge to wrap her up in his arms?

"What's wrong?" she asked, giving him a funny look.

Everything, that's what.

"Nothing. Let's have some wine." *And get drunk.*

"I shouldn't. I just recovered from the mimosas."

"Then the timing's perfect." He whipped a Prosecco out of the chiller, popped the cork, and poured.

She gave in without a fight, nose twitching at the fizz as she sipped. "I'm ashamed to admit it, but I could get used to drinking with every meal." Her gaze flickered over his chest, and her cheeks flushed a guilty pink.

He quit obsessing about unfamiliar feelings of domestic bliss and got back to basics—getting laid.

Meeting her warm eyes, he pinged his glass to hers. "It's your vacation, sweetheart, you can indulge in all kinds of debauchery. I'm happy to help."

"Your standards for debauchery are probably higher than mine."

"One way to find out."

She dropped her eyes to study her bubbles. "I'm not really a debauchery kind of girl."

"I'll show you the ropes."

She chuckled. "You're persistent, I'll give you that."

"Ma says it's my defining personality trait." He rolled out the dough. "She calls it stubbornness, but it's all how you spin it."

"She's quite a woman."

"Yes, she is. She likes you too, and believe me, she's picky."

"I picture her guarding her cubs like a lioness, keeping off the girls who would've snared you and Tana."

He grinned, because it was true. "We weren't always the fine catches we are today."

"Trust me, Verna Presky's kicking herself."

He fed the dough through the pasta maker. "She called me a few months ago."

"Why?"

"To ask if I'd be up to the ranch anytime soon."

"And you said?"

"That I had a girlfriend." He flicked a glance at her face. She was frowning. "Which was a bald-faced lie," he went on, "proving I'm the weenie Em says I am."

Christy chuckled, and he swore he heard relief there. "Wimpy, yes, but kinder than saying you've outgrown her."

"I should've said she blew her chance with me twenty years ago, so why didn't she go look up Earl Quigley and see how he made out for himself."

That got a rich laugh. "Earl must've been some kind of stud to beat out Dakota Rain."

"Old Earl was okay. But I happen to know his Ford dealership went belly up in the recession. Not that I take any satisfaction in it, you understand."

"I'm sure." A sarcastic smile curved her lips.

He wanted to bite it.

"How about you?" he said instead. "Who broke Christy Gray's cold, hard heart?"

It must not have been as funny as the Earl and Verna story, because instead of answering, she set her glass on the counter and turned it in a small circle, spreading condensation in a widening ring.

"I wouldn't call it a broken heart," she said at last. "More of a disappointment."

He dropped the pasta in boiling water and waited her out.

"He plays baseball," she said at last.

"Dodgers?"

"Not anymore. He transferred to an East Coast team in April. And no, I'm not telling you his name."

"Why not?" He was burning to know.

"Because he's a public figure and I respect his privacy."

No problem. Kota didn't follow baseball, but Tana would know which Dodger was traded east last spring.

"Why didn't he take you with him?" The guy must be six kinds of stupid.

"He asked. I just"—she shrugged—"didn't care enough about him to go."

Kota had trouble following. "So he asked you to go,

and you decided not to because you didn't care about him. How's that disappointing?"

"Because I *thought* I cared about him. I *wanted* to care about him."

"Oh." He drained the pasta, drizzled it with garlic-infused olive oil, then tossed it with the tomatoes, basil, a sprinkle of salt, and a dash of black pepper, all while puzzling out why her story disturbed him.

He filled two bowls, she carried the Prosecco, and they settled on the porch at their usual table.

It should've been cozy, relaxed, but instead he was edgy. Something pricked at the back of his brain, a sharp little barb that caught on an old wound.

He twirled pasta but never raised it to his lips. He'd gone cold inside.

"What you're telling me," he said, "is you broke this guy's heart. Ripped a big-ass hole in his chest and sent him off across country to suffer alone."

She must have heard the bite in his tone, because she set down her fork. "He could've stayed. I would've married him."

"Even though you didn't love him?" The poor bastard. What could be worse than loving someone who didn't give a rat's ass about you?

"It's not that simple," she said. "I told you, I thought I loved him."

"And when you figured out you didn't? You'd have ditched him." Cold sweat ran a river down his spine. "He'd have woken up one morning to find you long gone. Because you cared more about yourself than about him."

She reared back. "*If* he'd stayed, and *if* someday I realized I didn't love him"—she aimed a finger at his nose—"which might never have happened because I might've fallen in love with him over time. But *if* I didn't and our marriage fell apart, that would've torn me to pieces."

"Boo fucking hoo." He shoved his bowl away. "Poor little Christy, all torn to pieces." He leaned in, snarling. "What about your kids? You'd ditch them too, wouldn't you?"

She stood up, a tower of indignation. "Fuck. You." She took her bowl and strode away.

He kicked the table, then caught the wobbling glasses before they upended. "God*damn* it."

Cy abandoned the porch, disappearing around the corner of the house. Tri upped stakes and hopped off after Christy.

Kota's lids burned. "Sure. Leave me here alone, why don't you?" He glared at Christy's empty chair as if he could torch it with his eyes.

"What the fuck?" he demanded of the world at large.

CHRIS PACED HER room like a tiger.

Dakota Rain, notorious for avoiding committed relationships, dared to judge her? To accuse her of leaving kids she didn't even have yet?

Well, fuck him then. She owed him nothing.

Opening her laptop, she set her jaw. "I'll give Reed a story, all right."

Asshole's Brother Ties the Knot

At the celebrity wedding of the century, gorgeous, talented, and kindhearted stars Montana Rain and Sasha Shay walked down the aisle wearing Armani (him) and Carolina Herrera (her).

Best man Dakota Rain—the coldhearted bastard known for squinting his way through such mindless moneymakers as Machine Gun Mayhem *and* Kill Everyone In Sight—*packaged his muscle-bound physique in Tom Ford.*

The groom's egomaniacal brother also delivered the wedding toast, a tear-jerking tribute to the brothers' tragic childhood, undoubtedly penned for him by someone capable of real feelings.

Crossing her arms, Chris stared at the screen. Reed would nix the headline. And the made-up movie titles. And most of the third paragraph. But otherwise not a bad start.

She closed the laptop and rolled her neck. The tension was back, as if Kota had never rubbed it away.

Tri tapped her ankle. She boosted him up to eye level. "Plead his case," she warned him, "and you're outta here."

Tucking him under her arm, she walked to the window. Outside, the midday sun bleached the sand and shattered off the swells. It was no time to be on the beach, but there was Kota, arms hanging at his sides, looking out to sea.

Alone.

Against her will, her heart twisted. She knew about alone.

It sucked.

He reached up with both hands to push his fingers through his hair, a breathtaking move that spread his back in a wide V, tightened his cheeks, and showed off his powerful legs all at once.

No wonder he worked it into every film.

But now it wasn't scripted. Now he was just a man alone on a beach, staring out to sea as men had done through the ages.

And like women through the ages, she longed to go and stand with him. To comfort and be comforted. To make him, and herself, feel not alone.

Stupid impulse. She turned her back on the window, went to the laptop again, and opened a different file.

Reporting Live from the War Zone, This Is Emma Case

A catchy title. And yet all she'd written so far were a few chapter headings. *Vietnam. Bosnia. Somalia. Baghdad.*

It wasn't for lack of source material. She had Emma's journals, all fifty of them. Miles of video. Thousands of photos. Hundreds of people to interview.

Her mother had cut a wide swath through the world. And yet, as usual, Chris stared at the blinking cursor, fingers frozen, while her own vivid memories invaded her senses. Open markets, fragrant and colorful. Narrow streets buzzing with foreign tongues.

With her intrepid mother, she'd traveled the world. Ridden camels, lived in tents, worn a burka for months.

Played kickball with refugees and Scrabble with the daughter of a genocidal dictator.

Not your average childhood, and yet, except for summers with Zach, she was always with her mother. How many kids could say that? And if Emma was often absorbed by her work, she was also dynamic, brilliant, and determined that her daughter would be all that and more.

So why, when Chris sat down at her computer to pay tribute to Emma, did her fingers freeze up? Why couldn't she begin to tell her mother's amazing story?

As she often did when the words wouldn't come, she turned to the photos. Organizing them by date gave the illusion of progress. So did adding short captions.

And sometimes, when a photo triggered a particular memory, she wrote more, a paragraph. Or even a story. Usually it was just a fictional vignette built around the moment captured in the photo.

But one photo cried out for more. She kept it in a file all its own.

Opening it now, staring at the bleak image of a shockingly thin girl wearing a scrap of red cloth, Chris was transported back to a dusty refugee camp somewhere in Africa. The sickening smell of too many people with too little sanitation swept over her like a hot wind. She heard the cries of hungry children.

In the photo, the round-eyed girl stared mutely at the camera. But Chris remembered vividly the girl's spindly arm poking through a hole in the fence, reaching for the bread Chris held in her hand.

There was something about the girl, about the way

she'd made Chris feel. They were about the same age, but their lives couldn't have been more different. Chris left the camp forty-eight hours later. But that girl might have been there for a year. She might have died there.

Chris had given her the bread, then gotten more and given her that too. She'd felt fortunate, and it was at that moment that she'd truly become aware of the randomness of life, the fortuity that put her on one side of the fence and that hungry girl on the other.

For more than twenty years she'd wondered what happened to that girl. It nagged at her. Sometimes it kept her awake at night.

She'd long since accepted that she'd never know. But she'd imagined a thousand endings to the story. She'd written some of them down, fairy-tale endings to what was more likely a harrowing tale of struggle, starvation, possibly rape, even murder.

She'd written those endings to make herself feel better, but they were too simplistic. She wanted the tale to end happily, but more than that, she wanted it to be honest. A realistic depiction of what might have happened.

Unsettled, unsatisfied, she closed the file. Frivolous fantasies could wait. Emma's story must be told.

And yet, when she shut down her computer an hour later, Chris still hadn't written a word about her mother.

Chapter Fifteen

THE GOLF CART jounced over the trail at a blistering five miles an hour.

"We could walk faster," grumbled Christy. She'd been cranky since she woke up from a nap.

Kota let the exaggeration float by. "Thanks again for coming with me."

"Don't thank me. I'm still plotting my revenge."

"I said I was sorry." Was he ever. Another sexless afternoon down the drain.

Her grumpy silence berated him all the way to the big house.

He parked next to the vast porch overlooking the bay. The dogs piled out. Cy went on patrol. Tri waited for Christy to pick him up.

Sasha appeared on the porch, all smiles. "I hope you're hungry. Tana's been cooking all day." She kissed Kota's cheek, then Christy's, bubbling with pleasure. "There's beer, wine, gin and tonics. Whatever you want."

"Just water for me," mumbled Christy, throwing a damper on things.

"Oh. Sure." Sasha's smile wavered. "Kota?"

"Hold that thought," he said. "There's something I forgot to tell Christy." He got a good grip on her arm and hauled her back out to the golf cart.

"What?" she demanded.

"Here's what." He bored in. "Sasha's throwing her first dinner party as a married lady, and you just sucked all the fun out of the air."

She had the grace to look shamefaced. "Sorry. I'll do better."

"They're good people. You might like them if you give them a chance."

"I already like them," she said. "That's part of the problem."

"What problem?"

She shook her head. "Ignore me, I'm still half asleep."

"You don't have to drink. That's not what I meant."

"I know." She mustered a trooper's smile. "I'll be a good guest, I promise."

He arched a skeptical brow. "After your whopper about taking your shirt off, your word's no good around here."

She laughed, and relief spread through his chest. He hated being on the outs with her.

Sasha met them on the porch with ice water. Christy drained it like she'd crossed the desert to get there.

"Thanks, I was thirsty. A gin and tonic sounds good. Can I help?"

Kota gave her arm a grateful squeeze. "Get me one too, will you? I gotta see a man about a grill."

Around the corner on the terrace, Tana faced off with a stainless-steel behemoth that could've swallowed a school bus without burping. He looked over at Kota. "This fucker's complicated."

"Pfft. How hard can it be?"

"You haven't used it yet?"

"It's a grill, man. Turn it on, cook the meat, and let's eat."

Tana pointed at it. "Go ahead. Turn it on."

Ten minutes later they both had their noses in the manual when the ladies appeared with cold drinks.

"Is it hot yet?" Sasha asked. "Can we throw on the steaks?"

Silence.

Christy put a gin and tonic in Kota's hand. "You're stumped, aren't you?"

"We're not *stumped*. We just want to make the most of all the cool features."

She strutted to the control panel and turned a few knobs, then graced them with a superior smirk.

Kota tossed the manual over his shoulder. "Tell me Zach has one."

"Nope, but I've used one before."

Probably the boyfriend's. While she chatted with Sasha, he pulled Tana aside. "Who got traded off the Dodgers pre-season?"

Tana ran through a few names.

"Which ones went east?"

"Only Jason Pendergast. He's playing third base for the Red Sox."

Kota squinted, trying to call up a visual.

"Six-three," said Tana, "one eighty, brown and brown. Scar through his right eyebrow." He shrugged at Kota's stare. "I met him once."

"Good-looking?"

"Why? You thinking about switching teams?" Tana grinned at his punny.

"Har har. Christy was almost engaged to him."

"Makes sense. He asked where I got Sasha's ring."

Poor schmuck.

While Tana went inside for the beef, Kota sipped his drink and checked out the view, two gorgeous women in summer dresses framed against the sparkling sea. In the background, Chopin played, a far cry from the raucous rock that pumped through the sound system pre-Sasha, when this terrace had teemed with hot babes.

Kota didn't miss it like he'd thought he would.

He ambled over to join them.

"I'm trying to bribe Christy to sing for us," Sasha told him. "I know I shouldn't. I hate it when fans ask me to do lines from their favorite film." Her musical laugh was endearing. "You know all about that, Kota. Nobody has more taglines than you."

He squinted his deadliest squint and put razors in his drawl. "I can kill you now or I can kill you later. Either way, it's gonna hurt."

"*Terror Train.* I *love* that movie!"

"Sasha's into body count," he told Christy.

"Nobody does it better," said Sasha. "And the muscles." She eyerolled. "Wait'll you walk down the street with him. People stop him *constantly.* 'Flex for us, Dakota. Lemme see what you got.' And in bars, forget it. Every biker wants to arm wrestle him."

Christy grinned. "I beat him twice."

"Tit?" Sasha nudged her. "Tana taught me about the tit."

"Christy already knew." Kota looped an arm over her shoulder. "She's an expert on the tit."

Cy wandered into their midst, bumping Sasha affectionately. She patted his rump, well away from his grisly noggin.

Then he poked at Christy, favoring her with his ragged grin. She grinned back at him and scratched his chin. And Kota's heart got two sizes too big for his chest.

Even Ma had needed time to adjust to Cy. But Christy looked straight past his ruined face to his soul.

He couldn't help himself, he pulled her in and hugged her hard, like she might float away if he let go.

What a woman.

She tapped his shoulder, mumbling something he couldn't decipher. He loosened his grip an inch. She dragged air into her lungs.

"You're crushing her," Sasha said, laughing. She had a match-makey look on her face.

It didn't bother him a bit.

Tana called from the grill. "Um, Christy, you happen to know how to adjust the temp?"

"Be right there." She knuckled his tickle spot, and Kota let out an unmanly giggle. He morphed it into a growl and added a squint for good measure.

"Mr. Badass." She shoved him back with one finger and sashayed across the terrace to school little brother on the Grill-osterone 5000.

What a woman.

"To THE GRILL master." Sasha raised her glass to Chris. Candlelight sparked off the bubbles. "The boys are your slaves."

Chris grinned. "I rule the grill. And the tit." Three gin and tonics made her believe it.

Sasha was on number four. "He's crazy about you, you know."

Chris gave Tri a lap bounce. "I know. He went down my shirt the first time I met him."

"Get out! That's bad, even for Kota."

Chris giggled. "No, I meant Tri."

Sasha giggled too. "I meant *Kota*. *Kota's* crazy about you."

"Oh." That was sobering. Chris glanced at him, horsing around in the pool with Tana. "I don't think so. He got really mad today when I told him I didn't love my old boyfriend."

Sasha puzzled over that. "There must've been more to it."

"Not really. I said Jason transferred to the East Coast, and that I realized I didn't care enough about him to go along. And Kota got pissed and went off on a tangent about me walking out on my kids to follow my own selfish dreams."

"Oooh, that explains it." Sasha nodded wisely. "Kota has abandonment issues. They both do. Because of their parents."

"Their parents abandoned them?"

Sasha smiled, ruefully. "I know you're not the run-to-the-tabloids type," she said, making Chris wilt like lettuce. "But it's not my story to share. Tana didn't tell me until we'd been together for a year, so don't be hurt if Kota holds onto it for a while."

"We're not"—Chris cleared her guilt-clogged throat—"we're not a couple. This is just a"—she fanned her hand, groping for a word to describe it—"a week." No arguing with that.

Sasha's lips twitched in a smile. "A week is more than enough. When it's right, you know it. And those two"—she waved her glass at the brothers—"are as old fashioned as Grandma Moses."

Chris must have looked skeptical, because Sasha leaned in. "I'm serious. They've got huge hearts, and they're loyal as Labradors. I wouldn't have married Tana if I didn't think it was for life."

"How did you meet?" A juicy sidebar story if she could make herself write it.

"I work with a program that brings theater to inner-city schools. Tana came to talk to the kids." Her brown eyes went dreamy. "He was spellbinding. Had them eating out of his hand. Me too. Afterwards, he bought me a latte. We went out for Italian that night. I stayed over at his place . . . and never left."

She chuckled. "Sounds slutty, right? I'm really not. Tana was only the second guy I ever slept with, which makes me a Hollywood anomaly. But as Julia said in *Pretty Woman,* I wanted the fairy tale."

And she'd gotten it. Tana tracked water across the terrace and lifted her out of the chair. "Time to get wet, babe."

Sasha's shriek trailed her as he strode to the deep end and jumped in.

Kota flicked water at Chris. "I'd do the same, but you'd take a bite out of me."

"A big juicy hunk."

He shook his hair all over her instead. Tri abandoned ship, but Chris kind of liked it.

He slicked it back. "Ready to go home?"

"Tana made pie."

Kota's eyes popped. "Blueberry?"

"So I hear."

He sat down kitty-corner from her and took a slug from her glass.

"Hey, get your own."

"Nope, I gotta drive."

"Right. We wouldn't want to die in a fiery crash. At *five miles an hour.*"

"Golf cart accidents are no joke." His cool, wet knee

rubbed along her sticky thigh. "But just a heads-up. Sasha's folks—"

"Don't tell me." She dropped her head in her hand. "They died in a fiery crash."

"Nope. They were both at the wedding. Her father gave away the bride. But they're heavy-duty drinkers . . . even though her brother died in a fiery crash."

Chris felt the ache. She eyed Sasha's drink morosely.

Kota slid it toward her. "Taste it."

She did. Tonic, no gin. "I would've sworn she was tipsy."

"She gets contact drunk. But she hasn't touched alcohol in years."

"I'm glad. I really like her." Sasha was kind and down to earth. And if her life looked perfect, especially after marrying Montana Rain, she had sorrow and demons and family trauma just like everyone else.

And like everyone else, she trusted her friends not to trumpet her business in the *Los Angeles Sentinel*.

Chris sucked her lime just to torture herself.

The newlyweds joined them, Sasha's dress dripping. "Gotta change before pie." She bumped Chris's arm. "Come along?"

Inside, the big house was like the guesthouse on steroids. Sasha's bedroom could swallow half of Chris's wing, with room for dessert.

"Can you believe it?" said Sasha, throwing out an arm. "The view alone."

Chris went to the window. The sun had set. A filament of gold lined the horizon, where indigo sky met inky sea.

Sasha ducked into a closet, talking to Chris through the open door. "I'm still freaked out by Kota's thing with the horses. Freaked out in a good way. But still."

"It's amazing, all right."

"You've got some of that too. That way with animals."

Chris scratched Tri's tickle spot. "I'm going to miss them."

"Why? You've got Kota wrapped around your finger."

If only it was that simple.

Sasha emerged in a white sundress that set off her olive skin. "Remember what I said? Loyal as Labradors." She led the half-mile hike to the kitchen. "Wait'll you meet Verna and Roy. You'll want to move in with them."

"I already met them. They're great."

Sasha stopped in her tracks. "You met them?"

"Kota brought Verna backstage, then he took me to see both of them at his house." She grinned. "Verna's inquisitive, isn't she?"

Sasha's face lit up. "This is huge. Tana didn't introduce me for *three months*. It was the final rite of passage, and I swear, if Verna had gone thumbs-down, I wouldn't be standing here. She must've liked you too, or you wouldn't be here either." She rubbed her palms together, apparently planning the wedding.

"Hang on." *Hang the hell on.* "It was ten minutes, tops." *But* Roy *did* mention a wedding band. . .

"That's plenty. Verna knows her own mind." Sasha grabbed plates, Chris took the pie, and they headed for the terrace. "I can't wait to tell Tana. He's been so worried."

"About what?"

"His brother, what else? Kota's been depressed since we got engaged." Sasha paused in the doorway. "The thing about Kota is, he's a tender. You've probably figured that out, with the animals and all. But he tends people too. His folks, his friends. He's been tending Tana ever since they were kids."

"And now Tana doesn't need him."

"Tana will *always* need him. Just not in the same way." Sasha gazed out at the two of them, heads together at the table, deep in discussion. "Right now they're hashing out Tana's next move. He wants to direct, but he's been waiting for the right script. He thinks he's found it. So does his agent. So do I. But it's Kota's approval he wants."

"YOU'RE NOT STILL mad at me, are you, babe?" Kota flicked a glance at Christy's profile, then back at the bumpy trail. She'd been silent since they left the big house.

"No, I'm not mad." She stunned him with a brush of knuckles down his cheek, a tender touch.

He caught her hand and kissed it, then pressed it to his heart. "Tell me you're glad you came," he said impulsively. "To the island. To dinner."

"I . . ." She hesitated. "Everything's different than I expected."

"In what way? What's different?"

"You. Me. Everything." She didn't sound happy about it.

"How are you and me different?"

"You're not an asshole. And I am."

What the fuck?

"You're *not* an asshole," he said. That much he'd swear to.

"You don't really know me, Kota."

"I know plenty. I know you were pissed off when we got to the big house, but you put it aside for Sasha's sake. I know my brother thinks you walk on water. You love animals and they love you. My folks like you. Hell, Ma even asked you to lunch."

None of that seemed to help. In fact, she pulled her hand from his grasp and sat on it.

He didn't know what to make of her. In his book, it was a magical night. He'd begun to believe that everybody was right; he truly was smitten with her.

He struggled to keep his tone light. "What else you got?"

"Nothing. I got nothing." It came across dolefully.

He stroked her hair. "What happened, honey? Did Sasha say something to upset you?"

"Sasha's the nicest person I've ever met." Like it was tragic.

"Then what's the matter?"

Instead of answering, she buried her nose in Tri's neck. And Kota's heart, so full a moment before, shriveled like a raisin.

When they got inside, he took her shoulders. "Sweetheart. Talk to me."

She wouldn't meet his eyes. "I'm just tired. I'll see you tomorrow."

And she left him standing alone, with the best night of his life in pieces at his feet.

I'M AN ASSHOLE, I'm an asshole, I'm an asshole.

Chris typed it line after line. It was that or nothing, because about the wedding, the newlyweds, and the honeymoon, she couldn't summon a word.

Talk about writer's block.

Stepping away from the blinking cursor, she stood in the center of the room, not knowing which way to turn. Out the window, only black. As black as her heart. As black as ink on a page.

Out the door, only pain. She couldn't face Kota. She'd starve to death in her room, because she couldn't look into his eyes again.

She tried rolling her neck, but it was practically paralyzed, as if her head was a bottle cap screwed onto her shoulders by the strongest man on earth.

"What's wrong with me?" she asked Tri.

He licked her chin, a kiss she didn't deserve.

"Why aren't you with Kota? He rescued you. He rescued me." She gripped her neck with one hand. "But this time he took in a traitor, didn't he? A spy. A sneak. What would Verna say about that? What would any of them say?"

She released her neck to shove her hand through her hair. "What would Mom say? Damn the torpedoes and get the story, that's what she'd say."

Or would she?

Chris's pulse picked up speed. "Wait a minute. Mom never lied for a story. She never pretended to be someone she wasn't."

She paced the room. "Mom had pride. Self-respect. She got the story through grit and determination, not deception and deceit. She was a credit to her profession."

Stopping at the window, Chris ignored the darkness outside, staring at her reflection instead, seeing Emma in the depths of her own eyes.

"My God." The truth crystalized, clear as a diamond. "Mom would hate this. She wouldn't be proud of me at all."

Chapter Sixteen

SCONES. LIGHT AND airy, with currants and nothing else, the way God intended them.

Chris took two, poured a big mug of coffee, and headed for the swing.

Kota was already there, mug in hand, a stack of papers on the seat beside him. His smile made her newly freed heart flutter like a hummingbird.

He moved the stack to his lap and she sat beside him, curling one leg under her butt.

"These scones are outrageous." She polished off number one right down to the crumbs on her chest.

"Glad you like them." There went that smile again.

She wanted to return it wholeheartedly, but she couldn't do that quite yet.

First, she had to come clean.

In the wee hours of the night, she'd almost convinced herself it wasn't necessary. Wasn't it enough that she'd resolved to quit her job at the *Sentinel* rather than write the wedding story? Kota never had to know she'd deceived him.

But daylight revealed the holes in her logic. For one, if she got involved with him, he'd eventually learn of her double identity anyway, in a way that would surely cast her in the worst light.

For another, even if they never got off the ground, she'd gone a long way toward sacrificing her integrity. She needed, desperately, to reclaim it.

Nope, there was no getting around it. Even if Kota voted her off the island, she had to tell him the truth. And she would.

After breakfast.

Biting into scone number two, she pointed her chin at the pile on his lap.

"Scripts." He fanned a few pages without enthusiasm.

"The usual?"

"If it works, don't fix it." He shrugged like he didn't care.

She peered at the one on top. "*Edge of Destruction.* What does that even mean?"

"It means Sasha'll love it."

She studied him over the rim of her mug. "You could go back to school."

He smirked.

"I'm serious. How long would it take to become a vet?"

"Five years. I'd be forty."

"And if you don't go to school, how old will you be in five years?"

That seemed to stump him. She shook her head. "Never mind, you're not smart enough after all."

He gave her a crooked smile. "I never looked at it that way."

She licked her fingers, watching him from the corner of her eye as he thought it through.

She saw the moment he rejected it. The spark went out of his eyes. "Too many commitments," he said. "My next three films are lined up."

"What would it take to get out of them?"

"The Western starts shooting next month."

"What about the other two?"

He rubbed his neck. "I could wiggle out of the last one. It's not set in stone. But the second one . . ." He shook his head. "There's too much riding on me. Too many people."

"Okay, so the Western and the next one would take you through next summer, right? You could start school in the fall." She held up her hand before he could object. "I know, you'll be forty-one. Either way."

He looked at the pile of scripts like he'd gladly set them on fire. But he said, "In five years I can bank two hundred million. My body's worth a lot more than my brain. And money can do a lot more than one vet."

"If I can paraphrase, saving one vet won't change the world, but it'll change the world for that one vet."

That got a laugh out of him. She could see he wasn't ready to sign on yet, but she'd planted the seed.

"How about you?" he said, rocking the swing with his foot. "Em told me you don't perform much anymore. Why not?"

She shrugged. "I got tired of living out of a suitcase. I wanted to put down some roots."

"Get married? Have kids?"

She gave him the eyebrow.

He winced. "Too soon?"

"Oh yeah."

"I'm sorry I went off on you."

"So you said. I accepted your apology. But once burned, twice shy."

He nodded and dropped it. "So why not perform in L.A.? No suitcase."

She looked out to sea. "I'm concentrating on other things. Writing the biography." Her journalism career was dead in the water, but she'd redeem herself with a Pulitzer Prize–winning tribute to her mother's career.

"How can you not sing?" he asked. "It's like Rembrandt refusing to paint."

"That's sweet, but talk about a whopper. Besides, I still sing with Dad sometimes. In fact, I recently did a ritzy celebrity wedding. You might've heard about it."

"Was that you?" He eyed her up and down, raising her temperature.

She sang a few sultry bars of "Fever."

His eyes glazed.

"Just because I have it," she said, "doesn't mean I have to sell it." She aimed a pointed look at his chest.

"You think I should waste all this?" He drawled it out, with a lazy half smile.

Her turn to eye him up and down. "I see a nanogram

of fat hanging over your waistband. It's all this lounging around. Shouldn't you be pumping iron?"

His smile widened to a grin. "Wanna watch?"

"Pfft, why would I—okay, yeah, I do."

He dumped the scripts on the floor. "Come on then. I'll show you how the big boys do it."

The gym consumed more than half of his wing.

"Holy shit." She turned a full circle. "You use all this stuff?"

All this stuff included a Nautilus circuit, racks of dumbbells, a dozen futuristic cardio machines, an obstacle course with scaling walls and climbing ropes, and a full-sized trampoline surrounded by mats.

"I do a lot of my own stunts." He vaulted onto the trampoline, jounced a few times, and held out his hand.

She backed up to the wall. "Not on your life. You can break your neck on those things."

He bounced higher, his hair floating around his head, then he backflipped—awesomely—three times in succession. He dismounted, cheeks flushed, eyes shining, and walked toward her. "Come on, I'll spot you."

"Uh-uh."

He stopped directly in front of her. His sheer size made her feel petite, which she wasn't. His sheer power made her feel fragile, which she also wasn't.

What she was, was turned on like a mare in heat, which he could probably sense, being the stallion he was.

He braced a hand on the wall by her head and locked

onto her eyes. His finger trailed fire along her jaw. She shivered.

"Christy, darlin'." His deep, rumbling drawl. "You came to the gym for a reason. Want to tell me what it is?"

KOTA FELT CHRISTY's pulse flutter under his fingertip. "I . . . no," she said.

"No, you don't want to tell me?"

"That's right." Her throat moved as she swallowed.

"Why not?" He traced her collarbone, lingering in the well.

"Because." Barely more than a whisper.

He tilted his head, leaning in. Her eyes widened. Her lips parted.

At the last second, she turned her head. "It's not fair. You have all this *testosterone*, and it's not fair."

"I hear it transfers through saliva." He licked her cheek.

"Gross," she said, unconvincingly. She shoved at his chest.

He lingered a moment to remind her he was bigger and badder, then he pushed off the wall. Turning away, he smiled to himself. Christy might know the power of the tit, but she was about to learn the power of the bicep.

He strolled to the chin-up bar, jumped up and grabbed it, and pumped out a few quick ones. Then, as if it just occurred to him, he dropped down and waved her over. "Climb on," he said, giving her his back, "for resistance."

Her indecision hung in the air. Then she grabbed his shoulders and hopped up, piggyback style.

He took a moment to adjust his erection. Chinning with a boner. That was a first.

Then he caught the bar on a hop, and this time he chinned in slow motion so she could appreciate his arms in all their glory.

Sure enough, her breathing quickened. One hand snaked out to cover his bicep.

"*Woooow.*" She drew it out, awe and lust rolled up in one word. Her fingers flexed into claws, nails raking muscle in a curving path around to the back of his arm, scoring his triceps, tickling his armpit. Over his chest they scraped, then down to his abs, strumming the washboard from his chest all the way down to his shorts.

In his ear, she moaned. It hummed in his veins, a siren song, all the sexier because she gave it up unwillingly.

He released the bar with a moan of his own. Her legs slid down over his hips. But when he turned, she stepped back, palms out. "I'm sorry. Not yet."

He clenched his fists to keep from taking her against the wall. "When?"

"Let's take a walk. We can talk—"

He scooped up a towel and buried his face. His dick had a mind of its own just now, and it wasn't up for conversation. "I'll meet you outside," he said into the folds.

When the door closed with a click, he sucked a jagged breath. "God*damn* it."

"I'M SORRY," SHE said again when he stepped out on the porch. "I . . . You . . ." She threw up her hands. "Okay, I admit it. You're irresistible. Are you happy now?"

"Do I look happy?" He bared his teeth in a snarl that looked half serious. "If I'm so irresistible, why aren't we bouncing on the trampoline right now?"

"We should talk first. Get to know each other."

"And *then* we can do it?"

She smiled, noncommittally. If he still wanted to do it after she confessed, she'd strip on the spot.

"Is there a path along the shore?" Best to have this conversation away from sharp objects in the kitchen.

"Yeah." He stumped toward the beach, and she followed behind him. She couldn't blame him for not being a good sport. Even *she* was frustrated by the mixed signals she was sending.

It wasn't her usual style. She liked to flirt as much as the next girl, but she wasn't coy, and she wasn't a tease. When she was interested in a man, she didn't play games.

But with Kota she'd been hot and cold, her body and brain each wrestling for control. Whenever her body had her brain on the ropes, she let Kota see how she felt. When her brain got the upper hand, she retreated like a silly virgin.

It was as frustrating for her as it was for him. Maybe when the big reveal was behind them, they could start over. Maybe he'd still want her.

Or maybe not.

Kota led the way to a ribbon of trail. They walked it in silence, winding along the varied shoreline, around rocky outcroppings, across a sliver of beach. In places the path curved away from the sea and into the shadowy woods, a whole other world, only to emerge moments later into brilliant sunlight.

Again, Kota proved he couldn't hold onto a bad mood. Even if he'd tried, the dogs wouldn't let him. Cy bounded in and out of the water, shaking all over them each time. Tri rode on his shoulder, enjoying a bird's-eye view.

The ocean breeze washed over all of them. The sun splintered off the sea. And before long he was holding her hand and humming off tune.

"What's that song?" She couldn't make it out.

"'Crazy.' You don't recognize it?"

"Um, no. It goes more like this." She sang a verse.

"Okay, I got it." He tried humming it again.

"Patsy Cline's rolling over in her grave," she informed him and sang it all the way through.

Then he mangled "Stormy Weather" until she set him straight. She cut off "Misty" at the first sour note.

By the time she caught on to his game, they'd covered miles at a gentle pace. "You're a jerk," she said. "And I'm a dope."

"A dope with a gorgeous voice." He kissed her knuckles resoundingly. "If you don't want to sell it, how about donating it? The shelter's having a fund-raiser. They're bursting at the seams. Too many animals. Too many misfits."

Cy chose that moment to drop a stick at their feet, his jagged tongue lolling gaily over mangled lips.

"When is it?" she said.

"I'll tell you the details when we're back in L.A."

Which meant he expected to keep seeing her on the mainland. Warmth curled up like a kitten in her chest.

God help her, she'd fallen for a celebrity.

The path took a turn, emerging from the trees to descend toward another crescent of white sand. Kota started down, then slammed on the brakes.

Chris bounced off his back. "What the hell?" she said, but he didn't reply, transfixed by something on the beach below.

Peering past him, she followed his horrified gaze and gasped.

On a bright red blanket spread out on the sand, Tana banged his new wife like a jackhammer.

KOTA TORE HIS eyes away before they burned out of his head.

"Jesus, Jesus, Jesus," he muttered, praying for a mind wipe. Anything to erase his brother's humping white ass from his brain.

He tried prodding Christy back up the path, but she dug in her heels.

"What, you want to watch?" he hissed, incredulous.

"Don't you?" Just as incredulous.

"He's my *brother*."

"So?" Her eyes were glued to the action. "Don't tell me you haven't shared women."

"At the same time? No!" He tried nudging her, but she had hold of a tree.

Cy trotted past, heading down, and Kota panicked. Dumping Tri on the ground, he gave chase, afraid to shout even though the newlyweds were so into it they probably wouldn't notice.

But they'd notice dog slobber, for sure.

Scooping up Cy, all eighty pounds of him, he hot-footed back up the path.

Now to hustle the whole crew out of there, double-time. If Tana caught him, they'd both be scarred for life.

And Sasha . . . Kota broke a cold sweat at the thought.

Prying Christy's hands off the tree, he tried to turn her around. But she grabbed his arms. "Wait." She was a step above him on the path, so she could see over his shoulder. She stared unblinking, eyes glazed, cheeks flushed.

Sweet Jesus. The woman really liked to watch.

Then she gave a little gasp, caught her lip in her teeth. And his dick, in hiding since he glimpsed Tana's ass, stood up straight, ready to party.

It was weird, for sure, but weird never stopped him before. Keeping his back to the beach, he dropped Cy like a sack of potatoes, caught Christy's hem, and whipped her dress over her head.

Her nipples poked at her bra like nail heads. Popping her out of the silky little scrap, he caught one in his lips and thumbed the other. Her hands pushed into his hair, dragging him closer, smothering him in tits.

"Oh God," she breathed. "He's got her on her knees." She moaned, and it hit him like the tenth shot of Patron.

He lost his mind completely.

Shoving her back against the tree, he drove his hand

down her panties, her sopping wet panties, digging for
the heat, groaning as she soaked his fingers.

But it wasn't enough, not nearly enough. She'd lost her
mind too. Out came her nails, raking his back, scoring
his shoulders as she squirmed on his hand.

"Please, Kota." She panted it. "Please please please."

"Hell yeah." He tore off her panties. Whipped out a
condom and kicked his shorts aside.

"Now now now!" Her arms cinched his neck like she'd
drown without him.

Hands shaking, he fumbled the condom like a kid.
When he rolled it on, she jumped up, climbing him as he
caught her ass, wrapping her legs around him as he drove
up inside her.

"Oh God yes." She clung to him as he pumped, her
tits slick with sweat, sliding against his chest. He braced
one hand on the tree, held her ass with the other, sweat
streaming as he pounded, as she met him stroke for
stroke.

Then she snaked one hand down between them. Her
head fell back in abandon.

Like a stallion he sank his teeth in her neck, gave a last
hard thrust, and exploded.

Chapter Seventeen

CHRIS WIPED HER sweaty hair off her forehead.

Okay, so she'd gotten a little ahead of herself. But holy shit, seeing Tana and Sasha going at it had unhinged her.

Kota lifted his heavy head off her shoulder. Dreamy blue eyes gazed into hers. "Are they still doing it?"

She peeked over his shoulder. "They're in the water. Naked, but not touching."

"Disappointed?"

Heat climbed her neck, invading her cheeks. "You'll never let me forget this, will you?"

"Nope." He kissed her, a playful smack on the lips. "It's blackmail bait, babe. I'm your lord and master."

She shrugged. "In that case, I'll confess and get it over with. Tana, I'll say, we only watched for a little while, because we got so horny seeing you bang your wife—"

"Okay, okay. It's our little secret."

She took a deep breath. Time to yank off the Band-Aid. "Speaking of secrets—"

"Hold that thought," he said. "I need to take care of business before things get messy." He lowered her till her feet touched the ground. "You sure it's safe to turn around?"

"Totally G-rated."

Kota stepped back, rousing the now-dozing dogs. Cy jumped up, ready for action. Tri tapped her ankle, looking for a lift.

It took a few minutes to get everyone organized. When they were headed back the way they'd come, Kota took her hand, smiling and relaxed. "So, what were you saying about secrets?"

Chris reconsidered the Band-Aid. Not that she had cold feet. It was just simple logic. Any reasonable person would agree that this kind of news would go down better with wine.

She gave him a smile. "Ignore anything I say within ten minutes after an orgasm. Especially an orgasm like *that*."

His eyes gleamed. The king of the jungle, full of himself and high on endorphins.

By the time they got back to the house, he was ready for more.

"Whoa, wait." She grabbed hold of the door frame as he propelled her through the kitchen. "I need water."

"There's a fridge in my bedroom." He detached her from the door frame and kept her moving down the hall, pushing open a door to a gigantic room with a stupendous view and a mammoth bed.

"Sorry about the mess." Rumpled sheets, yesterday's socks, another pile of scripts. Everything hit the floor with one sweep of his arm.

"But I need—"

"A shower? Me too." He peeled her dress over her head, unhooked her bra—her panties had gone missing on the trail—and stepped back to look at her.

"Sweetheart," he drawled, "I could eat you alive."

And didn't that conjure an image?

Then he dropped his shorts, and she got an eyeful of what she'd barely glimpsed before.

Gulp.

His shower was oversized too, big enough for a cheerleading squad.

She didn't ask.

"Let's get you wet." He nudged her under a giant showerhead that soaked her like a cloudburst. She closed her eyes and slicked back her hair. The water cooled her steaming skin.

Then Kota's big, soapy hands slid over her breasts, heating it up all over again.

Opening her eyes, she drank him in, his shoulders twice as wide as hers, his chest hard and muscled and within her grasp. She stole some soap from her breasts and used it on him, her palms sliding up to meet behind his neck, then down, over his stomach, around his hips.

His cock bobbed against her belly, and she went back

for more soap, taking him in her fists. She'd dreamed of this, handling him, fucking him. For three days it seemed impossible. Now it was real, and oh, so hot.

"Nice hands," he murmured. His own slid down and around behind her. "Nice ass." His big palms made it seem small.

She lifted her face, greedy for his lips, sucking his tongue as his long fingers curled around and under, opening her, reaching for the heat.

Sliding her hands up his chest, she cupped his cheeks, plastering herself to him, massaging his cock with her belly until he tore his lips away, his voice a rasp. "Unless you want it standing up again, we gotta get out of here."

They didn't bother with towels. He tossed her on the giant bed and caged her under him.

"Condom?" her last, faraway brain cell asked.

"We're not there yet." He slid down the length of her, lips curved in a wicked smile. "Spread 'em, babe."

She spread 'em. Then he elbowed 'em wider to fit his shoulders. Slipping his arms under her thighs, he jacked her up, taking her with his tongue, no preamble, just a shock of pleasure right where it counted.

Gasping, she arched, heels gouging the mattress, hands fisting the sheets. He brought his fingers into play, toying with her, finding her sweet spots like he'd been there before.

It was torture sublime, by a man who knew how. Again, and again, he brought her to the brink, always holding her climax just out of her reach, working her, working her, for hours, for days, with lips and tongue and the pad of his thumb.

Her mind tilted toward madness. The universe contracted to one thought; her brain could process just one word.

"Please." A moan. "Please. Please please please."

At last he lifted his head. "Please what, darlin'?"

She wracked her fevered mind for the answer. "Please . . . Master?"

KOTA LAUGHED. "OKAY, that works for me." And burying his face between her thighs, he shot beautiful, sexy, incredible Christy straight up to the surface of the moon.

Waiting for her to come down to earth, he sat back on his heels and enjoyed the view—wet hair plastered to her cheeks, skin sheened with shower water and sweat, arms splayed at her sides with a few strands of his hair wrapped around limp fingers.

Yep, God built her just for him.

He jiggled her leg. "Wake up, sweetheart. Master wants to get off."

One eye opened, a baleful stare. "That was a joke."

"Uh-huh. We'll discuss the terms later." He reached for the nightstand, fished a condom from the drawer, and tore the foil with his teeth.

"For now," he said, "let's get you up on your knees."

To Kota's mind, women were their most beautiful in the languid moments after sex. Unconcerned about makeup, or hair, or what tomorrow would bring, they simply glowed. An inner beauty that enhanced their natural gifts.

Propping his head on his hand, he gazed down at Christy, the most gorgeous creature in the universe. With the tip of his finger, he wrote her name on her stomach, swirling the tail of the Y around her belly button.

A slow smile curved her lips. "That tickles."

"That tickles, *Master*."

She opened her eyes. Rolled them.

"That was your call," he reminded her, "and lucky for you, I'm up for just about anything. Blindfolds, handcuffs." He caught the flicker in her eye.

So she liked to play, did she?

He pulled her closer, caging her with his leg, nuzzling her ear. "I can raid wardrobe for anything you want. We can play bad girl and perverted cop. Coed and horny professor." He nipped her lobe, and her breath caught.

Still, she tried to save face. "What makes you think I'd be into that?"

"It's nothing to be ashamed of, honey. I'll tie you up, tie you down." He brushed her cheek with his knuckles. "Just don't ask me to spank you, because, sweetheart, I couldn't lift a hand to you to save my own life."

Her caramel eyes melted. She framed his face with her hands. "If people only knew what a softy you are."

"Think again, little girl." He curled his lip in a sadistic sneer.

She nibbled it.

He tried the narrow-eyed grill that made bed wetters out of hardened criminals.

She laughed. "You're cute."

"*Cute?*" He rolled over her, caging her with his body. "Take it back."

"Cutie pie." She pinched his cheeks. "Cutie patootie."

He bared his teeth. "Take. It. Back."

She ran a knuckle over his ribs, and he flinched like a girl.

"God*damn* it." Enough was enough.

He quit fooling around and kissed her.

CHRIS POURED THE Orvieto while Kota plated his chicken *limone* with linguine.

"God, I'm starving." She swiped a finger through the lemon butter and sucked it off. Orgasmic.

"We worked up an appetite, all right." He scorched her with a look. "I expect we'll be just as hungry come breakfast time."

If he was still speaking to her. She gulped her wine. It was time to quit fooling around and tell him.

After supper.

Any reasonable person would agree that this kind of news would go down better on a full stomach.

They settled at the table, dogs underfoot, cats pretending to doze on railings and windowsills, everyone hoping for a handout.

Kota rubbed his thigh along hers. "How about a sunset ride?"

She lifted an eyebrow.

"On Sugar," he clarified, then wagged his head. "Can't you keep your mind out of the gutter for five minutes?"

"No."

He grinned. "I like that about you." He pointed his fork at her pasta. "Eat up."

"I've been eating up since I met you. Pasta this and pasta that. It'll go straight to my ass."

"Here's hoping." He took a long swallow of wine.

"Seriously? You like a fat ass?"

"Sweetheart, your ass isn't fat. It's ample."

She sat back, horrified. "*Ample*? My ass is *ample*?"

He looked confused. "Abundant? Generous?"

She scowled, and he spread his palms. "Baby, it's *perfect*. I love your ass. I'd follow it anywhere."

That didn't cut it either. "It's not floating through space, disembodied. It's attached to the rest of me." She tapped her temple. "There's a brain that goes with that ass."

"And I'm crazy about the whole package. I can't help it if I'm partial to your ass. Like you're partial to my arms." He flexed, and her jaw sagged.

He twirled linguine on his fork and carried it toward her mouth. She buttoned her lips.

"Sweetheart."

She turned her head away.

"Master says open up."

"You know, I've had just about enough—"

Cy leaped up, barking, startling the pants off both of them.

Tana rounded the corner, and the dog subsided to a pet-me whine.

"Shit," Kota muttered, pinching the bridge of his nose. "I'm not ready for this."

"*You're* not?" Her cheeks were on fire. She'd watched the entire X-rated show.

"What's up, kids?" Tana skipped up the steps with no clue that his rump was burned into both of their brains.

Chris found her voice first. "Hi" was all she could muster, but she couldn't help eye-walking all six-foot-three of him.

Kota noticed and turned a hard eye on his brother. "Em accused me of horning in on your honeymoon. And yet." He spread his hands.

Tana dragged a chair over to the table. "Sasha's cooking dinner. I couldn't watch." He sniffed appreciatively. "Chicken *limone*. Don't mind if I do." He snatched a cutlet off Kota's plate. "Damn, how do you get it so tender?"

"I beat it with a hammer," Kota said through his teeth. "I can demonstrate."

Tana grinned and copped Kota's wineglass too. Tilting back in his chair, he turned his attention to Chris. "Sasha tells me you're writing a book."

"Mmm-hmm." She rubbed her forehead, trying to mind-wipe the beach sex.

"What's it about?"

"It's a biography. Of a journalist."

Tana flicked a glance at Kota. But Kota already knew that much, and he seemed to be too busy glowering at his brother to care.

"Interesting choice," Tana said noncommittally. "Someone you know?"

She'd hoped to use Emma's story to ease Kota into her own unsavory tale, but there was no avoiding Tana's question. "Actually, she's my mother."

That brought Kota's head around. "Your mother's a *reporter*?" He spat it out like *Nazi* or *terrorist*.

Chris's chin came up. She wouldn't apologize for Emma. "She was a war correspondent. She covered Vietnam, the Gulf War. All the hot zones."

"Sounds like dangerous work," Tana said diplomatically.

"*Very* dangerous. My mother's a hero, and now she has Alzheimer's. She can't write her own memoir, so I'm writing it." She pointed her chin at Kota. "You got a problem with that?"

His throat worked. "It's . . . admirable," he said, obviously groping for a word that wouldn't choke him.

So much for piggybacking on Emma's heroic career. Chris balled her fists in her lap, pissed off.

And worried. If Kota couldn't stomach a valiant war correspondent, how would he feel about a weasel who wormed her way into his brother's wedding?

And worse, into his own bed.

Chapter Eighteen

"ARE YOU AWAKE?" Chris whispered, half hoping he wasn't.

"Mmm-hmm." Kota tightened the arm that held her to his side.

She rubbed her cheek on his chest. If she were a cat, she'd be purring. Happiness fizzed like champagne in her belly.

Only to give way to churning anxiety.

She'd waited too long to break the news. Now that they'd bared their bodies, and even parts of their souls, her betrayal would cut Kota that much deeper.

He might cut her right out of his life.

Back in L.A., Kota had been the least of her worries. She'd worried about letting Reed down. Keeping her job. Disappointing her mother. And if she'd felt guilty about sneaking into a celebrity wedding, it was because deception didn't come naturally to her. Her vague notions of journalistic integrity had yet to be tested.

But they'd been tested now, first by Verna and Roy, then Sasha and Tana. And most thoroughly by Kota himself. Trespassing on his island to save her own ass, she'd discovered the man behind the movie star, and she'd fallen in love with the menagerie of broken animals he'd given a second chance at life.

Nothing could justify betraying any of them.

It was time to come clean.

She cleared her throat and tiptoed in. "Um, remember how we were talking about the press? Well, about that. I—"

"Listen," he cut in, "I know you have to defend your mom. I even respect it on a mother-daughter level. But don't expect me to get on the bandwagon. The press killed my best friend as sure as if they shot him between the eyes, and then they tore his body apart on the front page."

She went still. This was big. And bad. And utterly heartbreaking.

"I'm sorry," she said, compassion prevailing over dread. "Who was he? Or she?"

"Charlie Fitz was his name."

She searched her memory.

"Ten years ago," he added.

"I was in college back east." A world away from L.A. She stroked his chest lightly. "Can you talk about it?"

He covered her hand with his, pressing it over his heart. "Charlie had a history before he came to L.A. When he was fifteen, he killed his whole family. Parents, baby brother. All of 'em, all at once, with a shotgun. Boom, boom, boom."

"Jesus." Not what she'd expected.

"I know what you're thinking. But he wasn't a psychopath." He squeezed her fingers. "He was out of his head on meth. Awake for five days straight. Hadn't eaten. He was down to ninety pounds by then."

Okay, meth was bad shit. But still.

"He didn't remember it afterwards," Kota said, "but there was no doubt. Neighbors saw him go in alone, come out soaked in blood. The cops cuffed him in under ten minutes."

"Did he go to prison?"

"No. His buddy did, the one who gave him the gun and the meth and sent him inside. But Charlie's public defender was a crusader, fresh out of law school and fired up with ideals. She worked her ass off to keep him from being tried as an adult. He got six years in juvie instead. And a lifetime of guilt."

Jesus. "How did he end up in Hollywood?"

"He couldn't stay in Vermont. The whole state knew who he was. He needed to move far away, so his NA sponsor hooked him up with a friend in L.A. An agent, who showed him the ropes.

"We met him our first day in L.A. He was ten years older than me. I always wondered if that's why he took me and Tana under his wing. Atoning for the little brother he killed."

Chris pushed up on her elbow. She could see his troubled face in the moonlight. "What happened?"

"A reporter, that's what." His jaw ticked. "She started out researching a story on me. My early days in L.A. That kind of shit. She latched onto my friendship with Charlie and figured she'd discovered my deep, dark secret."

He pushed his fingers through his hair. "See, Charlie kept a low profile. Avoided the clubs. Only went to parties if he had to for business. So when we hung out, it was usually at his place, playing pool, watching tube. Or we'd leave town. Fly up to Yellowstone and camp out for a week, or go skiing up in Park City. All of which seemed mighty suspicious to Lois Lane. She decided I must be gay. And she figured outing badass Dakota Rain would be her big break."

The woman hadn't been wrong about that last part. The story would have put her on the map.

"She sniffed all over town," he said. "Even went out to Wyoming and pestered Ma and Pops. But she couldn't find anything to back up her theory. So she started digging into Charlie."

He swallowed hard and went on. "Charlie wasn't his real name. He'd changed it, taken other precautions. But he knew the risks. Hell, it's the internet age. It took that reporter less than a day to put him together with the murders." Kota snorted. "My story wound up as the sidebar on page three. Charlie got the front page."

"Dear God."

"Things went to hell fast. His clients jumped ship like rats. His neighbors petitioned him to move. And his friends"—he huffed a laugh—"what friends? They disappeared overnight."

Kota's skin had gone slick with sweat.

"The story went viral by lunchtime," he said. "The sharks smelled blood and closed in. *ET. 60 Minutes*. The fucking *Los Angeles Sentinel*."

Dear God.

"I was in the Ukraine, of all fucking places, filming some end-of-the-world piece of shit. We were twenty-four hours behind on getting the news. But for fuck's sake, we had a satphone. He could've called me. I would've come."

Agony laced Kota's voice. "They found him facedown in the pool. A couple of so-called journalists. They shot a hundred pictures before they bothered to check for a pulse."

He covered his eyes. "They couldn't have saved him, but Jesus, they didn't even try."

A tear leaked over his temple. Chris pressed her lips to it. His pain was still so raw and so deep, kept alive, no doubt, by guilt and shame.

Because as much as he blamed the press, it was obvious that he blamed himself even more.

"KOTA." CHRISTY'S VOICE was rough with emotion. "I'm sorrier than I can say. But it wasn't your fault. There's plenty of blame to go around, but none of it's on you."

He shook his head, trying to make her understand. "I heard she was asking around about Charlie and me. I should've seen where it was going. I could've diverted her. Had sex with her. Anything so she'd give up the gay angle.

"But I had to make a point," he went on, turning the knife in his chest. "Tana said I should confront her, but I dug in. I can still hear my own voice. 'Why go on record one way or the other, when it shouldn't matter either way?'"

"You weren't wrong about that." She laid her cool palm on his hot cheek. "You were what, twenty-five? Practically a kid. How were you supposed to see ten moves ahead?"

He turned his head to look at her. Her eyes were damp, filled with warmth and affection.

She stroked his fevered skin. Her smile was as gentle as her touch. "You stood up for your principles," she said, "even though it could have hurt your career. Don't beat yourself up for that. You were the good guy."

He wanted to believe that. And she was right about the blame. There was plenty to go around, and much of it could be laid at the press's door. From the most mercenary paparazzi to the highest reaches of the network news, they'd all made hay with Charlie's tragedy. And even though any idiot could tie Charlie's overdose directly to the headlines that preceded it, nobody at the *Sentinel* lost any sleep over a good man's ugly end.

Christy leaned in and kissed him, sweet and tender. Her hair, a mass of glossy waves, tumbled around them, their private cocoon. A sanctuary he wouldn't let ugliness penetrate.

He stroked her bare shoulder, cast from a mold for his palm. Pushed his hand under her hair to cup the back of her head, to cradle it, protect it.

To protect her. Keep her safe.

His chest, so tight with fury a moment before, expanded as if he'd drawn his first breath. His heart swelled so his ribs could barely contain it.

Pushing her down on her back, he caged her head with his arms and gazed into eyes so deep he'd never reach the bottom if he lived a hundred years.

"Christy Gray," he said in a reverent whisper, "I'm falling in love with you."

JOY AND PAIN washed through Chris in equal measure. Because—God help her—she was falling in love with him too.

She closed her eyes, afraid he'd see dismay there and misconstrue the reason. Why couldn't this be simple? Why must this ugly secret lie between them?

There was no way she could tell him now. Not with Charlie's story fresh on his lips.

It explained so much, some of which wasn't clear even to him. Sure, he had good reason to distrust the press. They'd contributed to, and exploited, his best friend's death.

But that wasn't the whole picture by a long shot.

What Kota refused to consider was Charlie's own role. The guy had obviously been a powder keg of guilt with a very short fuse. And who could blame him? Remorse must have hung on him like a lead suit he could never take off.

But Kota, a tender by nature, had taken his wounded friend into his keeping. Now he blamed himself for causing Charlie to be exposed, and for not being there to help him when the shit hit the fan. He believed he let Charlie down—twice—and he carried that guilt like a chain around his heart.

And guilt, as she'd learned during the past few days, was an accelerant. Dribble it on the smallest spark of recrimination, and—*whoosh!*—you had an inferno on your hands.

In Kota's case, he needed someone other than Charlie to share the blame with him, so his justifiable dislike of the media had exploded into an obsession that turned him against an entire profession and drove him to turn his brother's wedding into a siege and his own home into an armed compound.

Not that she could ever convince him of all that. The toughest thing about guilt was that you couldn't be talked out of it. No amount of logical explanation, sympathetic understanding, or old-fashioned common sense could dislodge it once it dug its claws in.

Only a crisis could uproot it, an emotional tsunami that washed away everything in its path, opening up the landscape, clearing the sight lines.

Hers had hit twenty-four hours ago, and only because she was trapped on a desert island with three people she planned to betray. Getting to know and care about them had made writing the story so repugnant that everything in her rebelled.

Only in that pressure cooker had she realized what would surely be so clear to anyone else: Guilt at disappointing her mother had not only driven her into a career she didn't want, but also forced her into an assignment that went against everything both of them believed in.

For her, it was a life-changing epiphany.

To Kota, though, it would mean jack shit. Because not only had she betrayed him, but her betrayal also stabbed at his deepest wound. How could he forgive her when his own guilt still had him by the throat?

If she tried to tell him now, her apology would fall on deaf ears. He'd see her deception instead, which was real and undeniable.

He'd see lies. He'd see the enemy.

He'd see a whore who sold her body for a story.

She felt his gaze on her face, the love in his eyes. She had four days to convince him she was worthy of it.

Four days.

They'd go fast.

Four days to talk and laugh and have sex on the beach.

Four days to show him all he'd come to mean to her.

Four days before she had to tell him the truth.

HE GOT IT. Gazing down into Christy's face, at the sooty lashes fanned against pale cheeks, the red lips slightly parted as if waiting for his kiss, Kota finally got it.

This was how Tana felt.

The dopey look his brother got on his face, like the sun rose and set in Sasha eyes, used to make Kota snicker. Now he looked into Christy's eyes, a thousand miles deep, and he tumbled in. Falling.

And that—another stunning revelation—was why they called it *falling in love*.

He smiled with his whole heart. At last the mysteries of the universe were solved. At last he understood why people wanted this, why they threw themselves into it, no matter the cost. Why they mourned its loss like a death.

He dropped a kiss on those lips, then rubbed his cheek along hers. Nosing the curve of her ear, he sucked gently on the silver bead in her lobe. Her breath riffled his hair so it tickled his jaw. Her breasts rose and fell against his chest, suspended above her.

His fingertips threaded her hair, tracing small circles on her scalp. His knee made a space between hers. "Christy, darlin'," he whispered. "I'm gonna make love to you now."

Her palms stroked down his back, a slow, tender slide. "Kota." Her voice caught on his name. "I didn't expect this. I didn't expect to feel this way."

"Neither did I, sweetheart. But I like it. I like everything about it."

His other knee joined the first, and she parted her legs to give him room. He trailed kisses along her jaw, and she gave a breathy little laugh, parting her lips to take his tongue.

He meant to take it slow, the prince kissing the princess awake after twenty years under a spell. But she had other ideas. Her head lifted off the pillow, applying the pressure he'd held back. Her hips came up off the mattress, inviting him inside.

Out the window went storybook notions of lovemaking. This was real. It was now. He wanted inside her, all the way in. She was already inside him, running in his veins, swelling his heart, his balls.

In one smooth motion he caught her hips and sat back on his heels, dragging her up his thighs and onto his cock. One thrust had him seated, the next had her eyes opening wide with surprise and wonder, and a whole lot of *wow*. She'd unchained his animal. And she damned well liked it.

Hauling her upright, he drove deeper, taking her nipple in his teeth, scraping as she arched, sucking as she cried out. His hands cupped her gorgeous ass, helping her ride him, his fingers drenched in the hot mess they'd made.

Gripping his shoulders, she worked her thighs till she couldn't. Then he took over again, going up on his knees, wrapping her legs around his waist. "Hang on, baby," he murmured, and he carried her down, flat on her back, trying not to crush her, dying to crush her, to absorb her through his skin.

It was sex, and more, and the more made it better, better than ever before. She fisted his hair, dragging his lips down to hers, kissing him, and it was more than a kiss. It was molten, and it spread through every inch of them, welded every juncture until they beat with one heart, felt with one skin.

And when they came, together, there was no Kota, no Christy. There was only a flame, one flame, burning bright.

Chapter Nineteen

EVERY CELL ACHED. Every hair follicle. Every hair.

Chris's body had gone from pitifully underused to worked-like-a-rented-mule in twenty-four short, but extremely awesome, hours.

The shower jets showed no mercy, hammering like a blacksmith on her aching flesh. Bruises bloomed on her thighs in fingerprint patterns. She'd earned every one.

But enough was enough. When Kota stepped up behind her, she moaned. "Food first. And coffee."

He reached around and held a steaming mug under her nose.

"Oh my God. I love you." It popped out of her mouth.

He kissed her nape. "I love you too, babe."

Oh God, oh Jesus, can I make this any worse?

"I . . . . uh." She gave up. What could she say? The toothpaste was out of the tube.

"I'll make you whatever you want," he said. "Pancakes? Omelets? Frittata?"

In spite of her turmoil, her stomach growled like a bear.

He curled an arm around her, spreading his big palm over her no-longer-flat stomach. "I love that you eat. Skinny women don't do it for me anymore."

Her lips flattened. First, ample ass. Now, not skinny.

Okay, both true. But what next? Saggy tits?

"I'll have toast," she said.

"Toast?" His disappointment was palpable.

She sighed. "Okay, *French* toast."

"Coming right up." He dropped another kiss on her nape.

When the door closed behind him, she thunked her forehead on the tile. *Thunk thunk.* And another *thunk* for good measure.

What am I going to do now?

Tell him, that's what. Forget waiting four days. No more procrastinating. No more sex, for God's sake, and no more "I love you" until all the cards are on the table.

Out in the kitchen, she walked into another episode of *Cooking with Kota—Shirtless Edition.*

She scooped up Tri and propped her butt on the stool. He smiled gorgeously and slid a refill across the counter.

Sipping her coffee, she watched him bend and reach and stir and sprinkle, and she blatantly ogled his muscles as they flexed and stretched and bunched and rippled. It was a breathtaking display, so dazzling that it took her a moment to realize he was hamming it up.

But when he curled the saltshaker so his biceps bulged, her gaze snapped to his face, and he burst out laughing.

"Very funny." She crossed her arms.

"Sweetheart, I get just as stupid when I stare at your ass."

"My ample ass. On my not skinny body. With my saggy tits."

He looked scandalized. "Your tits do *not* sag."

"Not yet. But I'm sure you'll point it out when they do."

He aimed the wooden spoon at her. "Speaking of your tits."

"What? Too big? Too small?" She crossed her arms tighter. "I don't care what you say, I'm not changing them."

Now he looked shocked. "I don't want you to change them. They're perfect handfuls. And baby, I got big hands."

He aimed the spoon again, at her chest this time. "My point was that I don't know why you say they do nothing for you. It looked to me like they were doing plenty."

She softened. "That was all you. They *like* you."

A smile spread like sunrise across his face. "Your tits like me?"

"Apparently. Because they've never even noticed another man. But you, they're all over."

He dropped the spoon and hotfooted around the island. "Let me at 'em," he growled, slipping up under her tee. "Mmm, no bra. I like."

She swelled into his palms, filling his hands. "I don't know what's wrong with them," she murmured. "The girls have lost their heads."

He plopped Tri on the other stool and lifted Chris onto the countertop. Then he peeled her shirt over her head and stepped back to look. Just look.

After a long, slow study, he lifted his eyes to lock onto hers. "I might love your tits as much as your ass."

She smiled. "I might love your shoulders as much as your arms."

He looked surprised. "You like my arms best? Out of *everything*?"

She shrugged innocently. "What could be better?"

He stepped in again, grabbed her ass, and tugged her to the very edge of the counter, meeting her there with his groin. His hard-again groin.

She groaned, part arousal, part misery. "Okay, I give. I love that more. But if you use it on me right now, I'm done for."

He cupped her face in his hands. "Did I hurt you, babe?"

"No, you didn't hurt me." She covered his hands with hers. "I'm just well used. And hungry. I'm ready to fight Bumble for his food."

They both turned to watch the scrawny cat gumming.

"He's tougher than he looks," Kota said.

"That wouldn't take much." Bumble was a stick on legs. "Will he ever fatten up?"

"Nope. He's got cancer."

"Oh no." It cut deep.

"He's had a good run. Four years here, living large. He'll come back to L.A. with us, so when it's time I can put him to sleep."

That was the downside of loving so many creatures so much.

Chris laced her fingers through his. "He's lucky to have you. They're all lucky."

She desperately wanted to be that lucky too.

TANA SHOWED UP again after breakfast and stuck like a burr for an hour. An hour alone with Christy that Kota would never get back.

When they finally saw the back of him, Kota pulled her down into the hammock. "Jesus, I thought he'd never leave."

She laughed her smoky, sexy laugh. "He was tweaking you. The more you tried to get rid of him, the more he dug in."

"Nah, he's just clueless."

She rolled her eyes. "Talk about clueless. You're the easiest person to get over on I've ever met."

"Take that back, little girl." He menaced her with a look. "Say 'Kota's the baddest ass I know.'"

"Pfft."

He juggled her around. The hammock swung drunkenly, but he got her where he wanted her, stretched out on top of him, breasts flattened to his chest, legs interlocked with his.

She stacked her fists on his chest and rested her chin on top of them. Her eyes were melted caramel, her lips curved deliciously.

She seemed lighter today. Not weight-wise. Oh, no. She was no bony supermodel.

But mood-wise. Like her heart was lighter. Like she'd finally stopped holding back and was ready to go all in.

Like she was in love.

He knew the feeling. He felt lighter himself.

It put him in a forgiving mood. "I'll let the clueless thing go on one condition." He shifted her hips a few inches to give his cock room to expand. "We have to prove that hammock sex is possible."

"What kind of hammock sex?"

"The intercourse kind. Doesn't matter who's on top, as long as we get it done."

They got it done.

They got trampoline sex done too.

Swimming-pool sex.

And surfboard sex. But not without some water up the nose.

He made a play for horseback sex too, while they were taking a sunset walk with the herd. But Christy drew the line. "As it is, I won't be able to ride a horse for a week. I definitely can't ride you *and* a horse."

He gave Sugar's rump an affectionate slap, and she drifted off with the herd. "I guess it can wait. I've got horses in L.A."

L.A. Right now it seemed like another world. But once they got off the plane, he'd be back to twelve-hour workdays. He'd have to change a few things around to make time for Christy. Which made him wonder about her schedule.

"So, what do you do with yourself back in L.A.? Who *is* Christy Gray?"

She stumbled, an arm-flailing flounder that damn near ended in a face-plant.

He steadied her with an arm around her waist. "You all right? Twist anything?"

"I'm good," she said, trying to disguise a limp.

He steered her to a deadfall. "Sit for a minute and let me see." He knelt to examine her ankle. "It's swelling up."

"It's always been bigger than the other one."

He gave her a pitying look. "You strained it. I'll ice it when we get home." For now, they had the sunset to admire.

The deadfall was only big enough for one, so he sat her on his lap and picked up where he left off. "Tell me what your days are like."

"I write."

"Friends?"

"A few from college, but they're mostly back east."

This was like pulling teeth. He kept at it. "No high school friends?"

She fidgeted. "I was on the road with my mother. She

homeschooled me, more or less. I got hands-on experience in geography and current events."

"But you missed out on the social stuff. Friday-night lights. Prom."

"Cliques. Mean girls. Losing my virginity under the bleachers." She tapped his chest. "How many cherries did you pop?"

"Not Verna Presky's."

Christy laughed, obviously more comfortable teasing him than talking about herself. "I bet you were captain of the football team."

"Cocaptain with—"

"Don't tell me. Earl Quigley." She put a hand on her heart and fluttered her lashes. "I want to meet this man. He must be quite the stud."

He did his big-dog growl.

She dropped a kiss on his nose like he was a puppy. "I used to think you looked dangerous. But you're all hat and no cattle."

That startled a laugh out of him. "You've been reading the script."

"You left it on the nightstand." She grinned. "It's a quick read. Not much dialogue. You do a lot of squinting into the distance, and squinting at the bad guys, and squinting at Sissy What's-her-name until you figure out she's a dancehall girl with a heart of gold. Then you squint at her pimp, and then you squint at the bad guys some more."

"Then I shoot 'em all, right?"

She nodded. "It's actually pretty satisfying. There's a

good story built around all that bloodshed. And I like how you save the pimp for last." She rubbed her palms.

"Bloodthirsty, aren't you?"

"And vengeful. You should add a scene where Sissy dances on his grave. And while you're at it, you could change the ending so you stay with her, or she goes with you. Because it's really sad that after all you go through, you end up alone."

He looked into her eyes. Yep, the sun rose and set there. "I never minded being alone. But I like this better."

"Oh," she said softly. Her head tilted, and her eyes warmed even more. She took his cheeks between her hands like he was the most precious thing she'd ever held.

And she kissed him tenderly.

Tenderly.

Imagine that.

KOTA TOOK THE ice pack off Chris's ankle and examined it gently. "Bed rest," he prescribed. "Flat on your back. Or your stomach. Or up on all fours."

She heaved a phony sigh. "I'll try to make the best of it."

He turned out the light and rolled into bed alongside her. Her head slotted into the notch of his shoulder. Her leg hooked naturally over his. Outside the window, the stars seemed close enough to touch. The quarter moon hung in the treetops.

She laid her palm on his warm chest. "I'm still thinking about vet school," she said.

"Me too." He sounded surprised at himself, but he went on. "Tana's settled now. Sasha's got his back. He doesn't need me like he did."

She lifted her head to peer at him in the moonlight. "You mean to tell me you stayed in Hollywood all these years to take care of Tana?" *Seriously?* Tana was thirty-four, a major force in the industry, and strong enough to break houses barehanded.

"I'm his big brother," Kota said, as if that said it all. "I've been watching out for him since I could walk."

"What about your parents? Weren't they watching out for both of you?"

He gave a short laugh. "My mother—my birth mother—was a hard-core junkie. She fed us when she remembered, but she was mostly interested in her next fix. Tana would've starved without me."

Good God. This must be what Sasha meant about abandonment issues.

"What about your father?" she asked.

"He was a user too. Not as bad as her, probably because he loved her. Keeping her alive meant keeping a roof over her head, feeding her when she didn't care about food." He shrugged a shoulder. "So he kept us alive too. When she had a roof, we had a roof. When she had food, we had food."

Chris tried to picture it. She couldn't. How did two weak-minded, selfish drug addicts produce such smart, successful men?

"The way I see it," Kota said, as if reading her thoughts, "my father was a good man who fell in love with the wrong woman. Maybe she was different before the drugs. I don't know. But the woman I remember was a waste of space. Strung out most of the time. Either jonesing and crying, or blissed out and staring at the wall.

"He never quit loving her, though. And he never gave up on her. The farther down the rabbit hole she went, the more he pulled out of it so he could take care of her."

What a prince.

"He cleaned up eventually," Kota went on, "which was harder than I gave him credit for at the time. He even started taking an interest in Tana and me. Not that he put us in kindergarten or anything normal like that. How could he, when we moved every few months? But he made us watch *Sesame Street* instead of game shows."

Father of the year.

"He had a friend in Casper—probably the last one he hadn't screwed over. The guy was a roofer, and he gave Dad a job. Steady work. And Dad was good at it. He was a big guy. Strong, now that he was off the shit.

"We were living in a hotel, but Dad was saving money for an apartment. He even signed Tana and me up to start school. Promised us a puppy. It was supposed to be a fresh start."

Chris braced herself. Tragedy loomed.

"Then my mother found the money. She disappeared with it. And Dad actually got mad. I mean, if you'd seen the shit he swallowed for years, you'd get that it was a watershed moment." Kota sounded amazed to this day. "He wasn't a violent guy, but when he found the book he'd stashed it in laying open on the bed, he threw it against the wall, yelling, 'You're not shooting my boys' future up your arm.'"

He covered her hand with his, holding it to his heart. His voice had gone deep with emotion. "I know it took too long for him to get to that point. But better late than never, right?"

She made a neutral sound and kept her opinion to herself. If he needed to believe his father had redeemed himself, she wouldn't contradict him.

He took a deep breath and pushed on to the end. "He was filthy from work, but he turned right around and headed out, going after her. Putting us first, for once. He stopped in the door and looked over his shoulder. Me and Tana were frozen like deer. Completely stunned. And he looked me in the eye. 'Take care of your brother,' he said. Like he knew he wasn't coming back."

Kota's heart beat hard and fast against her palm. The rhythm sang up her arm, all the way to her own heart.

"We were alone for five days," he said, "until the manager came looking for another week's rent. He called the cops. They took us to the station and told us Dad was dead. Mom's dealer shot him, then took off with Mom to parts unknown. An hour later, Tana and me went into the system."

And so the parting instruction from the father he'd just begun to trust became the defining purpose of Kota's life.

It explained so much. Not only the brothers' abandonment issues, but also how Kota became a tender. Why he sacrificed vet school to follow Tana to the wilds of L.A.

Why he tried to control every situation, to the point of buying his own island.

It even explained why he made movie after movie where he took out the bad guys, making the world safer for dads and kids everywhere, then disappearing into the smoke, alone.

It was profound, and it moved her to the core. Tears rolled down her cheeks, for the boy who became a man too young, and for the man still trapped in the boy's worst nightmare.

All this he'd shared with her, and she hadn't even told him where she lived.

Curling her arm around his neck, she buried her tears in his hair. "Lookout Mountain Avenue," she said brokenly. "In the house with the stone lion out front."

A jagged laugh broke from his throat, short and brittle. His arms closed around her, so big and so strong, squeezing the breath out of her. But he wasn't done yet.

"I left out part of the story," he said, his voice barely a whisper in her ear. "It was my fault. If I hadn't let her take the money, Dad wouldn't have gone after her. He wouldn't have died."

The last piece of Chris's heart broke. "My God, Kota, you were a *kid*. You couldn't have stopped her. I don't care if you were big for your age. Getting between a junkie and her fix is dangerous even for an adult."

She stopped short of pointing out that his father's bad choices put his sons in that position. Kota wouldn't want to hear it. He was more comfortable blaming himself than taking the sheen off his father, what little there was.

"I just wanted you to know," he said, "before you get too involved with me."

"Right. Thanks." Anger flared, not at him but at the parents who abused him. "I wouldn't want to fall for a guy who got screwed over by his mother when he was five. What a loser. He should've been more on top of that. He should've knocked her down and taken back the money. Because that's *so* much more impressive."

For a long moment he was silent, and she wondered if she'd gone too far.

Then he said, "Okay, I guess I was a little melodramatic."

"Ya think?"

He laughed for real, and after a second she joined him. It built until the bed shook with it. Relief and hilarity. Catharsis.

Followed by hot sex.

Chapter Twenty

CHRIS SAT UP in bed. "I need to make a phone call."

"You're kidding," Kota said. "It's the middle of the night."

"Here, but it's the shank of the evening in L.A."

He sat up and turned on the light. Her heart clenched at the sight of him, warm and tousled and bristled and grumpy.

"It can't wait till morning?"

"No. I want to check on my mother."

That was true, but just part of it. She had to call Reed immediately and quit her job. In her mind, she'd quit twenty-four hours ago, but now that Kota had opened up to her, she needed to make it official.

And then she'd tell him everything. She wanted a life with him, and she wanted it to start tonight.

He levered his big body out of bed, and she followed

his fine ass down the hallway to the kitchen, her stomach alive with butterflies, both anticipation and dread.

He dug out the phone, showed her how to use it, then dropped a kiss on her lips. "I'll be in bed. Waiting for you." She watched him disappear toward the bedroom. "I hope she's doing okay," he called over his shoulder.

She smiled. Kota might dislike her mother on principle, but after what he'd been through, he could appreciate a mother who stuck by her kid.

She dialed Reed's number. His voice, when he answered, was groggy with sleep.

"Hi, it's Christine. Sorry I woke you."

"Chris." She pictured him dragging a hand down his face, getting his bearings. "Is everything okay?"

"Yes." *For the moment.* "How's Mom?"

"I saw her today, she's fine." His voice hardened. "Owen's after me to find you. I told you not to call."

"It's okay. Owen can throw me under the bus. I'm quitting the *Sentinel*. I'm quitting journalism."

Silence. Then, "Listen, Chris, I know this is tough. You're taking a beating for something that's not your fault. But you need to grow a thicker skin. This isn't the last time you'll get kicked around in this business."

"Actually, it is. I'm really quitting, Reed, and it's not because of Owen, or not directly anyway."

She sucked a deep breath, then said it out loud. "I'm in love with Dakota Rain."

Reed blew a raspberry. "Get over it, Chris. You don't

ditch your career because you've got a crush on a movie star."

"It's not a crush. And that's only part of it anyway. I like these people. I don't have it in me to exploit them. And," she added before he could interrupt her, "Mom would hate it." The one argument he couldn't refute.

A pause, then, "Your mother *would* hate it, but that's because she worked in a different era. If she was still in the business, she'd understand that journalism has changed."

"And she'd hate that too. She'd quit if it came to this. She'd want *me* to quit. Think about it, Reed. Undercover reporting on important events is honest work if it's the only way to get the truth out. And covering social events is honest work too. Boring, but honest.

"But going undercover to report on social events? It's combining the worst of both worlds, and it absolutely wouldn't fall under Mom's definition of journalism. Sneaking into a celebrity wedding wouldn't make her proud. It would make her cringe."

"I don't like your implications, young lady."

"I'm not criticizing you. You're right about all of it. You have to adapt to stay in the game, and thank God you're there, holding the line somewhere close to where it used to be.

"But for me, I went into journalism because Mom always wanted me to. I felt guilty that I disappointed her. I wanted her to be proud of me. But Reed, she wanted me to be a *serious* journalist. A change-the-world journalist. And I'm not cut out for that. My heart isn't in it."

Silence. Then, curmudgeonly, "I stuck my neck out for you."

"Did you? Didn't you really stick it out for Mom?"

"Goddamn it, Chris." He was losing force. "She'd skin me if she knew I let this happen."

Chris leaned her forehead against the fridge. "I'm trying to tell you it was a blessing in disguise. I got into this for Mom. It was a bad decision. All this wedding thing did was bring it to a head. Better now than before I waste ten years trying to be something I'm not."

Tri batted her ankle. She hoisted him under her arm. "I'm sorry for the trouble my bad decision caused you. Owen'll be fit to be tied."

Reed blew another raspberry. "He'll be bullshit about the story, but he'll have Buckley off his back." He paused. "Are you sure, Chris? What'll you do now?"

"Write Mom's biography. Maybe do some singing." In L.A., where she could be with Kota if he'd have her. "Don't worry about me. I'm good. I'm really, really good."

She kissed Tri's wet little nose.

Now to tell Kota.

She found him on his stomach, out cold, taking up three-quarters of the king-sized bed.

A solid nudge got no reaction. He even slept through a rib-knuckling.

Relief snuck up and discouraged her from a full-scale assault. She curled against his side instead. Now that she'd made it official with Reed, the urgency drained out of her. Telling Kota could wait till morning.

What could it hurt?

SOMETHING DRAGGED KOTA from a very pleasant, very erotic dream, where he was back at the wedding reception, the only guest, and Christy was up on the stage, the only performer, and she was buck naked, all pink nipples and round ass and ruby lips, crooning her smokiest, down-and-dirtiest "Fever" just for him.

It was so real he could taste the salty sweat on her skin.

And then a mosquito buzzed his ear, insistent and annoying and soon to be flattened between his palms . . .

He opened his eyes. Daylight wiped out the sultry haze of the dream. He looked around, but the mosquito wasn't in the room.

It was an airplane, buzzing his island.

His island, god*damn* it.

He threw back the sheet and bounced out of bed.

"What?" came sleepily from the other side.

"Somebody's buzzing my island." He hadn't bought a goddamn island so some jackass could get his jollies by waking him up at the ass crack of dawn. He stepped into his shorts and strode toward the door.

Cy read his mood and went on full alert, flanking Kota as he marched down the hallway.

Christy caught up to them in the courtyard, a gorgeous mess fresh from the sack. "Get back inside," he growled. If this was some fucking paparazzi, they weren't putting pictures of his woman on the internet. Not today.

Shielding his eyes, he searched for the plane. When he spotted it, he dropped his hand, startled out of his bad mood.

"That's my Cessna."

A cold hand fisted his heart. He leaped for the golf cart. Christy piled in too, along with the dogs, and he careened out the courtyard.

"Whoa." Christy clutched the dash.

"Sorry. But this can't be good. Ma and Pops have the phone number. There's no reason for anyone to fly here unless something happened to them."

"Oh God." She gripped his thigh.

The plane was on the ground when they reached the landing strip. Em was coming down the stairs as he wheeled onto the tarmac.

"Em, what the fuck?" He was at her side, gripping her arm as her feet touched the ground.

Then Mercer appeared in the doorway, a fireplug in a sharp black suit. His square face was grim.

Confusion warred with panic. "What the *fuck*?"

"Your parents are fine," Em said, reading his mind.

Kota's knees buckled in relief. He grabbed the railing with one hand, Christy with the other. She moved under his arm, her own sliding supportively around his waist.

"Jesus, I thought—"

"I know, and I'm sorry. I wish I could've called, but it's better this way."

He pulled himself together. "Okay." Deep breath. "Okay, what's the problem? What's Mercer doing here?"

"There's something you need to know." Her eyes went to Christy. "She's a reporter."

He snorted. "What the fuck are you talking about?"

"She works for the *Sentinel*. They sent her to spy on the wedding."

Doubt crept in. He shook his head, slowly. "No. She came with the band. She's a singer." Only ten minutes ago, she'd serenaded his dreams.

"Kota." Em took hold of his arm. Her trusted voice rang clear and true. "You know I wouldn't be here unless I was sure. Mercer checked her out. It's true she used to sing with Zach, and we're pretty sure he didn't know what she was up to. But she's a gossip reporter for the *Sentinel*, and our sources confirm she was sent to do a wedding spread for their Sunday edition."

He turned to Christy. She'd gone sheet white.

"Wait," he said. "No. Tell them. No."

She met his eyes, but he saw a stranger there, frightened and desperate. The ground opened under his feet.

"I-I quit. I told Reed—"

"No." He stepped back, shaking her off, tearing his gaze from her lying face. "Em. Jesus. Get her out of here. Pack her shit and put her on the plane."

Em clasped Christy's wrist as she reached for him. "Don't even," she said, twisting Christy around, hauling her toward the golf cart. Christy stumbled on her bad ankle. Tri leaped from her grasp as she fell on one knee.

Kota turned his back, ice water in his veins. He found Mercer in front of him, and he shoved the man with both hands.

Mercer fell back a step, but his expression never changed. "Your brother's wife added her at the last minute," he said, all the explanation he was likely to give. Then he shot his cuffs. Rolled his neck. Body language for back off.

Kota didn't care if the man drew a gun and shot him. "Give me everything," he bit out. "Every fucking thing."

Mercer delivered it military style. "The subject is legally known as Christine Case."

So even her name was a lie.

"After touring with her father, Zachary Gray, for six years, she was hired by the *Sentinel* twenty-six months ago. She worked the society beat until approximately one month ago, when she moved to hard news, where her first major story backfired, incurring the wrath of Senator Buckley, who was implicated therein. Reed Washington—managing editor of the *Sentinel* and a friend of the subject's mother, Emma Case—intervened on her behalf."

How skillfully she'd woven truth and lies. Kota pinched the bridge of his nose. "You're boring me, Mercer. Get to the point."

"Reed Washington ordered Christine Case to infiltrate the wedding and bring back an exposé on the event."

But she'd gotten so much more, hadn't she? So much more *bang* for her buck. Because he was too stupid, too *smitten*, to keep his fucking mouth shut.

His heart turned to ice in his chest.

He glared at Mercer. "Took you long enough to figure it out."

Mercer stiffened. "We had the data in our hands by dawn on Sunday, but you'd already left with her. Your parents refused to give us the satphone number. And your mother"—Mercer barely restrained his disdain—

"insisted we not employ our usual methods of accessing that information."

Kota bared his teeth. "You work for me, not my mother."

Mercer bared his own teeth. "You informed me at the outset that your assistant has authority to act when you're incommunicado. She acceded to your mother's wishes."

So Em was to blame. He'd kick her ass before he fired her. She'd never work in L.A. again.

That was for later. "Then why are you here? The ladies let you off the leash?"

Mercer kept his cool in the face of Kota's sneer. "My people instituted a trap-and-trace on all of Reed Washington's telephones at 0600 on Sunday morning. We recorded all incoming telephone numbers, verified their origin, and determined whether further action was required.

"Reed Washington received no calls from any number associated with Christine Case. However, at 2300 last night, we intercepted a number we thereafter confirmed as your satphone.

"Assuming that the call was made without your consent, I contacted your assistant, who rejected my suggestion that she place an immediate call to that number. In her view, a late-night telephone call implicating the subject might trigger an unpleasant confrontation that could escalate out of control."

Em had that much of it right.

"However, she concurred that if the subject was

making contact with Reed Washington, action was called for. Upon further discussion, we decided on a daybreak arrival and supervised exfiltration."

"Good call," Kota said, keeping a tight grip on his rage. "Now get the bitch off my island."

Chapter Twenty-One

CHRIS STARED AT her lap as the cart bumped over the
path. Her hands cupped empty air. Tri had stayed back
with Kota.

She'd never hold either of them again.

Em drove sanely, though her knuckles were white on
the wheel. Chris tried again.

"I quit," she said, striving to keep her voice calm while
panic's icy fingers clawed her throat. "I called Reed last
night and told him I'm done. I won't write the story. I
won't do that to Kota."

"You called Reed," Em said, "that much is true. But
mixing the truth with lies is your specialty. So pardon me
if I call bullshit on the rest of it."

"Ask Reed. He'll tell you. He tried to talk me out of it,
but I don't want to be a journalist anyway. I never did."

"Boo hoo. Now shut the fuck up or I'll push you out
and you can walk the rest of the way."

Chris would gladly take her up on that offer. Kota's instant, unquestioning rejection had ripped her heart from her chest, and Em's disgust was acid in the wound. But it was a thirty-minute walk even on two good ankles, so she shut the fuck up instead.

At the house, Chris limped slowly behind Em, who ate up the long hallway with her short, furious strides. Then she watched stoically as Em wadded her clothing and forced it into her bag. And she made not a peep when Em tucked the laptop under her arm.

"You'll get it back when Mercer's done with it," Em said. "If you've got a problem with that, tough shit."

Chris closed herself in the bathroom and threw up.

Kota was nowhere in sight when they got back to the plane. Mercer stuck out a hand, and Em passed him the laptop. Then both of them watched Chris hump her bag up the narrow steps.

The plane was smaller than Adam's but every bit as lux. "Sit there." Mercer pointed at a table. "Buckle up." He sat down across from her.

Em took one of the leather recliners, strapped herself in, and they were wheels up in under a minute. They banked over the island, and Chris saw the horses in the meadow below, running flat out, necks extended, tails streaming. Sugar led the herd with Kota stretched out over her withers, his strong back rippling as he urged her on.

Anguish clenched a fist in Chris's gut. She'd done this. To herself, to him.

Then the plane leveled out. Mercer opened the laptop. "Is it password protected?"

She nodded. He stared at her, unblinking. She gave up the password. Why not? Nothing on her computer could make this any worse.

Defenseless, she watched him scroll through her files. There were many. Every article she'd written for the *Sentinel* for the last two years, all her background information, data on certain society types, details on functions, impressions. Her notes on Emma's biography. Her own recollections of traveling with both of her parents.

Nothing to be ashamed of, yet she squirmed as he read.

Eventually she laid her head on the table, hiding in the dark crook of her arms. There, she could wallow. Berate herself. Call down vengeance on Mercer's head.

And she could grieve. For herself, because she'd lost the only thing she'd ever truly wanted, and for Kota, because he'd loved her, and she'd broken his heart. He might never open it to anyone again. And what a shame that would be, because what a heart it was. Huge and soft and loyal and true.

But even now, as she flew over the wide Pacific, that heart was turning to stone. She knew him well enough to know that. To know that, and so much more.

Eventually she dozed, and she dreamed, none of it good. When they bumped down at Burbank, she lifted her pounding head and stared out at Cali-fucking-fornia.

Nobody spoke to her as she lugged her bag down the stairs. On the tarmac, Em handed her the keys to the

Eos, then walked away with Mercer without a backward glance.

CHRIS DROVE STRAIGHT to Seacrest, tears streaking her cheeks, regret burning a hole in her raw, empty stomach.

She was in despair, and she wanted her mother.

She found the afternoon activities in full swing. In the great room, a karaoke singer had residents clapping along to The Beatles. In a smaller room, a bored aide called out, "B eight, B eight. Check your cards, ladies."

Chris found her mother sitting on the patio with a cup of tea, looking more like an employee than a resident. At seventy-two, she was one of the youngest, and one of the few without a walker.

But her disease was progressing. Before long Chris would be a stranger to her.

Today, though, Emma broke into a smile, squeezing Chris's hand when she drew up a chair. "Where've you been?" she wanted to know. "I missed you."

"I missed you too, Mom." *Every day, more than words can say.* "I was on assignment."

Emma perked up at the familiar phrase, and that was all the encouragement Chris needed to spill out the whole story: her screwup at the *Sentinel,* Reed's bargain with Owen, the wedding, the island. Kota.

She rambled through to the end, sponging her eyes with a hanky Emma drew from her pocket. Drawing to a miserable close, Chris waited for her mother's no-nonsense response.

It didn't come.

Of course it didn't. Emma had lost the thread early on, if she'd ever held it at all. Her attention was on the birds, darting in to peck seeds from the feeder, then darting back to the surrounding trees.

"See the red one?" She pointed.

"It's a cardinal, Mom."

"Oh really? I've never seen him before."

Chris flopped back in her chair. The cardinal spent ten hours a day at the feeder. She saw him every time she visited. But to Emma, he was a fresh delight every day.

Chris let out a sigh that turned into a sob. Friction and resentment had been cornerstones of their relationship. But there'd been so much more. Love, compassion, intellectual curiosity. A shared appreciation for art and music. Stimulating conversation that Chris never appreciated until it slipped through her fingers like water.

What she wouldn't give now to hear Emma cut through the bullshit, to blister Chris's ear about trusting her reputation to rinky-dink editors, letting the brass bully her into an untenable assignment, and compounding her problems by—of all frivolous things—falling in love.

From the outset, Emma would have advised Chris to take her lumps rather than sneak into the wedding.

It seemed so obvious now.

And so trivial. Compared to all Emma had lost, Chris's problems shrank to pinpricks. Chris still had her memory, her will, and full possession of her faculties. She could start again. Build a new career. If losing Kota's love was the worst of the matter, she could deal with that too. She could outlast the pain and the loss.

But what she'd never overcome was knowing that she'd hurt him in the particular way that she had. She'd struck where he was most vulnerable. And she'd never forgive herself.

An aide approached. "They're dancing in the great room, Emma. Stephen's looking for you." She smiled at Chris. "A new resident, and he's already got his eye on your mother."

Who could blame him? Emma was Seacrest's hottest catch. Women outnumbered men ten to one, but Emma was always in demand. She went through boyfriends faster than a cheerleader did.

The truth was that while Emma was no longer the person she'd been—driven and involved and often stressed to distraction—the person she'd become was having a much better time.

For Chris, it took some of the sting out of it. "Come on, Mom, I'll walk you over."

She left Emma waltzing with a tall reed of a man, and went home alone to pick up the pieces.

Chapter Twenty-Two

KOTA STARED AT Christy's computer, open on his desk.

Em sat across from him. "There's nothing on it about the wedding," she said. "No notes, no article except that snippet you're looking at, which obviously wasn't a serious draft."

He couldn't dispute that. *Asshole's Brother Ties the Knot* was plainly a rant. He'd pissed Christy off, probably with his own rant about her boyfriend, and she'd taken it out on the page. It wasn't meant for publication.

"Mercer's source at the *Sentinel* confirms Christy quit," Em went on. "She never submitted a story, never even went back to clean out her desk. Her publisher threw her to the wolves, the senator served her with papers, and she had to hire a lawyer and file an answer before Buckley dropped it."

Kota swiveled his chair and looked out at the rose garden. "So she told the truth."

"About that, yeah. Refusing to write the story cost her her job, almost got her sued, and stained her rep as a journalist forever."

And all because, when push came to shove, she wouldn't betray him.

"So what?" he said, refusing to soften. "She fucking lied her way into the wedding. She lied to her own father about it. Then she lied her way into my house—"

"Keep it real, Kota. You finagled her here by roping Zach in."

"Don't nitpick. If I knew who she was, I wouldn't have let her through the door. And I damn sure wouldn't have brought her to the island. Once she lied about who she was, it tainted everything." Every word. Every kiss. Every touch of her hand.

"You're right," Em said.

He swiveled to stare at her. "You never agree with me about anything."

She shrugged. "It's no fun kicking you when you're down."

"I'm not *down*. I'm fucking furious."

"You're both. You're furious because Christy deceived you. And you're miserable because you fell in love with her."

He glared.

"Verna predicted it, you know. That's why she wouldn't give us the phone number. She said you were a big boy and could handle yourself, and Christy was a good person and would do the right thing."

"Yeah, Ma fed me the same line of bullshit."

"Well, she was kind of right."

"Don't you start too."

"I'm not starting anything. In fact"—she stood up—"I'll take that computer back to Christy right now so you can forget all about her."

He shut the laptop and planted his palm on it.

She tugged at it. He pressed down.

"Not yet," he said.

"It's got her notes for the book she's writing about her mother."

"She's waited two weeks, she can wait a little longer." He slid the laptop into a drawer. "Where am I supposed to be right now?"

Em scrolled through her phone. "At Peter's office, interviewing my replacement."

He stacked his heels on the desk. "I canceled that. You can stay."

"Oh goody." She scrolled some more. "The trainer's due at nine to put you through a three-hour workout, then Peter's doing a twelve-thirty lunch at his place with the Levi's people. You'll have to duck out by two, because Sissy"—she wrinkled her nose—"is coming by to *run lines*."

"You got a problem with that?"

"Please. You two don't need to run lines. You've only got one scene together in the first week of shooting, and neither of you says more than ten words."

"Since when are you reading my scripts?"

"Since I got insomnia. They put me right out. *Dakota shoots fifteen extras. Dakota blows up a city block.*"

At least Em could make him laugh. That was more than anyone else could do. He couldn't laugh, or eat, or sleep. He was running on empty. The three-hour workout might kill him.

"Anyway," Em was saying, "it's a ploy by Sissy to get you in the sack."

He smiled. "You say that like it's a bad thing."

"She's gross."

"She's gorgeous."

"She's skinny. I think she's anorexic."

"So?"

"She's been trying to get you in the sack for months."

"So?"

"You can do better."

His smile fell. *Better* hadn't worked out. Meaningless sex was all he was good for.

He dropped his feet to the floor. "Block out two hours. Sissy's dream is about to come true."

RAYLENE SURVEYED THE dirty dishes stacked on the coffee table. "Spaghetti again? Aren't you sick of it yet?"

Chris looked up from the *CSI* marathon. "It's easy," she said.

"And fattening. And it clashes with your pajamas."

Chris looked down at the blob of red on bright yellow SpongeBob. She dabbed it with a finger, then looked up at Ray and deliberately sucked it off.

Ray *grrrr*ed in frustration and stomped up the stairs.

Mission accomplished. Ray was being even more of a

pest than usual, always harping on Chris about getting off her ass, or getting her head out of her ass, or getting her ass out of the house.

Enough with her ass, already.

And there was nothing wrong with wearing pajamas all day. They were comfortable. They didn't cinch or bind. If people could wear pajamas to work, they'd be a lot happier.

Though a trip through the washer was probably overdue.

Stumping up the stairs, she cursed the insanity that had gripped her when she'd bought a three-story house. "Dumb, dumb, dumb."

She passed the second floor and Ray called out, "He's not worth it."

But he was. He was worth all her suffering, and more. She'd done Kota wrong, and she'd pay for it all her long, lonely life.

Stripping down, she caught her reflection in the mirror. Two weeks, and already her ass looked two sizes larger.

Round was good. Bulbous was . . . not good. Kota wouldn't give it a second look now.

She pulled on yoga pants—a short step up from PJs—and a T-shirt long enough to cover her ass. "There," she said.

The mirror replied, *What next? A muumuu?*

"Shit." She dug out her sneakers and tied them on.

When she walked into the kitchen, Ray had come down and was standing at the counter. She took one look at Chris and sputtered her wine. "Halle-fucking-lujah." Her favorite phrase since Zach had stopped by. "It's about time."

Chris made a face and kept moving out the door. The slightest distraction could take the wind from her sails.

Outside, she cringed like a vampire. The noontime sun lanced her eyes like a scalpel.

Running was out of the question even on her best day, which this wasn't. She'd like to blame her ankle, but two weeks of slouching on the couch had cured it. The problem was her heart. It weighed her down like lead, almost too heavy to carry.

The unseasonable heat didn't help matters either, another reason to curse Ray for prodding her off the couch.

She'd about had it with Ray anyway. Their relationship was prickly at best. Chris only put up with her because Ray had played masterfully on her guilt since sophomore year, when she'd walked in on Chris making out with Evan Graves. It wasn't like Ray had still been dating him—he'd dumped her a week before—but she hadn't given up on him yet. And even though Chris hadn't liked Ray any better in college than she did now, the roommate code of ethics forbade trespassing on posted property.

But enough was enough. If Chris had learned anything in the last few weeks, it was that decisions motivated by guilt never led anywhere good. Guilt had made her take Ray in. And guilt had driven her to the *Sentinel*. The cosmic convergence of those two bad decisions now had her trudging down the sidewalk under the sweltering sun, feeling fat, ugly, and worthless.

There was a lesson there, but she was too irritated to compress it into a pithy, tweetable phrase.

Resentment at Ray carried her all the way to the boulevard and across it, then fizzled out in the relentless heat.

Her shoulders slumped. The walk had delivered all it promised. Sweat, heavy breathing, chafing in more than one place. She regretted every step.

She turned around to head back to the couch, and as she waited at the light, panting like a dog, her gray T-shirt sporting sweat circles from armpits to waist, her unwashed hair straggling like weeds around her puffy face, fate dropped one more steaming turd on the pile.

Because who should pull up to the light but Dakota Rain, top down, aviators on, hair styled by the wind to look camera-ready.

Chris froze. Even her heart stopped beating.

Like a petrified rabbit, she prayed the wolf would glide past without spotting her motionless form.

The "Walk" light appeared. She ignored it.

Nothing—not an earthquake, an explosion, a nuclear bomb—could induce her to step into the crosswalk in front of his car.

Seconds ticked in slow motion. The "Walk" light glowed like the sun.

Kota forked his hair back in that way he had. He turned his head to say a word to the person beside him.

And suddenly Chris couldn't take it anymore. She made the mistake so many dead rabbits had made.

She tried to hide.

Just a quick step toward the light pole, but the motion

caught his eye. She saw recognition hit him like a slap in the face. The light finally changed. Horns blared behind him.

She turned on her heel and ran, fat ass flapping behind her.

KOTA THREW THE Porsche into first and left rubber on the road.

Em gripped the armrest. "Yikes! What the hell?"

"Christy. Chris." What should he call her? "The lying bitch." That worked.

Em swiveled. "Where?"

"You missed her. She looked like hell." Like she'd been sick for a month. "But her ankle must've quit hurting, 'cause she took off when she saw me."

"She probably thought you'd run her over."

"Pfft. She's not worth the trouble." Cops. Insurance. Bodywork on the Porsche.

"Maybe you should—"

"What?" He shot a death ray at Em. "Take her on a date? Bring her home for Thanksgiving?"

"—try to forget her."

"Already done."

Em shut her mouth in that way that spoke louder than words.

He refused to take the bait.

She folded her hands in that way that meant he was too dumb to live.

He focused on driving.

Ten full seconds elapsed. Then he threw up a hand. "Spit it out."

"You're in denial."

"Now you're a shrink."

"You're not that complicated. A monkey could diagnose you."

He smirked. "You said it, I didn't."

She jabbed him. "I know this is uncharted territory for you. You haven't given a woman a second thought since I've known you. But normal people get their hearts broken long before thirty-five, and they move on. So will you. But first you have to admit you're in love with her."

"Get real."

"I'm serious. It's the first step on the road to recovery."

"Now it's a twelve-step program?"

"I don't know how many steps there are, but until you admit you fell in love with her and she hurt you, you'll be stuck in this funk."

"I'm not in a funk." He squealed into Peter's driveway, slamming on the brakes six inches from a Lexus. "And we're done talking about it. I got real problems, like this Levi's deal. Peter's expecting me to sign on."

"I thought you already decided to do it."

He turned off the engine and stared out the windshield. "It's a three-year deal. I don't know if I want to commit."

She half-turned in her seat to study him. "This is new. What's going on?"

He shrugged. As much as he hated to give Christy

credit for anything, she'd gotten him thinking about vet school, and he couldn't stop. In fact, it was the only thing he had enthusiasm for anymore.

Em poked him. "Out with it."

He wasn't quite ready to announce a career change. "I'm taking some time off."

She goggled at him. "But you're a workaholic."

He shrugged again.

"Okay." Em could roll with the punches. "You're burnt out. You've had a shock to your system, and you're re-evaluating. I get it. But, Kota, October isn't the best time for big decisions."

"It's got nothing to do with October. Or Christy." He threw open the car door. "Don't piss me off, Em. I'm not a fucking idiot."

She sprinted around from her side to block his march toward the house. "Maybe not." She used her *voice of reason*. "But you can be impulsive. If you blurt this out in there"—she waved at the house—"it'll be all over town by dinnertime. You're committed to three films. People will pull out. The studios will lose millions—"

He took her slender shoulders. "Chill." And he moved her gently aside.

Peter met him at the door, a beanpole with shaggy blond hair and slate blue eyes. They'd been together since Kota's breakout role; Peter was agent, friend, and trusted advisor, all in one. And he would shit a brick when Kota broke the news.

Peter made the intros. "Kota, this is Nancy Rhodes." She'd be the senior VP, sent by the company to seal the deal. "And this is her assistant, Ashley Ames." She'd be the hot chick, expected to employ her wiles if he balked.

Kota knew his part. He complimented Nancy's suit, eyewalked Ashley, and generally played the mega–movie star graciously deigning to mix with mere mortals.

It wasn't his favorite role, but it was expected. As Peter liked to say, a sprinkling of stardust turned millions into more millions, since corporate types got endless mileage out of telling friends and colleagues how they'd lunched with Hollywood royalty.

Peter herded everyone poolside, where a table for five was set out under a green awning. A waiter brought Kota a microbrew. Em asked for Chardonnay. It was early in the day for her to have a drink. He raised an eyebrow at her. She scratched her cheek with her middle finger.

Small talk ensued, continuing as the caterer served an "informal" three-course lunch.

Em was usually a pisser at these kinds of events, dropping inside jokes for his benefit that slid under everyone else's radar. But today she was quiet, which made the hour feel like two.

She did rouse herself to run interference when Nancy tried to pin him down over dessert. And when Ashley sidled up to him over coffee, Em faked an incoming call that required his immediate presence elsewhere.

All in all, it was tiresome, and probably a waste of time, because over steamed mussels in garlic butter, his fuzzy notions about quitting had solidified into a concrete plan for the future.

It was the boring lunch and the prospect of thirty more years of boring lunches that convinced him.

Seeing Christy on the sidewalk had nothing to do with it.

Peter walked him to the door. "Well played," he said quietly. "They'll throw another million into the pot now. I'll hammer out the details and call you later."

Kota hesitated. He was Peter's biggest client. The commissions on Kota's deals had paid for this house and put Peter's daughter through Stanford. He'd earned every penny.

Now Kota owed him honesty more than anything else. "Things have changed," he said. "I'm not ready to sign."

Peter blinked, a strong show of emotion for him. Stepping outside, he pulled the door closed behind him. "What's wrong? Is it your folks? Are they okay?"

"Everyone's fine." Kota couldn't drop the safe on Peter's head while they stood on the stoop. So he hedged. "Three years is too long. See what they'll offer for one."

Peter was no dummy. He looked at Em, who pokered up, then back at Kota. "You've been on edge since the wedding. What's going on?"

"Call me later and we'll talk. But for now, one year, okay?"

"It's your call. But they might back out of the whole deal."

"I know. And I know you put a lot of work into it." Kota clasped Peter's shoulder. "I'm sorry. But one year's all I'll give it."

Peter nodded, slowly, his eyes sharpening as his brain went to work on recalibrating the deal. "I'll call. We'll talk."

In the car, Em blasted Kota. Gone was the *voice of reason.* "You are *not* allowed to make this decision in October. You've lost your mind. You'll be sued *out the ass* by three major studios. They'll take your house, your cars . . ."

He tuned her out.

She punched his arm. "Quit ignoring me. And why are you going this way?"

"I'm taking the scenic route." Lookout Mountain Avenue. He hadn't been tempted before, but now that he'd seen Christy again, something inside him had shifted.

"She looked sick," he said, more to himself than to Em.

"Oh Jesus, you're looking for her house." She bounced her head off the headrest. "What are you, sixteen?"

"I'm just wondering what the wages of sin buy you these days." He spotted the stone lion. "That's it on the right."

"Shit. Someone's in the driveway." Em slid down in her seat.

He kept his face pointed forward, raking the house with the side of his eye. "It's not her." The skinny blonde had nothing on Christy. "Must be her roommate."

"Who probably knows the whole story. And right now she's telling Christy you're stalking her."

RAY STEPPED IN front of *CSI*. "Guess who just drove by in his shiny black Porsche pretending not to case the joint."

Chris's pulse shot from zero to sixty.

She throttled it back. "His agent lives on Willow Glen. He was probably visiting him."

"Nobody takes Lookout to get from Willow Glen to Beverly Hills. He drove by here on purpose."

Chris gave up on *CSI*. She wasn't following the story line anyway. How could she, when the street-corner scene played an endless loop in her mind?

God, he'd looked good. Maybe a little pale, but she might be projecting. Otherwise, as gorgeous as ever.

Seeing him unexpectedly had swamped her with memories. His precious face in her hands. His hot body in her arms.

Thank God he'd worn shades today. One look into his eyes and she'd have fallen to her knees.

Ray stomped her foot. "Don't you care that he's stalking you?"

"He isn't stalking me," Chris said definitively. Unless it was to kill her, but even he wouldn't go that far. Probably.

"I bet he wants you back. I bet he thinks you'll jump at the chance."

Chris dropped her head in her hands. Why, oh why, had she told Ray the whole sordid tale?

Because she'd been desperate to talk about it, that's why, and who else could she tell? Her handful of real friends were back east, consumed with husbands and play dates. Ray wasn't ideal, but she was handy.

"Trust me, Ray. Kota might want me dead, but he doesn't want me back." Tossing the remote on the coffee table, she hoisted her ass off the couch and marched for the stairs. "Do me a favor," she called over her shoulder, "and quit scripting a happy ending, okay? Because it's not gonna happen."

It's not gonna happen. The words attached themselves to the street-corner loop like a sound track.

It's not gonna happen. She stripped down and dragged herself into the shower. *It's not gonna happen.* She leaned a shoulder against the wall and slid down to the cold tile floor. *It's not gonna happen.*

Tears dripped from her chin. She wept like a lost child.

And once more, she recycled the recriminations. Why had she agreed to the assignment? Why had she gone to the island? Why, oh why, had she put off confessing to Kota until it was too late?

The answer stared her in the face: She'd done each of those things because at every fork in the road, she'd taken the path of least resistance. Guilt might have gotten her into this mess in the first place, but once she was in it, rather than face the consequences of her actions, she'd taken the easy way out at every turn.

It was the story of her life. For years she'd done what Zach or Emma wanted her to do because it had been easier than choosing her own path and making her own way. Easier to blame them for controlling her life than to take control of it herself.

She loved them, and there was nothing wrong with wanting them to be proud of her. But how could they respect her—how could she respect herself—if she didn't figure out what she wanted, and then do the work to get it?

That's why she'd failed with Kota. Even after she realized she wanted him, even after she had him, she didn't do the work to keep him. Instead of sucking it up and telling him the truth, she postponed it again and again, hoping for an easy way out.

Now she was at it again. Holing up in the house. Cowering in the shower like a kid hiding in the closet during a thunderstorm instead of dealing with the shambles she'd made of her life.

She'd truly hit bottom. Her mother couldn't help her. Neither could her friends. Even her unflappable father was mildly annoyed that she'd used him to further her nefarious ends.

There was no easy way out. It was sit on the floor dripping snot on her chest for the next fifty years, or get up off her ample ass, make amends, and figure out what to do with the rest of her life.

Chapter Twenty-Three

SISSY BROUGHT HER swimsuit. "This weather." She fanned herself. "I figured we'd be better off running lines in the pool."

Em made a face, but Kota waded right in. It was hardly a hardship. Sissy got her start as Miss November. She could rock a bikini.

Being obstinate, Em parked herself at a table in the shade and went to work on her laptop.

Sissy pouted pillowy lips. "Can't you send her to Malibu or something?"

Kota played dumb. "What's in Malibu?"

Sissy tossed golden curls. "Just get rid of her so we can . . . you know." She jiggled her eyebrows, and more.

All that jiggling persuaded him. "Hey, Em, take the afternoon off."

She curled her lip and stuck like a tick.

He climbed out of the pool and dripped his way to her

table, leaning on it with both hands. "You're chaperoning me now?"

"She's a short step up from a porn star."

"When did you turn into a prude?"

"You used to have standards."

"When?"

"Since you hit thirty-five."

"Maybe I'm regressing."

"No, you're in denial. That's different." She tipped her head at Sissy. "Send the bimbo home. We need to talk."

He stood up straight and curled a lip of his own. "I haven't gotten laid in two weeks. The *last* thing I want to do is talk. And the thing about Sissy is, I don't think she's looking for conversation."

He reached over and closed her laptop. "Skedaddle, Em."

She left scowling.

Which left him alone in the pool with Sissy.

He waded into the shallow end and leaned back against the side, stretching his arms along the edge.

She breaststroked toward him, a slender raft floating on jumbo pontoons. Green eyes made emerald by contacts raked his chest. "I've heard about you, Kota. Girls talk, you know."

"Is that so?" His lids lowered to half mast, his sexy squint. "What did you hear?"

She stood up, the water chest deep on her five-foot frame. Her breasts bobbed like buoys.

With one fingertip she traced a line from his throat to

his waistband. "I heard you're a stallion." She tucked her finger inside. "I wanna go for a ride."

He'd heard worse come-ons. He'd delivered a few himself. But maybe Em was right, maybe he'd raised his standards, because Sissy, with her centerfold tits and blow-me lips and Barbie-blond hair, wasn't getting a rise out of him. Not even a twitch.

As she'd quickly discover if she gave his waistband a tug.

He couldn't let that happen. His reputation was at stake.

He needed a boner, and fast.

Catching her questing hand in one of his, he reached behind her neck with the other and tugged the string that tied up her halter. Out popped her double Ds, the nail-hard nipples pierced with solid gold rings.

As if it was scripted, she cupped one, offering it up. He made himself take the ring in his lips. He flicked it with his tongue, and she threw back her head like a . . . well, like a porn star.

His dick shriveled to pinky-sized.

"Kota," Tony called from the doorway. "Your ma's on the phone."

Thank God.

Kota spit out the ring, leaped out of the pool, and had the phone in his hand before Sissy could do more than gape. Throwing her an apologetic wave, he darted inside.

"Hi, Ma. How you doing?"

"I'm fine, your father's fine, everything's fine." She blew past the small talk. "I just got the nicest phone call from Christy."

"*What?*" He exploded out of the chair he'd sunk into. "Did you hang up on her? I can't *believe* she's harassing you. I'll call the cops, get a restraining order—"

"Kota." Her shut-up-and-listen-to-me tone. "It was a nice call, and I was very happy to talk to her."

"About what? Was she pumping you for information? I hope you didn't tell her anything—"

Verna cut into his rant. "She called to apologize to Roy and me for misrepresenting herself."

He bit his tongue to keep from calling bullshit at the top of his lungs.

"She explained the situation. Mind you, she wasn't making excuses. She only wanted us to understand that she was under some pressure from the higher-ups at the newspaper, and she made some bad choices—"

"*Bad choices?*" He couldn't hold back. "Ma, she snuck into Tana's wedding, planning to spread it all over the paper. She lied to everybody, including her *father.* Including *you.* And if that wasn't bad enough, she snuck into *my* house, taking notes for her story—"

"Hold it right there. Don't stretch the truth, young man. I have it on good authority that *you* lured her to the house."

Damn Em's big mouth.

"I also know," she went on, "that Christy's computer had no notes of any kind on it."

"She was taking mental notes," he said stubbornly. "And she hitched a ride to the island to keep spying."

"Invited herself, did she?"

He set his jaw. "If I knew who she was, I wouldn't have asked her."

"But you did, and I very much doubt your motives were pure, my boy." Verna was taking no prisoners. "Can you tell me you didn't plan to take advantage of her?"

Heat rolled over his skin. His face burned like fire. "At least I didn't hide my intentions. She knew what was what, which was more than I knew. I thought she was interested in *me*, not Tana."

"I'm sure that stung."

"That's not what I meant." He forked a hand through his hair. "I don't like being made a fool of."

"So she took advantage of you? She used her time on the island to insinuate herself with your brother and Sasha?"

He paced the room. "Not really."

"She pumped you for information about them?"

"No." She'd never asked one question about them.

"You're telling me she relinquished a golden opportunity to dig up information on the bride and groom?"

"I guess." He stopped at the window. Outside, Cy belly flopped into the pool and doggie-paddled toward Sissy, who fled up the steps, aghast.

"And what about *your* life?" Ma was relentless. "Did she pry into your secrets? Press for juicy details?"

"Not exactly." He'd volunteered everything. "But she pretended to care. About the animals. About me." Humiliation made him squirm. "She . . . she said she loved me. And I thought I loved her. So I told her stuff. Stuff I don't usually talk about."

Ma softened. "And when you did that, dear boy, what did she do?"

"She . . . " She listened. She wept. She told him where she lived.

And then she called her boss and quit her job so she wouldn't have to betray him.

He rested his forehead on the window. "What do you want from me, Ma?"

She laughed lightly. "I only wanted to tell you I got a nice call from Christy. The rest, my boy, is up to you."

LEGS SHAVED, BROWS tweezed, clean hair curling over her shoulders, Chris shimmied into a flirty-skirted sundress boldly splattered with fuchsia and black flowers.

The mirror said it flattered her bottom-heavy shape. She decided to agree with it.

When she walked into the kitchen, Ray's eyes bugged.

"Be nice," Chris said. "It's a fragile illusion."

"It's working." Ray pouted. "I want your legs and your ass."

"The ass you can have. I've got twice as much as I need." She found her keys on the counter where she'd tossed them two weeks ago.

Ray perked up. "Where to?"

"The Apple store."

"Boooor-ing."

"I need a new laptop."

"You should make him give yours back."

And wouldn't that be a fun phone call? "Not worth it. Everything was in the cloud anyway."

"He's a dick."

"He's angry. He has a right to be."

"Don't defend him—"

The door shook under a hammering fist. They eye-browed each other.

The fist pounded again. Ray slid off her stool and peered through the window. "You're kidding me." She yanked open the door.

There stood Dakota, larger than life, hot as the devil, and mad as a hornet.

All the saliva evaporated from Chris's mouth.

"What do *you* want?" Ray threw in his face.

Kota peeled off his aviators, baring the squint. "I'm looking for her." He pointed his chin at Chris like a gun.

"Why?" Ray held her ground bravely, earning Chris's respect.

He tightened the squint another dangerous notch. Ray wilted, and Chris found her voice. "Don't bully her."

His eyes widened. "Bully her? I barely opened my mouth."

"Don't play dumb either. You know the power of the squint." Stepping in front of Ray, she crossed her arms to hide the trembling. "Why are you here?"

"You called Ma."

She lifted her chin. "So?"

"You riled her up."

"Baloney. She was perfectly calm and very pleasant. It's *you* who's riled up. For no reason. I apologized, and that was that. I'm not planning to call her again."

He plainly wanted to menace her, but she'd taken the wind from his sails. "Yeah, well, you better not" was the best he could do.

She pressed her advantage. "I called Sasha too, as you'll find out soon enough. I apologized, and she graciously accepted. That's it, it's done. I'm not trying to be besties."

"So you apologized to everybody but me."

She dropped her eyes. "I wasn't sure how to reach you."

"I'm standing here now."

Yes he was, filling her door like a warrior, steel arms crossed like swords over armor-plated pecs.

Gathering her courage, she lifted her gaze to the face she loved. The beautiful, furious face. And her heart broke again, because his jaw was chiseled in granite, his lips pressed flat in an angry line. And his eyes, once as warm and soft as the sea, were a deep and frigid blue.

"I'm sorry," she said. Oh God, was she sorry. She'd had it all. She'd held that staggering face in her palms. Those arctic eyes had melted for her.

Now they sneered down on her. "That's it? Where's the pantload of excuses you dumped on Ma?"

"No excuses," she said simply. "Reasons. Selfish, shortsighted reasons that seemed important then, and ridiculous now."

She took a deep breath and went on. "I don't expect

you to care why I did what I did. It's my actions that matter, and I'm not proud of them. Sneaking into the wedding was stupid and embarrassing. And once we . . ." She made herself look into his eyes, when she wanted to sink through the floor. "Once we got involved, not telling you was unforgivable."

"Damn right it was." He glowered. "So don't expect it."

"I don't expect anything," she said. But she wished for everything.

His glare was acid on raw skin, too painful to endure. "I'm sorry," she said again, and stepping back, she started to close the door.

He stopped it with the flat of his hand. "We're not done yet." He raked her with his eyes. "You look better," he said gruffly.

She didn't wince, at least not visibly. "A shower will do that."

"Why'd you run?"

"I was embarrassed. I looked like shit. I wasn't expecting to see you. Take your pick."

"I'll go with embarrassed. You should be."

She threw up her hands. "If I had a do-over, I'd quit my job instead of crashing the wedding. I'll regret it for the rest of my life. Rubbing my nose in it is a waste of your time. I'm doing fine with that on my own."

"I doubt that." He leaned in. "I doubt you realize the damage you caused."

She held his fiery gaze. "I'm sorry I hurt you."

"Forget about me," he said, looming. "Tri won't eat. The little fucker won't eat since you left."

"Oh my God. Is he in the car?" She tried to look around him, but he filled the frame.

"Even if he was, what difference would it make? He'd see you once, but it wouldn't be enough. He'd still miss you. Think about you. Dream about you."

She stopped trying to peer around him and looked up into his face. "Kota, I—"

"What difference would it make?" he said again, bitterly. "It would only remind him how it was when he thought he could trust you."

"But he can." She swallowed past the lump in her throat. "He can trust me. I love him."

Oh, how Kota wanted to believe that. With his whole being, he longed to believe.

His heart, the same heart that ceased beating on the tarmac two weeks ago, now pumped like a piston. Every muscle, every fiber, strained to reach for her, to hug her to his chest, absorb her through his skin until she sang in his veins.

He needed to get out of there before he did something stupid.

"Wait here," he said, and stalked to the Porsche. He tried to lean in to get her laptop, but Tri was on top of it, dancing on his hind legs like a showgirl. He'd heard that smoky voice too, and like Kota, he'd let his heart get out in front of his head.

"Forget it," Kota muttered. "I only brought you along for the fresh air."

But the fool dog only got more excited, hopping in a circle, panting like he'd run a marathon. Whining, and Tri never whined unless . . .

Suspicious, Kota whirled. Christy was right on his heels.

"Back off," he snarled.

"No. Let me see him." She tried to go around him.

He blocked her. "He doesn't want to see you."

"You just said he misses me."

"That doesn't mean he wants to see you." He crossed his arms, ignoring the canine hysteria behind him. "He's not dumb enough to let you fool him twice."

She leveled a look. "Enough already. I'm not throwing myself at you, Kota. I get that you don't want anything to do with me. But Tri"—her voice caught—"I never got to say good-bye to him."

"You don't deserve—"

From behind him, a thud, then a yip. The crazy dog had flung himself over the door and onto the pavement.

Now he raced around the car and dove at Christy's leg. She scooped him up to chin level, and he went wild with his tongue as she laughed and cried all at once.

Only a hard-hearted bastard would break up their love-in.

"Quit it," he said, swiping Tri from her hands. "Quit teasing him."

Her empty arms fell. For a long moment she looked into his face, hers etched with misery. "I'm sorry," she said quietly. "I'm sorry I hurt you so badly that you'd hurt Tri to punish me."

Is that what he was doing?

He stuck the squirming dog under his arm. "He doesn't know you like I do. I'm protecting him."

"No, you're waving him under my nose." Her shoulders drooped. "I know what I lost, Kota. I can't think of anything else. I can't sleep. All I can do is eat, and you see where that's gotten me." She waved a hand at herself.

He used the excuse to eyeball her body, as amazing as ever. He swallowed the saliva that pooled on his tongue. "You look okay," he said gruffly. "None the worse for wear."

She gave a weak little laugh. "This dress hides the second ass I've grown."

More saliva. "It's nice. The dress, I mean." He cleared his throat. "Nice dress."

She almost smiled. Then she stiffened her shoulders. "Why are you really here, Kota?"

Why *was* he here, torturing himself, torturing Tri, who wriggled like a worm under his arm?

He grabbed the laptop and gave it to her.

"Oh." Like it was the last thing she expected. "Okay. Thanks." Tucking it under her arm, she backed up toward the house, and Tri, the traitor, squirmed even harder.

"Wait," he blurted, and she paused, sadness and uncertainty written on her face. "Just . . . wait."

He took a deep breath. Then, closing the space between them, he held out Tri. She took him with her free arm, and he snuggled against her breast. Lucky bastard.

Making himself step back, he said sternly, "He'll overeat if you let him. So don't, because if he gets fat, he won't be able to get around."

Her eyes had gone wide. Her lips parted, and trembled.

"He's lazy," he added harshly. "He'll want you to carry him everyplace. Don't, because—"

"He'll get fat." A tear slid down one pale cheek. "I won't let him. I'll take care of him."

"You better." His voice was rough with emotion. He channeled it into a growl. "Or I'll be back for him."

She buried her nose in Tri's neck. "I promise I'll never let anything hurt him."

He believed her, but it didn't make leaving either of them any easier. He bit down on the inside of his cheek. If he didn't walk away now, he'd bawl like a toddler.

Then she lifted her gaze, blinking back the tears swimming in her warm caramel eyes. His throat closed up tight.

And it was a damn good thing, or he'd have spit out something stupid.

Instead, he whipped open the Porsche's door and threw himself into the seat, refusing to watch her in the rearview as he burned rubber down the road.

Chapter Twenty-Four

"You LEFT TRI with her?" Em thunked her forehead with the heel of her hand.

"So?" Kota glared at her in the bathroom mirror.

"So it's an excuse for you to see her again."

"It's not about me. He was pining for her."

"*Pining*?"

He gave her a look meant to say her vocabulary was wanting. "It means he was missing her."

"I know what it means. And you're full of shit. *You're* the one pining."

He didn't deny it. Instead, he pasted his toothbrush and got busy with it.

She put a fist on her hip. "Tell me what happened."

"Nothing happened," he mumbled through the foam. Nothing except a hard-on that hadn't quit until midnight, when he'd finally taken it in hand.

"Did she at least say she was sorry?"

"Yeah." He rinsed. "She seemed like she meant it."

"Did you forgive her?"

"Hell no!" And he wouldn't. Not ever.

"But you left Tri with her."

He lowered his brow. "I told you he was pining. The little shit wouldn't eat."

She crossed her arms. "Did you send his food? His specially formulated, hundred-dollar-a-pound food?"

He scrubbed his face with a towel. "It's in the car. I'll drop it off on the way to the studio."

Silence. He lowered the towel.

She eyed him in the mirror. "You're pathetic."

He didn't deny that either.

THE HAMMERING ON Chris's door had a familiar ring to it.

Heart in her throat, she opened up, afraid he'd changed his mind about Tri, ready to resist if he had.

Tri scrambled out onto the stoop, wiggling and wagging. Kota scooped him up. "Ready to come home with me, buddy?"

Tri must have understood him, because if he'd been a baby, he would've held out his arms to Chris. As it was, he waved his paw at her frantically.

She grabbed him and he settled in, happy to gaze lovingly at Kota from the crook of her arm.

Angling her body to keep him out of Kota's reach, she said, "He ate. I walked him. He slept with me." She swallowed. "Please let him stay."

Blue eyes studied her. "I want visitation."

"Okay." She'd agree to anything. Cuddled up with Tri, she'd had her first good night's rest in two weeks.

Kota bent down and hefted a burlap sack. "His special food."

She couldn't help smiling. "Made from common natural ingredients blended together in their most effective proportions?"

His lips twitched. "Something like that. Where do you want it?"

"On the counter."

He strode into the kitchen and immediately spotted the Viking. He eyed it critically. "Looks like it's never been used."

"I told you I'm useless in the kitchen."

"Lot of money for a prop."

"I thought I might be a person who cooks." She shrugged. "I'm not."

He studied her. "What kind of person are you?"

"I'm trying to figure that out." But it wasn't somewhere she wanted to go with him. The problem was, he was too easy to talk to. Even now, with an unbridgeable chasm between them, she wanted so much more.

Shifting Tri to her other arm, she placed a hand on the doorknob, body language for *bye now*.

In typical Kota fashion, he ignored it, leaning a hip against the counter. "What about your roommate? She's okay with Tri? 'Cause if she's not—"

"She's fine," Chris cut in. Then honesty won out. "Actually, Ray's not much of a dog person. But it's my house. If one of them has to go, it won't be Tri."

He nodded like he believed her, which was progress. Then he glanced at the stove again. "Do you even know how to use it?"

"I can boil water. And heat up a frozen pizza."

He snorted. "That's like letting a Lamborghini rust out because you can't drive a stick." He walked to the stove. Opened the oven door. Closed it. Lifted the teapot to look under it like he was the health inspector.

She set her teeth. "If it offends you so much, you're welcome to buy it."

"Got my own." He fiddled with the knobs.

"Then if there's nothing else . . ."

He moseyed away from the stove at last, only to take a turn around the rest of the kitchen, poking in her cupboards, peering into the fridge.

Objecting would only egg him on, so she held her tongue as long as she could. But when he moved into the living room, she marched after him.

"If you're looking for the bathroom," she said between her teeth, "it's through there."

"I'll get to it eventually." He pressed the couch cushions, inspected the TV.

When he started pawing through her magazines, she blew her stack.

"Quit handling my stuff!" She set Tri on the couch and used both hands to wrest the magazines out of his. "What's your problem?"

The look he gave her said *she* had the problem. "I'm making sure it's safe to leave my dog here."

"By fingering my magazines? What next, my under-wear?"

Yikes, where had that come from? Her face heated up like a frying pan.

"Now that you mention it," he said, straight-faced, "I want to see your bedroom next."

"Like hell."

Ignoring her, he headed for the stairs. She charged after him, spiraling up the steps on his heels.

He paused at the second floor and surveyed the mess.

"That's Ray's room," she said, defensive, "not that it's any of your business."

He kept climbing. "Tri can't handle these stairs," he said, like it was the kiss of death.

"Yes, he can. He's right behind me." Hopping and bopping along, one step at a time.

Kota stepped into her room, making it feel as small as a dollhouse. Hands on his hips, he turned a slow circle. "At least it's clean."

Her back went up even higher. "You expected a pigpen?"

"I didn't know what to expect." He seemed to say it to himself. Walking into the bathroom, he flicked on the light.

Yesterday's panties hung out of the hamper. She mus-cled past him and flicked them inside. Then she spun to give him a piece of her mind.

And the heat in his eyes cut off her rant before it began.

He turned abruptly and almost tripped over Tri.

Scooping him up, he moved back into the bedroom, checking the view out the windows, sticking his head in the closet. He took his sweet time, while she silently counted to a hundred.

Stopping at last by the unmade bed, he turned to her. The morning light streaming in unfairly cast him in bronze. His cheekbones seemed sharper, his lips fuller. And his steady, assessing gaze reminded her that yoga pants didn't flatter her ass.

She crossed her arms. She did that a lot around him. Protecting herself. Standing her ground. "Well?"

"He can't get down those stairs."

She dropped her arms. "For God's sake, quit pretending this is about Tri. You're here to find fault. The stove's too clean, the bathroom's too messy. The stairs are too steep."

"You're paranoid."

"You're full of shit."

His brow lowered. "Don't cuss at me."

"I'll cuss if I want to." The infuriating man. "You're full of shit, and you're being an asshole."

He took a threatening step, shrinking the room. "You're nobody to talk. You're a sneak and a liar. Some people might call you a whore."

She drew herself up, trembling in every cell. "I'll own the first two, but you know I'm no whore. You *know* it."

"Do I?" He advanced. "You had sex with me while you were grubbing around for a story."

"First of all, I didn't go to the island for the story. And

if you'll recall, I tried *not* to have sex with you. You seduced me, with all your . . . your *muscles*."

"If *you'll* recall, it wasn't my muscles that did it for you. You"—his pointing finger damned her eternally—"got off on watching my brother have sex."

Heat flooded her cheeks. Embarrassment, and anger too. "You didn't complain at the time."

He sneered. "A stallion doesn't complain when the mare's in heat."

Her blood pressure hit a record high. Her voice dropped to a homicidal low. "You are too disgusting for words." She pointed at the stairs. "Out."

"No." He crowded her, looming. "I'm not done with you yet."

She shoved her face up at his. "So this was a ploy. A lie. You used Tri to worm your way into my house. You're no better than I am."

"Don't you dare," he growled. "Don't you dare compare this to what you did."

"At least I had a good reason. You're just looking for revenge, you big bully. You want to scare me. Well, you don't." She drilled a finger into his chest. "You wouldn't hurt me even if I pulled out a gun and shot you."

"Don't be so sure." His face was inches from hers, his breathing hot and heavy. "I've had about enough of you."

"Good, then go." She shoved his shoulder, but he was Mount Rushmore.

"I'll go when I'm good and ready."

"Then I'll go. Give him to me."

Kota pivoted so she couldn't reach Tri.

"Quit holding him hostage," she shouted. "Take your problem out on me. I'm the one you're mad at."

"Mad?" His face darkened. "You think I'm *mad* at you? Mad doesn't begin to cover it, sweetheart. You played me. You fucked me. You lied about everything."

"No, I didn't! I mean, yes, I lied about why I was at the wedding. But I never lied about my feelings. I tried to keep my distance, but I couldn't. Because I'm an idiot, like every other woman on the planet. Because I fell . . ." She caught herself. Caught her breath.

"What?" He grabbed her arm. "Finish, goddamn it."

She shook her head. He shook her arm.

She tried to pull away. Tears welled and spilled over. "Let me go," she sobbed out.

He tossed Tri on the bed and hauled her in, locking her to his chest. "Say it, goddamn you."

She shoved at Mount Rushmore. He gave not an inch. Heat poured off him like a furnace. His eyes, so intense, burned her skin.

"Don't lie to me again," he gritted through his teeth. "For once, tell me the goddamn truth."

"I fell in love with you, all right? Is that true enough for you?"

"I don't know. Is it?" He searched her face like he didn't trust either of them to know the truth from a lie.

"Yes, you son of a bitch. Are you happy now? I fell in love with you, and I lost everything. My job. My reputation. My future." She laughed, half hysterical. "Here, take my pride. There wasn't much left of it anyway."

"I don't want your pride," he growled. "I want this."

He closed the last inch, crushing her lips, thrusting his tongue. Taking her mouth the way he'd once taken her body.

And she took him right back, sucking him, scoring his shoulders, her fever burning as hot as his own.

Shoving his hands down her pants, he grabbed her ass, boosting her so she locked her legs around him. She broke the kiss to peel off her shirt, taking her tits in her hands, offering them up, and he took them, sucking the salty sweat from her skin.

This wasn't the plan, not even close, but he was out of control, crazed by her scent, scorched in her heat, and he only cared about getting inside her.

She clawed his shirt up, raking his back. "Arms," she panted, and he tossed her on the bed, ripping his shirt over his head, letting her see his muscles, his sweat.

She ate him up with her eyes. "Kota," she breathed, cupping her breast with one hand. She pushed the other hand down her pants, and he lost his mind.

He tore open his jeans and shoved them past his knees, caught her ankles and dragged her ass to the edge of the bed.

"Off," he uttered, and yanked her pants down. Her hand was in her pink panties; he snapped them like a thread. Then he flipped her over, pulled her up on her knees, and drove into her, every last inch, as she closed around him like a hot, slippery fist.

Clenching her hips, he pumped her, her beautiful ass filling his gaze, filling his mind. She met every thrust, as crazed as he was, matching his speed, faster, and harder.

He wouldn't last long. He reached around and covered her fingers with his, driving her higher, making her pant.

Then she threw back her head, and his sanity snapped.

Swearing through his teeth, he emptied every ounce of himself into her, until his cock ran dry and his legs gave out, and he collapsed on top of her in a slippery, sweaty, goddamn glorious, totally fucked-up mess.

Chapter Twenty-Five

I DON'T HAVE to love her to fuck her.

Kota rolled onto his side, taking his weight off Christy. She dragged in a breath and flopped onto her back. A bead of sweat rolled down her temple.

Or was it a tear?

He didn't care. Let her cry. He closed his eyes to block her out, but her profile was burned on his retinas. He'd missed her face. He'd missed her.

No. He'd missed fucking her. Liar or not, she was a great lay.

Which prompted the question: Why deprive himself of her body? It wasn't like he'd get attached to her now that he knew she was a liar. So why not fuck her till he got tired of her, then move on to the next girl?

Peaches grew on trees in California.

The sheets rustled, and the scent of roses wafted up his nose. His eyes opened. She'd rolled up on her side, arm tucked under her head, watching him with warm caramel eyes.

"What just happened?" she asked in that hot, husky voice.

His body strained toward her heat, so he put frost in his voice. "I fucked you, that's what."

Cruelty didn't come easy, but he couldn't let her see how she got to him. Or rather, how her *body* got to him.

"Is that really all it was?" Her voice was barely a whisper.

"You got a hot body, babe. Fuckable." He shrugged like that was all that mattered. Like everything was that simple.

Her eyes fell. Tri came out from behind the pillows and snuggled against her. A fat tear dripped from her chin and rolled down his ear.

Guilt drove a fiery spike through Kota's chest. He yanked it out and broke it over his knee. "You're a good fuck," he said, deliberately coarse. "We can fuck again sometime. I'll give you a call."

Her gaze shot up, furious now, and her mouth opened, probably to kick his mean, nasty ass to the curb.

He braced.

But she closed it without a word, studying him for a long moment instead, her misty eyes searching his face while he fought down the mounting urge to squirm.

CHRIS READ THE conflicting emotions on Kota's face, and her heart went out to him. The poor guy was even more messed up than she was.

She'd almost fallen for his act. The man knew how to sell cold, hard bastard; he made millions at it. But the Kota she'd come to know was more complex, more layered, and much more conflicted than his on-screen persona.

A good, long look in his eyes revealed what he was trying so hard to hide. He still loved her. He didn't want to, but he did, and he was tearing himself apart.

It was a tough spot for anyone to be in, but especially someone like Kota. He needed to be in control. Of his environment, of the people and situations around him. And especially of his emotions.

Now he'd lost that control, and he was trying to wrest it back. Playing the hard-ass was just a ruse to make her do what he didn't have the will to do himself. Break it off.

The problem was, she had no intention of going along with the plan.

"Sure," she said, wiping her check with the back of her hand. "Why not?"

His jaw dropped comically. He stared like she'd grown two heads.

But he recovered like a pro. Without a word, he stood up and hoisted his jeans, patting his pockets for his phone, his wallet, his keys. Then he rooted through the sheets for his shirt and dragged it over his head, tucking it in, zipping and buttoning.

Watching him go through the motions, she fought down the urge to burst into song. Another chance with him was the last thing she'd expected, but he'd opened the door a crack, and she'd stuck her foot in before he could slam it shut again.

Now he was struggling to regain control—of himself, and the situation.

In the end, he did it Kota-style, straightening to his full height, finger-combing his hair to give her a load of his arms. Then he rolled out his sexiest, shit-eating smirk, as if he held all the cards in his hand.

"I'll be back at twelve," he said, "for another bang."

She gave as good as she got, doing her own lazy stretch, giving him an eyeful of breasts and buns. Then she curled herself around a pillow and did a sleepy, sensual snuggle. "I'll be waiting."

It wiped the smirk off his face. The wrought-iron staircase shook as he pounded down the steps. Even the Porsche sounded pissed as he threw it in gear and peeled out.

She waited until it faded from earshot, then she bounded out of bed.

Two hours to get ready. Not a minute to waste.

FOR A SMALL woman, Em could be dangerous. Standing in Kota's parking space, legs braced, flaming arrows shooting from her eyes, she would have made a lesser man quail.

He inched into the space until he was practically touching her knees. When she didn't move, he took a picture of her with his phone.

That got her hopping. "Don't you dare tweet that."

When she darted around to pluck it from his hand, he pulled forward and shut off the car.

Picture deleted, she tossed the phone back at him. "If you bothered using that for actual communication," she said, "you'd know they've been waiting an hour for you. Now move it."

He got out, taking his sweet time while she did her border collie thing, herding him toward the studio door, yipping at his heels. "This is no way to start a picture. I don't care if you think you're burned out. You've got a sterling reputation—"

"Thanks to you."

"Exactly. It's not just *your* rep on the line. Someday you won't need me anymore and I'll have to find another job—"

That brought him up short. He stopped walking and turned to look at her.

She threw up her hands. "What's your problem? Quit staring and move your ass."

He closed the distance with one stride and wrapped her in a hug.

For a moment she went still. Then she started to squirm. "Let go of me, you lunkhead."

He kissed the top of her head.

She went still again. Her voice dropped to a whisper. "Kota. What's going on? Did you . . . do something to Christy?"

He bit down on his cheek so he wouldn't laugh. "She had it coming," he said.

She wriggled out of his grip and stepped back, staring hard at him. Then she said, "Any witnesses? Her roommate? Did anyone see you go in?"

He shook his head, not trusting himself to speak.

She looked him over, apparently for blood. Peered in the car. "Okay, good." Then she went still again. "What about the trunk?"

He shook his head again.

"You left her at her house?"

He nodded.

"Was it messy?"

He made a face. It was messy all right. But not how Em meant.

She spiked her hair with one hand. "You need an alibi. You've got to get inside immediately and be seen." She paced. "But I'll need your help later. Come out the second you're done. I'll cancel your lunch."

Pulling out her phone, she tapped a number, thinking out loud while it rang. "We'll need heavy-duty plastic. I know a place in South Central."

He couldn't contain himself. "You know a place? What the fuck, Em?"

She shushed him, said into the phone, "This is Emily Fazzone. Mr. Rain won't be available for lunch today. He sends his regrets. I'll call tomorrow to reschedule."

She hung up, then got behind him and bulldozed him toward the door. "Remember, you're an actor," she said, as if he might forget. "Act innocent. No, not innocent. Act like you always act."

"And how's that?"

"Like you're guilty of something but too irresistible to convict."

She left him at the door and set off toward her Honda at a clip.

"Wanna take the Porsche?" he called.

"To South Central? Yeah, because it's so inconspicuous." The look she threw over her shoulder said he was too dumb to live.

He let her start the Honda before he dialed her phone.

"What?" she snapped out, a woman with important things to do, like cover up a murder.

"Bring back a three-by-three, will you? I worked up an appetite."

Appalled silence.

"And you can skip the plastic," he said. "I rolled her in the sheets."

Her eyes blistered him through the windshield. "You had sex with her." She made it sound worse than homicide.

"She threw herself at me."

"Baloney." She shut off the engine and slammed out of the car.

He ducked inside. "Thanks for canceling lunch," he said before he hung up on her.

He found the rest of the cast assembled in a dingy gray room. Sissy patted the chair she'd apparently saved for him. Miles—the director—glowered at him from the head of the table.

This was Kota's third film with Miles. He was a no-bullshit kind of guy, and Kota liked that about him. Himself, he was a joker on the set. But when the lights came up, he was all business too. That's why they got on so well. They were both professionals.

Now Miles gave him a hard stare. He returned a sheepish grin.

The reading commenced, along with discussion, disagreement, some laughter, a few tears. But he couldn't keep his mind on it.

He kept thinking about Christy.

He'd only wanted to drop off Tri's food and make sure he was happy there. He hadn't expected to have sex.

But she was so hot.

He'd wanted women before. Lust was as normal to him as hunger or thirst. But this thing with Christy was out of control. He couldn't see her without wanting—*needing*—to be inside her.

Fortunately, that's all it was. Just sex. That whole thing on the island, where he thought he was in love? An illusion brought on by the circumstances. Tana and Sasha had looked so happy, so whole, that he'd foolishly fantasized about having the same for himself.

Not gonna happen. Christy played her tricks on him, made him feel special, but at the end of the day he was just a means to an end. She didn't care about him. And now that the story was off the table, she just wanted his body. Hell, she hadn't batted an eye when he'd offered to be fuck-buddies.

Well, that was fine with him. That's all he wanted from her too. And that's what he was going to get, in exactly—he snuck a look at the clock—forty-five minutes.

He could hardly wait.

EM DOGGED HIM out to his car. "Don't do it. Don't go."

He got in, slammed the door. The sun-soaked leather scorched his butt, but he didn't care. His mind was already at Christy's. "Quit worrying, Em. It's just sex."

"It's not *just sex,* and you know it. You've lost your mind."

She must really believe that if she thought he'd offed Christy.

"Have you ever known me to lose my head over a woman?" he said, trying to comfort her.

"I've never seen you in love with one before." She leaned her hands on the door. "I kind of hoped I never would."

That startled him. "Why?"

"Because I've seen how you love Tana, and your folks, and me. You go all in. You take us on. Make us your responsibility. You do the same with the animals, like we're all under your protection."

"You are," he said simply. "I'd do anything for you." But he'd failed Charlie, hadn't he? Like he'd failed his birth parents.

Em touched his shoulder, a squeeze instead of her usual punch. "That's why you're torn up about Christy. She triggers all your protective instincts. But you can't get over that she lied to you. She was a threat to Tana. Maybe she still is."

She'd hit the nail on the head.

He gave her an approving nod. "Those internet psych classes are really paying off." He shifted into reverse, then shot a quick grin over his shoulder as he pulled away. "Don't wait up for me, you hear?"

He hit all the lights and made it to Christy's in record time. Banging on the door, he heard Tri go into attack mode, barking like a big dog. He'd never done that at Kota's, where Cy had it covered. But anybody who wanted to get to Christy would have to go through Tri.

Then she opened the door, and a sunbeam hit her, sparking off her hair. His throat went dry.

Gone were the yoga pants, replaced by a short, sleeveless dress the color of Ma's favorite pink roses. Her feet were bare. Her arms too, except from the elbows down, where they were coated in flour.

She stepped back, he stepped in, and he blinked at the counter.

"I'm making pasta," she said.

No, she was making a mess. Flour blanketed the countertop and the floor surrounding it. She'd tracked it to the door.

Now she tracked it back to the counter, where a blob of paste squatted. She poked it. "It doesn't look like yours," she said.

"It sure as hell doesn't." He nudged her out of the way and tossed the blob in the garbage.

"Hey! I was still working on that."

"You could work on it till the cows come home. It'll

never be pasta." He rolled up his sleeves, washed his hands like a surgeon. "Any flour left, or is it all on the floor?"

"Very funny." She took a bag from the cupboard. "You can't expect me to get it perfect the first time. I need practice."

"Practice on your own lunch hour. I'm hungry." He hadn't been kidding when he'd told Em he'd worked up an appetite. And he needed strength for what the afternoon promised.

He pointed at a stool. She shimmied her butt onto it, plopping Tri on her lap.

It was almost like old times. Except now he knew she wasn't what she'd pretended to be.

He broke eggs from the carton she'd left open on the counter, then worked the dough while a hundred questions ran through his mind. Questions about her, about them. Questions he wasn't sure he could trust her to answer honestly.

He asked the most basic one first. The one that started it all. "What made you do it?"

"Sneak into the wedding? Your guy Mercer must've figured that out by now. I did it to save my job."

He watched her draw smiley faces in the flour.

"You don't seem too broken up about losing it."

She rubbed out the faces. "Losing my job seemed like the worst thing in the world. Until it happened. Then it was a relief. I never wanted to be a journalist."

He would've scratched his head if he weren't wrist deep in dough.

"Then why do it?" he asked. "You put Billie Holiday to shame. Why do anything but sing?"

"It's hard to explain." She went back to making faces again.

He let the dough sit while he unboxed the never-used pasta maker and washed the pieces in the island's sink. He kept one eye on Christy. When she didn't follow up, he leaned over and blew the smiley faces into her lap.

"Hey!" She flapped her dress, while Tri fired off three pistol-shot sneezes.

"You were sayin'," he said.

She heaved a sigh. "My mother changed the world. If I had a nickel for everyone who reminded me of that, I could buy your island for cash. She spent half her life in war-torn countries, surrounded by the dead and dying, peeing on the side of the road, dodging shrapnel.

"And she wanted me to do the same. To carry on her work. Go into the heart of misery and strife and tell the world the truth about it. But I'm not as tough as she was. I'm not built for that kind of abuse."

She said it like that made her a failure. "I had enough of that life as a kid, trailing around the world behind her. Not that she brought me into the smoke and fire. But I was close enough to be scared shitless a lot of the time."

To Kota, it sounded like child abuse. Foster care sucked, but at least he was in America.

He kept his voice neutral. "Who took care of you?"

"When I was little, I had a nanny. She traveled with me and Mom, and came on tour with me and Dad in the summers."

So the poor kid never had a home. At least he and Tana had landed at the ranch, the best place a kid could grow up. Hard work, little money, but loads of love. And he'd put his feet under the same table every night.

Still, he refused to feel bad for her. As fucked up as her childhood was, she knew right from wrong. She knew the truth from a lie.

That said, he needed a minute, so he stuck his head in her fridge. And cringed.

Three sad little Dannons surrounded an outpost of Ragú. "What the hell?" Nobody could live on that.

He glanced over his shoulder, but she was ignoring him, tickling Tri, who wriggled gleefully, like the horny bastard he was.

Kota rolled his eyes, but he was in no position to judge. After all, he was here to get tickled too.

Rifling the drawers, he dug out a stick of butter and a moldy hunk of Parmesan. When he plopped them on the counter, Christy made a face at the cheese. "Ugh, don't use that. There's some good stuff in there." She pointed.

He opened the cupboard, curled his lip at the green cardboard container, and dropped it in the trash.

"That's not cheese," he said when she squawked. "It's the stuff they sweep up off the floor. This here is perfectly good." He trimmed the mold from the hunk with the least-dull knife he could find. "You'd know that if you spent more time cooking and less time ordering takeout."

"Hey, I was trying to make pasta. You're the one who kicked me out of the kitchen."

That was true, but he wouldn't give her an inch, not

on anything. She'd use it to hogtie him, and he wasn't making that mistake again.

"So if you didn't want to be a journalist, why'd you go to the *Sentinel*?"

"Because my mother has Alzheimer's."

"So you said, and I'm sorry about that. But if she doesn't know one way or the other, what's the point?"

Her chin came up. "I felt guilty, okay? Guilt's a powerful motivator."

"And now you've got even more to feel guilty about. Like lying to me. Lying to my *folks*."

OUCH. KOTA KNEW just where to jab her.

But she'd asked for this when she'd engineered the pasta debacle. She wanted to get him talking instead of screwing, even though conversation was bound to be painful.

She quit playing with the flour and looked him in the face. His eyes, once so warm, were chilly. She made herself hold his gaze.

"When I accepted the assignment, I hadn't met your parents. I hadn't met you, or Tana, or Sasha. None of you were real to me. And to be honest"—because that was the whole point—"my biggest qualm was that dishing on a celebrity wedding was beneath me. Because I was a serious journalist."

Disdain curled his lip. She soldiered on.

"Once I met you, I felt bad about deceiving you. And when I met your parents . . . well, I fell in love with them."

He snorted.

"I did," she insisted. "They're everything my parents aren't. I love my parents too, but they're different. They have these huge egos, and both of them expect me to carry their torch into the future. My father's just as bad as Mom. He can't understand why I don't throw myself into singing—"

"Neither can I."

"Because I don't *want* to." She slapped the counter, sending up a puff of flour.

"Then what *do* you want?"

Now she spread her hands. "Why do I have to want anything? Why can't I just live a normal life like everybody else?"

"Get over yourself. Everybody wants something."

"Maybe. But"—she leveled a look at him—"even people who know what it is don't always go after it."

He crossed his arms. "We're not going there."

"Why not? How can you judge me when you're gearing up for another blockbuster you don't want any part of?"

"Mind your own business, sweetheart." He backed it up with a death-ray squint.

She scooped up a handful of flour and threw it at him. Most of it drifted down onto the counter, but some of it speckled his black T-shirt.

"You don't want to be doing that," he said, low and deadly.

She did it again.

He came around the counter. She clutched Tri like a force field.

"We're wasting time talking," he growled, "when we should be screwing."

She swallowed. "I thought you were hungry."

"I'll get a burger when we're done." He took Tri out of her hands and dumped him on the floor. Then he cuffed her wrists. "Come on, baby. Let's fuck." He pulled her off the stool and over to the couch. "Where's your roommate?"

"At a casting call."

"She gonna walk in on us?"

"Would you care if she did?"

"Not a bit." He caught the hem of her dress and whipped it over her head.

Then he caught his breath. Hot eyes licked over her breasts, down her belly.

She smiled. Her pasta run had included a detour to Rodeo Drive, where she'd dropped three hundred on a white teddy guaranteed to make him drool.

Money well spent.

He stroked his palms up her arms to her shoulders, hooked his pinkies under flimsy lace straps. She waited for the pop, but it didn't come. Instead, he drew the straps down her arms, exposing her breasts. With the rough pads of his thumbs, he brought her nipples to life.

Dipping his head, he rubbed his nose along her collarbone, breathing her in. She let her head fall to the side, giving him room, and he nipped the long muscle that tied her neck to her shoulder. It tickled, and she giggled. He bit harder, and she gasped.

Slowly, he peeled her teddy to her waist, then slid his

hands down the back, cupping her rump, kneading it, his wrists stretching the fabric. He pushed against her, circling his hips so bulging denim rubbed her where she wanted it.

Nothing had ever felt so good, or so sexy.

She didn't want it to stop. Reaching around him, she clutched his ass, pinning him to her as she rocked against him, a victim of her own well-planned seduction.

He hooked a knuckle under her jaw, tilting her chin, taking her lips in a kiss that was more than a kiss. More than sex, more than lust. She rose up on her toes, giving him more too, her heart lifting, chest swelling.

Then he stepped back, abruptly, and for an instant she thought he'd reconsidered. But he dropped his jeans and moved in, not going anywhere except inside of her.

Yet in that instant, something had changed. Gone was Mr. Slow-and-Easy. His blue eyes blazed, scorching her skin. He tore her teddy. Boosted her up and brought her down on his cock, forging in, taking control. Backing her against the wall, taking her weight like it was nothing, pumping her hard.

Words fell from his lips, dirty, sexy words, and she ate them up and gave them back, an X-rated dialogue that drove them both higher, past anyplace they'd been before. She cinched his waist with her legs, doing her part, shoving her hands up under his shirt, raking his shoulders, scratching his pecs.

He tried to take back control. "Come." He growled out the command, wanting to call the shots, order her around, pretend he was using her.

She held out, refusing to be bossed, refusing to be used. "Come with me," she panted, biting his jaw, tasting his sweat.

"God*damn* it, woman." He couldn't hold out. Throwing back his head, he roared out her name. And together they came, denting the wall, bringing books down off of shelves.

When they could breathe again, he lifted her off of him. In less than a minute, he was headed for the door.

"Bye?" she called after him. "See you later?"

"Don't count on it," he threw over his shoulder and slammed the door behind him.

Chapter Twenty-Six

KOTA JAMMED THE shifter into third, taking the winding road faster than he should.

Shoving his hand down his pants, he unstuck his cock from his thigh. For Christ's sake, he should've at least taken a minute to clean up.

But no, he ran like a rabbit instead. And from what? They had sex. Just sex.

He shouldn't have kissed her. That was his mistake. A kiss was too intimate, too not-just-sex.

But once he *had* kissed her, he should have been cool about it. Now she'd know she got to him. Just like she planned to when she slipped into that teddy. Hell. Nobody wore a teddy under a sundress—nobody wore one, period—unless they were expecting some action.

Well, in her defense, she *was* expecting action. He'd promised to come back at lunchtime. He shouldn't complain that she was ready and waiting for him.

She'd even tried to make lunch. He snorted. She'd botched it, of course. The woman probably couldn't boil water without burning it. But she tried. And then he'd gone and left without even cleaning up the mess. Ma would read him the riot act if she knew about that.

He touched the brakes. He should go back and help. Flour was a bitch to get up off the floor—

His phone rang. Em. For Christ's sake.

"What?" he blasted at her.

"Where are you?"

"Don't pretend you can't track my phone." Like he didn't know she'd put him on her friends-and-family plan specifically to keep tabs on him.

"Okay, then. You're driving too fast."

He sped up. "Why're you pestering me?"

"Peter called. Levi's is firm on three years."

"Tell him to say thanks, but no thanks."

Silence.

He shot through a yellow light, whipped into In-N-Out, and squealed up to the drive-thru.

"Bring me a grilled cheese," Em said.

He backed up and squealed out. "I'm getting a new phone. Without the spyware."

"Like you have a clue how to get your own phone."

"I'll have my new assistant take care of it."

"Great. When does she start? Because I cut short my last vacation to save you from the woman you're currently banging—"

He hung up.

Five minutes later, he braked at his gate and waved

to the camera. Somewhere in the house Tony pushed a button to let him in.

Em met him in the driveway. He gave her a "*What now?*" look. Then he did a double take.

For the first time he could remember, she had circles under her eyes. Like she was sick, or hadn't slept. Or was worried about someone she cared for who might be going off the deep end.

"Get in," he said.

She shook her head. "No time for joyriding. You've got shit to do."

"Who's the boss?"

Huffing a sigh, she got in. He pulled forward into the garage and shut off the car.

Rolling her eyes, she grabbed the door handle. He stopped her with a hand on her arm.

"What now?" She snapped his own words back at him.

"I want to be a vet," he said.

"You're too old to enlist."

"Quit telling me I'm old. And I'm not talking about a veteran. I'm talking about a *veterinarian*."

She looked stumped.

"That was the original plan," he said. "Get Tana settled, then go back to school."

Sharp eyes assessed him. "Why didn't you ever tell me?"

"Because I gave up on it. Or forgot about it."

"Or repressed it so you could stay in Hollywood and babysit Tana."

"Or that."

"So why now? What changed?"

"Tana's married. He doesn't need me anymore."

"What about everyone else who counts on you? Peter, and Tony, and me?"

He cocked his head. "I never figured you'd lay a guilt trip on me."

"I don't have to. You *already* feel guilty. I'm asking how you're going to live with it."

Damn her, she knew him better than he knew himself.

He rolled his shoulders, trying to roll off the guilt. "Brad told me he's thinking about switching agents. I'll give him a shove toward Peter. And Tony, hell, he can get any gig he wants. I've been overpaying him for years just to hang on to him."

She watched him steadily, waiting.

"What?" he said.

"Veterinarians don't have PAs."

"Movie-star vets do. Or they will, when I'm one. It coulda been you, if you weren't such a pain in the ass."

As if he could manage his life without her.

"Meanwhile, about the Levi's deal," she said. "You're just blowing it off?"

"They'll take a year when they see I'm serious."

"What about the Abrams project? You signed the papers."

"I know." A zillion-dollar superhero extravaganza set to start shooting a month after his current film wrapped. "The thing is, if it scores, they're counting on a franchise.

When I tell 'em it's my last film, they'll opt out and find somebody else."

She narrowed her eyes. "You've been thinking about this for a while."

"Two weeks."

Her eyes widened. "You're shitting me. It's Christy, isn't it? She wants you to quit acting and go to vet school."

"She doesn't *want* me to do anything. And believe me, if I was looking for a life coach, it wouldn't be her. She's a goddamn mess." He shrugged. "She made me think about it is all."

Em held her tongue, but he could see the wheels turning.

Finally, she shrugged. "Maybe she's not as bad for you as I thought."

CHRIS WAS ON her hands and knees with a sponge when Zach strolled in.

"Hey, honey pie. That's quite a mess you got there."

She blew her hair off her forehead. "Flour's a bitch to get off the floor."

"How'd it get there in the first place?"

"We were making pasta."

"You and Ray?" Zach guffawed. "The blind leading the blind."

"Thanks, Dad." She trickled sarcasm over it. "But actually it was me and Kota. He's a wizard in the kitchen."

"In the bedroom too, so I hear." He winked at her.

She stood up and threw the sponge in the sink. "Sometimes I think we share too much information."

"To tell you the truth, I'm kinda surprised you two are hanging out again." He wandered into the living room and ran an eye over the jumble of books on the floor. "Looks like you're having fun, though."

"We were, until we kissed. Then he ran out like his hair was on fire."

Zach let out a laugh. "Boy's got it bad. I saw it hit him the minute he laid eyes on you. He went ass over teakettle."

"Yeah, he's a mess." She poured two club sodas. "I'll clean the flour up later. Let's sit outside."

They settled at the tiny café table in her microbackyard. Zach stretched his legs out and made a show of relaxing. He was used to life on the road. On the rare occasions he was home, he got antsy, so he tended to drop in and stay awhile.

He smirked at the ribbon of dirt lining the low fence. "Still working on that garden, I see."

She stuck her tongue out. He laughed. "Honey pie, you need to face the fact that you're just not domestically inclined. Why don't you sell this place and move in with me? I'm hardly ever home. And you won't have to rub elbows with Death-Ray."

"She's not that bad."

"She's a stone bitch." Zach called 'em like he saw 'em.

"I'm not the nicest person either."

"You made a mistake. That's different. Ray's miserable by nature."

Chris sipped her drink. She couldn't deny that Ray got bitchier each day. She resented Hollywood's failure to fall on its knees and declare her a star. And pouring liquor on bitterness only sank its roots deeper.

But no matter how bitchy she got, Ray sure as hell wouldn't run Chris out of her own house. This was the first place she'd ever called home.

"Don't worry, Dad, I'll kick her out if it comes to that. Meanwhile, it's nice to have another warm body around. I'm home a lot, now that I'm unemployed."

He steepled his fingers. "I was thinking about that. Now that your schedule's opened up, I've got a gig in Dubai next week you might want to get in on."

She'd seen it coming from a mile away. "Thanks, Dad, but I'm gonna focus on Mom's bio. If something local comes up, I'm in. But no travel."

"Oh well." He gave her that famous Zach Gray grin. "Worth a try."

With that out of the way, they ordered a pizza and spent a few hours playing rummy like they used to on the tour bus. Then he strolled out the way he'd come in.

When he was gone, Chris got antsy herself. She brought her laptop out to the table.

Then she went inside and made a cup of tea.

She brought the tea outside and turned on the laptop.

Then she went inside for a cookie.

Tri dutifully hop-skipped along behind her. In and out of the slider. Up and down in the chair.

But when she popped up again to find her phone, he waited outside.

She got the hint. "I know, I know. I'll get serious now." She scooped him up on her lap. Opened the file. Scrolled through her notes.

Ho Chi Minh City, blah blah. Baghdad, blah blah.

The words ran together on the page.

Giving up on dry facts, she went back to the pictures, sorting and organizing. Europe, Asia, Africa.

A minaret caught her eye, framed against a blazing sunset. Morocco, April 2001. She remembered a boy, dark and exotic, and even less experienced than she was . . .

She pushed the memory aside. This was Emma's story, not hers. She kept scrolling. Turkey, Romania, Sierra Leone.

All her life she'd resented being dragged around the world like a suitcase. Yet she couldn't deny that these places had formed her. The noisy streets, the desperate people. They were real. They were part of her.

So were the summers, traveling with Zach, seeing the world from backstage. Growing up with the other band kids, playing hide-and-seek as youngsters, making out once puberty hit.

Sure, she'd been lonely a lot. But she'd always felt loved. Her parents might've been globetrotters, with big careers and bigger egos, but they never left her behind or shunted her off to boarding school.

They'd always wanted her. And not every kid could say the same.

The slider opened and Ray stuck her head out. "What-cha doing?"

"Daydreaming," Chris said. Which was all she ever

seemed to do when she opened her laptop. She closed it. "How was the audition?"

Ray came out and plopped in the other chair with a pout on her puss. "A waste of time. They picked a red-head, if you can believe it."

"She can dye her hair."

"She can't dye her pasty skin." Ray flicked at a fly. "Whatever. She was obviously blowing the producer."

Or maybe she was more talented. But that was Ray, always making excuses. Blaming someone else when she didn't make the cut.

She aimed a sour look at Tri. "I can't believe that jerk dumped a lame dog on you." She held out her hands. "Gimme. I'll take him to the pound."

"No, you won't." Chris tucked Tri under her arm. "This is his home, Ray. Deal with it."

"Or what? You'll kick me out?" Ray snorted a laugh.

Chris eyed her levelly.

"You're kidding." Ray shot to her feet. "This is what I get for listening to your sob story? You pick his crippled mutt over me?"

"I'm not picking Tri over you." *Yet.* "I'm just saying we all need to get along."

"Then keep the little shit out of my way." Ray curled her lip in a nasty sneer. "If I trip over him, I'm suing that dickhead Dakota Rain for everything he's got."

KOTA RACKED THE barbell, but he didn't sit up. Instead, he lay on the bench, lathered in sweat, staring at the ceiling.

Somewhere in the vast house, a grandfather clock chimed nine times. Which meant he had another twelve hours before he was due on the set.

Twelve hours of not going to see Christy. Twelve hours of not touching her. Or fucking her. Or sleeping beside her.

Tony poked his head through the door. "You expecting anyone tonight?"

"Nope," Kota said. He could have lined up Sissy or Danni or some other warm body, but he didn't have the heart for it. "Go to bed, man. I'll see you in the morning."

Now he was really alone. Sure, Tony was only over in the other wing. If Kota asked him to, he'd stay up all night, playing pool, watching movies. But why make both of them miserable?

Instead, Kota pumped out another set. Ran four miles on the treadmill. Did a hundred chin-ups, then a hundred more.

And the clock chimed ten.

Cy pestered him to go out, so they rambled the yard. Cy sniffed every blade of grass. Kota peed on a palm tree. Cy peed on top of it. And they wandered their way back to the house.

Inside, they roamed from room to room, ending up in the kitchen. Kota peered in the fridge. Closed it. Rolled his shoulders. Checked his watch.

Ten hours and forty-five minutes to kill.

Cy gave him a "*What next?*" look. The poor dog was at loose ends too.

Kota scratched his ears. "You miss Tri, don't you? I bet he misses us too."

In fact, Tri was probably pining for them right that minute. He probably wouldn't be able to sleep without seeing them, without getting his goodnight kiss.

Kota grabbed the keys. "Come on, man. Time to exercise our visitation."

"YOU'RE KIDDING ME." Christy blocked the door. "It's ten-thirty at night. We're on our way to bed."

That was obvious. Her hair was stacked in a messy bun, and her see-through nightgown hit her at midthigh and left nothing to the imagination.

Tearing his eyes from her nipples, Kota glanced over her shoulder. Tri was on the couch, wiggling around with all three legs in the air, like Kota had interrupted something good.

So much for pining.

He switched tactics. "Too bad," he said. "Cy's been pacing all night. He can't settle down till he sees his brother."

"Baloney."

"Truth. He's out in the car." He gestured. "You want to break his heart, go ahead."

"Oh, for the love of . . ." She shooed her hands at him. "Go get him. I want to see him, anyway."

A minute later, Cy bounded through the door, grinning his ghastly grin, dancing at Christy's feet, sticking his nose up her nightgown.

When she sat on the couch, he crawled into her lap, paws on her shoulders, kissing her like his long-lost love.

Tri wriggled between them, the pair of them pushing Christy's nightgown all the way to New Jersey.

"Okay, enough," Kota said when he couldn't take it anymore. "Down, guys."

He'd been propping up the wall so he wouldn't crawl into her lap too. Now she smiled over at him, and before he knew it he was sitting on the coffee table, his knee an inch from her bare one.

Her caramel eyes locked onto his. "Kota." Her voice, her smoky, sultry, sexy voice, shivered through him. "What're you doing here?"

"I told you." He worked to keep his own voice steady. "Cy missed his brother. And you too, I guess." Obviously, the dog was no judge of character.

"This is the third time you showed up here today."

He tried to look away. Couldn't. "Don't read anything into it. You got nothing I want. Except sex. Just sex."

She brushed his knee with her fingertips. "Do you want to have sex now?"

He swallowed. "Well, since I'm here."

"Okay." She stood up. "Ray's home, so we should do it in my room."

He followed her up the steps like a robot, lust wrestling with conscience. His body's message was clear and simple. *Sex. Now.*

But his mind asked, *Why? Why is she letting me use her this way?*

It made no sense. She wasn't slampiece material. She wasn't a starfucker.

Yet at the top of the stairs, she lifted her nightgown

over her head, leaving only a white thong pointing like a road sign to heaven. She shook down her hair so it tumbled over bare shoulders.

And she came to him, a slow, sinuous walk that gave him time to drink in every bombshell curve. Stopping inches away, she laid her hands on his chest.

His own hands hung helplessly at his sides.

"Kota."

God, he loved the way she said his name.

She smiled, and his knees turned to water.

He stepped back so her hands fell away. "Christ, woman. Don't you even want to talk first?"

Her brow creased. "I thought you just wanted sex."

"No. I mean, yeah." He rubbed the back of his neck. What was wrong with him? She was offering it on a platter. Her bed was six feet away. He should toss her down face-first and do her like that. Then he wouldn't make the mistake of kissing her again. Or looking into her eyes.

"God*damn* it," he squeezed through his teeth. "Why're you making this so hard?"

"I'm trying to make it easy," she said, stepping out of her panties.

"Christ." He could do this. He was hard as a spike. All he had to do was drop his pants—

A bloodcurdling scream split the air. He leaped out of his shoes.

Something crashed below, and he shot down the stairs, adrenaline-powered, testosterone-fueled, ready to take on the bad guys bare-handed.

Streaking through the living room, he slammed on

the brakes in the kitchen. A blonde was standing on the counter. "A hellhound! A hellhound!" she screeched at the top of her lungs.

He followed her pointing finger. Poor Cy cowered in the corner, tail tucked, ears down, embarrassed as hell.

"Shut up!" Kota shouted over the woman's wails. "He's a dog, for fuck's sake!" Adrenaline stripped away anything like patience or empathy. What kind of movies did this whacko watch, anyway?

He grabbed her by the waist and tried to set her feet on the floor, but she wasn't having it. She climbed him like a tree, shrieking in his ear.

"Ray!" Christy's voice cut through the din like a knife. "Calm down. He's not a hellhound. He's a pit bull."

Ray subsided to whimpers, but she didn't loosen her death grip.

Kota propped her butt on the counter. Christy helped him pry loose the limbs locked around him.

"Wh-what's he doing here?" Ray managed through chattering teeth.

"He's visiting," Christy said firmly. "So chill out, because he's here for the night."

Ray finally focused on Kota. "Don't you have any *normal* dogs? Are they all *freaks*?"

Christy stepped between them before he could blast her. "They're not freaks, Ray." Her voice had gone from firm to frigid. "They're perfectly wonderful, and the fact that they've had a tough time only makes them more special."

Yeah. Go Christy.

"Listen, Ray. I get that Cy startled you. But now that you know he's not a *hellhound,* you can relax. He's very gentle."

"Right." Sarcastic. "He's obviously never been in a fight."

"Those scars are from abuse, not from fighting." Christy walked to Cy, who was still plastered to the wall. She crouched down and hugged him, and Cy leaned into her, resting his head on her shoulder.

And that was all Kota could stand. He'd reached his limit.

"Come on," he said, "we're going home."

Christy gazed up at him with stricken eyes.

"All of us," he said. "All four of us are going home."

Chapter Twenty-Seven

"RISE AND SHINE, sleepyhead."

Chris had just enough time to open her eyes before the covers went flying.

Em stared down at her, goggle-eyed. "Holy shit! What're *you* doing here?"

Grabbing the sheet, Chris pulled it over her naked body as Kota stepped out of the bathroom. Shaving cream covered half his face. Otherwise, he was naked too. And not one bit embarrassed about it.

Em didn't seem one bit embarrassed either. Her head whipsawed back and forth between them. "What the hell? You *never* have sleepovers."

"Well, I had one last night." He stepped back into the bathroom.

Astonishingly, Em followed him in. She left the door open. In the mirror, Chris saw Kota calmly stroking a razor down his cheek.

Bare-assed.

"What the hell?" Em said again.

"There was a problem at her place," he said. "She might be here for a while."

Em raised her eyes to the ceiling. "You're a dumbass, you know that?"

"So you've told me many times."

"And yet it bears repeating." She met his eyes in the mirror. "I hope you know what you're doing."

"Do I ever?"

Em didn't deign to answer.

Instead, she pulled out her phone and scrolled, all business. "You're due at the studio at nine. Peter's coming by at twelve—and yes, he'll bring a three-by-three. Levi's okayed the one-year deal. He'll bring the papers. And he wants to talk about that Japanese thing, to coordinate with *Blood Money* opening in Tokyo . . ."

Kota tuned her out. Chris saw the actual moment when it happened, when he met Chris's eyes in the mirror . . . and smiled.

Her heart stuttered, then swelled, filling her chest. Butterflies danced in her stomach, and she smiled back, wholeheartedly, giddily.

Em pushed the door shut with her heel.

A few minutes later the shower turned on. Em came out of the bathroom, eyeing Chris like she was a hairy spider in the sheets.

Chris refused to cringe. Kota had invited her here knowing all there was to know. This time, she had nothing to be ashamed of.

"Good morning," she said.

"Is it?" Em wasn't giving an inch.

Chris considered asking if she always conducted business with Kota while he was naked, but really, the answer was obvious.

"He doesn't like sleeping with women," Em said.

Chris's brows winged up.

"I mean actually *sleeping* with them. Waking up with them. Apparently, you're different." Em didn't sound happy about it. "Which means you can hurt him. Again."

"I won't." Chris sat up, pinning the sheet to her chest. Somebody needed some modesty around here. "I deceived you too. I'm sorry about that."

"Sorry doesn't mean shit. If you hurt him again, if you do *anything* to take that smile off his face, I will hunt you down and I will bury your ass." Em aimed a finger at Chris. It should've been laughable. She was half Chris's size.

"Kota's the best person I know," Em said through taut lips. "He's too good for this world. He's too good for you. I will *bury* you."

And on that chilling note, she stalked out.

The shower shut off. Kota came out of the bathroom in a cloud of steam. "Is she gone?"

Chris nodded.

"She can be scary," he said, rubbing his chest with a towel. "But I don't think she'll really kill you."

"Gee. I feel better now." She got out of bed to hunt down her clothes. "Can you give me and Tri a lift home?"

"Sure. Or you could stay here." He smiled uncertainly. "I'll be back early."

She wasn't quite ready for that, and she didn't think he was either. "I'll take the ride. We left in kind of a hurry last night. I didn't bring much with me."

He nodded, then disappeared into the bathroom again. A few minutes later someone knocked on the bedroom door. Chris opened it and Em barged in, glancing at Chris's jeans and baggy T-shirt. "Good, you're dressed. Tony's waiting to take you home."

Kota stepped out of the bathroom. He was dressed in jeans and T-shirt too, but his fit like body armor. Chris's belly fizzed way down low, where it counted.

"I've got her," he said.

Em crossed her arms. "You don't have time."

Kota took her shoulders. "Chill. My eyes are wide open this time."

His words hit Chris like a fist in the stomach. He still didn't trust her.

Maybe he never would.

IN THE CAR, Christy was too quiet.

Kota took her hand, rubbing her knuckles with his thumb. "Pick you up later?"

She looked down at her lap. "For more sex?"

"I won't say no. But I was thinking about dinner. There's a little Italian place called Maria's up in Malibu. Off the beaten path." No paparazzi, and an owner who understood privacy.

Her head came up. "Sounds nice."

"Only if you like candlelight, and a piano bar, and shit like that."

Her lips softened into a smile. "Yeah, I like shit like that."

Warmth flooded his chest. She was so damn gorgeous. And when she smiled at him—

"Red light," she said.

He hit the brakes. "Quit distracting me."

She laughed. He gazed at her.

"Green light."

"Shit." He threw the Porsche into gear.

In her driveway, he slipped his hand under her hair. Her neck was warm in his palm. He stroked her jaw with his thumb, and she leaned into it like a cat.

Sitting there behind the wheel, his heart beating fast, his blood humming in his veins, anything seemed possible. Like he was seventeen again, with a pretty girl and a six-pack on a warm summer night.

Leaving her took all his willpower. "I'll be back by six, okay?"

Her lips quirked. "I think I can live that long without you."

Good for her, but he wasn't sure *he* could make it.

Dawdling his way to the studio, he daydreamed, picturing himself in the future, coming home to Christy . . .

In the first scene, they were at his place in Beverly Hills. He walked in after a long day on the set to find her stretched out by the pool in a string bikini . . .

Wait. He adjusted the picture, and she was topless.

Adjusted it again, and she was naked. *Yeah, naked.*

She stood gracefully and walked toward him, swaying to Sarah Vaughan . . .

Wait. She was singing Sarah Vaughan in her smoky, sexy voice. Singing just for him . . .

His mind sprang forward five years and the setting morphed to a log cabin, mountains rising in the background. He walked through the door tired and happy from a long day at his practice to find her lounging in front of the fire in a snow-white teddy . . .

Wait. A white thong . . .

A horn blasted him back to reality. The guy next to him at the light was grinning, curling his biceps in the universal sign for *mine's bigger than yours.*

As usual, it wasn't, and Kota was almost annoyed enough to prove it in front of the guy's girlfriend.

Instead, he gave a one-shouldered shrug, and when the jerk patched out in his pathetic Corvette, Kota wasn't even tempted to floor the Porsche and leave him in the dust.

Today, even the world's biggest asshole wouldn't be able to kill his buzz.

RAY SHUFFLED INTO the kitchen in her bathrobe, a snotty look on her hungover face.

Pouring a cup from the pot Chris had just made, she said over her shoulder, "I can't believe you're sleeping with that asshole."

"Sorry you don't approve." Chris could do sarcasm as well as the next guy.

But being at odds with Ray made life too difficult, so she took a deep breath and started over. "About last night. I thought you were asleep, or I would've given you a heads-up. I'm sorry Cy startled you."

Ray snorted. "He did more than startle me. He tried to take off my leg."

Another deep breath. "Cy's not vicious, Ray. He was probably trying to make friends. But I admit he can be scary to look at."

"I still think he's a hellhound."

Which explained the line of salt across the threshold.

Chris pressed her palms on the counter. There was no reasoning with Ray when it came to demons and hell-hounds, so she changed the subject instead.

"What's up for you today? Another casting call?" *Please say yes, please say yes.*

"A job interview." Disgusted. "My father set it up. He says he's done writing checks." Ray rolled her eyes, drama-queen style. "Can I borrow your car?"

"What happened to yours?"

"The cops booted it yesterday. Can you believe it? Just because I forgot to pay some stupid parking tickets."

She'd probably get another on Chris's car. Small price to pay to get her out of the house.

Chris set the keys on the counter. "Bring it back as soon as you can, okay? I need to run some errands before six."

"Why, what's happening at six? Mr. Movie Star coming back for another bang?"

Chris clung to her temper by her fingernails. "Actually, he's taking me to dinner."

"Someplace ritzy, I hope. It's the least he can do."

"A little place called Maria's in Malibu, as a matter of fact. Very romantic." She shouldn't get so defensive, but Ray pushed her buttons.

"Woo, big spender." Another eye roll, Ray's default expression. "Whatever. As long as he keeps that butt-ugly mutt out of here."

That was the last straw. "Cy's welcome in my house," Chris said through her teeth. "I think it's time you look for another place to live."

Ray gasped.

Brushing past her, Chris said over her shoulder, "Good luck with the interview. I hope you get the job."

Because come the end of the month, sister, you're out on your ass.

HIS HAIR WHIPPING as they rolled up Highway 1, Kota glanced over at Chris. "I can put the top up if the wind's too much."

She'd tucked her own hair into a scrunchie. "No, I love it." All of it. The wind that stripped the day's frustrations away. The man, framed by the ocean, backlit by the sinking sun.

And the car. She rubbed her palm over supple leather. Her Eos was a convertible too, but comparing it to the Porsche was like holding box wine up to Dom Pérignon.

He must've noticed her petting the seat. "This is the

one I'll keep," he said, "when I get out of the business."

Her jaw dropped. "You're going back to school?"

"People keep reminding me I'm not getting any younger."

She touched his arm. "Oh, Kota. This is great. I'm so happy." Giddy, in fact, as if the Dom was fizzing in her stomach.

He smiled like he was pleased to have pleased her. "Gotta finish this project first. Wrap up a few things. Prance around in some Levi's with my shirt off. Then it's bye-bye Hollywood."

"Wow." It was a major move for anyone. But for one of the world's biggest stars, it was unprecedented.

"I'm keeping a lid on it for now," he said. "I told Em and Tana, but nobody else knows yet." He squeezed her hand. "So keep it to yourself, okay?"

"I will." Warmth suffused her from head to toe. He'd entrusted her with a huge secret. It was a start. More than a start.

It was a new beginning.

Wanting to share something meaningful in return, she spoke out impulsively. And shocked herself when she said, "I'm not going to write my mother's bio."

His brows went up. "Why not?"

"My heart isn't in it." Hard to admit, even to herself. "Every time I open the file, I end up daydreaming."

"About?"

"Myself." Embarrassing, but true. "I had a weird childhood. Nine months a year living in war zones, three months living like a rock star."

"Most people never do either of those things. We grow up somewhere in the middle."

"While I lived at both ends of the spectrum, with no idea what the middle was like."

He nodded like that explained a lot. "You should write about it."

"Ha. Who'd read it?"

"I would."

She couldn't hug him while they were driving along a cliff edge, so she feigned shock instead. "You read?"

"I skip over the big words."

She patted his leg. "I'll help you with those." She'd help him with anything. "That reminds me. You mentioned a fund-raiser for the shelter. Did I miss it?"

"It's in December. I'm Santa Claus." His smile dazzled her. "You in?"

"I'm in." Oh boy, was she in. Over her head, and loving it.

"Something else," he said. "Adam and Maddie are tying the knot next month. I'm looking for a date."

"I'm in for that too." Her heart floated like a balloon. She'd never been happier. Never in her whole life.

The sun set in splendor as they drove, turning to twilight as they reached Malibu. Kota hooked a right onto a road with no name, swung a U-turn, and parked in front of a tiny restaurant disguised as a house.

When she reached for the door handle, he said, "Hang on. It's our first date. Let me open your door."

Folding her hands in her lap, she watched him walk around the hood, six feet four inches of gorgeousness

packaged in a white button-down and black Levi's that
revealed nothing but hinted at everything.

To the untrained eye, he looked formidable, built to
lead armies through impassable mountains over pitiless
terrain. To conquer entire civilizations, annihilate their
men and enslave their women.

But to her, he was the gentlest man she'd ever known.

Opening her door, he held out his hand. She took it,
her heart in her throat.

With one long, muscled arm, he caught her waist and
swept her close. She met his eyes, saw passion there, and
fun.

"Nice dress," he said.

She flipped the flirty skirt. "This old thing?"

"You'd make burlap look good."

Could her heart melt into a gooier mess?

He lowered his chin. She tipped her head back for his
kiss—

And a loud voice split the twilight. "Dakota! Hey,
Dakota! Is Chris your new girlfriend? Are you two serious?"

They both spun toward the voice. A flash fired, repeat-
edly.

Kota turned on her. "What the fuck?" His voice was a
steel blade. "You lying bitch."

"But I didn't—"

He stepped up onto the hood of the Porsche and over
the windshield, dropping down into the driver's seat.

"Wait! I—"

Gunning the engine, he squealed away.

As he took the corner onto Highway 1, her purse sailed out the back, bounced off the trunk, and exploded on the pavement. Like shrapnel, the contents sprayed from sidewalk to sidewalk. Tampons. TicTacs. A half-eaten Snickers. And her birth-control pills in their pink plastic case.

She stopped breathing. Her vision shrank to a pinprick and her skin went ice cold.

I will not faint. I will not faint.

She dragged a powerful breath through her nose. The world took shape again. Her hands unclenched.

And the reporter closed in, camera rolling. "Chris, tell us what's going on with you and Dakota. Is it serious? Why'd he take off and leave you here?"

"No comment." It came out weaker than she intended, but she left it at that.

He was undeterred. "Chris, our sources say—"

She tuned him out and took stock of the situation. Traffic zoomed along Highway 1 at thirty, a crawl for the drivers, but the Indy 500 to someone planning to step out in front of them.

A pickup zipped past, leaving tread marks on her wallet, the one item she couldn't abandon. Timing her move, she darted into the street, scooped it up, then froze on the yellow line as a Suburban skinned past with inches to spare.

She was making for the other sidewalk—paparazzi-free, but peopled with gawkers—when she spotted her iPhone farther down the lane. A Beemer sped toward it like it was worth extra points.

Damn it, her whole life was on that phone.

Recklessly, she sprinted for it. The Beemer hit the brakes, then hit the horn even harder, but she snatched up the phone unharmed and beat feet for the sidewalk.

Ducking into a chocolate shop, she ignored the clerk and the guy buying make-up truffles at the counter. Flattening her back to the wall, she pressed a palm to her chest to keep her heart from punching out through her ribs.

And she waited. Sweat rolled down her sides.

Minutes passed and no one followed her. The guy left with his chocolates. The clerk disappeared into the back. And gradually her adrenaline slowed to a trickle, then dried up completely.

Which wasn't a good thing.

Because in its wake came heartbreak too immense to process. Betrayal too deep to forgive.

And fury too extreme to control.

Chapter Twenty-Eight

"RAYLENE!" CHRIS STRODE into the kitchen and slammed the door behind her.

Tri plopped off the couch and hopped toward her. She scooped him up under her arm, out of the line of fire.

"Raylene, get your ass down here!"

"What's your problem?" Ray trudged down the steps, wineglass in hand.

"You called *TMZ*." Chris quivered with fury. She put the counter between them so she wouldn't tear Ray to pieces bare-handed. "You called fucking *TMZ* and told them we'd be at Maria's."

Ray faked offended. But she was a shitty actress, which was why she hadn't worked a day since she got to L.A. "Why're you blaming me? I didn't do anything."

"Liar."

"Look who's talking."

"Don't go there." Chris white-knuckled the counter. "I want you out of here. *Now*."

"It's midnight!"

"Don't I know it." Chris had counted every minute during the long cab ride, itching to get her hands around Ray's throat. "Find a hotel. Crawl home to Daddy. I don't care, but get out."

"You can't—"

"I can." Chris dropped her voice to a hiss. "Leave now, or I'll beat you unconscious and throw your body in the road to get creamed by the first passing car."

Ray backed up. Her wine sloshed. "I don't have a ride."

"I told the cabbie to wait."

RAY LEFT WITH one bag, vowing to return with her lawyers.

"Go ahead, sue me." Chris slammed the door. Ray didn't know how easy she'd gotten off. A traffic jam on the 101 had probably saved her life, because Chris's homicidal rage had an extra hour to flame out.

What remained was a slow-burning anger that glowed like banked coals. Less volatile, but enduring enough to roast a slow-turning pig on a spit.

A six-foot-four, two-hundred-pound pig.

As for Ray, good riddance. The woman was a selfish narcissist, and her escalating resentment and imminent poverty made her a menace. Tipping off *TMZ* was the least of what she'd do for money now that Daddy had cut her off.

Still, the house was damned quiet without her.

Until knuckles rapped on the door.

Only Kota would have the nerve to barge in at this hour, probably to rip her a new one.

Well, if he thought she'd stand still for it, he had another think coming. With blood in her eye, she yanked open the door, planning to send him back to hell with her boot in his ass.

But it wasn't Kota. "Chris, I'm—"

"I know who you are, and I said *no comment!*" She slammed the door for the third time that night.

Damn it, she should've known they'd show up. Panic tickled her throat. She rushed around the ground floor, checking all the locks, drawing every curtain.

Then she paced like a tiger in a cage. Just knowing they were outside shrunk her tiny house to a matchbox.

Tri eyed her as she strode and turned, strode and turned. Her imagination raced along with her pulse, picturing the story as it would run on TV, as it would even now be running on *TMZ*'s website.

They had plenty to work with. Not only had she been publicly abandoned by the world's biggest star, her purse tossed out of his car like garbage, but she'd added to the drama with a hair-raising dash into traffic, a near-death experience on the yellow line, and a heart-stopping standoff with a Beemer.

And yet, as horrible as it had been, and as embarrassing as it would be, she had to give Ray credit for one thing. Her despicable stunt exposed Kota's true feelings. He didn't trust her, or he would've let her explain. And he damn sure didn't love her, or he wouldn't have thrown her—and her purse—out onto the street like trash.

She deserved better. She might have started out on the wrong foot with Kota, but when push had come to shove, she'd done the right thing.

He couldn't say the same.

Backhanding the tears that streaked her cheeks, she raised her chin, squared her shoulders. And summoned the anger that had wilted under grief.

She'd cried her last tear for Dakota Rain.

She was better off without him.

KOTA STARED AT his computer, a fist-sized knot in his gut.

On screen, Christy teetered on the yellow line as a Suburban skinned past, blowing her skirt up to her waist. Then she darted in front of a Beemer that barely stopped short of flattening her.

He raked a hand through his hair. It never occurred to him that her purse would blow apart like a bomb.

And to be brutally honest, at that moment he wouldn't have cared. He'd told no one else where they'd be, so he'd assumed Christy was to blame. His heart had broken on the spot, his ego had taken it in the teeth, and he'd reacted instinctively.

But driving home, doubt had crept in. Why would she tip off *TMZ*? It made no sense at all.

He'd almost turned around to go back, to let her explain. But she'd burned him before. He didn't trust himself to know her lies from the truth.

Now one look at the news clip told him all he needed to know. No actress could fake the blank astonishment on Christy's face as he'd shoved away from her and left her in the dust.

Guilt burned a hole in his chest. He rubbed it with the flat of his hand as he replayed the clip, suffering through the voice-over, agonizing over Christy's confusion, shamed by her courage in the face of his reckless stupidity.

Then he shut it off and stood up.

He was an asshole, and she'd probably never forgive him. But that wouldn't stop him from begging her for one more chance.

Traffic was light at two in the morning. It made for a quick ride to Christy's house. And it made it easy to spot the van tucked into the hedgerow across from her driveway.

The parasites were already staking her out.

Banging on her door wouldn't help the situation. The fast talking required to convince her to open it wasn't something he wanted broadcast to millions of viewers, especially since it would drag her further into the limelight.

So he kept driving, circling back to his house, where he paced the library, scraping his hands through his hair until his scalp stung, rewatching the video until it was burned into his brain.

Em found him there at six. "What the hell? Have you been up all night?"

"Did you see it?" He charged at her.

She leaped back. "See what?"

"The thing. The video." He sounded deranged even to himself. Over-caffeinated and strung out like a wire.

He made himself take a deep breath. "I went on a date with Christy, and it went sideways. Some idiot from *TMZ* showed up, and I assumed she called him—"

"Why would you assume that?"

"Because I'm an asshole," he said, as if it needed explaining. "Her batshit roommate must've called them, but I didn't think it through. I jumped the gun like I always do. And I left Christy on the sidewalk and drove away."

Em nodded. "Okay, that's bad. But it's not stay-up-all-night bad. Just apologize, and she'll get over it."

"I don't think so." He dragged her to his desk and pushed her down in the chair. Then he hit Play.

"Oh," she said. Then, "Oh shit, not her purse." She sat back. "You *are* an asshole."

"You gotta help me, Em. Her phone's turned off. Or maybe it's broken." It had hit the street like everything else. "You gotta go to her house."

"*You* go to her house. You're the asshole."

"I tried, but they're staking her out."

"Wait a while. By the time you're done at the studio, they'll have moved on."

He shook his head. "I'm not going to the studio till I know she's okay."

"You're going." She stood up. "It's hair and wardrobe today."

"I don't care." He leaned his palms on the desk. "This is bad, Em. What if she . . . does something?"

Sympathy swam into Em's eyes. "Kota, this is nothing like Charlie. Christy isn't going to hurt herself over some stupid video on *TMZ*."

"Are you sure? A hundred percent sure?"

"Ninety-nine point nine. But I'll go, okay? If you promise to shower and get to the studio by seven, I'll go."

"Done." He straightened. "Call me the minute you lay eyes on her."

A SHARP RAP on the door startled Chris out of a doze on the couch and set off Tri's big-dog bark.

"Shut up, Tri, it's me," Em yelled.

He hopped off the couch and made for the door. Chris followed, none too happy.

Pulling it open six inches, she started to tell Em to take a hike, but the pushy bitch bulldozed in, saying into her phone, "I'm eyeballing her right now. She's fine. Get to work." Then she hung up and shoved the phone in her pocket.

Chris raised her brows to her hairline.

"Kota's been up all night," said Em. "Agonizing. Watching that stupid video a thousand times."

"What video?"

Em snorted a laugh. "He was afraid you offed yourself over it, but you haven't even seen it."

"Offed myself? It's that bad?"

"You can imagine."

Could she ever. "Thanks for the warning. I'll skip it. Bye, now."

"Since I'm here."

Chris held up a hand. "Spare me, please. I haven't had coffee yet."

"Me either."

"For Pete's sake." Chris stumped over to the pot and got busy. "If he was so worried," she said over her shoulder, "why didn't he come himself?"

"He did, but the paparazzi scared him away."

"So they're good for something."

"He's torturing himself."

"He shouldn't have jumped to conclusions. If he'd waited five seconds, I would've told him it must've been Ray."

Chris rested her forehead on the cabinet, tired and sad. But no longer mad. Anger had drained out overnight, leaving her empty.

Her heart, so full the day before, was hollow as a drum.

"Tell him I get it now," she said. "I get why he can't forgive me. Once someone proves they can't be trusted with your heart . . ." She shook her head, forlorn. "It's too late for Kota and me. We both screwed up, and it's too late."

"It's not too late," Em said. "What it is, is October. Kota always goes off the rails in October. Just wait till next week to make any big decisions, okay?"

Chris smiled, sadly. "You're very loyal, Em. He's lucky

to have you. But Kota and me . . . we're not the other half of each other's happy couple."

KOTA SCRATCHED HIS head. "She said what?"

"That you're not the other half of each other's happy couple." Em plopped in his desk chair. "I'm just the messenger. If you don't get it, ask her yourself."

He threw up his hands. "I'm gonna have to, because you screwed everything up."

She pointed a finger at him. "You're getting a pass on that because you've been awake for two days."

That was true. And ten hours in costume and makeup had only made him crankier.

He dragged a hand down his face. The knot in his stomach tied itself tighter. "I called, texted, e-mailed. She won't answer. What am I gonna do?"

"Go to her house. Fuck *TMZ*."

He laughed miserably. "If only it was just *TMZ*. You're out of the loop." He reached over and woke up his computer. "The whole story's out. The wedding, the island, every-fucking-thing."

Em clicked through half a dozen websites, making a face. "You've gotta admit this story has it all."

Did it ever. A wrongly accused senator, an undercover reporter, a celebrity wedding, a private island, and a steamy affair involving a mega–movie star. Not to mention a messy breakup on the tarmac, a rapprochement, and, best of all, a public shaming.

But wait, there was more, because the woman at the

center of the tale was the illegitimate daughter of a world-renowned journalist and a legendary entertainer.

Politics, sex, celebrity, depravity. There was something for everybody. The angles were infinite.

An alien spaceship landing in Times Square wouldn't have the legs of this story.

"The irony is," Em said, "if you hadn't locked down Tana's wedding, the *Sentinel* wouldn't have snuck Christy inside in the first place, and this whole shit storm would never have hit."

True enough. But the other side of the coin was that he'd never have met her. And nothing—certainly none of this bullshit—would ever make him regret that. Christy was the best thing to happen to him since Roy and Verna gave two troublemaking wiseasses a home.

He loved her, and if she slipped through his fingers, he'd regret it for the rest of his life.

There was only one thing to do.

"Call Tony," he said. "Tell him to bring the Rover around."

"Whoa, wait. She'll be surrounded by now. You won't be able to drive down her street."

"Then I'll walk."

"They'll mob you."

"No, they won't." He smiled grimly. "I've got a secret weapon."

KOTA PULLED OVER half a mile from Christy's house, blocking a driveway. The Range Rover would probably get towed, but there was nowhere else to park. The media assholes had consumed every available inch.

As he stepped out, a TV van cruised past. The driver spotted him and hit the brakes, then a reporter leaped from the back, mic at the ready.

Kota gave him a come-on-over wave. Then he opened the back door and Cy hopped out, tail wagging, ready to buddy up to the guy.

Kota said, "Smile," and Cy smiled. "Bark," and Cy barked.

The reporter flung himself back into the van. The van patched out.

Kota scratched Cy's ears. "Good job, buddy. I think the dude wet his pants."

And he set out for Christy's, his bodyguard trotting happily beside him.

Chapter Twenty-Nine

WITH THE SOUND-DEADENING headphones blocking out the commotion in the street, Chris felt strangely peaceful. Like she was underwater, or suspended in another dimension where no one could reach her and no problems could touch her.

Secluded in the bubble, it was easier not to think about Kota, about the plans she'd begun to make. Not big plans, not forever plans. But plans nonetheless.

And it was easier not to fume at Ray. She'd obviously spilled her guts for money and revenge. The resulting media blitz had plugged up Chris's narrow road so completely that the cops had given up trying to disperse the crowd and begun diverting traffic.

But safe in the bubble, she could remind herself that it was only temporary. Kota wouldn't feed the media frenzy. Neither would she. With a freezer full of frozen pizza, she wouldn't have to open her door for a month.

By then, the press would have moved on to the next big scandal.

And she'd move on too, out of Cali-fucking-fornia. Maybe to Maine. Yes, Maine should be far enough away.

She'd find a nice place for Emma out in the countryside and buy a dilapidated farmhouse nearby. Once she restored it, she'd fill it with animals no one else wanted. The rejects. The halt and the lame.

And she'd live in peace and tranquility, with no chance of bumping into Kota at a traffic light.

Until then, she was stuck. She needed something to do besides nurse her broken heart. Something absorbing. Something meaningful.

Opening her laptop, she faced the document already up on her screen: *Reporting Live from the War Zone, This Is Emma Case.*

She deleted it.

Then she flinched, waiting for guilt to crush her like an anvil. Her finger hovered over Undo.

But seconds passed, and . . . no guilt. In fact, she felt lighter. As if a weight she'd borne for years had floated off her shoulders.

She closed her eyes, releasing the breath she'd held pinched in her lungs.

Someone else would write Emma's story, someone more objective. Maybe Reed. He'd loved her—he still did—but he was a journalist to the marrow. He'd be evenhanded, analytical, while Chris could be neither where her mother was concerned.

She drew a deep, steady breath and opened her eyes.

The screen before her was blank. Hers to fill with whatever moved her.

For a long, pregnant moment, she stared at the blinking cursor.

Then she began to type.

CHRISTY'S STREET WAS a scene from Kota's own personal nightmare. News crews, spotlights, TV trucks with satellite dishes poking up like periscopes.

He paused in the shadow of a palm tree, taking in the chaos, and his blood ran cold. Charlie had lived just a few streets away, and Kota had seen his house surrounded just like this.

The memory turned his stomach.

Charlie was dead by then, beyond Kota's help, but the press was stalking his aunt, who'd come from Vermont to pack up his things. She'd forgiven Charlie years before, the only family member who had, and for her kindness and grace, she'd been hounded by the press.

He'd seen the stark fear on her face that day, and fury had lit a fire in his breast that still burned bright.

He'd shouldered through the idiots and hustled her out of the house, driven her to the airport, and watched her leave L.A. in tears. Then he'd cleaned out Charlie's house himself, a lonely, heartrending task. Penance for his own arrogance, and for the foolish pride that had set off the fatal chain of events.

Sure, he'd taken a stand against haters who wanted to

divide the world into straights and gays, but he should have considered that others might pay the price for his actions.

Now Christy was paying for his latest blunder. Pinned down, probably scared shitless, she needed rescuing too.

So Kota did the one thing he never imagined he'd willingly do.

He stepped into the center ring of a full-blown media circus.

Sweat beaded his hairline and prickled his armpits. But his muscles responded to stress as they always did, going loose and limber, primed to react as required, to lift or carry or punch anybody who asked for it.

He'd rather not hit anyone tonight. It would only fuel the flame. But if that's what it took to get to Christy, somebody was going down.

He arrowed straight for her house, and at first, no one noticed him. He was just another body in motion.

Then someone shouted, "Dakota!" Others took up the call. Every head swung his way, and the whole horde surged toward him.

This was no red-carpet event, where the media was leashed and fenced. It was a bloodthirsty battle for ratings and revenue, a full-on feeding frenzy.

They were the sharks; he was the meat.

But he wasn't in it alone. As they closed in, waving their mics in his face, he said, "Smile," and Cy smiled. "Bark," and Cy barked.

Miraculously, a path opened before them, and Kota marched to the door unimpeded.

CHRIS FELT, MORE than heard, the fist pounding her door. It rattled the china like a minor earthquake, 3.1 on the Richter scale.

Tri blasted off the couch like he was shot from a cannon, barking insanely, scratching at the door. Chris pulled off her headphones.

It couldn't be.

"Christy, open up!"

It was.

She tiptoed to the kitchen window, as if Kota could hear her sock feet over the pandemonium outside. She peeped through the curtain. Reporters formed a semicircle ten feet from her front door, shouting questions at Kota where he stood with Cy on the stoop.

One daring soul stepped forward. Kota said, "Bark," and Cy barked. Chris smothered a laugh as the woman leaped back into line.

Then *bam bam bam*. "Christy, open the door!"

She opened it, but before he could steamroll her, she stepped outside and closed it behind her.

"Hello, Kota." It felt like she was pushing her voice over gravel. Like she hadn't spoken in a week.

He locked onto her eyes, dropped his voice ten decibels, from a roar to a murmur. "Let's take this inside."

Sweat dampened her neck under the mass of her hair, but she crossed her arms and said coolly, "I'm good right here." If he had something to say, let him say it in front of the cameras. That would keep it short and sweet.

He glowered down at her, all squints and hard angles. Lesser mortals would pee themselves.

But Chris was unmoved. "Did you want something, Kota? Or were you just out walking Cy?"

"We need to talk," he muttered for her ears alone.

"I have nothing to say to you," she said loud and clear. "But if you're compelled to unburden yourself, I'm all ears." She propped her shoulders against the door as if she had all night.

His jaw ticked. Flattening one palm beside her head, he dropped his voice even lower. "I'm sorry—"

"You're sorry?" she repeated loudly. "For what?"

His eyes seared her. "You're gonna make me do this out here?"

"You mean *out here in front of the cameras*? So *TMZ* can run the clip backwards and forwards, with their pithy asides?" She cocked her head. "Yeah, that's what I mean."

Color climbed his neck, then his face, all the way to his hairline.

That was a good start, but it was far from enough.

"I thought . . ." He paused and threw a glance over his shoulder at the mob. As one, they leaned forward, hanging on every word. He turned back to her, visibly girding his loins. "You know what I thought. I was wrong. And stupid, and cruel."

She waited, not nearly satisfied.

"I'm sorry I left you. And I'm sorry about your purse. I didn't know it would . . ." He did an exploding fist.

She waited.

He pushed his fingers through his hair. The torment on his face plucked at her heartstrings.

She ignored their sad song.

"Ma tore me a new one," he went on. "Even Pops got into it. Sasha too. And Maddie." He winced. "She's got a tongue like a buzz saw."

Chris smirked, recalling their conversation on the plane. "Still think you can have her whenever you want?"

He went redder, probably picturing Adam's reaction when he heard that on TV. "The point is," he said quickly, "I know I was an asshole, and I'm sorry. I'll never do it again."

She waited.

"Forgive me?" He tried to sell it with a charming smile.

She wasn't buying. "Forgive you for ditching me? Or for doubting me?"

"For ditching you. I'm not apologizing for doubting you. It's not like I don't have reason."

Her heart sank. "Then I guess we're done here." She put her hand on the knob.

He covered it with his. "Not so fast." His eyes glinted. "You wanted to do this out here. Let's do it. Let's talk about trust. Let's talk about lies."

She faced him. "I paid the price. I apologized. You forgave me."

"No, I fucked you."

She gasped. Heat swept her skin like a blowtorch. She tried to flee inside, but he held the knob fast.

"I fucked you because I couldn't help myself." He crowded her, invading her space. "I couldn't help myself because I love you."

She gasped again.

"Is that what you want?" he said. "A public declaration? You've got it. I love you." He said it loud and clear.

Words failed her.

But he was suddenly loquacious. "I love you, but I'm having a hard time trusting you. Part of that's on me. I've got trust issues, and I'm working on them."

He jerked a thumb over his shoulder. "This is on me too. Which is why I'm standing here making a fool of myself. But baby, you gotta meet me in the middle."

The middle? Where was the middle? The line kept moving.

He waited.

She gazed up at him, helplessly. "What do you want me to say?"

He smiled again, gorgeously. "Say you love me."

"I love you."

He turned, spreading his arms to the cameras. "Did you get that?" he called. "I love her. She loves me. We're getting married."

Chapter Thirty

"THAT GOT 'EM moving," Christy said. "But talk about a whopper."

Kota watched the reporters scramble to their trucks to break the story. Then he turned to Christy. Her cheeks were pink. A half smile curved her luscious lips.

"It wasn't a whopper," he said. "I was serious." He might've been shooting from the hip when he threw it out to the reporters, but it felt absolutely right.

Her brows went up. "I don't remember a proposal."

"Okay. Let's get married."

"No."

His face fell. "Why not?"

Her expression said he was nuts. "We've known each other for three weeks. For most of that time, you hated me. And for the last twenty-four hours, I hated you." She shoved his chest. "Go home, Kota. We'll call it a draw and get on with our lives."

"No." He wouldn't let her push him away. Something important was happening here. They had to see it through.

But not in front of the press.

Reaching around her, he opened the door and hustled her inside. Thankfully, the kitchen lights were down low. It would be easier to say what he needed to say if Christy couldn't read the shame in his eyes.

"Listen," he said before she could lay into him for barging into her house, "I've never been in a relationship before. I thought it wasn't in the cards for me."

That startled her. "Why not?"

He spread his arms. "Look at me. I'm a brick shithouse. I can lift and carry and fuck all night. I'm built for physical stuff. But I'm not built for love."

"That," she declared, "is the dumbest thing you've ever said. You're the most loving person I know. The way you love your parents, your brother, Em. It's staggering. And the animals, my God, the animals." She poked his arm with one finger. "Your heart's bigger than your biceps. And that's saying something."

He shook his head. "That's not what I mean. I can dole it out. Hell, I can't help myself there. But I do stupid shit, and people get hurt. Look what I did to Charlie."

She waved that away.

"There's more," he said. "Something I haven't told you." Something he hadn't told anybody. "It's about my parents. My birth parents." He took a deep breath, made himself say it. "I told my mother where the money was."

The truth burned his throat like a flame. He'd

never said it out loud, his darkest secret, his deepest shame. "She was tearing her hair out, scratching the skin off her arms. So I told her where Dad hid it. Because I loved her, and she was suffering, and I hated seeing her like that."

He swallowed, his mouth dry as ashes. "I made a snap decision without thinking it through. And she ended up gone, and my Dad ended up dead."

"Oh, Kota." Christy touched his cheek with her fingertips. "You were a little kid. You saw your mother in pain. You wanted to stop it." Her fingers were cool on his fevered skin. "Think about it. What if Tana had been the one to tell her? Would you blame him? Would you want him to blame himself?"

"Of course not. But it wasn't Tana. It was me." How could she not understand?

"And Charlie," he said, the words sticking in his throat. "You can blow it off, but that was my fault too. I wasn't a kid. I was twenty-five, old enough to know better. But I thought I was smarter than everybody else. And he died because of my stupid ego."

For a long moment, Christy looked into his eyes.

Then she took a step back, cocked her head to the side. "You know, you're right," she said. "You should've seen that coming. You should've known that if you refused to deny you were gay, Charlie would end up dead in his swimming pool."

She shrugged like it was a no-brainer. "It was inevitable. Because everything's all about *you*. It's Kota's world, and we're all just living in it. The reporters had no free will. Neither did Charlie. They were just action figures, while you"—she jabbed his chest—"make the whole fucking world go round."

He held up his hands. "I hear what you're saying, but look what I did to you. I went off half cocked, and you almost got nailed by a Suburban. You could be dead right now."

It stole his breath. His palms went clammy.

She laid a hand on his chest. "You were an ass, Kota. But you didn't push me out in front of that Suburban. If I got nailed, it would've been my own fault. I could've asked a cop to stop traffic while I picked up my things. But being just as pigheaded as you, I blundered out into the street without engaging my brain."

She shook her head. "You're a good man, Kota. You just need to accept that you can't control everyone else. Just like you can't control the weather, or the stock market, or a virus that could turn us all into zombies. Because life isn't a movie. You can't squint us into submission, or shoot everybody who crosses you, or have sex with every woman you meet."

She paused. "Well, maybe that last one."

He laughed. So did she, and it felt good, so good, to laugh together again.

Gazing into her warm caramel eyes, he could believe that anything was possible. That he could love her without killing her. That they had a chance at happiness.

His chest swelled, and he pressed her hand to it, flattening her palm so she'd feel his heart beating.

"Christy Gray, I've been waiting all my life for you."

CHRIS'S HEART FLUTTERED. Her knees went weak.

But she stiffened her spine and took another step back, reclaiming her hand, leaning her hip on the counter. "There's more to a relationship," she said, "than declaring our love and riding off into the sunset on Sugar. We're fundamentally different people."

He spread his palms. "Sweetheart, that's a good thing. Why would I want to hook up with another asshole like me?"

"Good point. But assuming for the sake of argument that I'd jump at the chance, you'd have to dial down your control freak."

"Sure, no problem." He did his most disarming smile.

She gave him a pitying look. "Listen, I get it. You had a crappy childhood where nothing was in your control. So it's only natural that as an adult you'd react by trying to control everything."

"You sound like Em."

"You're not that complicated. The problem is, you like order and predictability, and I'm chaos. In the last three weeks, I snuck into a celebrity wedding, fell in love on a desert island, got kicked off the island by the men in black and ditched on the sidewalk by the man I love.

"If that wasn't enough, I quit my job, got sued by a senator, shit on by my roommate, chased by *TMZ*, lampooned on late-night TV, and now my house is surrounded by paparazzi."

He shrugged. "So things are a little crazy right now. They'll settle down."

"Maybe someday. But my life's up in the air. I'm working on sorting it out, but it's a process."

"I can help." He glanced at her laptop, open on the coffee table. "What're you writing?"

"A screenplay." Her face flushed hot. It was so clichéd. Everyone in L.A. was writing a screenplay.

She brazened it out. "It's about a girl I met in a refugee camp. How I imagine—well, how I *hope*—her life turned out."

"Sounds original. You'll probably want to go indie with that. I know some people—"

She growled low in her throat.

He shrugged. "Fine, do it the hard way. But if you change your mind—"

"Kota, you have to let people sink or swim on their own. You're not responsible for what the rest of us do." She threw up her hands. "Shit happens. I could get into a car accident on the way to see you. Or get food poisoning when we eat out somewhere."

He paled. "How about you move in with me? Then you won't have to go anywhere. And I'll cook for you every night. No restaurants."

She let out a laugh, because he was funny, and more than half serious.

He closed the distance between them, brought one hand up to cup her face. His thumb stroked her cheekbone, the lightest caress. "I know what you're saying, sweetheart. Everything doesn't revolve around me. And I'm learning. I'm letting Tana fend for himself while I go off to school. That's progress, isn't it?"

"It's a start." She rested her hands on his waist. His heat soaked through his shirt, warming her skin. Warming her heart.

He lifted her chin and kissed her, a light brush of his lips. Then he wrapped his arms around her, gently, like she might take flight if he moved too suddenly.

"You snuck into more than a wedding, darlin'. You snuck into my heart."

THERE WAS ONLY one way to carry Christy up the corkscrew staircase—over his shoulder.

"You know I'm not crazy about this form of transport, don't you?" Her voice vibrated with every step.

"All the more reason to move in with me. My bedroom's on the first floor."

"It's too soon."

He opened his mouth to override her objections, to point out the many advantages of his estate, number one being that it was paparazzi-proof . . .

Then he clammed up without a word. She was right; he was a controlling son of a bitch. Sure, he only wanted the best for everyone, but if he'd learned one thing this October, it was that people had their own ideas about how to live their lives.

Which meant he had to let Christy decide for herself when to move in with him. Not that he wouldn't do everything he could think of to tempt her. But he could be reasonable.

Hell, he'd even let her set their wedding date.

She pinched his butt. "Put me down."

He stood her on her feet beside the bed. Eyed her in the moonlight streaking through the windows.

"Nice dress," he said. "Take it off."

She lifted it over her head.

"Nice shirt." She tapped his chest with one finger. "Take it off."

He ditched it.

"Nice bra." He flicked it open. Her tits spilled into his hands.

He thumbed the nipples, smiled at her sharp sip of air. "I thought they didn't do much for you."

"That was before they met you." She covered his hands with hers, feeling herself up with his palms.

Hot. Very hot.

His Levi's shrank two sizes too small.

She dropped her hands to her panties, shimmied them off, and pushed them into his pocket. "A souvenir." Her voice had gone husky. "Meanwhile, your pants." She unbuttoned the button, tugged on the zipper.

He did the rest, then pulled her down on the bed, caging her under him, gazing into her face. There were stars in her eyes, or reflected in her eyes. Either way, she sparkled.

"I love you," she said, and he breathed it in. It swirled through his chest like sweet smoke, making him high.

He breathed it back to her, "I love you," and she drew it in, closing her eyes, smiling softly.

His arms circled her head where it lay on the pillow. She seemed small beneath him, but the furthest thing from weak. With one fingertip, she could move his two hundred pounds of muscle and bone. He'd be helpless to resist her.

Talk about control.

He slid a knee between hers, spreading her legs. And she put that fingertip to work, pushing him off, rolling him onto his back. Then she climbed aboard, taking him inside, all the way in, palms on his chest, skin gleaming in the starlight.

It was her ride, her rodeo, and she set the pace, slow and easy, while his fists bunched the sheets.

She smiled, locking onto his eyes. "You're dying to flip me, aren't you?"

He nodded. Sweat beaded his chest.

"You want to hold me down and hammer like Thor."

Sweat slid off his temple.

She rolled her hips, testing his mettle. Her head fell back, the column of her throat pale in the moonlight. He must be part vampire, because he thirsted to bite it.

Then—*thank you God*—she picked up the pace. Faster, and faster till sweat glistened between her breasts.

He abandoned the sheets and gripped her hips, urging her on, driving her higher. Everything in him screamed to roll her, pin her down, take her harder, claim her fully.

But he held the line, even as she strained, as she moaned.

Then her head dropped forward, a cascade of mink sweeping his chest, sticking to her skin. His hands slid up her sides to palm her breasts, slippery and full.

"Babe," he ground out through his teeth. "I'm dying here." Drawn up tight and ready to explode.

"Then come." She shook back her hair. Her neck stood out in cords. "Come with me."

And she ignited, pure fire, sucking him into the blaze until they burned as one, searing through all that divided them, clear through their skin to sheer flame.

Chapter Thirty-One

CHRIS SLID HER palm along the glossy rail of Adam LeCroix's seventy-five-foot cruising yacht. "How come you don't have one of these?"

"You want one?" Kota propped his elbows on the rail and smiled gorgeously. "Consider it your wedding present."

"Speaking of"—air quotes—"our wedding. You all but told everyone the invitations are in the mail."

He shrugged. "Love was in the air."

She had to agree. Adam and Maddie's sunset wedding was unforgettable; an intimate ceremony with a handful of guests, a candlelight dinner on deck, and dancing under twinkle lights to a talented trio.

Now Chris was alone with Kota under the stars. The trio had departed for shore and the other guests had retired, except for Adam and Maddie, still waltzing to their own tune at the far end of the deck. The yacht rocked gently on the placid sea. The lights of Portofino twinkled in the distance, reflected in Kota's eyes.

It couldn't have been more romantic.

But still. "I haven't said I'd marry you."

"Sweetheart, we both know it's just a matter of time."

He was right, of course. For a month he'd been wearing her down. Not pressuring her—he'd shown surprising restraint. But wooing her with conversation, good food, and mind-blowing sex.

In her head, she'd already set the date. But it wouldn't do to give in too easily.

"You're a cocky bastard," she said. "Lucky for you, pasta puts me in a forgiving mood."

"Pasta does lots of good things to you." He gave her ass a squeeze.

She swung it out of reach. "They're not melons, you know."

"Believe me, fruit's the farthest thing from my mind." He pulled her into his arms, rubbed his nose in her hair. "Mmm, roses. I used to be partial to peaches, but you made a rose man out of me."

A breeze riffled across the water, making her shiver. He opened his jacket and wrapped it around her. She snuggled in, his heat warming her through his shirt.

Maddie appeared beside them, her satin gown shimmering. "Hey, you two. We're hitting the sack. Christy, I want to thank you again. It was beautiful."

Chris smiled. "It's a privilege to sing at a wedding. Especially for friends."

Adam came up behind Maddie, set his hands on her

shoulders. His black tux was immaculate . . . except for the red lipstick on his white collar.

"It was magical," he said to Chris. "We'll never forget it." To Kota, "If you can get away from the set again, we'll be cruising for three weeks. Fly into any airport in Greece, and we'll get you both out to the ship."

"I'll see what I can do," Kota said. "By the way, nice vows."

Adam laughed. "I couldn't have been more surprised when Maddie proposed we write our own. She's not known for sentiment."

Maddie sniffed. "It's not sentiment. The lawyer in me wanted the terms on the table."

He kissed the top of her head. "Consider me forewarned that love, honor, and cherish will go out the window in a zombie apocalypse."

Leaving Chris and Kota at the rail, they went off to do what newlyweds do.

Kota nuzzled her again. "It was nice of you to sing for them."

"Like I said, it was a privilege. I felt the same about Tana's wedding, even with all the baggage." She tipped her head up and propped her chin on his chest. "I probably shouldn't tell you this, but once I met you backstage, I wasn't singing for anybody else. I was singing for you."

For a long moment he gazed down at her from eyes midnight blue.

Then, "I knew it," he blurted, busting out in a grin. "I *knew* you were singing for me. I looked around at all those other suckers who were thinking the same thing, but I *knew* it."

She rolled her eyes. "I was right, I shouldn't have told you."

He let out a big laugh and lifted her feet off the deck in a hug.

She jabbed his ribs. "Put me down. I'm going to bed."

"Damn right you are." He swung her into his arms and headed for their stateroom. "If we're lucky, we'll hear the newlyweds goin' at it next door. I know how that turns you on."

Her face caught fire. "I can't believe you brought that up."

He stepped inside and kicked the door closed behind him. Then he tossed her on the king-sized bed. "I might be persuaded," he said, untying his bow tie, "not to bring it up for the rest of the night."

She leaned back against the pillows, mouth watering as he peeled off his shirt. He'd trained hard for the Western, and his chest was even bigger, his abs more defined.

She licked her lips. "Exactly what would I have to do to persuade you?"

Unbuckling his belt, he said, "All you have to do is ask, darlin'. Just ask."

That was too easy. "Okay," she said. "Please."

He pulled his belt through the loops. "Please . . . what?"

Ah. So he wanted to go there again, did he?

Well, she'd play along, to a point. And revenge would be sweet.

Playing the submissive, she crawled toward him,

slowly, until she reached the foot of the bed. Then she sat back on her heels.

Reaching both arms behind her, she unzipped her dress an inch at a time, until the filmy black silk slid off her shoulders to puddle around her hips.

And she waited.

He tried to hold her eyes, but his gaze kept dropping to her breasts, squeezed together and served up in a black satin, barely-there bra.

Hooking her pinky under one strap, she drew the ribbon of lace ever so slowly over the curve of her shoulder.

His belt slipped through his fingers to the floor.

Reaching into her bra, she drew forth one breast and cupped it in her palm. He wet his lips.

A standoff.

Then, "Hell," he muttered. "You win." And he tackled her, peeling off her bra, shedding his trousers.

Laughing, giddy, she let him have his way with her, and she had her way right back.

When they'd worn each other out, he spooned her, his big body warmer than the warmest quilt. "I gotta hand it to you, darlin'." His murmur was sleepy and sated. "You don't fight fair."

Snuggling her rump to his groin, she covered his hand where it cupped her breast. And she smiled, smugly.

"It's the power of the tit."

Give in to your impulses . . .
Read on for a sneak peek at seven brand-new
e-book original tales of romance
from HarperCollins.
Available now wherever e-books are sold.

VARIOUS STATES OF UNDRESS: GEORGIA

By Laura Simcox

MAKE IT LAST

A BOWLER UNIVERSITY NOVEL

By Megan Erickson

HERO BY NIGHT

BOOK THREE: INDEPENDENCE FALLS

By Sara Jane Stone

MAYHEM

By Jamie Shaw

An Excerpt from

VARIOUS STATES OF UNDRESS: GEORGIA

by Laura Simcox

Laura Simcox concludes her fun, flirty
Various States of Undress series with a
presidential daughter, a hot baseball player,
and a tale of love at the ballgame.

"Uh. Hi."

Georgia splayed her hand over the front of her wet blouse and stared. The impossibly tanned guy standing just inside the doorway—wearing a tight T-shirt, jeans, and a smile—was as still as a statue. A statue with fathomless, unblinking chocolate brown eyes. She let her gaze drop from his face to his broad chest. "Oh. Hello. I was expecting someone else."

He didn't comment, but when she lifted her gaze again, past his wide shoulders and carved chin, she watched his smile turn into a grin, revealing way-too-sexy brackets at the corners of his mouth. He walked down the steps and onto the platform where she stood. He had to be at least 6'3", and testosterone poured off him like heat waves on the field below. She shouldn't stare at him, right? Damn. Her gaze flicked from him to the glass wall but moved right back again.

"Scared of heights?" he asked. His voice was a slow, deep Southern drawl. Sexy deep. "Maybe you oughta sit down."

"No, thanks. I was just . . . looking for something."

Looking for something? Like what—a tryst with a stranger in the press box? Her face heated, and she clutched the water bottle, the plastic making a snapping sound under her fingers. "So . . . how did you get past my agents?"

He smiled again. "They know who I am."

"And you are?"

"Brett Knox."

His name sounded familiar. "Okay. I'm Georgia Fulton. It's nice to meet you," she said, putting down her water.

He shook her hand briefly. "You, too. But I just came up here to let you know that I'm declining the interview. Too busy."

Georgia felt herself nodding in agreement, even as she realized *exactly* who Brett Knox was. He was the star catcher—and right in front of her, shooting her down before she'd even had a chance to ask. Such a typical jock.

"I'm busy, too, which is why I'd like to set up a time that's convenient for both of us," she said, even though she hoped it wouldn't be necessary. But she couldn't very well walk into the news station without accomplishing what she'd been tasked with—pinning him down. Georgia was a team player. So was Brett, literally.

"I don't want to disappoint my boss, and I'm betting you feel the same way about yours," she continued.

"Sure. I sign autographs, pose for photos, visit Little League teams. Like I said, I'm busy."

"That's nice." She nodded. "I'm flattered that you found the time to come all the way up to the press box and tell me, in person, that you don't have time for an interview. Thanks."

He smiled a little. "You're welcome." Then he stretched, his broad chest expanding with the movement. He flexed his long fingers, braced a hand high on the post, and grinned at her again. Her heart flipped down into her stomach. Oh, no.

"I get it, you know. I've posed for photos and signed autographs, too. I've visited hospitals and ribbon cutting ceremonies, and I know it makes people happy. But public appearances can be draining, and it takes time away from work. Right?"

"Right." He gave her a curious look. "We have that in common, though it's not exactly the same. I may be semi-famous in Memphis, but I don't have paparazzi following me around, and I like it that way. You interviewing me would turn into a big hassle."

"I won't take much of your time. Just think of me as another reporter." She ventured a warm, inviting smile, and Brett's dark eyes widened. "The paparazzi don't follow me like they do my sisters. I'm the boring one."

"Really?" He folded his arms across his lean middle, and his gaze traveled slowly over her face.

She felt her heart speed up. "Yes, really."

"I beg to differ."

Before she could respond, he gave her another devastating smile and jogged up the steps. It was the best view she'd had all day. When Brett disappeared, she collapsed back against the post. He was right, of course. She wasn't just another reporter; she was the president's brainy daughter—who secretly lusted after athletes. And she'd just met a hell of an athlete.

Talk about a hot mess.

An Excerpt from

MAKE IT LAST
A Bowler University Novel
by *Megan Erickson*

The last installment in Megan Erickson's daringly
sexy Bowler University series finds Cam Ruiz
back in his hometown of Paradise, where he comes
face-to-face with the only girl he ever loved.

Cam sighed, feeling the weight of responsibility pressing down on his shoulders. But if he didn't help his mom, who would?

He jingled his keys in his pocket and turned to walk toward his truck. It was nice of Max and Lea to visit him on their road trip. College had been some of the best years of his life. Great friends, fun parties, hot girls.

But now it felt like a small blip, like a week vacation instead of three and a half years. And now he was right back where he started.

As he walked by the alley beside the restaurant, something flickered out of the corner of his eye.

He turned and spotted her legs first. One foot bent at the knee and braced on the brick wall, the other flat on the ground. Her head was bent, a curtain of hair blocking her face. But he knew those legs. He knew those hands. And he knew that hair, a light brown that held just a glint of strawberry in the sun. He knew by the end of August it'd be lighter and redder and she'd laugh about that time she put lemon juice in it. It'd backfired and turned her hair orange.

The light flickered again but it was something weird and artificial, not like the menthols she had smoked. Back when he knew her.

As she lowered her hand down to her side, he caught sight of the small white cylinder. It was an electronic cigarette. She'd quit.

She raised her head then, like she knew someone watched her, and he wanted to keep walking, avoid this awkward moment. Avoid those eyes he didn't think he'd ever see again and never thought he'd wanted to see again. But now that his eyes locked on her hazel eyes—the ones he knew began as green on the outside of her iris and darkened to brown by the time they met her pupil—he couldn't look away. His boots wouldn't move.

The small cigarette fell to the ground with a soft click and she straightened, both her feet on the ground.

And that was when he noticed the wedge shoes. And the black apron. What was she doing here?

"Camilo."

Other than his mom, she was the only one who used his full name. He'd heard her say it while laughing. He'd her moan it while he was inside her. He'd heard her sigh it with an eye roll when he made a bad joke. But he'd never heard it the way she said it now, with a little bit of fear and anxiety and . . . longing? He took a deep breath to steady his voice. "Tatum."

He hadn't spoken her name since that night Trevor called him and told him what she did. The night the future that he'd set out for himself and for her completely changed course.

She'd lost some weight in the four years since he'd last seen her. He'd always loved her curves. She had it all—thighs, ass and tits in abundance. Naked, she was a fucking vision.

Damn it, he wasn't going there.

But now her face looked thinner, her clothes hung a little loose and he didn't like this look as much. Not that she probably gave a fuck about his opinion anymore.

She still had her gorgeous hair, pinned up halfway with a bump in front, and a smattering of freckles across the bridge of her nose and on her cheekbones. And she still wore her makeup exactly the same—thickly mascaraed eyelashes, heavy eyeliner that stretched to a point on the outside of her eyes, like a modern-day Audrey Hepburn.

She was still beautiful. And she still took his breath away.

And his heart felt like it was breaking all over again.

And he hated her even more for that.

Her eyes were wide. "What are you doing here?"

Something in him bristled at that. Maybe it was because he didn't feel like he belonged here. But then, she didn't either. She never did. *They* never did.

But there was no longer a *they*.

An Excerpt from

HERO BY NIGHT
Book Three: Independence Falls
by Sara Jane Stone

Travel back to Independence Falls in Sara Jane
Stone's next thrilling read. Armed with a golden
retriever and a concealed weapons permit, Lena
Clark is fighting for normal. She served her
country, but the experience left her afraid to be
touched and estranged from her career-military
family. Staying in Independence Falls, and finding
a job, seems like the first step to reclaiming her life
and preparing for the upcoming medal ceremony—
until the town playboy stumbles into her bed . . .

Sometimes beauty knocked a man on his ass, leaving him damn near desperate for a taste, a touch, and hopefully a round or two between the sheets—or tied up in them. The knockout blonde with the large golden retriever at her feet took the word "beautiful" to a new level.

Chad Summers stared at her, unable to look away or dim the smile on his face. He usually masked his interest better, stopping short of looking like he was begging for it before learning a woman's name. But this mysterious beauty had special written all over her.

She stared at him, her gaze open and wanting. For a heartbeat. Then she turned away, her back to the party as she stared out at Eric Moore's pond.

Her hair flowed in long waves down her back. One look left him wishing he could wrap his hand around her shiny locks and pull. His gaze traveled over her back, taking in the outline of gentle curves beneath her flowing, and oh-so-feminine, floor-length dress. The thought of the beauty's long skirt decorating her waist propelled him into motion. Chad headed in her direction, moving away from the easy, quiet conversation about God-knew-what on the patio.

The blonde, a mysterious stranger in a sea of familiar faces, might be the spark this party needed. He was a few feet away when the dog abandoned his post at her side and cut Chad off. Either the golden retriever was protecting his owner, or the animal was in cahoots with the familiar voice calling his name.

"Chad Summers!"

The blonde turned at the sound, looking first at him, her blue eyes widening as if surprised at how close he stood, and then at her dog. From the other direction, a familiar face with short black hair—Susan maybe?—marched toward him.

Without a word, Maybe Susan stopped by his side and raised her glass. With a dog in front of him, trees to one side, and an angry woman on his other, there was no escape.

"Hi there." He left off her name just in case he'd guessed wrong, but offered a warm, inviting smile. Most women fell for that grin, but if Maybe Susan had at one time—and seeing her up close, she looked very familiar, though he could swear he'd never slept with her—she wasn't falling for it today.

She poured the cool beer over his head, her mouth set in a firm line. "That was for my sister. Susan Lewis? You spent the night with her six months ago and never called."

Chad nodded, silently grateful he hadn't addressed the pissed-off woman by her sister's name. "My apologies, ma'am."

"You're a dog," Susan's sister announced. The animal at his feet stepped forward as if affronted by the comparison.

"For the past six months, my little sister has talked about you, saving every article about your family's company," the angry woman continued.

Whoa . . . Yes, he'd taken Susan Lewis out once and they'd ended the night back at his place, but he could have sworn they were on the same page. Hell, he'd heard her say the words, *I'm not looking for anything serious*, and he'd believed her. It was one freaking night. He didn't think he needed signed documents that spelled out his intentions and hers.

"She's practically built a shrine to you," she added, waving her empty beer cup. "Susan was ready to plan your wedding."

"Again, I'm sorry, but it sounds like there was a miscommunication." Chad withdrew a bandana from his back pocket, one that had belonged to his father, and wiped his brow. "But wedding bells are not in my future. At least not anytime soon."

The angry sister shook her head, spun on her heels, and marched off.

Chad turned to the blonde and offered a grin. She looked curious, but not ready to run for the hills. "I guess I made one helluva first impression."

"Hmm." She glanced down at her dog as if seeking comfort in the fact that he stood between them.

"I'm Chad Summers." He held out his hand—the one part of his body not covered in beer.

"You're Katie's brother." She glanced briefly at his extended hand, but didn't take it.

He lowered his arm, still smiling. "Guilty."

"Lena." She nodded to the dog. "That's Hero."

"Nice to meet you both." He looked up the hill. Country music drifted down from the house. Someone had finally added some life to the party. Couples moved to the beat on the blue stone patio, laughing and drinking under the clear Oregon night sky. In the corner, Liam Trulane tossed logs into a fire pit.

"After I dry off," Chad said, turning back to the blonde, "how about a dance?"

"No."

An Excerpt from

MAYHEM

by Jamie Shaw

A straitlaced college freshman is drawn
to a sexy and charismatic rock star in this
fabulous debut New Adult novel for fans
of Jamie McGuire and Jay Crownover!

"I can't believe I let you talk me into this." I tug at the black hem of the stretchy nylon skirt my best friend squeezed me into, but unless I want to show the top of my panties instead of the skin of my thighs, there's nothing I can do. After casting yet another uneasy glance at the long line of people stretched behind me on the sidewalk, I shift my eyes back to the sun-warmed fabric pinched between my fingers and grumble, "The least you could've done was let me wear some leggings."

I look like Dee's closet drank too much and threw up on me. She somehow talked me into wearing this mini-skirt—which skintight doesn't even begin to describe—and a hot-pink top that shows more cleavage than should be legal. The front of it drapes all the way down to just above my navel, and the bottom exposes a pale sliver of skin between the hem of the shirt and the top of my skirt. The fabric matches my killer hot-pink heels.

Literally, killer. Because I know I'm going to fall on my face and die.

I'm fiddling with the skirt again when one of the guys near us in line leans in close, a jackass smile on his lips. "I think you look hot."

"I have a boyfriend," I counter, but Dee just scoffs at me.

"She means *thank you*," she shoots back, chastising me with her tone until the guy flashes us another arrogant smile—he's stuffed into an appallingly snug graphic-print tee that might as well say "douche bag" in its shiny metallic lettering, and even Dee can't help but make a face before we both turn away.

She and I are the first ones in line for the show tonight, standing by the doors to Mayhem under the red-orange glow of a setting summer sun. She's been looking forward to this night for weeks, but I was more excited about it before my boyfriend of three years had to back out.

"Brady is a jerk," she says, and all I can do is sigh because I wish those two could just get along. Deandra and I have been best friends since preschool, but Brady and I have been dating since my sophomore year of high school and living together for the past two months. "He should be here to appreciate how gorgeous you look tonight, but nooo, it's always work first with him."

"He moved all the way here to be with me, Dee. Cut him some slack, all right?"

She grumbles her frustration until she catches me touching my eyelids for the zillionth time tonight. Yanking my fingers away, she orders, "Stop messing with it. You'll smear."

I stare down at my shadowy fingertips and rub them together. "Tell me the truth," I say, flicking the clumped powder away. "Do I look like a clown?"

"You look smoking hot!" she assures me with a smile.

I finally feel like I'm beginning to loosen up when a guy walks right past us like he's going to cut in line. In dark shades and a baggy black knit cap that droops in the back, he flicks a cigarette to the ground, and my eyes narrow on him.

Dee and I have been waiting for way too long to let some self-entitled jerk cut in front of us, so when he knocks on the door to the club, I force myself to speak up.

"They're not letting people in yet," I say, hoping he takes the hint. Even with my skyscraper heels, I feel dwarfed standing next to him. He has to be at least six-foot-two, maybe taller.

He turns his head toward me and lowers his shades, smirking like something's funny. His wrist is covered with string bracelets and rubber bracelets and a thick leather cuff, and three of his fingernails on each hand are painted black. But his eyes are what steal the words from my lips—a greenish shade of light gray. They're stunning.

When the door opens, he turns back to it and locks hands with the bouncer.

"You're late," the bouncer says, and the guy in the shades laughs and slips inside. Once he disappears, Dee pushes my shoulders.

"Oh my GOD! Do you know who you were just talking to?!"

I shake my head.

"That was *Adam* EVEREST! He's the lead singer of the band we're here to see!"

An Excerpt from

SINFUL REWARDS 1
A Billionaires and Bikers Novella
by Cynthia Sax

Belinda "Bee" Carter is a good girl; at least, that's
what she tells herself. And a good girl deserves
a nice guy—just like the gorgeous and moody
billionaire Nicolas Rainer. Or so she thinks,
until she takes a look through her telescope
and sees a naked, tattooed man on the balcony
across the courtyard. He has been watching
her, and that makes him all the more enticing.
But when a mysterious and anonymous text
message dares her to do something bad, she
must decide if she is really the good girl she has
always claimed to be, or if she's willing to risk
everything for her secret fantasy of being watched.

An Avon Red Impulse Novella

I'd told Cyndi I'd never use it, that it was an instrument purchased by perverts to spy on their neighbors. She'd laughed and called me a prude, not knowing that I was one of those perverts, that I secretly yearned to watch and be watched, to care and be cared for.

If I'm cautious, and I'm always cautious, she'll never realize I used her telescope this morning. I swing the tube toward the bench and adjust the knob, bringing the mysterious object into focus.

It's a phone. Nicolas's phone. I bounce on the balls of my feet. This is a sign, another declaration from fate that we belong together. I'll return Nicolas's much-needed device to him. As a thank you, he'll invite me to dinner. We'll talk. He'll realize how perfect I am for him, fall in love with me, marry me.

Cyndi will find a fiancé also—everyone loves her—and we'll have a double wedding, as sisters of the heart often do. It'll be the first wedding my family has had in generations.

Everyone will watch us as we walk down the aisle. I'll wear a strapless white Vera Wang mermaid gown with organza and lace details, crystal and pearl embroidery accents, the bodice fitted, and the skirt hemmed for my shorter height. My hair will be swept up. My shoes—

Voices murmur outside the condo's door, the sound piercing my delightful daydream. I swing the telescope upward, not wanting to be caught using it. The snippets of conversation drift away.

I don't relax. If the telescope isn't positioned in the same way as it was last night, Cyndi will realize I've been using it. She'll tease me about being a fellow pervert, sharing the story, embellished for dramatic effect, with her stern, serious dad—or, worse, with Angel, that snobby friend of hers.

I'll die. It'll be worse than being the butt of jokes in high school because that ridicule was about my clothes and this will center on the part of my soul I've always kept hidden. It'll also be the truth, and I won't be able to deny it. I am a pervert.

I have to return the telescope to its original position. This is the only acceptable solution. I tap the metal tube.

Last night, my man-crazy roommate was giggling over the new guy in three-eleven north. The previous occupant was a gray-haired, bowtie-wearing tax auditor, his luxurious accommodations supplied by Nicolas. The most exciting thing he ever did was drink his tea on the balcony.

According to Cyndi, the new occupant is a delicious piece of man candy—tattooed, buff, and head-to-toe lickable. He was completing armcurls outside, and she enthusiastically counted his reps, oohing and aahing over his bulging biceps, calling to me to take a look.

I resisted that temptation, focusing on making macaroni and cheese for the two of us, the recipe snagged from the diner my mom works in. After we scarfed down dinner, Cyndi licking her plate clean, she left for the club and hasn't returned.

Three-eleven north is the mirror condo to ours. I

straighten the telescope. That position looks about right, but then, the imitation UGGs I bought in my second year of college looked about right also. The first time I wore the boots in the rain, the sheepskin fell apart, leaving me barefoot in Economics 201.

Unwilling to risk Cyndi's friendship on "about right," I gaze through the eyepiece. The view consists of rippling golden planes, almost like . . .

Tanned skin pulled over defined abs.

I blink. It can't be. I take another look. A perfect pearl of perspiration clings to a puckered scar. The drop elongates more and more, stretching, snapping. It trickles downward, navigating the swells and valleys of a man's honed torso.

No. I straighten. This is wrong. I shouldn't watch our sexy neighbor as he stands on his balcony. If anyone catches me . . .

Parts 1 – 7 available now!

An Excerpt from

FORBIDDEN
An Under the Skin Novel
by Charlotte Stein

Killian is on the verge of making his final vows
for the priesthood when he saves Dorothy from a
puritanical and oppressive home. The attraction
between them is swift and undeniable, but every
touch, every glance, every moment of connection
between them is completely forbidden . . .

An Avon Red Impulse Novel

We get out of the car at this swanky-looking place called Marriott, with a big promise next to the door about all-day breakfasts and internet and other stuff I've never had in my whole life, all these nice cars in the parking lot gleaming in the dimming light and a dozen windows lit up like some Christmas card, and then it just happens. My excitement suddenly bursts out of my chest, and before I can haul it back in, it runs right down the length of my arm, all the way to my hand.

Which grabs hold of his, so tight it could never be mistaken for anything else.

Course I want it to be mistaken for anything else, as soon as he looks at me. His eyes snap to my face like I poked him in the ribs with a rattler snake, and just in case I'm in any doubt, he glances down at the thing I'm doing. He sees me touching him as though he's not nearly a priest and I'm not under his care, and instead we're just two people having some kind of happy honeymoon.

In a second we're going inside to have all the sex.

That's what it seems like—like a sex thing.

I can't even explain it away as just being friendly, because somehow it doesn't feel friendly at all. My palm has been laced with electricity, and it just shot ten thousand volts into him. His whole body has gone tense, and so my body goes tense, but the worst part about it is:

For some ungodly reason he doesn't take his hand away.

Maybe he thinks if he does it will look bad, like admitting to a guilty thing that neither of us has done. Or at least that he hasn't done. He didn't ask to have his hand grabbed. His hand is totally innocent in all of this. My hand is the evil one. It keeps right on grasping him even after I tell it to stop. I don't even care if it makes me look worse—*just let go*, I think at it.

But the hand refuses.

It still has him in its evil clutches when we go inside the motel. My fingers are starting to sweat, and the guy behind the counter is noticing, yet I can't seem to do a single thing about it. Could be we have to spend the rest of our lives like this, out of sheer terror at drawing any attention to the thing I have done.

Unless he's just carrying on because he thinks I'm scared of this place. Maybe he thinks I need comfort, in which case all of this might be okay. I am just a girl with her friendly, good-looking priest, getting a motel room in a real honest and platonic way so I can wash my lank hair and secretly watch television about spaceships.

Nothing is going to happen—a fact that I communicate to the counter guy with my eyes. I don't know why I'm doing it, however. He doesn't know Killian is a priest. He has no clue that I'm some beat-up kid who needs help and protection rather than sordid hand-holding. He probably thinks we're married, just like I thought before, and the only thing that makes that idea kind of off is how I look in comparison.

I could pass for a stripe of beige paint next to him. In here his black hair is like someone took a slice out of the night sky. His cheekbones are so big and manly I could bludgeon the counter guy with them, and I'm liable to do it. He keeps staring, even after Killian says "two rooms please." He's still staring as we go down the carpeted hallway, to the point where I have to ask.

"Why was he looking like that?" I whisper as Killian fits a key that is not really a key but a gosh darn credit card into a room door. So of course I'm looking at that when he answers me, and not at his face.

But I wish I had been. I wish I'd seen his expression when he spoke, because when he did he said the single most startling thing I ever heard in my whole life.

"He was looking because you're lovely."

An Excerpt from

HER HIGHLAND FLING
A Novella
by Jennifer McQuiston

When his little Scottish town is in desperate
straits, William MacKenzie decides to resurrect
the Highland Games in an effort to take
advantage of the new tourism boom and invites
a London newspaper to report on the events.
He's prepared to show off for the sake of the
town, but the one thing William never expects
is for this intrepid reporter to be a she . . .

William scowled. Moraig's future was at stake. The town's economy was hardly prospering, and its weathered residents couldn't depend on fishing and gossip to sustain them forever. They needed a new direction, and as the Earl of Kilmartie's heir, he felt obligated to sort out a solution. He'd spent months organizing the upcoming Highland Games. It was a calculated risk that, if properly orchestrated, would ensure the betterment of every life in town. It had seemed a brilliant opportunity to reach those very tourists they were aiming to attract.

But with the sweat now pooling in places best left unmentioned and the minutes ticking slowly by, that brilliance was beginning to tarnish.

William peered down the road that led into town, imagining he could see a cloud of dust implying the arrival of the afternoon coach. The very *late* afternoon coach. But all he saw was the delicate shimmer of heat reflecting the nature of the devilishly hot day.

"Bugger it all," he muttered. "How late can a coach be? There's only one route from Inverness." He plucked at the damp collar of his shirt, wondering where the coachman could be. "Mr. Jeffers knew the importance of being on time today. We need to make a ripping first impression on this reporter."

James's gaze dropped once more to William's bare legs. "Oh, I don't think there's any doubt of it." He leaned against the posthouse wall and crossed his arms. "If I might ask the question . . . why turn it into such a circus? Why these Games instead of, say, a well-placed rumor of a beastie living in Loch Moraig? You've got the entire town in an uproar preparing for it."

William could allow that James was perhaps a bit distracted by his pretty wife and new baby—and understandably so. But given that his brother was raising his bairns here, shouldn't he want to ensure Moraig's future success more than anyone?

James looked up suddenly, shading his eyes with a hand. "Well, best get those knees polished to a shine. There's your coach now. Half hour late, as per usual."

With a near-groan of relief, William stood at attention on the posthouse steps as the mail coach roared up in a choking cloud of dust and hot wind.

A half hour off schedule. Perhaps it wasn't the tragedy he'd feared. They could skip the initial stroll down Main Street he'd planned and head straight to the inn. He could point out some of the pertinent sights later, when he showed the man the competition field that had been prepared on the east side of town.

"And dinna tell the reporter I'm the heir," William warned as an afterthought. "We want him to think of Moraig as a charming and rustic retreat from London." If the town was to have a future, it needed to be seen as a welcome escape from titles and peers and such, and he did not want this turning into a circus where he stood at the center of the ring.

As the coach groaned to a stop, James clapped William on the shoulder with mock sympathy. "Don't worry. With those bare legs, I suspect your reporter will have enough to write about without nosing about the details of your inheritance."

The coachman secured the reins and jumped down from his perch. A smile of amusement broke across Mr. Jeffers's broad features. "Wore the plaid today, did we?"

Bloody hell. Not Jeffers, too.

"You're late." William scowled. "Were there any problems fetching the chap from Inverness?" He was anxious to greet the reporter, get the man properly situated in the Blue Gander, and then go home to change into something less . . . *Scottish.* And God knew he could also use a pint or three, though preferably ones not raised at his expense.

Mr. Jeffers pushed the brim of his hat up an inch and scratched his head. "Well, see, here's the thing. I dinna exactly fetch a chap, as it were."

This time William couldn't suppress the growl that erupted from his throat. "Mr. Jeffers, don't tell me you *left* him there!" It would be a nightmare if he had. The entire thing was carefully orchestrated, down to a reservation for the best room the Blue Gander had to offer. The goal had been to install the reporter safely in Moraig and give him a taste of the town's charms *before* the Games commenced on Saturday.

"Well, I . . . that is . . ." Mr. Jeffers's gaze swung between them, and he finally shrugged. "Well, I suppose you'll see well enough for yourself."

He turned the handle, then swung the coach door open.

A gloved hand clasped Mr. Jeffers's palm, and then a high, elegant boot flashed into sight.

"What in the blazes—" William started to say, only to choke on his surprise as a blonde head dipped into view. A body soon followed, stepping down in a froth of blue skirts. She dropped Jeffers's hand and looked around with bright interest.

"Your chap's a lass," explained a bemused Mr. Jeffers.

"A lass?" echoed William stupidly.

And not only a lass . . . a very pretty lass.

She smiled at them, and it was like the sun cresting over the hills that rimmed Loch Moraig, warming all who were fortunate enough to fall in its path. He was suddenly and inexplicably consumed by the desire to recite poetry to the sound of twittering birds. That alone might have been manageable, but as her eyes met his, he was also consumed by an unfortunate jolt of lustful awareness that left no inch of him unscathed—and there were quite a few inches to cover.

"Miss Penelope Tolbertson," she said, extending her gloved hand as though she were a man. "R-reporter for the *London Times*."

He stared at her hand, unsure of whether to shake it or kiss it. Her manners might be bold, but her voice was like butter, flowing over his body until it didn't know which end was up. His tongue seemed wrapped in cotton, muffling even the merest hope of a proper greeting.

The reporter was female?

And not only female . . . a veritable goddess, with eyes the color of a fair Highland sky?

He raised his eyes to meet hers, giving himself up to the sense of falling.

Or perhaps more aptly put, a sense of flailing.

"W-welcome to Moraig, Miss Tolbertson."

About the Author

CARA CONNELLY is an award-winning author of contemporary romances. Her smart and sexy stories have earned several awards, including the Romance Writers of America's Golden Heart, the Valley Forge Romance Writers' Sheila, and the Music City Romance Writers' Melody of Love. A former attorney and law professor, Cara lives with her husband Billy and their rescue dog Bella in the woods of upstate New York.

Discover great authors, exclusive offers, and more at hc.com.